EVEN VAMPIRES GET THE BLUES

Other Signet Eclipse books by Katie MacAlister

Paranormal Romances
Fire Me Up
You Slay Me

Contemporary Romances
Blow Me Down
Hard Day's Knight
The Corset Diaries
Men in Kilts

EVEN VAMPIRES GET THE BLUES

Katie MacAlister

A SIGNET ECLIPSE BOOK

SIGNET ECLIPSE
Published by New American Library, a division of
Penguin Group (USA) Inc., 375 Hudson Street,
New York, New York 10014, USA
Penguin Group (Canada), 90 Eglinton Avenue East, Suite 700, Toronto,
Ontario M4P 2Y3, Canada (a division of Pearson Penguin Canada Inc.)
Penguin Books Ltd., 80 Strand, London WC2R 0RL, England
Penguin Ireland, 25 St. Stephen's Green, Dublin 2,
Ireland (a division of Penguin Books Ltd.)
Penguin Group (Australia), 250 Camberwell Road, Camberwell, Victoria 3124,
Australia (a division of Pearson Australia Group Pty. Ltd.)
Penguin Books India Pvt. Ltd., 11 Community Centre, Panchsheel Park,
New Delhi - 110 017, India
Penguin Group (NZ), cnr Airborne and Rosedale Roads, Albany,
Auckland 1310, New Zealand (a division of Pearson New Zealand Ltd.)
Penguin Books (South Africa) (Pty.) Ltd., 24 Sturdee Avenue,
Rosebank, Johannesburg 2196, South Africa

Penguin Books Ltd., Registered Offices:
80 Strand, London WC2R 0RL, England

First published by Signet Eclipse, an imprint of New American Library,
a division of Penguin Group (USA) Inc.

ISBN: 978-0-7394-6766-4
ISBN: 0-7394-6766-2

PUBLISHER'S NOTE
This is a work of fiction. Names, characters, places, and incidents either are the
product of the author's imagination or are used fictitiously, and any resemblance to actual persons, living or dead, business establishments, events, or lo-
cales is entirely coincidental.

The publisher does not have any control over and does not assume any responsibility for author or third-party Web sites or their content.

This book was written because so many very kind people sent me notes asking for another vampire book. The hero is Scottish because the ladies on my message forum got together and presented me with a tear-jerking plea for a Scottish vampire (and threw in the demand that he make an appearance in a kilt). It is to all those wonderful readers that this book is dedicated.

Many, many thanks also go to Vicki L. Ankrapp, Michelle L. Graham, and Linda Morrison for all (separately) coming up with the title of this book. I can't thank you ladies enough for all the support and warm fuzzies you send my way!

Prologue

"Hi." A woman stood in the doorway, American if her breathy voice was anything to go by. "Are you Payann, by any chance?"

Paen looked up from a tattered manuscript, wincing slightly at the mispronunciation of his name. The woman had to be from the southern US. No one else drawled his name into two syllables. "I'm Paen, yes. Can I help?"

"Hi," the woman said again, slipping in through the barely opened door, a big Cheshire cat smile on her face. "I'm Clarice Miller."

Paen was on his guard the second the smile hit her lips. Whose was she? he idly wondered as she smoothed down her sexy, nearly see-through gauzy dress before starting across the room in what he assumed was meant to be a seductive slink. Daniel's? No, Danny preferred redheads, and this woman had a mane of golden brown curls that spilled over her shoulders. Finn's? Clarice turned her smile up a notch as she stopped before the chair opposite him. She might possibly be Finn's, but his middle brother tended to prefer earthier women, Pagans and Wiccans. Clarice looked fresh out of an expensive salon or day spa. Which meant she had to belong to—

"Avery said you're the laird of Castle Death?" She tilted her head slightly, so she was peering up at him through her lashes in a pose he mentally dubbed the Princess Di look. It was charming on the late princess . . . less so on the American in front of him.

Regardless of the irritating interruption, he kept his voice pleasant. "I'm the acting laird of the castle—which is named de Ath, incidentally, not Death—but my father is the true owner. He and my mother have moved to Bolivia, however, so if you have a question about the estate, I will do my best to answer it."

The scarlet-tipped fingers of her left hand trailed along the edge of his rosewood desk as she sidled around it toward where he sat. "Your daddy's in Bolivia? How fascinating. But you're left here to handle everything yourself since you're the oldest son? That must be a lot of work. Avery says your land runs for miles and miles all around the castle."

Paen heaved a small, inaudible sigh, and mentally wrote the words gold digger next to the woman's face. Lately, Avery had taken to bringing home women who seemed to be more attracted to the family's home and supposed wealth than the men who lived there. "Yes, we have a bit of land. And yes, it takes some doing to manage the estate, but as I enjoy the work, it's not really that much of a chore. Is there something in particular I can help you with? Some question you have, perhaps?" He glanced at the ancient manuscript before him, wishing nothing more than to be left in peace so he could finish translating it.

"Well now, that's mighty kind of you, but I'm here to help you," she answered, scooting aside the manuscript so she could ease herself onto the desk. Her smile changed into one of blatant invitation. "I was thinking I might give you a hand"—she paused as her eyes flickered briefly to his crotch—"with whatever you might need. I'm told that I'm very good at what I do."

Paen sat back as she crossed her legs. He gave her full marks for the casual way her dress seemed to slide back on her thighs as if by accident. Did she know what he and his brothers really were? Or was she just looking for a fling with a bona fide Scotsman, as he'd heard female American tourists were wont to do? "What exactly did you think to turn your hand to?"

"Oh . . . this and that," she answered, her little pink tongue running quickly across her bottom lip. Paen watched her attempts at seduction with mild amusement. "Anything you like, really. I'm open to all suggestions."

She dropped one shoulder and leaned forward, allowing him an unobstructed view of two plump breasts.

Being a man, he felt obliged to admire them for a moment. That done, he gave Clarice a tight, dismissive smile. "Indeed. I'm afraid that I already employ a steward, and she's quite competent, if a bit on the trying side sometimes. Although I appreciate your offer, there really isn't much that I need help with."

She licked her lips again, more slowly this time. "I bet I could think of something."

Paen looked down in surprise. Clarice, evidently emboldened by his brief admiration of her breasts, uncrossed her legs, kicking off a sandal and sliding her bare foot along the inside of his thigh until it rested on his crotch. "You wouldn't by any chance be indicating that you'd like to have sex with me?"

"Why, sugar, I thought you'd never ask," she purred, caressing him with her toes.

Enough was enough. Lord knew he was no stranger to casual sex—quite the contrary, in fact—but he had work to do, and it didn't involve banging a lusty American. He carefully pried her foot off his groin and pushed it away. Before she could protest, he stood and marched over to the door, holding it open for her. "Thank you for the offer, but there are two reasons why I am unable to take you up on it."

"Two reasons?" she asked, not moving from his desk. Her brows pulled together as she made a little pout at him. "What two reasons?"

Paen sighed again. He was used to women fawning over his three brothers, but seldom did one ever cast her eyes on him. Normally he was the pursuer. He always supposed women sensed something of his tormented, soulless nature, and left him alone because of that.

"One, I don't screw my brothers' women." He walked back, stuffed her sandal on her foot, and gently pushed her off the top, returning to the open door. Rude, yes, but he didn't have the time or inclination to play with this woman. "And two, you have no idea who I really am. It would be best if you left now."

"Oh, I know who you are," Clarice said, her voice

thick as she undulated toward him. Rather than feeling any attraction toward her, her blatant attempts at seduction left him cold. Perhaps if she had truly been attracted to *him* rather than what he represented, he might have been interested, but he was not so deluded as to imagine she cared for anything other than herself. "Or more to the point, I know *what* you are."

Paen stood silent as she leaned into him, her breasts rubbing against his chest. She gave him a knowing smile, and then tipped her head back and to the side, baring her neck. "Avery told me all about you. Go ahead, sugar. You know you want to."

The hunger rose as the scent of a warm, willing woman curled around him. His mind warred with the need—why shouldn't he take what he wanted from her? She was offering it, after all. Once Avery knew she had tried to seduce him, he would want nothing more to do with her, so where was the harm in taking what was being offered?

Deep within him, the hunger growled and demanded satisfaction. She leaned closer into him, her neck a few inches away from his mouth. He swallowed hard, trying not to give in to the hunger, reminding himself that he was a civilized man, not a beast to jump on every morsel of food. He inhaled her scent, finding nothing unpleasant other than the chemical odor of a strong perfume. He preferred a woman's natural scent to anything that came out of a bottle, but he wasn't in a position to complain. His tongue ran over the points of his sharp canines, the hunger building until it was a dull roar in his ears, throbbing to the beat of his heart. The urge to bite, the need to drink deeply was almost overwhelming. All he had to do was sink his teeth in that tender white flesh . . .

"Take it, Paen. Take me. Take me now! Make me yours forever!"

It was the triumph in her voice that stopped him from giving in to the hunger. Like a bucketful of cold water tipped over his head, distaste washed over him at her words.

"You may know what I am, but I also know what you are," he said, stepping back, his voice cold and flat.

"What?" she asked, her eyes confused for a moment. "What do you mean? You aren't going to bite me? You aren't going to Dracula me and drink my blood? You aren't going to make me your eternal bride?"

"No," he answered, more amused than annoyed. "I'm not going to drink your blood, or marry you. My name is Paen Alasdair Scott, not Dracula, and I'm not a prince of the night, or a count, or even a dashing, romantic figure. I'm a simple Scot with an interest in the history and travels of Marco Polo, and a weakness for computer games."

"But . . . you're a vampire!" she protested. "You can't refuse me!"

"We prefer the names Moravian or Dark One. They are less dramatic, and result in fewer people arriving at the front door with torches and wooden stakes. As for refusing you . . ." He gestured toward the open door. "Thank you again, but I'm a busy man. If you wouldn't mind leaving now?"

"Well, I have nevah!" The confusion in Clarice's grey eyes changed to haughty anger as the twangy cadence of her accent deepened. "There's just somethin' wrong with you, you know that?"

"Yes, I'm aware of it," he answered, still amused despite the irritating aspect of the interruption. "I'm more or less damned by an ancient curse. My parents hadn't completed the seven steps to Joining when I was born, so unlike my younger brothers, I have no soul."

"But . . . your brother said that only a woman can save you. He said that you need a woman to become whole again."

"Clearly it's time for me to have yet another talk with Avery," Paen said, sighing a little. "He means well, but I've told him before—I have no intention of accepting a Beloved even if I did find her."

"Beloved?"

"Only a Beloved can redeem a Dark One's soul. But I don't need a woman to live a happy life," he told her, gently pushing her out the door. "I'm quite content on my own. I have my research, and family—although they can be annoying as hell sometimes—and given my brothers' randy natures, all the beautiful women I can look at. I even had a girlfriend a few years ago, although she left me for a software genius. So as you can see, I may be damned, but I'm just fine with it. Thanks again for the offer. See you later."

"But . . . you can't . . . you need to drink blood—"

Paen quietly closed the door on Clarice's outraged protests, turning the lock after a moment's thought. No sense in giving her the chance to pop back in and throw herself at him again.

"Alone at last," he said to himself as he turned back toward his desk.

"Not exactly."

Across the room, a shadow moved against a wall, separating itself to form into a man. Paen watched with interest, cautious but not overly concerned about the sudden appearance of what he believed was a demon in his study. "Today seems to be my day for entertaining guests. I assume this isn't just a social call?"

The man-shaped demon chuckled. Paen was momentarily taken aback by such an act—demons were notorious for their lack of sense of humor. It was a rare one who could appreciate sarcasm and irony. "I'm not going to drag you down to Abaddon, if that's what you are wondering. So I suppose in a sense, this could be construed as a social call. I'm Caspar Green."

Paen looked at the hand the demon offered. It didn't look like it concealed any spring-loaded razor blades, or deadly acid pumps, or even some horrible contagion that would cause various body parts to wart up and subsequently fall off, but you never really knew with demons. "Erm . . . you'll forgive me for being rude, but I don't recall ever hearing about a demon who assumed a mortal name."

Caspar smiled. Paen glanced quickly toward a delicate glass-fronted secretary that held his more valuable manuscripts. Generally when demons smiled, things broke. "That would be because I'm not a demon. I am, in fact, an alastor."

"Alastor?" The name tickled in the back of his mind.

"Yes." Caspar tipped his head to the side. "I find myself somewhat offended that you thought I was a common demon. I assumed you were a man of some discernment."

"Forgive me," Paen said with a wry twist to his lips. "I am a bit of the stereotypically cloistered scholar. I haven't had time to mingle much with citizens of the Otherworld, but correct me if I'm wrong—isn't alastor another name for a demon?"

"I am of the demonic persuasion, yes, but not truly a demon. Alastors are not bound to demon lords—they can, however, be employed. A better name would be nemesis; it is what most alastors are commonly called. As for my name—I was mortal at one time. It is my preference to use a name that puts humans at ease."

"I'm not human," Paen pointed out, finally shaking the alastor's hand. He might not be able to tell a demon from an alastor, but he wasn't a fool. He'd heard enough stories of how tricky those beings born in the service of dark powers could be.

"No, you're not, although some would say you're close enough to count as human." Caspar smiled again and gestured toward a chair. "May I?"

"Certainly. Er . . . I don't often have denizens of Abaddon visiting. What is the proper protocol? Should I offer you a whisky, blood of a virgin . . . or would you prefer a small rodent?"

"Whisky will do just fine," Caspar answered, seating himself in the chair opposite Paen's desk. "Although the blood of a virgin . . . ?"

Paen poured some whisky into a small lead-crystal glass and gave it to the man. "I'm afraid we're fresh out."

"Ah. As I feared. The market price on virgin's

blood has been outrageous of late. Ever since the virgins formed a union, they have been unreasonable in their demands. Slainte." Caspar sipped at his whisky. "Excellent. How old is it?"

"My father set it down the year I was born," Paen answered, leaning a hip against his desk, his arms crossed over his chest. "What exactly is it you want?"

Caspar took another sip. "Extremely smooth for a whisky that's . . . hmm. I judge it to be approximately three hundred years old?"

"Two hundred and forty-six."

"Ah. Delightful, nonetheless."

Paen frowned. His curiosity was roused by the being who sat before him, drinking his father's whisky, but not so much that he was willing to spend all afternoon in polite chitchat with him.

"The reason I am here involves your father, actually. You have no doubt heard how he met your mother?"

"Yes," Paen said, growing uneasy. Caspar Green might not be a demon, but nothing good could come of someone from the Otherworld being concerned with his father. "They met at the conclusion of what is now referred to as the French and Indian War. My mother was French. My father fought on the side of the English. His head was almost completely severed during one battle, and she found him and tended to him despite her family's objections. They fell in love. What do my parents have to do with you?"

"A great deal, actually. Or rather, their meeting does. The story you've been told isn't quite accurate—your father *was* wounded, and your mother *did* nurse him back to health, but he himself inflicted the injury."

Paen thinned his lips. He didn't believe anything so ridiculous. "Why on earth would he do such a foolish thing?"

"Because I told him his Beloved was nearby."

"*You* told him?" Paen stared at the man in outright disbelief.

Caspar smiled—on the surface a pleasant smile, but Paen was aware of the aura of power that surrounded the alastor. "Yes. Your father engaged the demon lord Oriens to find his Beloved. I was charged with locating her, which I did. I informed your father of her situation, and counseled that a drastic action would be needed to get within her circle of friends. He took the action, and the rest, as they say, is history. Literally, in this case, but that's one of the perks of being immortal."

"Even assuming that's true—and it sounds highly unlikely to me—what does that have to do with my father *now?*"

Caspar carefully set the glass onto the desk, clasping his hands over his knee, an affectation that for some reason annoyed Paen. "There is a little matter of the debt your father incurred by purchasing Oriens's help."

Paen's jaw tightened. Yet another gold digger, albeit a demonic one. He went around to the other side of the desk, pulling out the estate checkbook. "How much?"

"You misunderstand me, Paen. The debt your father owes Oriens is not one that can be repaid by means of mortal money."

"Oh?" Paen closed the checkbook, watching the man suspiciously. "What is it he owes for this debt, then?"

"A simple thing, really. A small statue of a monkey. You may be familiar with it? I understand it is a family heirloom—the Jilin God is its most common name."

Paen frowned as he dug through his memories. "A statue of a monkey? No, I've never heard of it, let alone being familiar with it."

Caspar pulled a piece of paper from his pocket. "Here is a sketch of it. It's about six inches high, black, made of ebony. Its origins are said to be Chinese, about six hundred years old."

"Ming dynasty," Paen said absently, still poking around in his memories. As far as he could remember, his father never mentioned anything about a monkey statue as a family heirloom. He himself knew every square inch of the castle, and he'd never seen such a statue.

"Yes. How perspicacious of you to know that. Are you familiar with the era?"

"Only in a collateral sense. I am doing some research on a knight in the service of Marco Polo. He was in China during the Ming dynasty. What proof do I have that any of what you're telling me is true?"

Caspar smiled yet again. Paen was starting to get tired of that knowing smile. He felt decidedly out of his depths with the man, and it wasn't a feeling he relished. "I thought you might ask for some proof. I have here"—Caspar pulled out a small leather case, the size to hold a passport—"a document signed by your father, and bearing his seal."

Paen took the document over to where a magnifying light sat on his worktable. He read the document quickly. It simply stated that one Alec Munroe Mc-Gregor Scott, of Darmish, Scotland, did swear to provide the lord Oriens or his due representative with the statue known as the Jilin God in exchange for services rendered him. Paen, no stranger to antique parchment, and certainly familiar enough with it to detect modern paper doctored to look old, examined the item closely with the magnifying glass. He went so far as to pull out a small pocket microscope to examine the fiber content of the document, as well as the red wax seal.

"Very well. I concede this document is real. But why has Oriens waited two hundred and forty years to collect this debt?"

"Oriens is a busy demon lord. Perhaps it slipped his mind, or perhaps he had no need for the statue until now. Regardless of the why, the debt is now being called due, and it must be paid."

"I have no idea what or where this Jilin God statue is. If Oriens waited this long, he can wait another three months until my parents return from the depths of the Bolivian forests to their home in La Paz."

Caspar spread his hands. "Alas, it is not so easy. The debt must be repaid within one lunar cycle upon being called due, or else Oriens is entitled to claim the collateral used to secure his services."

Paen could have sworn his blood turned to ice. The situation was quickly going from bad to worse. "What collateral?"

"There is really only one thing a demon lord wants—a soul."

"My father promised his soul in order to have you locate his Beloved?"

"No, his soul was held in trust for another, so he could not use it," Caspar answered, shaking his head. "He tried to, but Oriens wouldn't accept that as collateral."

Little glaciers rose in Paen's heart. "Then whose soul did he use?"

Caspar smiled, just as Paen knew he would. "Why, that of his Beloved, naturally. Although strictly speaking he wasn't in possession of her soul, the fact that she was his Beloved, and would by her very nature agree to sacrifice herself on his behalf, served as a guarantee. I'm afraid that means if you do not provide me with the Jilin God in the next five days, your mother's soul is forfeit. Unfair to her, true, but that is the nature of these arrangements."

"*Five days?*" Paen asked, his mind awhirl. He would die before he let a demon lord lay one hell-spawned finger on his mother, let alone her beautiful, pure soul. "What happened to a lunar cycle?"

"I'm afraid that it took me some time to track down your whereabouts," Caspar said with faux apology.

"That's ridiculous! Right, there are four of us. We'll just divide up the work . . ."

"Oh, no, I'm afraid that's not possible." Caspar gave him a sad little smile. "Didn't I tell you? This debt is yours alone to fulfill. You are your father's son, you see."

Paen frowned. "Why mine? My brothers are just as much the sons of my father as I am."

"Yes, but you are the eldest. According to the

agreement your father signed"—he gestured toward the note—"the debt must be repayed by the debtor himself, or the nearest member of his blood. That would be you, the oldest son."

"That is completely outrageous. My brothers—"

"—are not eligible to locate the missing statue. If they do, the debt will be considered forfeit, and the collateral will be collected." Caspar plucked the promissory note from Paen's hands and tucked it away in the leather case. "All that remains is five days. If you do not have the statue in that time . . . well. We won't dwell on the unpleasant."

"Get out," Paen said, gritting his teeth against the pain that threatened to swamp him at the thought of what the alastor was saying.

"I understand that you are upset, but—"

"Get the hell out of my house! Now!" Paen roared, starting toward the unwelcome visitor.

"I will be in touch about your progress with the statue," Caspar said hurriedly, backing toward the wall as Paen prepared to grab him and throw him out of the room. Hell, he wanted to throw him out of the country . . . off the planet, if he could manage it. "Until then, farewell!"

Paen snarled several obscenities and medieval oaths as the man's form shimmered, then disappeared. He continued to swear under his breath over the next half hour as he placed four international phone calls and authorized three messengers to be sent out into the depths of the Bolivian forests in an attempt to locate his parents.

"I don't suppose you have any idea where they

are, or where this monkey god statue is?" he asked
his brothers that evening.

"Not a clue on either count," Avery said as he
slipped on a leather jacket. "No one tells me anything. The whole thing sounds a bit dicey to me, to be
honest. We can't help you search for this statue because you're the eldest? What's up with that?"

"Some archaic medieval law still around a few
hundred years ago, no doubt," Paen grumbled.
"There were all sorts of agreements then that oper-
ated under obsolete laws."

"Well, I hate to be callous, but since we can't help
you search for the statue, I guess I'll go out."

"You'll do nothing of the kind," Paen said, stalking past his brother. "You and Dan will go to the
Lachmanol Abbey in the Outer Hebrides, and beg the
abbot for access to his very rare collection of sixteenth-
century manuscripts. There you will scour the collection for references to this damned statue."

"Me? Why me?" Paen's second-youngest brother
looked up from the evening paper. "Why can't you
go? And I thought this demon said none of us could
look for the statue."

"You're not going to be looking for the statue itself. I want to know more about it—where it came
from, what its history is, that sort of thing. You're the
only one besides me who knows Latin. Avery can use
his charm to get access to the manuscripts, and you
can translate them."

"Sounds like a bloody bore, but I'll do it for
Mum." Avery admired himself in the mirror again,
then frowned at Paen. "You're not going to brood the

whole time we're gone, are you? Because if you are, we won't bring back any souvenir girls for you."

"We're going to an abbey, you idiot," Daniel said, smacking his brother on the arm as he stretched and grabbed his coat.

"Bet you I could find some."

Paen only just kept himself from rolling his eyes. "I'm not brooding. I never brood."

His brothers, all three of the rotters, laughed.

"Paen, you're the world's champion brooder," Daniel said, stretching again and squinting at the clock.

"Aye, and a broodaholic, to boot. I'm thinking we need to do an intervention, or maybe get you into one of those twelve-step programs. 'Hi, my name is Paen, and I'm broody.' Maybe that'll help you lighten up a bit." Finn grinned at his brother.

Paen stifled the urge to sock him in the arm. Finn was just as tall as he was, and although he had a good twenty pounds on his brother, it had been a near thing the last time he wrestled Finn—or any of them, for that matter.

Instead, Paen gave them all a narrow-eyed look, wondering for the umpteenth time how his fair-haired mother and dark-haired father could produce four sons who differed so greatly in appearance. He took after his father in looks, with black hair that insisted on curling despite his efforts to make it lie flat, and grey eyes. Avery was every bit his blond-haired, blue-eyed mother's son, while Finn and Daniel were somewhere in between. "There is a vast difference between being concerned for Mum's soul and brooding. What you see here is concern, with just a dash of worry thrown in to keep from going stale. There's not a single shred of brood on me."

"Here it comes," Avery told Finn.

The latter nodded. "The bit about us lot being so lucky because we have our souls, and him being damned and all. Same old, same old."

"Well, I _am_ damned! You don't have the slightest concept what it is to be in my position," Paen argued. "You have no idea the torment, the pain—"

" '—the agony of living each day without any hope, without love shared with a soulmate, without any chance at redemption,' " his brothers all chanted together.

Paen growled. He loved his brothers, but there were times when he would pay good money to be an only child.

"And yet you claim you're perfectly happy that way. We've told you that we'd move heaven and earth to help you find your Beloved," Avery said. "Just say the word, and we'll scour the length and breadth of Scotland for her. The whole of Britain, even!"

"I met a woman yesterday you might like," Daniel said thoughtfully. "I could ring her up before we leave—"

"No!" Paen said quickly, a little chill running through him. "I've had enough of Avery all but pimping for me—I've no need for any more of you bringing home women you just know will turn out to be my Beloved. I don't need a woman to save me. I'm perfectly happy, in a completely non-brooding way, just as I am, and besides, I'm well on the way to locating the _Simia Gestor Coda._"

"Oh, not that faery story again," Daniel said, rolling his eyes.

"It's not a faery story."

"I know, I know," Daniel said, holding up his hands. "This book you're always going on about supposedly contains the details about the origins of Dark Ones, including a way to unmake the curse binding you guys."

"Exactly. I just have to find it, and I will be able to lift the curse myself. Completely without the assistance of any interfering woman, thank you."

"Paen, you've looked for the last twenty-five years for that manuscript—I think it's time you admit it doesn't exist," Avery said. The others nodded. "I don't know why you're so bent on fighting the fact that you need a woman to save you. Women are nice! They are smooth, and they smell good, and god knows they do things to my body that make my eyes cross with bliss. You need to get off this high horse of 'I'll save myself' and get with the program, brother. Find your Beloved, let her save you, and make lots of little Paens."

Paen glared at his irresponsible brother. "Just because I can keep my dick in my pants and you can't—"

"Oh, I can, it's just a lot more fun out and about," Avery answered, pausing to punch Finn in the shoulder until keys to a car were handed over. "Ta, mate. We're off to this abbey of fun. I'll call and let you know how many women I manage to find there, too."

"Between the fast cars and faster women, you're going to kill yourself one of these days," Paen warned.

"One of the perks of being immortal, brother, is

the ability to do whatever you want whenever you want, and to hell with the consequences. You should try it sometime."

A muscle in Paen's jaw twitched. "One of us has to have some responsibility and keep things together while Mum and Dad are off."

Avery rolled his eyes and left the sitting room. Daniel grabbed his jacket and followed after his brother, saying, "I'm with Av on this, Paen. You need to loosen up a bit, and let go of some of that responsibility you're always harping on. I've got my mobile phone. I'll give you a ring if we find anything."

"Well?" Paen turned to his remaining brother. "Don't tell me you're going to pass up an opportunity to get in a few digs about how I need to ignore the castle, the family, and Mum's eternal happiness and instead live like there's no tomorrow."

Finn grinned. "Could I pass up such a wonderful chance? All that repressed sexuality—what you really need is to fall in love with some delicious bird, fuck your brains out, let her save you, and try out happy instead of gloomy."

"Do you know how tiring it gets repeating that I don't need a Beloved? Women I can, and do, have whenever I'm struck with the desire for sex. A female doesn't need to bind herself to me to satisfy my sexual desires."

"I can't believe I'm going to say this, but here goes—Paen, you're missing out on a whole world of pleasure by keeping yourself at an emotional distance from women. You might as well use slags for all the involvement you have with them. I know you equate feeling affection for a woman with a Beloved, but you know, you can actually *like* a woman you sleep with without her saving you. Maybe even love her a little, if you're determined not to find your true better half."

"I don't have a better half," Paen said, fighting the desire to punch something, *anything*. "I'm whole as I am. I might be in eternal torment, but love, souls, and emotional commitments are all overrated. If I didn't know that for myself, all I'd have to do is look at you lot. Always falling in love with some woman or other, then moping around when they end up stomping all over your hearts—no, thanks. If all you're going to do is lecture me, you might as well go, too."

"I was about to ask what you wanted me to do to help you," Finn said with a grin.

"To find the statue?" Paen ran a hand through his hair, happy to change the subject of conversation. "You can't."

"Not technically, no. So what can I do to help *you* find it?"

Paen felt as if the weight of the world had descended upon his shoulders. "To be honest, I've no idea where to even start looking for it. I've never come across a mention of it in the family papers, and since Dad is completely incommunicado until someone tracks him down and forces a satellite phone into his hand, I'm at a loss as to where to begin searching. It could be in the castle, hidden somewhere. It could have been lost or stolen or sold over the years, and I'd have no way of knowing."

"Hmm," Finn said. "Sounds like we need some professional help."

"What sort of professional help?" Paen asked as

his brother went to the phone. "If it's anything involving demons, it's right out. We're in enough trouble because of them."

Finn dug around in his jeans pocket and pulled out a handful of miscellaneous items, extracting a blue sticky note from his keys and change. "Not a demon. I met a woman last week in Edinburgh, an underwear model—man, she had great tits, just how I like them, big enough for my hands but not fake-looking—and she said her cousin was trained as a Diviner, and the two of them were just opening up a private detective business. I bet a Diviner could figure out where the statue is. I'll give Clare a ring and get the cousin's number."

"Might as well," Paen said glumly as he slumped down into a chair. Despite his protestations to the contrary, he wanted nothing more than to brood about the latest trial fate had dumped on him. As if things weren't bad enough already . . . "It's not like a Diviner could make things any worse."

Chapter 1

"What do you think of the sign?"

Clare set down a box of desk supplies and a bouquet of fresh cut flowers, and frowned. "Well, to be honest, Sam, I wasn't going to say anything about it, but I don't think the crow landing on your head this morning is a good omen. It means your life is about to go crisis central. But I'm here to help, and you know I'll do what I can to keep you from going outright insane."

"No . . . I meant the sign on the door." I nodded to where a local sign painter was putting away her stencils and paints.

"Oh. Mmm." Clare tipped her head and considered the freshly painted words on the upper half of the open office door. "EYE SCRY, SAMANTHA COSSE AND CLARE BENNET, DISCREET PRIVATE INVESTIGATIONS. It's nice, but I still think it's a bit too strange. People are going to think we're not normal private investigators."

"We aren't normal, Clare."

"Speak for yourself. I'm as normal as they come." She plucked a tulip from the bouquet and went to the window, using her elbow to wipe a small clean patch on the grimy glass. "Isn't it a lovely morning?"

I glanced out the window at the grey, sodden-looking sky, and shrugged as I arranged paper in my new printer/copier/fax machine. "It's a typical Scottish May: grey, cold, and wet."

"When I woke up this morning," Clare said dreamily, unconsciously striking an elegant pose that made her a star on the fashion runways, "the dew had kissed all the sweet little flowers just as if faeries had danced upon them with damp little slippers. Don't you think that's lovely? I thought that up all by myself."

"Very, um . . ." Clare blinked silver-tipped lashes at me. I relented under her hopeful expression. "Very poetic. But not terribly accurate, is it?"

She blinked again, her large blue eyes clouded with confusion. "What do you mean?"

"Well . . . just look at you." I waved a hand toward her torso. "You're the opposite of short, sturdy, dark-haired me—you're tall, lovely, elegant, and have that silver blond hair that everyone seems to rave about, but you're hardly in a dancing-on-the-dew-kissed-flowers sort of form, are you? You'd squash the little buggers flat were you to try it in your human form."

She rolled her expressive eyes and bopped me on the arm with her tulip. Clare always had flowers with her—she couldn't help it any more than my mother could. It was just part of their genetic makeup. "You're going to start that silly business again, and I won't listen to it, I simply won't listen to it."

I took her by both arms and shook her gently. "You're a faery, Clare. It's time you face up to that fact. You're a faery, your real name is Glimmerharp, and you were left with my aunt and uncle because your faery parents wanted you to have a better life than running around in wet shoes, stamping dew onto flowers. I doubt if they would have done so had they known that your idea of a better life is to parade up and down in scanty lingerie in front of strangers with cameras, but that's neither here nor there. You are a faery, and the sooner you admit that, the happier everyone around you will be."

"I am not a faery; I am an underwear model."

"You're both."

"Oh!" She plucked a piece of the smooth red tulip's flower and popped it in her mouth. "You take that back!"

"I won't," I said calmly, releasing her to hook the printer up to the laptop that sat on the scarred and battered oak desk I'd claimed as my own. "It's the truth, and you know it, even if you are in denial."

"You're a fine one to talk about denial!" she said, marching over to her desk, a trail of tulip petals gently drifting to the floor behind her. "You deny your heritage every chance you get."

I laughed. I couldn't help it—the mere thought of me being able to ignore who I was, was beyond ridiculous. "There's no way I could deny my parentage—not after growing up the only kid in my neighborhood whose mother is a bona fida poetry-spouting, pointy-eared, gonna-live-forever elf. Years of Keebler jokes made sure I knew just how different I was, and we won't even go into what a mention of *Lord of the Rings* does to me. What I've never understood is how you can accept the fact that my mother is an elf, and yet insist that there are no such things as faeries."

"I refuse to talk to you when you get in that mood," Clare said, and picked up an empty milk jug she'd brought to serve as a vase. "I won't let you ruin the excitement of the day with all that nonsense."

"Excitement?" I looked around the small office as Clare left to fill the vase with water. The painter had toddled off, leaving the faint odor of acrylic paints behind her. Through the open door I could see a dark, dingy hallway that led to a couple of flats and a shared bathroom.

"That's not quite the word that comes to mind," I said loud enough that Clare could hear me down the hall. "But never fear! A little elbow grease and some creative decorating courtesy of that thrift store you saw on the way in should do much to wipe out the years of neglect. I just wish Mila would come and get her boxes of sex toys."

Clare's muffled voice drifted into the room as I crawled under the desk to plug in the computer equipment. "You shouldn't have told her she could keep her stock here."

"I had a hard enough time persuading her to rent this office to me—ow!" I rubbed the back of my head where I cracked it on the underside of the desk. "Evidently her sex store is doing a tremendous amount of business and she needs all the storage space she can get. Besides, she knocked a hundred pounds off the rent just for us putting up with a few extra boxes."

Clare's answer was drowned out by the sound of running water. I scooted backward under the desk, dragging with me the phone cord to plug in the new set of phones I'd purchased. "Regardless of the naughty toys, I don't know how exciting this job is going to be to someone who spends time in Milan and Paris and Berlin being paid thousands of pounds to stand around and pout in her panties."

"It's not nearly as exciting as you might think," Clare said, coming back into the room. "That's why I decided to go on hiatus for a year. My modeling batteries need to be recharged, and this job should do wonders for that."

"Eh . . . OK." I plugged the cord into the appropriate wall socket, and jumped violently when the phone above me rang loudly, causing me to whack my head on the desk a second time.

"Phone," Clare said helpfully.

"Oh, thank you. I might have thought it was my umbrella ringing, otherwise." I hunkered down under the desk rubbing my abused head.

"I'll get it," Clare said, hurrying over to her desk. "Your umbrella is ringing. Honestly, Sam! Your imagination! Good morning, Eye Scry, discreet private enquiries, this is Clare. How can I help?"

I crawled out from under my desk, wondering as I brushed off the dusty knees of my pants who was calling us. I'd only set up the phone lines the day before, and had given the number out to just one person other than Clare. It was probably just the phone company checking to see if the line worked. I turned on my laptop and sat down at my desk while Clare made little murmurs of encouragement to whoever was on the phone.

"I see. Well, I don't believe that will be a problem,

Mr. Race. My partner has a particular talent with finding lost objects. Oh, you did?" Clare looked at me, her eyes round. "Then perhaps it would be best if you talked to her yourself. Can you hold? Thank you."

"Lost items?" I asked. "That's not a client, is it?"

"Yes, it is. It's a Mr. Owen Race. He's a medieval specialist of some sort, and he wants us to find some sort of an antique book for him. But Sam—he says that Brother Jacob recommended you to him. I thought you were kicked out of the Order of Diviners?"

"I was, but Jake said he'd keep an ear out for me for anyone who might be able to use the services of a failed Diviner. Sounds like he found someone. Hello, this is Samantha Cosse. I understand you need some help locating an object?"

Like Clare's, the man's voice was English, very upper-class, positively reeking of places like Eton and Cambridge and of the BBC. It made me all the more aware of my flat, accentless (to my ears) Canadian speech. "Good morning, Miss Cosse. Yes, as I told your associate, I am seeking to locate a very rare medieval manuscript that was stolen from me recently—the *Simia Gestor Coda* is its name. I understand from Brother Jacob at the Diviners' House that you studied there for several years and have a good deal of experience in locating missing items?"

Oh dear. He wanted a Diviner, and I was anything but one. I'd have to let him know right away that I wasn't what he thought I was. "I've had some luck locating missing items, yes. But if you are seeking the assistance of a true Diviner, Mr. Race, I'm afraid you may have been misled. I did study at the Diviners' House with the Order, but I was . . . well, to put it bluntly, I was kicked out before my novitiate was completed. Although I have been trained in elementary divination, I'm afraid I am unable to conduct the more advanced rituals."

"I see. I appreciate such frankness, and can assure you that I have no need for the services of a professional Diviner. Brother Jacob recommended you to me because you apparently have a talent for locating items that goes beyond mere divination."

I slumped back in my chair in relief. I hadn't anticipated Jake sending me a customer, despite his declarations that he would do all he could to help me, but now that I had bared the ugly truth in my past, I could focus on the job being offered. "I will be happy to put the full resources of my firm at your disposal," I said. "Perhaps we can meet to discuss this further?"

"Excellent. I'm in Barcelona at the moment, but I would be happy to pay your airfare out here."

I blinked back my surprise. "Er . . . I appreciate the offer, Mr. Race, but we are still in the process of setting up our business, and I wouldn't be comfortable leaving all the remaining work to my partner." I motioned to Clare and wrote *he wants me to go to Barcelona* on the notepad. Clare looked panicky. I'd had to promise her, when we thought up the idea of the investigation agency, that I would handle all of what she termed the "messy businessy stuff."

"Sam, no," she whispered.

"Don't worry," I mouthed, then said into the phone, "That's very generous of you, but I'm afraid it's out of the question. However—" I raised my eyebrows in question. Clare nodded quickly. "However, my partner would be available to fly to Barcelona. She would be very happy to stand in my place and discuss with you all the necessary details."

"Erm . . . no, that won't be necessary," he said, sounding disappointed. I shook my head at Clare. "I will be returning to Edinburgh at the end of the week, so we can meet then."

"I would be happy to get started on your project if you can give me the details over the phone," I said in my most professional voice, opening a text document. "Why don't you give me the specifics of the item that was stolen, and later you can fax me any insurance documents you have, as well as the police report."

Twenty minutes later I hung up the phone and hit SAVE on my document file.

"Well?" Clare asked, absently nibbling on a carnation. "Do we have a job?"

I smiled. "We are employed! Let fly the doves and all that."

"Hurrah! I told you this was going to be exciting! Although I'm disappointed I won't be going to Barcelona. Such a pretty city. So, we're looking for a book?"

"Yes, some sort of medieval manuscript that was stolen. Evidently Mr. Race has quite a collection, and he didn't notice the theft until he had ordered an inventory of his holdings a month ago. He's going to have his housekeeper round up some information about the manuscript, but until then, we can get to work on the little info he gave me. He believes the manuscript could well have been taken by a rival collector."

"Oooh. How thrilling! It's like an art theft, only with a medieval book."

"Mmm," I said, gathering up my bag and jacket. "I'm going to go visit a couple of antique shops and see if I can't get some info on who the big collectors are in Britain."

"What would you like me to do?" Clare asked, chewing another bit of flower.

"You'd better stop eating those flowers, or you won't have anything left but a vase full of stems," I said at the door.

She shot me a look of pure outrage. "I do not eat flowers!"

I raised my eyebrows and looked at the half-eaten carnation in her hand. She glared at it for a minute as if it had magically appeared there. "You're a faery, Clare. No one else eats flowers but really hard-core vegetarians, and I've seen you wolf down a steak, so I know you're not that. If you want to do something helpful, do an Internet search for me on the"—I consulted my notes—"*Simia Gestor Coda*. With a name like that, it has to have some sort of a history. I'd like to know everything you can find out about its past. All Mr. Race told me was that it was written by a mage who was supposedly in Marco Polo's service. Oh, also, pull up a list of the major antiquities dealers for England. It wouldn't hurt to know who might be dealing in something like a rare antique manuscript."

I spent the next couple of hours visiting various antique shops in and around the Royal Mile, the most famous street in all of Edinburgh. By the time I tottered into the last shop on my list, a small, dusty shop tucked away between a bookstore and a gyro shop, I was feeling uninspired. The antique dealers were particularly loath to talk about their clients, and none of them had heard of the *Coda*.

A little bell over the door jangled as I entered the shop. Like others of its ilk, this antiquities shop was filled to the rafters with statuary, objets d'art, stuffed animals, strange old mechanical pieces, books and illuminated manuscripts, and a myriad of other items whose use and purpose were shrouded in the distant reaches of the past. I browsed through the items, glancing periodically at a man I took to be the owner as he stood with his back to me in the doorway to another room, speaking to someone I couldn't see.

"Shoot," I said to myself as I glanced at my watch. I was three hours away from the office already, and I wanted to get back to help Clare. I stopped in front of a bookcase bearing a stuffed spider monkey, and sent yet another impatient look toward the man in the doorway. "I don't have time for thi*aaaaieeeeee!*"

My heart just about leaped out of my chest as the spider monkey I'd assumed was stuffed suddenly jumped from the bookcase to my shoulder. "Oh, man alive, you just scared a good ten years off me. Hello there, Mr. Monkey. Um . . . that is, I assume you're a mister. I can't tell, what with that little sailor suit you're wearing. Do you belong here? Of course you do, what a stupid question. What else would a monkey be doing in an antiques shop? Would you mind asking your owner if he could talk to me for a few minutes? No? Drat. Well, doesn't matter—you'll do as an excuse to interrupt him."

The monkey, evidently satisfied with his evil plan

to give me a heart attack, leaped back onto the bookcase, where he smoothed down the fur on his tail.

"Um . . . I can't use you as an excuse unless you're on my shoulder, so hop on . . . er . . . what's your name?"

I reached out a tentative hand to stroke his arm. He didn't seem to mind being petted, so I gently touched the jeweled collar he wore around his neck. Tiny rivets spelled out a series of letters.

"B . . . E . . . P . . . well, hello there, Beppo."

The monkey stopped examining his tail and held out a rust-fingered hand. Stifling a giggle at the dignified look on his little face, I carefully shook his hand. Satisfied, he returned to his grooming.

"You are one strange little monkey. All right, Beppo, hop on and let's go interrupt your owner."

He dropped his tail and held out his hand again.

"Hee!" I shook his hand again. That completed, he picked up his tail.

"Beppo," I said again, unable to resist. Down went the tail; out went his hand.

"OK, cute but could well become annoying. Here, if you don't mind—" I hoisted the monkey off the bookcase and set him onto my shoulder. His tail wrapped around my neck as he clung with one hand to my ponytail. "Groovy. Now let's go pretend that I just found you in a dangerous situation and see if I can't have a quick word with your owner before toddling on my merry—holy crap! What is it with everyone trying to startle me into an early grave?"

A being popped up in front of me. I mean, literally popped up right out of the floor. All my supernatural senses went into high tingle mode at the sight of what appeared to be a short, middle-aged man.

Only he wasn't a man. I didn't know exactly what he was, but he *wasn't* human.

"Hello," I said politely, feeling it was better to give him the benefit of the doubt. I'd come across a few different types of beings in my time with the Diviners, and although only a couple of them had turned out to be from the wrong side of the tracks, metaphorically speaking, some who looked bad had turned out to be quite nice. "That was an impressive entrance. Was it for me in particular, or are you just a fan of antiques?"

The man looked from Beppo to me. "You bear the monkey."

"Beppo?" The monkey promptly held out his hand. I gave it a little two-fingered shake. "He jumped on me earlier, but I was just taking him back to his— what's this?"

The man shoved a shoebox-sized package at me.

"I am charged to give it to you. It is yours now," the man said, then without another word, dissolved into black smoke that sank down into the floor.

Chapter 2

"What the . . . OK, this day is really starting to go strange. What the heck is in this? It's heavy . . . hey!"

At the front of the store a man's voice rose in anger. He was speaking some language I'd never heard, but the threat in his voice was unmistakable. The bell on the door tinkled distantly, sending Beppo flying off my shoulder with an agitated squawk. The little monkey loped down the aisle until he was out of sight.

"Damn it, just when I needed—ouch! Who on earth would want to buy a guillotine?—just when I needed him, he runs off."

I made my way around the blocky guillotine, rubbing my arm where I had hit it on a pointy bit of wood, past an eight-foot-tall reproduction of the Sphinx, and into the aisle that would take me to the front of the store. The small man I had seen earlier standing in the doorway was at the desk bearing an antique cash register. He looked startled to see me.

"Good morning. I had no idea there was anyone in the shop. Can I assist you? Are you looking for something in particular, or just browsing?"

"I was just browsing while you were busy with the other customer, but I am looking for something in particular. It's a fifteenth-century manuscript named the *Simia Gestor Coda*. It was stolen from a nearby collector. I don't suppose you've heard of it?"

"Stolen! Oh no, we do not deal in stolen goods," the man said, his soft voice filled with outrage.

"No, no, I didn't mean to imply you did. The owner just found out about the theft, which could have occurred up to six years ago, so there's no way anyone would have known that it was stolen."

"Regardless, I do not have any medieval manuscripts," the owner said stiffly.

"Well, it was a long shot. I'm interested in contacting some of the area collectors," I said carefully. "People who collect medieval antiquities such as the manuscript. Would you be able to tell me who in this region might be interested in acquiring something of that sort?"

"I would be happy to appraise any object you wish to sell," he said quickly, moving around the desk.

"Thank you, that's very kind, but I prefer to talk to collectors myself."

His helpful expression turned to one of stone.

I sighed. "I didn't think you'd go for that. None of the other dealers and sellers have. Well, thank you anyway." I had started to leave when I remembered the box that had so oddly been thrust upon me. "Oh—something popped up while I was in the back of the shop with your monkey, and gave me this. I thought maybe he mistook me for you . . . ?"

The man looked at me as if I had spider monkeys growing out of my ears. "Some*thing* popped up?"

"Yes, some sort of being or entity. Perhaps a spirit, although I haven't heard of spirits acting as delivery services. Then again, it could have been a demon—I'm afraid I haven't had much experience with the dark beings, so I'm not absolutely sure I would recognize one if I saw it."

"Erm . . ." The man's eyes turned wary as he edged toward the part of the desk bearing a phone.

"Not a demon?" I asked.

He shook his head slowly and glanced toward the front door. "I'm afraid I don't quite follow you, madam. I don't have a monkey, nor is my store haunted with demons and ghosts. If there's anything else I can help you with?"

Clearly this man was not hip to all the woo-woo stuff that went on in the Otherworld. I smiled what I hoped wouldn't look like the smile of an insane person, and said very carefully, "My apologies for startling you—my imagination gets away with me sometimes. I assume you don't want this box?"

I held out the shoebox to him. He backed away as though it contained projectile leprosy. "I'm afraid I cannot accept gifts from . . . *visitors*."

The words "freakish Canadians who babble about weird stuff" hung unspoken in the air, but I took his meaning. "All right. I'll just leave you my card in case you do happen to hear of anyone with the *Coda* for sale."

I extracted one of the brand-new business cards from my purse and set it down on the counter, thanking the man as I left. The box was heavy in my hands, reminding me of the rashness of hauling around a strange gift from an even stranger being. With all sorts

of visions of plagues and blights in mind, I stood outside the antique store for a moment, chewing my lip.

"When in doubt, go to an expert," I said to myself,
and hustled my way through the misty drizzle to the
nearest bus stop. A short time and a pound coin later,
I stood outside a familiar white brick building. The
buildings were designed in Georgian style, all clean,
classical lines, but the Diviners' House itself (donated
to the Order by a grateful client) was unremarkable,
its polished oak and brass door speaking of the same
quiet affluence as the hotels that sat on either side of
it. I shook away the bad memories of the last few
years and entered the house, quickly locating one of
the few remaining Diviners who would acknowledge
my existence.

" . . . so I thought it would be better to have it
checked out before I opened it, in case there was
some sort of Pandora's box thing going on," I finished five minutes later, carefully watching the man
who stood next to me with the box in his hands.
"What do you think? Is it something bad?"

Brother Jacob, head of the Scottish branch of Diviners, and erstwhile schoolmate from a childhood
spent in Calgary, gave me a look that almost made
me squirm. Almost. "Sam, you didn't leave here utterly ignorant. You possess the skills to determine if
this object is tainted by dark powers."

"Uh . . . Jake, I hate to disillusion you about any of
my so-called skills, but I flunked divination, remember? I was kicked out of the Order."

"You left voluntarily," he said, still giving me the
look that said I shouldn't be bothering him with
petty things.

"Right. Only I was *volunteered* to leave by the head of the Order."

"Master Tsang was acting in your best interests—" Jake started to say, his brow furrowed.

I laughed and held up a hand. "Don't worry, Jake, I'm not here to start up that whole how-I-left-and-why-I-left thing. Honestly, I'm over it. And perfectly willing to accept that Master Tsang was right and I was wrong about divination being my calling. I'm a mutt, half human and half elf, neither one thing or another, and as we both know, divination is a gift, not a skill. Hence my inability to tell if that box is nasty or not. What do you think?"

Jake sighed and gave up trying to glare me into being something I just wasn't. He looked off into the distance as his hands spread across the box, an abstracted look on his face indicating he was deep in a world that only Diviners could access. "The box itself has been in the possession of a demon."

"So that *was* a demon? Interesting."

"However, the object inside it does not seem to be imbued with any dark powers."

"That's good to know. So what is it?" I asked, curious.

Jake blinked and shot me a jaded look. "I'm not an X-ray machine, Sam. If you want to know what's in it, you'll have to find out for yourself."

"But I told you, I can't divine anything—"

He rolled his eyes, shoving the box back at me. "I meant you'll have to open the box, you idiot."

"Oh." I smiled and punched him lightly in the shoulder, just to let him know I appreciated the insult. I bummed a pair of scissors from him to cut the leather thongs that bound the box, then popped off the lid, wondering what on earth a demon could be delivering, and whom it was supposed to be delivered to. "Huh. It's a statue."

"Of what?" Jake asked, peering over my shoulder. "A bird?"

"Yeah." I lifted the small statue from a nest of velvet material, surprised by its weight. It was gold-colored, about nine inches tall, apparently of a bird of prey. "Looks like a hawk or falcon or some raptor like that."

"Ooooh. Is it gold?" he asked, his voice hushed as if he was in the presence of something awe-inspiring.

I turned the statue around, flipping it over to look at the bottom. "I don't think so. I think it's brass."

"How can you tell?" he asked. "It looks like gold to me."

"One word." I pointed at the letters on the bottom of the statue. "Last I heard, Taiwan wasn't knocking off gold bird statues."

"Why would someone go to the trouble of having a demon deliver a non-gold Taiwanese statue?" Jake asked, looking as confused as I felt.

"That is the question, isn't it?" I gave the bird statue another quick once-over, then put it back in the box and strapped the lid on with some packing tape. "Maybe if I knew that, I'd know who it was meant for. Thanks for your help, Jake. And for the referral. I appreciate you spreading the word about our agency."

"What are you going to do with the statue?" he asked, waving away my thanks as he walked me to the door.

"You said it's not evil or anything, so..." I

shrugged, pulling my jacket close against the chilly, damp May air. "I'll put it in a safe place until after this job is over, and then try to track down the person it was intended for. Thanks again. And stop frowning—my mother always says a frown is what brings the rain."

"That's because your mother's frowns literally do," he answered, yelling after me as I hurried off toward the bus stop a few streets away. "Be careful, Sam. The statue may not be made of gold, but it clearly has some value if a demon was engaged to deliver it. Whoever it was intended for may not take kindly to you possessing it."

I waved to let him know I heard, then made my way back to the office, stopping off at the store occupying the floor below to leave off the shoebox with Mila, sex shop diva, landlady extraordinaire, and more importantly, possessor of a huge black safe that squatted in the corner of her small office.

"I'm back," I called to Clare as I trotted upstairs to our office. "Did you get a list of antique dealers? Did you find out anything about that book? Why are the shades drawn? You would not believe the guy I saw in one of those long dusters that are so sexy on men. He was browsing through the condoms at the back of Mila's shop, and wow, talk about slobber city! Tall, dark, and handso— oh. Hello."

"Good afternoon." A man wearing a long leather coat and holding a black fedora loomed into view. For a fraction of a second my mouth hung open. Even though the room was dark, the lights on the desk illuminated him enough to see one hell of a specimen of man—short curly black hair, liquid silver eyes that glowed brightly in the dark room, and shoulders that seemed to go on forever. On the other side of the office, Clare quickly stuffed a tulip petal in her mouth, her eyes huge as she looked back and forth between the man and me. "You are the Diviner Samantha Cosse?"

"I'm Sam, yes," I said, skating around the non-applicable Diviner label. "Can I help you?"

"I hope so. My brother—he's the tall, dark and handsome one downstairs condom shopping—referred you to me as someone who might locate a missing object for me."

I sent Clare a woohoo, two-cases-in-one-day look, but she was too busy gawking at the man to catch it. Clearly, though, something was up to have her so flustered. "I see. Well, Mr. . . . er . . ."

"My name is Paen Scott."

"Pain? As in . . . *pain?*"

"Paen. It's a medieval name, one that runs in my family. My mother liked it."

"It's . . . unique. Won't you have a seat at my desk, Mr. Scott?" I sidled over, grabbed Clare's arm, and hustled her toward the door. "I just need a quick word with my partner. I'll be right back to take down all the details of your missing item."

"You're leaving him alone in there?" Clare whispered as I opened the door to the hallway.

I glanced back inside. The man stood next to the client chair in front of my desk, his hat in his hands, a dark, vibrant figure that seemed to catch my gaze and hold it.

"He is something, isn't he?" I whispered back, pushing Clare through the doorway to the hall beyond. "I know he's a potential client and all, but hoo! The guy downstairs was nice-looking, but this man is drop-dead gorgeous."

Clare stared at me as if a second head had magically sprouted on my shoulders. She popped another bit of tulip in her mouth and chewed quickly. "You think he's . . . *handsome?*"

She said the word like it was made up of maggots. Rotten maggots. "Well, of course I do. I'd have to be dead not to notice. What's wrong with you? Why are you so wonked out?"

She stared at me again. "Don't you know what he is?"

"A client?" I asked, suddenly concerned. Clare liked men. Men worshipped Clare. For her to be in the presence of a devastatingly handsome man and not be responding with her typical flirtatious manner was very unusual.

"No. Yes, I mean, he *is* a client, but he's also . . ." Her voice trailed away as she waved the remains of the tulip around.

"What? Gay? Married? A homicidal maniac?"

"Vampire," she whispered, her eyes getting even bigger as she looked over my shoulder. A little shiver washed down my spine.

"We prefer the term Dark One, actually," a voice behind me said. I spun around to face the man. He had been right behind me, which meant I was now all but pressed up against him. Up close, he was even more handsome than standing across the room, the blunt line of his jaw and those bright silver eyes making my breath catch in my throat. "Moravian Dark One is the technical name, to be exact. If you are finished with your conference, perhaps we could get to my missing statue?"

"Statue?" I asked stupidly, wondering if it was wrong to be so instantly and wholly attracted to a man, especially when that man was a ... *vampire?* Good lord, it was almost dinnertime. What if he was peckish?

A Diviner with a sense of humor. How amusing.

I blinked a couple of times (like that was going to do me any good). "I'm sorry, I'm clearly a bit out of it. . . . Did she say vampire? You're a real vampire? A Dracula-type vampire?"

"I am a Dark One, yes. Is that going to be a problem to a working relationship?" Paen asked, his voice deep, with a lovely Scottish accent that seemed to roll right through me. I shivered and rubbed my arms, wondering about my reaction to him.

"Well . . . I don't know," I said, thinking furiously. "I've never worked with a vam— er . . . Dark One before. I've never even seen one. To be honest, I wasn't entirely sure that you guys existed."

"Really?" His silver eyes roamed over my face, finally touching on my ears. Without a thought, my left hand went to my ear for a moment. "And yet I would have guessed from your facial structure and eyes that you have some Fae blood in you."

"Something like that. My mother is an elf."

"Ah," he said, glancing at my nearest ear again.

I rubbed it self-consciously. "I had them bobbed when I was twelve. It was a coming-of-age present. I can't do anything about the tilt of my eyes, though."

"Don't. They are lovely as they are. Do I take it that your immortal heritage means you have no issues with taking my case and performing as many divinations as will be necessary to help me?"

I pulled myself together. Paen was a man, a potential client. His preferred choice of food was no business of mine, so long as I wasn't on the receiving end of those fangs.

A shame. I can think of so many places I would like to nibble.

"I'm only half elf, and not immortal, but yes, absolutely I will take your case. I have no issues whatsoever. Although, regarding the divinations . . ." I bit my lip, hesitating, ignoring my inner voice to worry over something that could become an issue. He seemed to want a Diviner to do the job for him. Clearly he didn't know that I wasn't fully qualified to conduct divinations.

"Is there a problem?" Paen asked, interrupting my uncomfortable thoughts.

If I told him I wasn't a Diviner, would he take his business elsewhere? How unethical was it for me to take a job under false pretenses?

"Miss Cosse?"

I sighed. It was unethical enough to make me admit the truth. "I'm not sure where you heard I was a Diviner"—Paen glanced at Clare, who suddenly busied herself with something in a desk drawer—"but I must tell you that although I've had some training as a Diviner, I am not, in fact, one. So if you'd like to withdraw your request for help, I will understand. However, I do have some skills in finding lost objects, and I will be happy to apply my full effort to your problem if you see fit to entrust it to us."

He rubbed his chin for a moment, his eyes darkening until they were a cloudy grey. "I appreciate your honesty. If you are confident you can help me, I see no reason to go elsewhere."

I smiled, and heaved a mental sigh of relief. "Excellent. Shall we?" I gestured him back into the office. "You mentioned something about a statue. It wouldn't happen to be a brass statue of a bird, a hawk or falcon, would it?"

He didn't even bat an eye. "No. The statue I seek is black, of a monkey. It is called the Jilin God. Have you heard of it?"

My fingers itched to type the phrase into Google, but I didn't want to look so ignorant in front of a potential client. "No, I'm afraid I haven't, but admittedly, I haven't made a study of art. Can you tell me a little about it?"

"No."

"Ah." I waited a moment to see if he wanted to add to that. He just watched me. "Er . . . nothing about it? Nothing at all?"

He made a brief, annoyed, shrugging gesture. "Virtually nothing. I can't tell you when it was stolen from my home, what its history is, or even exactly what it looks like. All I know is its name, that it's black, and depicts a monkey. It's up to you to find it for me."

Paen leaned back in his chair, a slight arrogant twist to his eyebrows, as if he was challenging me to turn down his outrageous request.

I glanced over to Clare. She had thankfully stopped consuming flowers, but sat at her desk taking notes, a wary look on her face. That didn't bode well. Clare as a full-blooded faery (albeit one who didn't admit the fact) had an uncanny sense about people, a sense I had learned to appreciate. "I see. Well . . ." I stopped and nibbled my lip again, unsure of what I wanted to do.

"Yes?"

The fact that Clare was hesitant about Paen raised enough warning bells in my head that I considered refusing the job offer. I had one job already, after all. I wasn't desperate for another one. I hesitated for a moment, and then looked back at the man sitting in front of me, intending to tell him that I was unable to help him. But as I opened my mouth to do just that, waves of coldness rolled off him, a coldness of despair and utter emptiness that buffeted me, leaving me shivering with a sadness that seemed to have no end. "I'd like to come home with you," my mouth said without consulting my brain.

I almost died. Mentally, I slapped a hand over my mouth and asked myself what my problem was.

Paen's eyes widened. Clare's just about bugged right out of her head. "Pardon?" he finally asked.

"I'm sorry. That sounded like a base proposition, which I assure you it wasn't."

That's a shame, a voice in my head said.

I ignored it. "What I'd like to do is go over your home, examining it for clues as to the nature and whereabouts of the statue. Assuming it was there in the past, I might be able to pick up some whatchamacallit . . . vibes and things."

"Vibes and things?" he asked, disbelief evident for a moment in those gorgeous quicksilver eyes.

"Yes. Emanations and such—very powerful things. They can tell a lot about an object." Oh, great,

Sam—babble like an idiot in front of a client. A very handsome client, not that his appearance had anything to do with it.

But man alive, he sure rang my chimes, what with those shoulders, and that jaw, and those flashing silver eyes. . . . A quick glance at his expression had me pulling back from *that* particular mental excursion. I dug through my memory of Diviner precepts and trotted out something I thought had a bit more of a professional ring to it. "Sometimes objects leave behind a non-tangible record of their existence. Diviners can use that trail to learn more about the object itself, and tune into its wavelength, if you will, thus allowing them to locate the item."

"Hmm." He didn't look convinced, but at least he lost that what-the-hell-are-you-saying-you-idiot-woman-you look. In fact, for a moment there, it looked like he was trying not to smile. "I suppose that's possible, although the statue must have been removed from my home many years ago. Its intangible record may be so weak you can't read it."

"I won't know until I can examine the house," I said brightly. For some reason—oh, who am I trying to fool? It was because he was so damned gorgeous, and it had been so very long since I had been with a man—I was quite determined to do anything to prolong our contact, and that included checking out his home. Honesty forced me to admit that common curiosity about what sort of a place a vampire inhabited was not going to do for an explanation of my interest in him. It was the man himself that caught my attention, and held it. "You never know what sorts of things you can learn until you open yourself up to new experiences."

An interesting array of emotions flitted across his face. At first he looked obstinate, then somewhat surprised, followed by smug, ending with a smile so fleeting I almost missed it, which quickly dissolved into a bland, expressionless look that left me even colder than before. "Very well. As you feel it's necessary, I will allow you to conduct whatever divination rituals you need in my home. What will you require as a retainer fee?"

"Nothing," I said, quickly flipping over the little sign that stood on the edge of my desk proclaiming that a 10 percent retainer was due at the time of engagement. "We can talk fees and such after I've had a chance to get a better feel for the case, if that's agreeable with you."

His eyebrows rose for a moment, but settled down almost immediately. "As you like. When would you like to examine my home?"

"Anything wrong with right now?" I asked, standing when he did.

The surprised look was back for a moment or two in his eyes.

A straightforward woman. What a refreshing change.

I jerked as if I'd been shocked. That wasn't my inner voice speaking to me as I had assumed it was—this was someone else. Someone male, someone with a Scottish accent that made me think of *Braveheart*, and men wearing kilts, and wild, sexy masculinity. In other words, it made me think of . . .

"As you put it like that, no," Paen said, his eyes shuttered. "There is nothing wrong with right now."

Why on earth was he talking in my head? Why and how? And why didn't I particularly mind such an intimate feeling? I ignored the questions squirreling around in my brain, confident that I would work out the answers in the near future. It was just one more curious element in what I was coming to believe was a fascinating man.

"Excellent. We have another case we're presently engaged with," I said, shooting Clare a meaningful look that, judging by the confused expression on her face, went totally over her head. I gathered up my coat and tapestry bag, closing my laptop and slipping it into the bag. "But I think we can handle both cases without any difficulty. Clare, another minute of your time, please?"

Paen walked to the door as I conducted a quick whispered conference with Clare. "You don't mind if I go check out this statue thing, do you? I was going to swing by Mr. Race's house to pick up the information about the manuscript he asked his housekeeper to get for me, but I can't do both tonight. Can you work on the manuscript case by yourself for a bit?"

"Of course. I have arranged for a meeting with a fence in two hours. I can go to Mr. Race's house first, then meet the fence."

"A fence!" I stared at Clare.

"Yes. Raul the fence. He wouldn't talk to me on the phone, so I am going to meet him later tonight—"

"How on earth does an underwear-modeling faery know a fence?"

Clare gave me a wounded look. "I do wish you would stop being so silly about that faery business. And as for Raul, I met him at a party. He is a very nice man for a criminal."

Now, how on earth was I supposed to reason with that sort of an attitude? I didn't even try.

"Be careful, no matter how nice a criminal he is. I'll call you in a bit, after I check out Paen. Er . . . check out Paen's house. It shouldn't take long, so hopefully I will be back in time to help you with your fence guy."

"All right," she said, her eyes worried. As I started to leave she tugged on my arm, saying in her soft, sweet voice, "Sam, I'm not sure you going to this man's home by yourself is a smart idea. He's a vampire! He's powerful! He could do any number of wicked things to you, and you wouldn't have any way of stopping him!"

I sighed as I looked at the dark figure waiting for me in the hallway. "Yeah, I know. Makes me goose bumpily all over just imagining what sorts of wicked things he could do, too. Especially with those delectable lips."

"Sam—"

"Don't worry, I'll be fine. Unless I get lucky and Paen tries to seduce me over to the dark side."

"Sam!"

I laughed and patted her arm as I passed. "Stop making that scandalized face, I'm just teasing you. Nothing is going to happen. Nothing *ever* happens to me, remember?"

I really hate it when my own words come back to haunt me.

Chapter 3

"So, you're Scottish," I said by way of making polite (if inane) conversation as Paen drove us to his home.

"Yes, I am."

"A Scottish vampire . . . er . . . Dark One."

"Yes." He kept his eyes on the road as we drove into the darkness. Night had fallen fully, the air thick with the promise of more rain, the stars and moon obscured by the usual soggy clouds that I'd seen hang over Edinburgh for much of the two years I'd lived there.

"Is that unusual? I mean, I always imagined you guys were from Eastern Europe. Romania, or somewhere like that. Or is that just legend?"

His silver eyes flashed my way for a moment. "The origins of the Dark Ones are lost to us, but much of our heritage goes back to the Moravian Highlands in what's now the Czech Republic."

"Huh. Interesting." I looked outside at the black nothingness that whizzed by us as he drove beyond the suburbs of Edinburgh into the lowlands, quickly heading into the windswept hills of East Lothian on a long, empty road. "I'm Canadian. And American. Both. My dad is from the US, but my mother is Canadian, and I grew up there. I've got a dual citizenship thing going, in case you were wondering. That's how I was able to open up a business here."

He said nothing. I took that to mean he wasn't wondering about the ins and outs of my heritage.

"Did I thank you for giving me a ride to your house? Clare has a car, but she tends to start writing poetry to the stars or a flower and doesn't pay much attention to actually driving, so I really do appreciate you giving me a lift."

"Yes, you thanked me."

"Good." Silence fell between us—not a companionable, comfortable silence, but one that was fairly awkward and weighty. It itched along my skin like raw wool. "Finn was nice. Are you sure he won't mind being left in Edinburgh? I hated to rush you into leaving, but I wanted to see the house before deep night was upon us."

"No, he won't mind."

"OK." More silence. I surreptitiously picked at a fingernail for a moment, wondering why I could be silent with so many other people without feeling anything, but was bothered by Paen's silence. I mused on that for a few minutes, then decided I'd put the question to the man who sat so close to me that his hand brushed my leg every time he shifted gears (something I was very well aware of). "Paen—"

His shoulder twitched.

"Oh, I'm sorry. I didn't mean to offend you by using your first name. I realize that's rather unprofessional of me, but it kind of slipped out."

"I don't mind if you call me Paen," he said, rather gruffly, I thought.

"Oh. Good. I'm Sam, by the way. Do you dislike talking to me?"

That got me a startled glance. "Pardon?"

"I wondered if you disliked talking to me. Especially since you were doing that whole non-verbal talking-into-my-head thing earlier."

Thank heavens for seat belts, that's all I can say. The belt kept me from bashing my brains out on the windshield when Paen slammed the brakes on, sending the car into a little spin in the (thankfully empty) rain-slickened road.

"Are you all right?" he asked once the car came to a stop, flipping on the overhead light so he could peer anxiously at me.

"I think so." I sat back and rubbed a spot on my neck where the seat belt had burned it. "I'm just a little shaky. Nothing like pulling a one-eighty to get your adrenaline flowing, eh?"

He didn't answer, just opened the car door and got out to look at the front of the car. I sat for a minute, figuring he was just checking on the car, but when he started walking away from me, I got out.

"Is the car OK?"

"Yes. I'm looking for the demon," he said, peering into the night. "Damn. I wish I'd thought to bring a torch."

"Demon? What demon?" I hurried over to where he stood, the car's rear lights our only illumination.

"The one that I almost hit when it jumped out in front of me. At least I assume it was a demon—it rose up from the ground, and there are few beings but demons which will do that." He frowned at me. "Do you have much experience with them?"

"Demons? No, not a lot," I answered, thinking about the one who had given me the bird statue. "All I really know about them is that they're bad news, and they have a nasty-smelling smoke."

"Exactly," he said, lifting his head.

I sniffed along with him, the faintest hint of a smoky stench reaching my nose. "That does smell like a demon. That or really bad fertilizer. But why would one jump out in front of us?"

"A good question, but one I can't answer right now," he said, giving me a gentle push toward the car.

I reentered the car, belting myself in, pulling down a small mirror to look at my neck.

"You're hurt," Paen said as he buckled up, leaning close to me in order to eye the spot on my neck that stung. That's what my mind said, anyway. My body didn't care why he was close; it just wanted him closer.

"Not really. It's just a little abrasion. All in a day's work," I quipped, suddenly overwhelmed by his nearness. His aftershave, a citrusy scent that mingled with something that was much earthier, much more male, and 100 percent pure pheromone as far as I was concerned, curled around me. I breathed it in again, my breath coming in short, shallow little bursts. Shivers skittered down my back while goose bumps broke out on my arms. I'd never had this sort of a reaction to anyone before, and I wasn't quite sure if I was comfortable with such an overpowering reaction. I tried to analyze just what it was about him that held such an attraction for me, and ended up putting it down to the fact that he was different from everyone I'd met before. Paen was missing something; he had a great need in him that I could feel even when I wasn't near him. That need called to me.

His eyes lifted from the spot on my neck to mine, two brilliant points of silver light in the dark, and I was suddenly reminded that needy and attractive as he was, I was trapped in a confined space in the middle of nowhere with a man who had no soul, a man for whom the word dinner meant who, not what.

"You're not going to bite me, are you?" I asked on a breath, my heart beating madly from the combination of adrenaline and Paen.

"Do you want me to?" His voice made me shiver again, the sound of it like the touch of raw silk on my bare flesh. In the blackness of the car, his eyes shone like the purest mercury.

"Part of me does," I answered. "Part of me wants to . . ."

"What?" he asked, his head moving closer until I could feel the warmth of his breath on my neck, just above the spot the seat belt had scraped.

"Bite you back."

His head tilted slightly as he considered me. "How would you bite me?"

"How as in how, or how as in give you a demonstration?"

His eyes glittered.

"Demonstrate how you would like to bite me."

I swear, looking into those eyes was like falling into a pool of quicksilver. They seemed to mesmerize me, pull me in and consume me. Without thinking of the wisdom (or lack) of making out with a client, I tipped my head slightly to the side and nuzzled a spot behind his ear, where the tendons of his neck met his jaw. All reason, all common sense, all thought but that of the man whose presence drew me disappeared as I licked a spot, then gently bit it.

Paen sucked in air, shuddering slightly as I nibbled the spot behind his ear, swirling my tongue over it once more before withdrawing.

"*That* is how I would like to bite you. Well, just one of the ways."

He didn't move, didn't pull back in disgust or triumph, either of which I half expected.

"You are a very honest woman," he said after a moment's silence.

I frowned. That wasn't quite the response I had imagined to my nibbles. "Yes. Half elf, remember? It pretty much makes it impossible to lie, what with that whole elves-can't-dissemble thing happening. Plus I've found it's just easier all around to tell the truth. Did you like it?"

"Yes." *Too much.*

I smiled.

"Would you like me to reciprocate?" he asked, his breath hot on my skin. I shivered again, a delicious shiver of anticipation and excitement and arousal. Beneath that, a deep, endless need of my own burst into life, consuming me with its power.

"You know, I think I would."

Heat flared along my neck as his tongue swept across the spot that had been scraped. Pleasure of a nature more profound than just sexual burst into being within me, setting my whole body trembling as his tongue caressed the sore spot, taking with it all the pain and discomfort, and leaving me strung tighter than a concert violin.

"You're hungry," I said suddenly, wondering how I knew.

"I am." His teeth nipped my skin.

"Then go ahead." I waited, my body clenched hard.

"I don't normally—" He stopped, hesitating.

"Don't what? Drink blood?"

"No, I must drink blood to feed." Paen's eyes had darkened until they were the color of clouds over the moon. "I don't normally feed from women I respect."

His words touched me in an oddly endearing way. "Are you saying you like me?" I asked, wondering why it meant so much that he did.

"Yes," he answered, his breath hot on my neck.

"Good. I like you, too."

"It is for that reason that I hesitate," he said, his lips caressing the skin on my neck. I melted. "But if you're sure—"

"I'm sure," I said, pressing myself against his mouth.

"I won't take anything you don't want to give," he reassured, his tongue flicking across my pulse point.

"Dinner's on," I said, my head lolling back as his tongue swept across my skin once again, sending ripples of excitement through me. Pain, red and hot and deep, flared from my neck for a second before it dissolved into a pleasure that seemed almost obscene in its quality. I twisted slightly so I could clutch Paen's head, my fingers tangling into his curls as he drank from me.

"Dear god, don't stop," I gasped, my body seemingly one gigantic erogenous zone as he took life from me.

I won't. I can't.

A familiar rush of lightness raced through me. I struggled against it, clutching Paen's head even harder as my mother's blood kicked in and sent my consciousness flying out of my body.

"No, dammit!" I yelled silently as my ethereal being floated out of the car, Paen's head bent over mine the last thing I saw before I was caught on an astral wind and whipped away from the car. "Dammit, this isn't fair! Why can't I stay? *Nooo!*"

I drifted down the road, past houses, up over trees, gaining speed as the wind carried me farther and farther away from my body. There was no moon, so I couldn't see where I was going, but as I was whipped along over fields, housing tracts, and stretches of untouched land, I had a feeling I was heading to somewhere specific.

I've found that time passes differently when you're an astral projection. Either it seems telescoped, running so slow a second seems to take minutes, or it's speeded up like a movie being fast-forwarded. In the time it took me to swear silently (in my astral form, I couldn't speak aloud), I found myself zooming up to a looming black structure, a castle, an ebony mass silhouetted against a midnight sky. Before I could blink, I was whisked through the castle, down stairs, and suddenly plunked down in a rectangular room lined with bookcases. At one end of the room sat a large desk, a man seated behind it, shadowed by the light that illuminated only one corner of the desk. He shuffled through papers, and occasionally peered at a computer monitor as he tapped a couple of keys. He looked vaguely familiar. For a moment, I couldn't place him, but in a flash of memory I realized he was the man who had been arguing with the antique shop owner.

"Huh. I wonder what I'm doing seeing him? It's certainly not the man I'd like to be looking at right this moment."

Although the words I had spoken didn't make a sound, the man's head snapped up just as if he had heard them. He half stood while scanning the room, evidently startled by my interruption, but I knew that wasn't at all possible. My astral form was soundless and invisible. In reality, I wasn't really there, so how could he see or hear me?

"Uh . . . hello? Can you hear— whoa! Where did *you* come from?"

The small monkey named Beppo—at least, I assumed it was the same monkey; I couldn't get close enough to see if he wore the same leather collar—raced across the room and jumped onto the desk. The man had been in the process of sitting back down, but he shot up again at my words, his head turning back and forth as he scanned the room. A chill rippled through me as his gaze approached me. I was suddenly very, very afraid, and wanted nothing more than to be away from that room. There was an aura of something powerful around him, as if he suddenly presented a threat. I tried to tell myself that I was being ridiculous, that there was nothing anyone could do to me in astral form, but my brain didn't want to listen.

I froze when the man's eyes met mine, holding my breath as if that would make my invisible self even more invisible. He held out his arm for the monkey, going still when Beppo scrambled up to his shoulder.

Then he smiled at me. Slowly. With so much menace that a scream built up inside me. Just as it was about to burst from my formless lips, a voice in the distance called my name.

"Samantha!"

The man snarled something and lunged toward me, but my ethereal body was yanked out of the room, whisked back toward the voice that so imperiously demanded my attention. "Samantha, you will answer me!"

The trip back to my body was conducted much more quickly than the journey out—the world seemed to shimmer and blur, shaking itself for a moment, then suddenly I was sitting in Paen's car, my neck tingling, my body tight and tense as if it had been on the verge of an orgasm.

"Welcome back," Paen said dryly.

"Hi," I said, touching my neck. There didn't seem to be any open wound, so I gathered he had some power to heal up any signs he had been dining at Café Sam. "Oh, thank you. Thank you so much."

"For what, boring you?" he asked, reversing the car, turning so we were headed back into the hills.

"Boring me? No, Paen . . ." I put my hand on his arm, slightly surprised to find that I was shaking from my encounter with the dark man. "I was thanking you for pulling me back. I . . . there was someone I would not care to meet again, and you anchored me when I needed it, so thank you. But I wasn't bored with you—it's not that at all. It's just . . . I have . . . oh, it's a little difficult to explain."

"Is it?"

I sighed, rubbing the chill from my arms. Just

being near Paen seemed to drive away the nightmar-
ish quality of my out-of-body experience. "The truth
is that it's all my mother's fault."

His jaw tightened as he drove. "Indeed."

"I didn't mean that it's her fault I'm here, and thus
with you—I meant it's my mother's fault because she
passed on a couple of elf traits to me. I was born with
her pointy ears, elf-tipped eyes, talent for finding lost
things, and a really warped version of her ability to
do out-of-body trips. Unlike Mom's skill with astral
projection, however, mine only hits whenever I'm
sexually aroused."

He looked at me in patent disbelief. "You what?"

I nodded, then pointed to the road. He turned
back to it, but glanced curiously from the corner of
his eye a couple of times. "Whenever I get aroused,
my body and consciousness part ways, and I go drifting off while it has all the fun. I can't begin to tell you
how frustrating it is."

"I can imagine," he said dryly.

"Oh, you think you can, but I doubt it," I said
mournfully. "It's awful, and there's nothing I can do
about it. I've tried everything, too. Once I'm gone—
pfft! I just have to wait it out. No one has ever called
me back like you did. That was pretty amazing."

"Hmm." He didn't look like he disbelieved me,
but he didn't look like he was buying everything I
was saying, either.

"The worst is when I come back and find out that
evidently I've been having wonderful sexual experiences, but wasn't there to enjoy them."

He shot me a curious glance. "Are you saying this
happens *every* time you engage in sex?"

I nodded. "It doesn't even have to be sex. Just doing what we were doing is enough to send my brain into astral mode."

"So you've never actually . . . er . . . for lack of a better phrasing, been there for any of the times you've had sex?"

"No."

"Not any of the times?"

"None. It's not like I've had tons of sex, though. I pretty much gave it up after I realized what was going on. I mean, what's the use? Just when I start getting into it, whammo! I'm taken off and return to find my body either apparently fulfilled and no longer interested, or tense and frustrated, while my boyfriend is snoring away."

"I see."

"I've only had three boyfriends," I said, compelled for some reason to make it absolutely clear I wasn't a thrill-seeking trollop. "But I tried everything I could think of to stay there for the whole thing, and never had any luck."

"Perhaps the fault lies with them, not you," Paen said, his eyes back on the road as we drove.

"What do you mean?"

"Were your partners mortal?"

"Yes. One was a Diviner, but he was mortal all right. He died last year in a plane crash."

"I'm sorry to hear that."

"So was I. He was a nice guy. Not a great Diviner, but a nice guy. But what do my boyfriends being mortal have to do with me drifting away during the fun time?"

He shot me a silver-eyed look that was completely

unreadable. "You have immortal blood. Perhaps you would have better luck with a man who shared that trait."

My jaw dropped for a moment before I had enough wits about me to snap it back. "Are you offering yourself as a potential partner?"

There was a pause. "In the interests of scientific understanding, yes, I would be willing to undertake that role."

He noticed the surprised look on my face.

"I don't normally proposition women in this manner, but I will admit to being physically attracted to you, and believe that you feel likewise."

"Oh, really." We were deep in the heart of the country now, heading into a rural area with patches of forest and wilderness, so there were no streetlights. The only light illuminating Paen's face was that from the dashboard, but it was enough for me to eye his profile. It was just as handsome as the rest of his face.

His jaw tightened. "I see. I have misread your interest in me, then. I apologize for—"

"No!" I interrupted, not wanting him to misunderstand. "That 'oh, really?' wasn't challenging your statement about me being attracted to you—I am—but more just . . . well, annoyed."

"Annoyed?" A slight frown wrinkled his forehead. "Are you always annoyed when someone tells you he finds you attractive?"

"Of course not, but you have to admit that someone telling you they want to go to bed with you purely in the interests of science sounds a bit condescending. I mean, sheesh, talk about martyring yourself . . ."

His lips thinned. "I didn't intend for you to take my offer that way. I am a man. I find you an attractive woman, and since you apparently reciprocate that feeling, you are not presently dating anyone—" He paused and gave me a quick glance.

"Nope, not dating," I said.

"—and as you appear to be of legal age—"

"Thirty-four in September."

"—then I assumed I could express my interest without you taking offense."

"Oh, I'm not offended," I said, smiling. He was so cute when he was in a snit. "Just surprised."

He said nothing.

"Tempting as your offer is, I hasten to point out that you *are* immortal, and I just *did* do the astral thing, so the answer to what I would do with you is pretty evident."

"Not necessarily. I was feeding, not attempting to arouse you. It would be different if I were to focus my attention on bringing you pleasure."

I digested that morsel for a moment and admitted that he could well be right. "We just met, Paen. Yes, the physical thing is there, but we haven't known each other for more than a couple of hours at most. I've never been one for casual relationships. In fact, I was madly in love with all three of my boyfriends before we ever got physical."

"Perhaps that's the trouble," he said, still not looking at me.

"What, having an emotional commitment with my boyfriends before having sex with them?"

"Yes. Sex is a bodily function no different from any other bodily function. You need air, you breathe. You need sexual pleasure, you have sex. It's that simple."

I gawked. "You are really screwed up, aren't you? We're talking serious commitment issues here, the kind that you see on *Montel.*"

"You don't have to be committed to a hamburger to gain sustenance from it, do you?"

"No, of course not, but—"

"Why should something so simple as sex be any different?" he asked, his eyes all but lighting up the inside of the car. "I have no doubts that were you willing. I would be able to provide you with sexual pleasure without any messy emotional issues becoming involved."

" 'Messy emotional issues,' " I repeated, aghast. "Is that what being in love is to you? Messy?"

"Yes. Love for a sexual partner serves no real purpose. It is unnecessary."

"Thus speaks a man who has never been in love," I said. "Are you sure you're a Dark One and not a Vulcan or something?"

"On the contrary, I love my parents and brothers," he answered, ignoring my Vulcan quip.

"That's splitting hairs, and you know it. Love in a relationship is a wonderful thing, Paen. Sex can be nice on its own—or so I've been told; I've never been present to feel it for myself—but sex without love is empty. Shallow. Meaningless."

He snorted. "Why do women have to sugarcoat everything?"

"How's this for sugarcoating—what you're talking about is the difference between fucking and love-making."

"You say that like there's something wrong with fucking."

"Of course there's nothing wrong with it. Even people deeply in love can indulge in it. But one is pure physical pleasure, while the other has a deeper meaning. Lovemaking is more than just sex—the pleasure received from it comes not just from sexual stimulation, but from sharing something profound with a person who is more than just a casual acquaintance. Lovemaking is just that—making something, creating a bond, forming a loving relationship."

He shot me an annoyed look. "You are using a woman's typical arguments. Until you've tried it my way, you can't make a statement like that."

"The same could be said for you making generalizations against love. Boy, you are so lucky I'm not in love with you. You'd have some serious shaping up to do."

"That is a moot point. You are not in love with me, nor I you, but I *would* be quite willing to show you the pleasure I could give you sexually."

"You're still saying you want to screw me?"

A muscle in his jaw twitched. "I wasn't going to put it quite so crudely, but yes. I want you in a sexual sense."

"Why?"

"Why?" he asked, confused.

"Yes, why do you want me? That is, what about me is attractive to you?"

The annoyance that flared in his eyes had me smiling to myself. "You intrigue me. I find you stimulating, both physically and mentally. And . . . er . . . you smell nice."

"I smell nice?" I tipped my head to the side to sniff myself.

His eyes flickered my way for a moment. "Yes. You smell like a woman, untainted by harsh chemical scents. You smell like a sun-warmed field of wild-flowers."

"Wow," I said, momentarily renderd speechless by his comment. "That's the nicest thing anyone has ever said about me."

"Your scent permeates the air around you," he added.

"I take it back—that just makes me sound like I have gas." I did another covert sniff of myself, but didn't notice any sun-warmed wildflower smell being emitted from any part of me.

"On the contrary, your natural scent is very pleas-ing. Very arousing. That's why I want you, and that is why I offered what I did."

I sat wordless for another few minutes before fi-nally saying, "All right."

He slowed the car down to a stop right in the mid-dle of a windswept stretch of road. "All right? You wish to have sex?"

"Well, not right this second, but yes, I will go to bed with you. You can do your best with me. But when it ends up being a hollow experience and my mind goes drifting off on its own, I'm going to let you know."

"I accept your terms," he said, setting off again.

"The only reason I'm doing this is because I have a point to prove to you," I said, which was mostly true. I still didn't really understand why I was willing to do this; I wasn't like Clare, falling in love with a new man every week. It took months for my emotions to ripen to a point where I found a man sexually stimulating.

But there was just something about him, something that seemed to call out to me, something that *needed* me . . .

"As I have with you."

"There's no way that sex without affection can possibly be better than sex with it. And although I can't show you that for yourself, I can certainly prove to you that your way is not going to work for me."

His lips quirked upward. "I have no doubt that there will be little difficulty in showing you the delights in a wholly physical relationship unencumbered by any emotional expectations beyond that of sexual satisfaction."

"In your dreams," I muttered to myself, half annoyed with his arrogant attitude, half aroused just by the thought of sleeping with him.

"We'll explore fantasy role-playing later," he said, and I spent a long time after that wondering just what his grin meant.

Chapter 4

The remainder of the drive to Paen's home was anti-climactic (literally, but we won't go there). I was momentarily surprised to see that the castle I had astrally visited was his.

"It's just like I saw when I was floating around," I said as he drove across a long causeway that connected a tiny little island with land. "I had no idea you lived in a castle. Wow. It's really impressive. It's . . . er . . . not haunted or anything, is it?"

"Haunted?" Paen frowned. "Why do you think it would be haunted?"

"Aren't most castles?"

"Mine isn't."

"Oh. How old is it?"

He spent the time it took us to circle around the castle to a parking area at the back to give me a quick history of the place. By the time he escorted me into the main building, I knew it was approximately six hundred years old, had been inherited by his father via his grandmother's mortal family, and although it was beset with a dampness issue that no amount of modern technology could seem to fix, it housed nothing more extraordinary than a family of vampires.

Which, I suppose, was pretty extraordinary when you considered it.

"How many people does it take to keep up a castle?" I asked as he walked me through a huge hall.

"We have a day staff of four—two inside, and two outdoors."

"Ah. And nighttime?"

"None of the staff remains after dark," he answered, shooting me an unreadable look.

"Oh, right. That's when you guys do your thing." I stopped for a moment and looked at Paen. He turned back to see what was keeping me. "Do you miss the daylight?"

A tiny little frown wrinkled his brow. "Miss it? What do you mean?"

"Well, you're up at night rather than day. I wondered if you missed it."

"I am up no later than noon each day," he answered, looking oddly hurt. "I keep late hours, yes, but I assure you that I don't spend my life in darkness."

"Oh. I thought all vamps were nighttime only. So you don't miss being able to go outside in the sun? You don't . . . you know, brood about being a Dark One, not being able to do things other people can do?"

"Good lord, no. I don't brood about anything. I am perfectly happy being what and who I am," he said, giving me a mildly annoyed look. "To do otherwise would be a waste of time."

"But . . . you have no soul," I said, following him through a door. "I may not have been around any

Dark Ones before, but even I can tell there's something missing in you. It's like your insides are made of ice. Doesn't that bother you?"

"Not at all. I may lack a soul, but I have not allowed that to hinder me in any way," he said, turning to wave a hand around the room. "You said you wanted to see the house. This is the library. My father is seldom home to use it, so it's really my room."

"It's lovely. Very comfortable," I said, looking around. It was a typical room of its sort—floor-to-ceiling bookcases lining two walls, dark leather furniture gathered around a fireplace, long, heavy (assumedly light-inhibiting) curtains framing huge windows and a pair of French doors, and a familiar desk lurking at the opposite end of the room—familiar because this was the room my brain had zipped off to while Paen was snacking on me.

It was interesting that I had been sent to this place earlier. "Can you guys disappear?"

Paen just stared at me.

"Is that a no?" I asked.

"Yes, it's a no. Dark Ones are more or less human, Samantha. We have some integral differences, but despite popular lore, we don't shape-shift, we can't fly, and we are not able to disappear into nothing."

"Hmm. Then who was that man at your desk? The bad one, the one who creeped me out so much?"

He looked startled for a moment. "What man?"

"The one I saw while you were sucking down Vintage Sam. There was a man at your desk, poking around in things. I assumed it was his own. He seemed to hear me, though, and then I could have sworn he saw me, which is impossible. He seemed threatening somehow. I'm so glad you pulled me back before he had time to . . ."

"To what?" Paen asked, quickly examining his desk.

"I don't know. Something bad." I moved closer to the desk, looking hard at it like it would spill whatever secrets it kept.

"Why would someone want to harm you?"

"No idea. I haven't been in the business long enough to have jealous rivals, and we just got our first and second cases today, so it's not a pissy client or something. What are you doing?"

"Looking to see if anything has been disturbed," Paen said, checking the computer. "I don't see anything missing."

"Maybe he didn't find what he came for," I suggested.

"That, or he was looking for information rather than an object," Paen answered, tidying up some papers. "We won't know that unless you see the man again. Unless you can . . ." He waved a hand over the table, one eyebrow cocked in question.

I held out my hands over the table, but didn't get the slightest inkling of anything untoward. "Sorry. That's not really my forte."

He grunted a noncommittal response as he shoved some papers into a leather attaché. I used the moment to get a better look around the room. I wandered down a line of bookcases, noting a few empty shelves. "Is this the room where the statue had been kept?"

"No."

I waited a moment for Paen to elucidate, but he just shucked his coat, held out a hand for my jacket, then went back to the desk to check the answering machine for messages.

"All righty," I said, looking around the room again, trying to orient myself. "Where was it kept? If you take me there, maybe I can pick up some information about it."

He stopped frowning at the answering machine and frowned at me instead. "That's what *you're* here to do—find it. I have no idea where it was kept."

"Why do I think there's more to this statue thing than you're telling me?" I asked, taking a seat on a chair next to his desk. "You don't know what it looks like, don't know when it was stolen from your family's castle, don't even know where it was kept . . . Nope. Not adding up. Why don't you tell me the whole story?"

He stood silent for a moment. *I don't know if I can trust you.*

Of course you can. I'm eminently trustworthy, just ask anyone. Besides, we're going to sleep together. Even you, Mr. No Emotional Commitment, must have some level of trust you are willing to grant to a sexual partner.

Paen's jaw slackened for a moment as a look of absolute surprise filled his lovely silver eyes. "How did you do that?"

"Do what?" *Talk to you without actually speaking aloud?*

He stared at me as if I was an escapee from a freak show. "Yes."

"I'm not quite sure," I said, shrugging. "I could hear you, so I figured the reverse might be possible if I thought at you. Evidently it is. Are Dark Ones usually telepathic like that?"

His eyes widened for a moment before narrowing. "No, they are not. Not without some connection, usually a close blood relationship."

"Oh, so you can talk to Finn that way?"

"My brothers, yes. But not others," he answered, moving behind the desk. I got the distinct feeling he was uneasy, as if he was avoiding something. "About the statue—it has been demanded as payment to the demon lord Oriens. I have five days to find it, or a horrible penalty will be placed upon my family."

"What penalty?" I asked, feeling nosy, but needing to know everything there was to know about the statue and its history.

He toyed with a pen for a moment. "My mother's soul will be forfeited."

"Ouch. OK, so we need to find this statue in five days. That's an impossibly short amount of time to find anything, but I'll give it my utmost attention." I rubbed my chin as I thought. "Does anyone in your family know anything about it?"

"Assumedly my parents do, but they are on a research trip in an uninhabited forest in Bolivia, and thus are out of communication for the next month or so."

"Can't you do the brain thing with them?"

"No." His lips got a wry twist to them for a few seconds. "When I was a child I could, but now I can only do the *brain thing*, as you call it, with my brothers."

"Hmm." I rubbed my chin some more. "Can they do it with your parents?"

"Not anymore. Like me, they lost the ability when they reached adulthood."

"Huh. Weird. I'd have thought once you had it, you had it forever."

Paen made an exasperated tsking noise. "I appreciate you wishing to know all that there is to know about my family and our relationship to the statue, but shouldn't you get on with finding it? That is your job."

"Yes, but as I told you before, I'm not a Diviner. It's not just a matter of me consulting the higher spirits and asking where the statue is now."

"You may not be a Diviner, but you have elf blood, and you are talented in finding objects—or so you said."

"Hey now, no slurs," I said, getting up to pace the length of the room. "I *am* good at finding things. Better even than my mother, and she's nothing to sneeze at in the locating department. But every little bit of information I can get helps narrow down the search. Since you don't know anything else . . . well, we'll just do this logically."

"What are you doing?" Paen asked, coming over to where I was stretching out on the carpet.

"I'm going to open myself up to the castle, and let my consciousness roam the hallways, looking for signs of the statue."

"You intend to search for the statue while lying on the floor?"

"Sure. My mother does it artistically arranged on a fainting couch, but whenever I try that I get a case of the giggles, so I just use the plain old floor."

He stood over me, his hands on his hips, glowering. I smiled up at him. *You really are handsome, you know? If you weren't so messed up about relationships, I might go for you.*

"Stop that."

Stop what, this?

"Yes. I don't like it."

I could feel how uncomfortable it was making him, so I didn't continue, although I couldn't help but ask why. "All right. But why does me doing that bother you so much?"

He glowered some more at me, and ignored my question. "Why are you trying to find the statue here? I told you it was stolen. Why aren't you using your powers to locate it?"

"I'm looking here first because you don't know for a fact that it was stolen."

"It has to have been stolen. I know every inch of this castle, and there are no monkey statues anywhere."

"It could be hidden," I pointed out, admiring for a moment the gloss on his shoes. "Until we rule out absolutely that it's not here somewhere, it doesn't make sense to search elsewhere."

"Doubtful."

I sighed, closed my eyes, and crossed my arms over my chest. "Shoo."

"What?" Disbelief was rife in his voice.

"Shoo. Go away. Leave me alone so I can work."

"You're shooing me from my own library?"

"Yes." I uncrossed my arms to make shooing motions, peeking at him through barely opened eyes. He looked outraged at the thought of me telling him what to do. "If you're not going to be quiet and let me concentrate, you have to leave."

He drew himself up, not that he wasn't impressive enough before. Now he positively loomed over me. "I will not be shooed from my own room."

"Fine, then. Just give me a little quiet so I can focus and do the mental thing."

The leather couch sighed softly as he sat a few feet away from me. "I thought you said you could only do the astral projection when you were aroused?"

"I can. But this isn't astral projection—I'm just opening myself up to the castle and touching its awareness. My mind will send out little tendrils to wander around, but my consciousness will remain here."

"Mind tendrils? That sounds stranger than anything I've ever heard of, even sexually driven astral projection."

I laughed and opened my eyes long enough to grin at him. "Yes, it is a bit weird, huh? But it works."

The only sound in the room for the next few minutes was of the central heating kicking in and blowing warm air through a grate on the floor near me. I let myself relax, pushed down my brain's desire to think about Paen, and slowly allowed the essentia of the castle to sink into my body.

Every building has an essentia. It's the essence of existence, similar to the souls of living beings, a collection of emotions and thoughts that have been imbued upon its structure and pulled from the surrounding environment. Most dwellings' essentias consist of a mixture of happiness, contentment, and sorrow, as collected over the years from the people who've lived in them. I've only once encountered a place that had a bad essentia, but most places, like this castle, were an assortment of emotions, most good, a few bad, but nothing unexpected.

"This castle has been at peace for the last five

hundred years," I told Paen without opening my eyes. "But before that, it had a violent history. Many people were killed here, some justly, others without reason."

I heard him shift on the couch. "My great-grandmother's family fought long and hard to retain the castle. It was under siege many times."

"You resemble the man who built the castle," I said, catching a flash of him in the castle's consciousness. "He loved this land dearly. He died defending it, and was happy to do so."

Just what I need—a house whisperer.

I laughed. "I can't help it if houses talk to me."

"Stop reading my mind!"

"I'm not reading it. You're talking into mine."

"I am not," Paen said crossly. "I've told you I can't do that with strangers. You're poking into my mind, and I want it to stop."

I bit back the urge to argue, and kept focused. As soon as I saw what there was the castle wanted me to see, I let my mind wander around it.

"What are you doing now?" Paen asked quietly some ten minutes later.

"I've just checked the top two floors, and am now in the basement. So far there's nothing to see, although I did find two hidden rooms."

"One off the dining room?" he asked.

"Yes. And one in the basement, leading into a tunnel."

"That is the castle's bolt-hole. It collapsed several hundred years ago due to the land shifting."

"Ah. Well, there's nothing in either other than cobwebs, damp, and mouse droppings, so it looks like you're right—the statue must have been stolen. What bothers me is that I don't get any sense of it ever having been here in the first place."

Paen shifted again on the couch. "Why don't you just ask the castle where it went?"

I snorted. "A house isn't a living being. I can't ask it questions—I'm limited to just sorting through information from its memories." I opened my eyes and sat up, blinking a bit at the lights Paen had turned on. "And this castle has no memories of the statue you described. There are lots of other objet d'art memories, too many for me to look at individually, but I glanced at every one that would match the description, and there was no black monkey statue. There's an ebony statue of a man with a giant penis in a second floor bedroom, but he's not a monkey in any form."

Paen looked mildly embarrassed. "That would be one of my mother's mementoes from the time they lived in New Guinea."

"She sounds like an interesting woman."

"She is. What do you intend to do now?" he asked.

I bit my lip, glanced at my watch, and thought for a moment. "Well, I don't think the castle has anything else to tell me."

"I don't see that it told you anything," he said, rather grumpily.

"Sure it did. It told me that the statue wasn't here, and hasn't ever been here."

"That's ridiculous. It has to have been here. The castle is . . . er . . . confused."

I sat up, hugging my knees. "I suppose it could be, but most houses are pretty good about things like that. It's their purpose, you know—to hold and protect the things inside them. This castle doesn't know anything about a black monkey statue. Does your father own other houses?"

"No," Paen said, shaking his head. "This is our only family home. The statue had to be here."

"Hmm. Well, regardless, the castle can't tell me anything else, and it's almost deep night, so I had better be getting along."

"What does the hour have to do with you finding the statue?" Paen looked puzzled.

"My mother is a sun elf. Deep night is the time when they are at their weakest. It would be useless for me to try to do anything during the four hours of deep night, so I should probably get back to the office and see how Clare is getting along."

I thought Paen was going to stand up, but he didn't. Instead he knelt on the floor next to where I was sitting. "You can't leave. You aren't finished here."

"I'm not?"

"No."

"The castle told me everything it could."

"I'm not talking about the castle," he said, his eyes burning with a bright silver light. A little ripple of excitement had me shivering as I realized what he was talking about.

"Oh. That. Er . . . you wanted to do that tonight? Now?"

"Is there anything wrong with now?" he asked, using my own words against me.

His eyes had me shivering again. I was still surprised at how strongly I was reacting to him—I'm not the sort of person to have a casual relationship—but just the thought of doing all sorts of intimate things with Paen had me flushing with arousal. That, and the sense that he needed me. I could fight the former but not the feeling that I could help him in some manner.

"Well . . . deep night is coming," I said weakly as he leaned toward me, the fingers on one of his hands stroking up my arm.

"That's not the only thing that will come tonight," he said. Wickedly. With an intent that made my whole body tingle.

"Oooh." I breathed the word rather than spoke it as Paen leaned into me, gently pushing me back onto the floor until I was stretched out with him leaning over me. "I suppose I could stay for a little while longer."

"I believe it will take us all of deep night to explore this attraction we share," he murmured, his lips brushing mine for a moment before they burned a little trail over to my neck. Propped up on an elbow as he was, he had only one free hand, but oh, how he made use of it! My back arched as his hand slid along my ribs to the closest breast. "I have watched you the last half hour, and have decided on many ways to give you pleasure."

A faint familiar feeling started building within me as my body quivered at his touch.

"Still with me?" he asked my neck.

"Right here," I said, breathing erratically as my hands decided to get in on the action. I tugged his shirt out of his pants and slid my hands underneath it, skimming along the very interesting planes of his naked chest.

"Good. If at any time you feel as if you are leaving your body, let me know and I'll do my best to anchor you."

My mind spent a few happy moments contemplating the form an anchoring would take, but there was too much pleasure to be had in exploring the lovely world of Paen's chest to devote too much time to that.

The hair on the back of my neck started to stand on end.

"This is a lovely jumper," he said, pulling back just enough to admire my sweater.

"Thank you. My aunt knitted it for me. She wove good luck wards into it. It's one of my favorites."

A slight smile curled the corners of his mouth. "Would you mind terribly if I removed it?"

"I'd like that a lot." I went limp as a rag as he peeled the sweater off me. No, that's not quite true— my hands were busily unbuttoning his shirt in between him pulling off my sweater. "Fair is fair," I added when he had to stop de-sweatering me for a moment while I tugged his shirt off.

"Absolutely." He stilled for a moment, looking down at where I lay languid before him, my hand sliding ever so slowly down the sleek muscles of his arm.

An abstract sense of detachment bubbled over and washed along my limbs, making me even more relaxed.

"Um . . . Paen?" My breasts, normally well behaved, suddenly decided they wanted out of my bra and into his hands. Or mouth. Or up against his chest. They weren't picky about which, they just wanted his full attention.

"Yes?" he asked, leaning over my belly, his tongue a brand on my flesh.

The room began to spin. "I'm starting to drift again."

His head moved up until his eyes filled my vision. "Focus on me, Samantha. Focus on what I'm doing to you. Feel every little touch I make. Concentrate on the pleasure I can give you."

"I'm . . . I'm trying . . ." My consciousness started to detach from my body. Paen's head dipped, his breath hot on my breasts as his tongue snaked between the mounds of flesh trying so desperately to escape my bra. "Er . . ."

"Focus, Samantha."

I started rising, lifting from my body.

"Stay with me!" Paen ordered. I floated above him, looking down to where he was peering at my face. My body looked relaxed, like I was daydreaming, a pleasant, if vague, expression on my face.

There was no drifting around the room. One moment I was there watching Paen, the next I was floating along the night, wafting who knew where.

I insist that you come back here! Samantha! Come back to me!

Pain accompanied the words in my brain, a hot burst of pain in my breast that immediately turned to pleasure so intense, it yanked me back. I blinked dumbly, surprised to find myself in my body again, Paen's curls tickling my chin as his teeth sank deep into my breast.

With that contact, my world changed.

Holy cow, I gasped into his mind. *This is incredible. I can feel everything you feel! I can taste my own blood as you drink! I can feel passion building inside you. It's like we're sharing it somehow, like you're feeding me rather than vice versa. It's like—*

My cell phone, located in my purse next to me on the floor, rang at that very moment. Paen lifted his head, the contact between us broken. Likewise the psychic connection between us disappeared, leaving me feeling oddly bereft, as if something that was a part of me, something I needed, had been taken away.

"I'm sorry," I said, apologizing both for my phone and the fact that we had been interrupted.

"We could ignore it," he suggested, his eyes so bright they almost hurt me to look at.

I wriggled uncomfortably as I reached for my purse. "Normally I would, but I told Clare to call if she needed me."

Paen leaned back to allow me to grab my purse. I extracted the cell phone, checked the incoming caller's number, and mouthed, "It's her," at him before answering. "Hey Clare. What's up?"

"Oh, Sam, something terrible has happened. My dress has been shot!"

"You *what?*" I shrieked, sitting bolt upright, inadvertently slamming my breasts into Paen's nose. "Oh, man, I'm sorry," I told him, covering the phone for a second. "Are you all right?"

"My dress has been shot!"

"Your dress? Why would someone shoot at your dress?" I asked, confused as hell.

"I'm fine," Paen told me, gently feeling his nose. "I don't think it's broken."

"Well, I think he was aiming at me. I was wearing the dress at the time," Clare said thoughtfully. "It was just mean of him to shoot the part of me covered by the dress. I don't know if it's going to recover."

"Clare has been shot. She's delusional, babbling on about a dress," I said aside as I grabbed my sweater and yanked it over my head, my voice muffled as I asked into the phone, "Clare? Are you seeing things? Strange, unreal things?"

"Well, I consider my dress with bullet holes in it a strange, unreal thing, so if that's what you mean, yes. It's a mess, Sam, a mess, absolutely destroyed. I've tried for half an hour to get the blood out, and it won't come out! I'm so annoyed I could just scream!"

I stared at Paen in confused horror. He had donned his shirt and was quickly buttoning it.

"How bad is she? What hospital is she at?" he asked. "I'll take you there."

Clare continued to rant about her dress. I shook my head, trying to figure out just how badly she was hurt.

"Clare? You didn't get shot in the head, did you?" I asked. "Are you lucid?"

"Of course I'm lucid. Haven't you been listening to me? My dress is ruined!" she wailed.

I rubbed my forehead as Paen helped me to my feet, waiting not-so-patiently for me to answer his questions. I was so bemused by the fact that Clare seemed more concerned for a dress than her own bullet-riddled body that I couldn't seem to think straight. "Yeah, but . . . Clare, exactly where *were* you shot?"

"Twice in the chest, once in the stomach."

"Samantha?" Paen said, clearly wanting an update. I covered the mouthpiece. "She's been shot in the chest and stomach, but she doesn't seem to care much about that."

One of Paen's expressive eyebrows rose slightly. "She is a faery. She is immortal. Bullets can't kill her."

"No, but they can hurt her," I snapped, immediately feeling bad. "I'm sorry, I didn't mean to get irritated, but Clare seems to be more worried about her dress than anything else."

"Sam? Did you hear me? What am I going to do?" Clare's plaintive voice sobbed in my ear.

"Don't worry, we'll be there as quickly as we can. Where are you?"

"On Dunstan Moor."

"Where?"

"Dunstan Moor. It's in the Lammermuir Hills. They're shooting a movie here, and Finn is part of a historical group that's providing extras for the movie, and we decided it would be fun to join in. Since he didn't think it was a good idea me meeting with the fence on my own, we arranged to meet him here."

"On the set of a movie?" I asked, more than a little incredulous.

"It's not as movie-like as you'd think. Evidently the primarily filming was already done, and they're just doing a few more battle scenes—"

I sighed. Only my cousin would think nothing was wrong with meeting a fence in a location where there were plenty of witnesses to watch. "Dunstan Moor. Got it."

"You're coming? You'll bring help?" she asked, her voice plaintive.

"Police, paramedics, or both?" I asked.

There was silence on the other end of the phone. "Neither, silly! I need an emergency dry cleaner!"

I lost my patience then. "Honest to god, Clare, you act like the dress is more important than you being shot!"

"Of course it is! It's a Versace, you idiot! Bring help! I'm going to save this dress at all costs."

Chapter 5

"Can anyone tell me why . . ." I asked half an hour later as Paen and I stopped in front of Clare. She stood with a familiar dark-haired, dark-eyed man, both of them leaning over a small, portable plastic table spread with a wispy, gauzy bit of fabric in green, blue, and gold that I assumed was the all-so-important dress in question. We were a good fifteen yards away from a brightly lit area around a cluster of trailers. Beyond, half hidden by a couple of scrawny trees, blinding arc lights cut through the night as someone yelled instructions via a bullhorn for people to charge and retreat at specific cues. I paused, trying to see into the darkness. Something tugged at my consciousness, as if it was trying to get my attention. I scanned the area, slowly turning to locate whatever it was that called to me, then decided it was the location itself. Like my office, this land was founded.

"Can anyone tell you why what?" Clare asked.

"Hmm? Oh, why were you wearing a Versace gown to meet with a fence? On a movie set, yet?"

"They're having a ceilidh here after the battle shooting."

"Ceilidh? Oh, a party?"

"Yes. They've been making some sort of a Scottish historical movie, and since it's almost over, the movie people are letting the extras use the area for ceilidhs for the next couple of nights before they leave," Clare answered, waving toward the man next to her. "But I can't let anyone see the dress like this! Just look at it! Even if I could pretend the bullet holes were meant to be there, the blood has stained the fabric!"

"Hi, Finn," I said, smiling at Paen's brother. I'd only met him briefly before, just a quick introduction before we had set off for the castle, but now I had a chance to study him covertly. I could see a physical resemblance between him and Paen—they both had the same forehead, and similar dark, curly hair, but the fundamental difference was something not quite so obvious.

Finn had a soul.

Why does your brother have a soul? I thought Dark Ones didn't have them?

Paen shot me a glance, but didn't answer. I wanted to ask him again what the problem was with mind-talking, but since it made him so uncomfortable, I let it pass.

"Hello, Sam. What did you think of Castle de Ath?"

"It's big. And old. But nice. I liked it. Clare, what exactly happened?"

Clare wrung her hands in a delicately helpless manner that had Finn murmuring soft little platitudes in her ear. "Oh, it was awful, Sam, just awful! I arranged to meet Raul the fence, and he turned up with another man, a very evil man."

"The evil man shot you?" I asked, eyeing her. She had obviously borrowed a spare costume from an extra, since she was clad in a plain-spun ankle-length skirt and green bodice.

"He shot my dress, yes." Clare nodded. "Oh, stop making that face. Yes, I realize he meant to shoot me and not the dress, but you know how I am with wounds—I heal so quickly that the bullets did more damage to the dress than me."

"It's because you're a faery, Clare. Immortal. It's not that you heal fast—you just don't get injured."

Clare glanced quickly at Finn. "You'll have to excuse my cousin. She's normally very nice, but there are times when she's absolutely unreasonable."

"Ah?" Finn asked, looking at me.

I rolled my eyes and turned to Paen. "Is Clare a faery?"

"Yes," Paen said, poking a finger through a hole in the dress.

"Oh!" Clare gasped, her silvery eyebrows pulling together in a frown as she glared at Paen. "Do you think I'm going to listen to the opinion of a *vampire?*"

"Moving on," I said, not bothering to argue the obvious with her. "Who was the man who shot you? And why exactly did he try to kill you?"

"I don't know who he was, but I wrote up a report for you while Finn was sweet-talking the wardrobe mistress in order to get some club soda to remove the bloodstains. I know how you like reports," Clare said, pulling from her purse a small notepad.

"Hmm," I said, quickly scanning the pages. Paen moved to stand behind my shoulder so he could read it as well. I was momentarily distracted by the feeling of him so warm and solid behind me, but I firmly squelched the desire to turn around and run my hands over his chest again. "Finn was called away by some friends, so you met with Raul alone. . . . He said he'd brought someone who wanted to talk to you. . . . The other man had a monkey on his shoulder? A spider monkey?"

"I didn't ask him what sort it was," Clare answered, tsking over some new atrocity to the dress. "But it was small, so I guess it could be. It had on the cutest little sailor suit."

"Huh." If it was Beppo, then that would explain why the shopkeeper thought I was insane when I mentioned his monkey. But what was the man who was in Paen's castle doing shooting Clare? I read further in the report. "You chatted, he asked you about a statue—"

"Statue?" Paen asked, his voice rumbling close to my ear. Goose bumps ran down my arms at the nearness of it.

"A bird statue," Clare said, dabbing at the dress with a grubby bit of paper towel. "It's all there in the report. He asked me where the statue of the golden bird was."

"Are you sure he said a bird statue?" Paen asked.

"I thought the same thing," Finn said quickly. "Clare said she was sure—it was a golden bird."

"A falcon." Clare nodded. "I told him I didn't know anything about any falcon statue, gold or otherwise. He snarled something rude that I won't repeat, and told me I was lying, and that he would kill me if he had to in order to get it. I told him that wouldn't do any good because I didn't know where the statue was, but he shot me anyway, then both he and Raul ran away. I knew I was better off here than anywhere else, so even though Finn wanted to take me to the hospital, I called you instead."

"What do you mean you're better off here?" I asked, confused why she would think a movie set out in the middle of the wilderness was the location of choice after a shooting.

"It's nice here," Clare said with a shrug. "It's pretty country. I like the way it makes me feel."

I looked around. There wasn't much to see in the darkness, the Lammermuir Hills being a remote and exposed area that was known for its wild beauty, sheep grazing, and grouse. I understood what it was she felt—this land was founded. . . . No, more than founded. It was a lodestone, a holy place to faeries and elves. I didn't bother mentioning the fact to Clare, though. She had a soft, protective security blanket of denial wrapped around her that she clearly wasn't going to shed until she was ready.

"Interesting," I said, glancing at Finn. "Do you have anything to add to Clare's summary of events?"

"Only that I wish I'd been here to catch the bastard who shot her," Finn said. "A friend of mine wanted my opinion on some weaponry, so I left Clare watching the filming." He shot her a reproachful glance. "She was supposed to tell me when the fence came so I could be with her just in case of trouble, but I wasn't of much help on the other side of the field. I heard the shots, and found Clare lying bloody on the ground. I couldn't leave her to chase after the bastards, so I told Paen I needed his help."

"Finn told you he needed help?" I asked Paen. I'd

been with him every minute since I had the phone call from Clare, and he hadn't used a phone once. Which meant . . . "Oh. That sort of message. You've got mind-mail."

"You asked me if my statue was of a hawk," Paen said slowly, an abstracted frown on his face as he turned toward me. "A brass hawk or a falcon. Am I correct in assuming you know what this man was talking about?"

"Yeah, I think I do." I nibbled my lip for a moment while considering how much to tell the expectant faces watching me, and then decided that since it didn't have anything to do with one of our cases, there was no real reason not to explain how I came by it. "It's at the office, downstairs, locked in Mila's safe."

Quickly I told them all how I had come by the statue, emphasizing that I had Jake check it over for any bad emanations. "I assume the guy who shot you must be the one the statue was intended for," I finished, glancing back at Clare's report. "He said he knew you had it, and would stop at nothing to get it?"

"Yes," Clare answered, mournfully examining a portion of the dress.

"That's odd. I wonder why he thought you had it? You weren't anywhere near the antique shop."

"He could have been using the collective you, referring to both you and your cousin," Paen pointed out, looking toward the battlefield, which now rang with cries and shouts accompanied by the sound of clanging metal as the extras gave their all to looking like a horde of wild Scots defending their land.

"True. Well, whatever he meant, I'm not at all

inclined to give him the statue now that he tried to kill Clare. If he had asked nicely, I'd have had no problem giving it up, but not anymore. Now I want something."

"Revenge," Finn said, smiling his approval.

"Justice for my dress!" Clare snorted.

"Answers," Paen said succinctly.

I nodded. "I want answers. How long will they be filming?"

"At least another hour. They just got started when we arrived an hour ago. Why?" Finn asked.

Clare gave me an outraged look as I scooped her dress off the table and laid it over the back of a chair. "I'm going to try to contact the essentia of this area and see what it can tell me."

"The *what?*" Finn's face mirrored his confusion.

Clare explained briefly how I could communicate with locations while I made myself comfortable on the rickety portable table.

"I thought you could only do that with structures?" Paen asked, watching as I stuffed my purse under my head as a support. I folded my hands together and closed my eyes, trying to ignore the exposed feeling of lying on a table in front of three other people. Fortunately, the rest of the movie people were attending to the filming, so we were alone in our corner of their camp.

"This is a structure of sorts. It's a historic battlefield—didn't you see the marker when we came in?"

"I know it's a historic battlefield. My ancestors fought here. But there's no building for miles."

"There's a ring of standing stones on the other side of the trailers, and beyond that, some sort of rocky area that's the heart of the moor. It has enough history for me to look through its memories."

Clare held a whispered conversation with Finn, telling him more about how elves can feel the souls of places. I ignored them, pushed down my consciousness's awareness of Paen standing so close by, and cleared my mind.

Normally it takes me several minutes to calm my thoughts enough to be able to hear the voice of the house, but this location, being founded so strongly in the beyond, took no time before it started talking to me.

Or rather, the men did.

"Whoa," I said, my eyes opening a few seconds after I'd closed them. Surrounding us was a ring of men, their numbers growing as I stared at them.

"Sam?" Paen asked, a faint frown between his brows. "What is it?"

I looked around at the men, a good twenty or so of them ranging in age from early teens to late sixties, all of them dressed in ragged tunics, grubby bits of plaid worn wrapped around their waists, each armed with a huge, massive sword. "I think I just met the residents of Dunstan Moor. Hello, gentlemen."

One of the men stepped forward and said something in a language I didn't understand.

"Ghosts?" Paen asked.

"That would be my guess. Unfortunately, we don't seem to speak the same language. Do either of you speak old Scottish?"

"It would be Gaelic, and I am reasonably proficient in it."

"Good," I said, taking his hand. It was warm and

strong and sent little excited chills down me at the feel of it. "You can translate, then."

"Translate? Translate what?"

I opened my mind to him, willing him to see through my eyes. He jerked away at the touch of my mind. "What do you think you're doing?" His voice was low enough that only I could hear it, but it was rife with indignation.

I'm trying to let you see the ghosts. Mom used to do this with Dad whenever he wanted to see elf stuff. She said she just merged consciousness with him, and he could see things she saw.

"You are not a full elf, and I am not your father."

We can do the mind-speak thing. I think it's probably a given we can do other things, as well.

"I don't want to—"

Afraid? I interrupted.

"No, of course not."

Then merge up, handsome. The ghosts are waiting.

He gave me a long, unreadable look before I felt the tentative presence of him in my mind. I smiled to myself over his reluctance to admit what was pretty clear to me . . .

"Stop that," he growled.

. . . and turned my attention to the ghostly figures who stood around us.

Paen felt a moment of surprise that quickly melted into active curiosity.

"There are more than I expected." He pursed his lips a little as he looked at the ring of ghosts around us. "Do you normally see ghosts when you talk to houses?"

"Ooh, she found ghosts," Clare said, scooting closer to Finn. "Isn't this exciting?"

"It's something, all right," Finn answered, a comical expression of disbelief and amusement on his face.

"Not normally, no," I told Paen. "It's especially rare at night, when I'm not at my best, power-wise. Sometimes you'll find one if it has an extremely strong tie to the location. But this place is kind of special. The ground is practically steeped in blood. I'm guessing that's given these ghosts the powers to make it through to me even late at night."

"Yes, Dunstan Moor is one of the bloodiest battlefields in Scottish history. It makes Culloden look like a virtual playground. Er . . . can you talk to them?"

"She's going to talk to the ghosts now," Clare said to Finn, sotto voce, but not nearly quiet enough.

"Clare!"

"Sorry."

"I'll try. No promises." I looked at the nearest ghost, a man with a long scraggly black beard, a filthy yellow tunic, and a yellow and brown bit of plaid material twisted around his waist as some sort of primitive kilt. "Hello. I'm Sam."

The ghost squinted at me for a minute, then said something to the man nearest him. They both laughed.

"I don't suppose you got that?" I asked Paen without taking my eyes off the ghosts. Normally I wouldn't be worried about them, since ghosts can't interact with this reality without first being grounded, but with this area so strongly steeped in the beyond, I was willing to bet it served as a grounding force.

"Actually, I did. He seems to be speaking an ancient dialect of early Gaelic."

"Oh, good. What did he say?"

"That you're splayed out like a pig about to be roasted."

I glared at the ghost as I sat up, swinging my legs off the table, making sure to keep my mind firmly enmeshed with Paen's. I was a bit woozy with the drain on my power, but I figured I had enough to get us through a brief chat. "How do I say 'up yours' in ancient, ghostly Gaelic?"

He told me. It was highly satisfying to see the ghosts' eyes widen with surprise for a moment when I repeated it, and then the lot of them burst into laughter and clapped each other on the back.

"Why do I suspect you just had me telling a dirty joke?" I asked Paen as I carefully slid off the table and moved over to stand next to him.

He grinned in response. My stomach contracted at the sight of his grin, but it soon settled back to normal as we conducted a one-sided interview of the ghosts. Paen translated for me, while I tried my best to repeat phonetically everything he said.

"Did you see a man with a monkey shoot this woman here?" we asked the ghosts.

The leader, who identified himself as a man named Uilleam, answered in the negative.

"Has there been a disturbance of any sort in the area in the last hour or so?" I asked, via Paen's help.

"Nay," Uilleam answered. "Just the mortals dancing about and making fools of themselves on the plain."

"You think he means the actors?" Clare asked, clearly fascinated.

We asked. Uilleam answered in the affirmative.

"He says they don't know what they're doing," Paen said as Uilleam and two of his buddies stumbled over each other's words to speak. "He says if those swords weren't dulled, they'd have all killed themselves days ago."

"Well, they are just actors," I said, less concerned about the quality of acting and sword choreography than I was the man who shot Clare. "I wonder why they didn't see the guy with the monkey?"

Paen listened a moment as Uilleam said something else. He smiled in response. "It sounds to me as if they've been spending their time watching the film people. You're right about one thing—they are tied to the land. They all gave their lives to defend it, and to it they are bound, acting as guardians of a sort."

"Fascinating, but not terribly helpful as far as finding out why someone wants the bird statue, or for that matter, who he was. Well, I guess we're done here—"

One of the ghosts shouted something to Uilleam, who looked thoughtful for a moment, then turned to face his men and yelled something at them.

"What's going on now?" I asked Paen in a low voice, a little bit worried about the ghosts. So far they'd been perfectly well behaved, but I was still concerned about the possibility that they might have a physical presence in our world.

"Uh-oh."

"What? What are they saying?"

"Uh-oh? What uh-oh?" Clare asked at the same time as I spoke.

An odd look of chagrin passed over Paen's face. "The suggestion has been made that they do something about the lack of sword skill being demonstrated by the actors."

"Oh no," I said, a dread feeling in the pit of my stomach. "You mean—"

Paen nodded. "Yes. They intend to show everyone how it's done."

Uilleam shouted something that sounded very much like a battle cry. The air around him seemed to shimmer and part, as if he was walking through a translucent curtain.

"Goddess above, I see a ghost," Clare said, her eyes huge as she grabbed on to Finn. "He materialized! Do you see him?"

"Yes," Finn said, sounding just as curious as Paen. "Fascinating."

"No, no, no, no," I said, putting myself in Uilleam's path, my hands raised to stop him even though I knew it would serve no practical purpose. "I am not going to be responsible in any way, shape, or form for ghosts manifesting to teach a bunch of actors how to swordfight. I'll never live that down. . . . Holy moly! I can feel him!"

Evidently Uilleam wasn't expecting to do more than materialize visually either, because he stopped and looked down in surprise at my hands on his chest.

"Oh no," I groaned, the dread feeling growing. "I was right. He's ground*eee!*"

Before I could get the word out of my mouth, Uilleam decided to make up for what must have been at least six hundred years of nooky-less existence by grabbing me, pulling me into an all-too-real embrace, his lips cooler than body temperature as they mashed up against my mouth.

Paen was there in a flash, jerking me out of Uilleam's arms as he snarled something that sounded like it was probably obscene. Uilleam laughed and made him a little bow, giving me a lascivious waggle of his eyebrows.

"He heard you? He understood you?"

"Yes," Paen said, releasing my shoulder. He looked pissed, both at me and the ghost. I frowned at his frown.

"Good. Then you can tell him that now is not the time to show a bunch of actors how to wield a sword. Tell him if he doesn't back off and go back to his ephemeral form, we'll call in a Summoner and have them all sent to the Akasha."

Paen duly told the ghost what I said. Uilleam spat out a few words that I didn't need to have translated, then stalked back to his men, his form shimmering slightly as he released his grounding. The men grumbled when Uilleam gave them my ultimatum, a couple of them looking daggers at me.

"They're not very happy," Paen said quietly. "Perhaps it would be best if we were to leave."

"Poor ghosts," Clare said, her mouth turned down with sadness. She turned to me. "Would it be such a bad thing if they were to join the actors—"

I raised an eyebrow.

She sighed. "I suppose so. It seems so unfair, though. They just want to have a little fun, and they are offering to help . . ."

"Another time," I said firmly, having way too much to deal with at the moment to add battle-hungry ghosts to my list. "I think Paen's right. There's nothing more we can find out here."

"So what do we do now?" Finn asked as we said a polite good-bye to the ghosts, gathered up our things, and climbed the slight hill to the overlook area where all the cars were parked.

"We'll just add the guy who attacked Clare to our list of things to investigate. In the meantime, I don't think it would be smart of you to go anywhere on your own, just in case this man decides to shoot you again. Or worse."

"Nothing can be worse than shooting an innocent gown," Clare said, smoothing a hand down the fabric she held tenderly in her arms.

"I will be happy to act as a bodyguard," Finn said, giving Clare a look that was unmistakable. I glanced from him to Paen, but my would-be lover was clearly thinking of other things.

"Oooh," Clare said, momentarily distracted by Finn's lascivious look. "That would be fun. I've never had a bodyguard before."

"You can't go out in daylight," I pointed out, not wanting to interfere with what could be a budding romance, but obliged to make sure Clare was protected during the day.

"I can. I just have to have protection. How do you think we came here earlier today?" Finn glanced at his watch. It was now the second hour of deep night (better known as one in the morning). "Or rather, yesterday."

"You can go out during the day?" I asked Paen. "I thought Dark Ones couldn't? Or is that just a vampire old wive's tale?"

"It's partially true," Finn answered for him. "My brothers and I can tolerate a lot more than Paen, but even he can go out if he has enough protection from direct sunlight."

"How can you tolerate more than Paen?" I asked, distracted by the idea of vampires who could walk in daylight.

"Finn—" Paen said warningly.

His brother ignored him. "We all, the three of us, are Moravians. Paen is a Dark One. That means we have souls, but he doesn't. Our parents weren't Joined when he was born."

"Huh?" I asked, more confused than ever. "Joined?"

"That's enough, Finn," Paen said, stepping over a low chain barrier at the edge of the overlook.

"Joining is the procedure a Dark One undertakes with his Beloved, the woman who can salvage his soul and make him whole again. Mum was Dad's Beloved, but due to a war, they didn't complete the Joining until after Paen was born."

"They don't want to hear about our family history," Paen said, striding over to his car. "There are more important things to be discussed, like what steps are to be taken next in the search for our statue."

"I don't know, I'm kind of interested in hearing about this," I said, smiling at Paen. He glowered back at me.

Finn looked from his brother to me, a smile growing slowly on his lips. "Sorry, Paen. I didn't realize you don't want me telling Sam about Beloveds. No doubt she wouldn't be interested if I told her how there is one woman who can save you, a woman who completes you and makes you whole again. I won't explain about the seven steps to Joining, because that would probably just bore her. Nor will I go into the fact that a Beloved knows she is such by the fact that she is marked by a Dark One, and that the marking usually takes the form of a strong psychic connection."

"God damn it, Finn, just shut up!" Paen exploded.

My jaw dropped a little. *A strong psychic connection? Something like being able to mind-talk?*

No. Ignore him. He's a fool and he doesn't know what he's talking about.

You answered me, I thought at him, oddly pleased by the touch of his mind against mine. It felt . . . right.

Paen frowned at me, but said nothing else.

Chicken. "All right," I said aloud. "Finn, if you want to volunteer to be Clare's bodyguard, that would do a lot to relieve my mind. As for what steps we're going to take next to find your statue . . ."

I closed my eyes for a moment to think. I was never at my brightest in deep night, and after the drain of speaking with ghosts—and sharing my vision with Paen—I was left limp and exhausted, sapped of the energy needed to make a decision.

"You will go home and get some rest," Paen said authoritatively.

"I beg your pardon?" I asked, looking at him in surprise.

His eyes glittered like shadowed mercury. "You're exhausted, and at the end of your strength. You will go home and rest."

"You seem to misunderstand the basic client-investigator relationship," I told him, straightening my shoulders in an attempt to look chock-full of vigor. "I'm the one who makes the game plans. That's what you're paying me for."

"I am your employer. I have paid you to work for me," Paen said. "That entitles me to give orders."

"In your dreams!" I said, too tired to come up with a snappier comeback.

"Sam doesn't look tired to me," Finn said, eyeing me, standing next to Clare's car a few feet away. "She looks pretty good, as a matter of fact. How do you know she's tired, Paen? Do you have some special insight into Sam's feelings? Something you would instinctively know about, oh, say, a Beloved?"

We all looked at Paen. He glared back at us. "I will take Sam home. Finn, you do the same with Clare. In the morning, we will plan out a new strategy for locating both the statue and the man who attacked Clare."

"Wait a minute," I protested, dropping the intriguing idea of a Beloved. "You are not the boss here—I am. And I already have a plan for locating your statue."

"Really?" Paen asked, crossing his arms over his chest. "What would that be?"

"To start with, we will do the same thing we have been doing for another client—I'll check with the antique network and see if anyone has an interest in black monkey statues. Since you can't tell us much about it, Clare is going to do a little research into just what the statue looks like, and its provenance. Once we have a little more information on the statue itself, I can pull out the big guns."

Clare gasped in horror, and instinctively reached for a wildflower growing at the side of the overlook.

"And what would your big guns consist of?" Paen asked, his eyes so dark they looked like a stormy sky.

I took a deep breath. "I'm going to scry."

"No." The almost inaudible whimper slipped between Clare's lips as she stuffed petal after petal into her mouth.

Paen frowned. "What's wrong with Samantha scrying?" he asked Clare.

Her eyes got huge as she looked at me with wordless pleading.

"It won't be like that," I told her. "Stop frightening the clients!"

"I'm not frightened," Paen said. "I am, however, a bit confused. I thought scrying was a standard divination technique?"

"It is."

"Then what's the big deal with you doing it?" Finn asked.

"I'm not actually a Diviner," I explained to him. "I studied as one for a while, but I . . . er . . . left the Order."

Paen's eyes narrowed. "You left them because you realized you were not meant to be a Diviner?"

"Something like that," I said, giving Clare a look that was meant to keep her quiet. It didn't work, of course. No one can shut a faery up when she's determined to blab.

"Sam was kicked out of the Diviners' Order after she scryed," Clare said, swallowing the last of the petals. "She was part of a scrying circle, and she lost control."

"It's not as bad as she's making it sound," I told Paen, more than a little mortified to have my dirty laundry aired in such a manner.

"How can you lose control scrying?" Finn asked at the same time Paen asked Clare, "What happened?"

"She opened a temporal rift that sucked in two Diviners," she answered, meeting my potent glare with a haughty look. "They should know, Sam! You're dangerous when you scry!"

"A temporal rift?" Paen looked at me as if I was wearing my underwear on my head.

"It's not that uncommon," I said abruptly, tossing my things onto the backseat of Paen's car. "Happens all the time."

"Hardly that," Clare said. She turned to the men with an eloquent gesture that stated how distressed she was by the very thought of me giving in to my Elvish birthright. "It took the head of the Diviner Order three weeks to get the Diviners back from where Sam had sent them."

"Inadvertently sent them," I corrected. "It was just a minor little glitch."

"And you're planning on scrying the location of the statue?" Paen asked, clearly stuck on that point.

"Yes." I gave them all a level look over the top of Paen's car. "I admit that I had a little control issue before, but I know what I did wrong. I was scrying by the moon. I'm part sun elf—unlike most Diviners, the moon does not give me power, it dilutes it. This time, I will scry by sunlight. Everything will be fine, just you wait and see."

Famous last words, eh?

Chapter 6

The next two days passed like . . . well, like two days. Busy, mostly. Frustrating, definitely, both on a personal and a professional level.

"Are you coming back tonight?" Clare's voice was rather breathless against my ear as I cradled the phone to hear her over the noise and confusion of the Glasgow train station.

"Yes. I should be home around dinnertime. What's been going on there today?"

A smothered giggle followed by a deep rumble of a masculine voice answered that question. "Um . . . we don't have much to report, actually. Finn and I have been working through the list of antique buyers, but with no new information. Oh, Mr. Race called to see if we'd had any progress. I told him you were in Glasgow working on a tip for another case, and he was a bit put out. He said he wasn't paying us good money to work for other people, and he demanded that we put all our attention on his case. He also said he was in London for a day or two, and he'd really like you to meet him there."

"London? I thought he was in Barcelona?" Something rustled in a nearby trash bin. I hoped it wasn't rodents.

"He left. He said he could put you up for a couple of days if you wanted to contact some of the English collectors in case some of them have heard anything about the manuscript."

"I hope you told him we already have, with no luck."

"I tried to, but he doesn't seem to want to listen to me. He just kept saying that people are more forthcoming if you approach them in person, and what a good idea it would be for both of us to go to London and search."

"He can just go soak his head," I grumbled, eyeing an itinerant man to make sure he didn't decide to relieve himself near the phone cubicle I occupied. I spent a few minutes damning whoever it was who stole my cell phone a few days earlier, then pulled my mind back to the present. "Did you tell him we were devoting all possible energies to finding the book for him?"

"Yes, but he didn't like the fact that you were away working on another case. So, the private auction lead was a total failure?"

"Not just the lead, the last two days have been a bust." The homeless man curled up on a bench and quietly picked at various parts of his body. I turned away to stare at the graffiti in the phone booth, depressed and oddly unsettled. "It took me an entire day to track down the collector who was selling off part of his collection, and another day to convince him to let me take a peek at it before the bidders got at it. I'm just sick at the waste of time, Clare. Paen's mother doesn't have two days for us to waste like this."

"You had to check it out," she consoled, stifling another giggle.

I sighed to myself over that, too. In the time I had been gone, Paen had been absolutely silent, not even bothering to check in with me by phone. It was as if he had lost interest in me personally—which even I realized was ridiculous. I'd known the man only three days. There wasn't time for us to establish an emotional bond.

Yet I had spent the last few days thinking about Paen, feeling as if a part of me was missing because he wasn't around, and dreaming the most lascivious, erotic dreams about a man I barely knew.

"What's that?" Clare asked, her words dissolving into a squeal.

I poked morosely at the coin return. "Nothing. I'll be there by suppertime. Tell Finn hi for me. And if Paen calls . . ." I stopped, furious with myself at the demanding urges buried deep within me. He wasn't a potential mate. He wasn't even boyfriend material. He was a client, a man who didn't believe in the importance of emotional attachment.

And I was starting to think I was close to falling in love with him.

"Tell him what?"

"Nothing. See you in a few hours."

I argued with myself all the way home, until I was too tired to see reason anymore. The last few nights I hadn't slept much—no doubt that was affecting my sanity.

"Oh, now this is bad," I said to myself several hours later as I hauled my wheeled bag off the train platform. "I'm so obsessed with the man, I'm starting to see him everywhere. In a kilt, yet."

"Sam," the kilt-wearing, Paen-shaped vision greeted me, taking the handle of my luggage. He must have noticed my confusion, because he added, "Clare told me you were coming back tonight. I take the fact that you haven't called to announce you found the statue to mean your visit to Glasgow was unsuccessful?"

I stared at him in sleep-deprived bemusement for a few seconds. He paused and raised an eyebrow. "Is something the matter?"

"No. Yes. Maybe. It depends—why are you here? And why are you wearing a kilt?"

He ignored both questions, gently rubbing his thumb under my left eye. "You have dark circles under your eyes."

"I know. It's because I haven't slept well the last couple of nights, thanks to you."

"To me?" He frowned, then took my elbow and propelled me toward the main doors. "I have left you completely alone for the last forty-eight hours. How can I be to blame?"

"Because you've left me completely alone for the last forty-eight hours."

"That doesn't make any sense," Paen argued.

I stopped outside the doors, moving to the side so we were out of the flow of traffic. "Of course it does. Paen, three days ago we met. You told me you wanted to sleep with me. I, against my better judgment, agreed to do that simply because I wanted to prove to you that sex without emotional commitment was shallow and meaningless."

"You agreed to sleep with me because you fancied me," he said, his beautiful eyes lightening.

"That too. The point is, you made a big deal about us sleeping together, then you just left me!"

He frowned, his brows pulling together in a black slash over his eyes. "You'd had a trying day. You yawned three times on the way back from Dunstan Moor. Clearly you were not in an optimum mood to appreciate my sexual technique."

"In other words"—I poked him in the chest—"you chickened out."

"Don't be ridiculous," he said, grabbing my elbow again and pushing me along the sidewalk toward the parking lot. "I was being considerate, just as I have been the last two days, a fact you totally seem to have misunderstood."

"Given that you never once called to see how I was doing in Glasgow, I think it's reasonable to assume you were avoiding me because you regretted ever making those rash statements regarding personal relationships."

"Or I could have been letting you do your job while I was tied up with SEPA," Paen said, unlocking the trunk of his car and throwing my suitcase into it.

I stood to let him unlock and open the passenger door for me. "SEPA?"

"Scottish Environmental Protection Agency. They've been claiming a bit of my land is contaminated with runoff from a nearby smelting plant, and I had to meet with the officials to prove again that it isn't. I doubt if you've had much experience dealing with

Scottish political red tape, but it's just as unpleasant as the Canadian version."

"Oh. I'm sorry." I nibbled on my lower lip for a moment. "How did it turn out?"

He flashed me a quick grin before starting the car and backing it out of the parking spot. "Chemical analysis of the soil and water table showed they're unpolluted, as I've said for the last six years."

"Good."

"It was damned annoying timing on their part. I planned on helping search the antiquities network for news of the statue, but was tied down with the minutiae of officialdom."

"That's OK. Clare and Finn worked on that while I was gone."

He glanced at me before pulling out into traffic. "Why haven't you been sleeping well?"

I hesitated about telling him. I'd already made a fool of myself by sounding jealous and possessive of him when there was no relationship to be jealous or possessive about, but the urge to protect my delicate ego was strong. In the end, though, I told the truth, because . . . well, just because I figured it might mean something to him. "The time not spent in incredibly erotic dreams about you was mostly spent tossing and turning, wondering what you were doing, why you hadn't called me, and whether you regretted making the proposition you did."

"You didn't call me either," he said, picking the one thing out of my embarrassing confession that I knew was the weakest.

"I did. You didn't answer. And I . . . er . . . didn't leave a voice mail."

"Why?" he asked, shooting me another quick glance.

I looked out the window at the lights of the city as they passed by. It was painful having to admit how much I missed him during the two days away. "I didn't have anything to report. I just wanted to talk to you."

"Well, I'm here now," he said, pausing to let an elderly couple cross the street.

"Yes, and that's something I'm rather curious about. Clare knows full well there's a bus that goes from the station to less than a block away from our apartment. I've hauled a lot more luggage than what I have now. So why has she sent you to fetch me?"

His eyebrows flattened out to a straight line. "I just thought it would be polite to pick you up since you'd been away on my behalf."

"Doing the job you're paying me to do," I pointed out, secretly delighted by the revelation that Paen had missed me while I was gone.

"I was in town anyway," he said, avoiding my eye.

"Uh-huh. And the kilt?"

"I'm a Scot. I'm allowed to wear one."

"I know that, silly. I just meant, what's the occasion?"

He maneuvered the car slowly through a busy, pedestrian-laden street. "I don't need an occasion to wear a kilt."

"Riiiight," I drawled.

He sent me a quick glance. "Most women fair drool at the sight of a man in a kilt."

Oho! So that was the way things were. I fought to keep my smile from showing, and tried to look only mildy interested. "Do they?"

"Yes." He glanced at me again. "They find it sexy."

"I'm sure they do." I pointed out the next turn, and Paen swung around a corner, entering the narrow street in the old part of Edinburgh where Clare and I shared an apartment. "Did you miss me?"

He pulled into the tiny parking area behind our building, giving me a startled look. "Did I what?"

"You heard me. Did you miss me while I was gone?"

"Where should I park?" he asked, ignoring my question.

"There, next to Clare's car. It's the spot assigned to me, but I don't have a car, so you can use it. And stop avoiding answering the question."

He pulled into a spot and turned off the engine. "I regretted that you were away on business when I couldn't help you."

I smiled to myself as I unhooked my seat belt. "Not good enough. Did you *miss* me?"

He got out of the car, going to open the trunk.

I followed, my arms crossed over my chest as I leaned a hip against the car. "Well?"

"Let me ask you this—did you miss me?" he said, slamming the trunk closed.

"Very much," I said, waiting.

His eyes lightened another few degrees. "I see. In that case—yes, I missed you."

"Good. Are you going to spend the night this time, or are you not yet ready for such a thing?"

"That was our original agreement, but I thought perhaps you might have changed your mind."

"I don't change my mind that easily," I said as we walked to the building, waiting as he opened the door for me. The faint sound of music from Mila's sex shop was the only sound to permeate this part of the building. I started up the stairs to our apartment, but Paen stopped me, pushing me up against the wall of the stairwell, his body blocking out the dim light that hung over the stairs until all I could see was the silver gleaming brightly in his eyes.

"You're tired," he said.

"I haven't yawned once. How can you possibly imagine I'm tired?"

"You said you weren't sleeping well," he reminded me.

"I slept on the train coming home," I answered, thankful that I had dropped off for a few minutes so I could tell him that.

"You look tired," he insisted.

I smiled. I couldn't help it; he was so cute trying to deny the obvious. "I do not look tired. I checked a mirror before the train arrived. The dark circles under my eyes are hereditary, not due to lack of sleep. I am exhibiting no obvious signs of fatigue."

He leaned into me. "I can feel that you're near exhaustion."

"Nuh-uh, that won't work either, because according to you, we don't have a psychic thing. So you can't possibly know what I'm feeling," I argued softly, my body turning into one gigantic tingling erogenous zone as he pinned me against the wall.

"Then you won't mind at all if I ascertain for myself your feelings on the subject of our having sex?" His voice was likewise low, but roughened with arousal.

"Good god, no. Ascertain away," I said, gasping as his hands slid up my waist to cup my breasts, causing me to rub myself against him like a cat begging for stroking. I clutched the back of his jacket to keep myself upright, my senses overwhelmed with the scent and feel of him.

"I'm going to kiss you now," he said, as if he had to warn me. My answer was to move sinuously against him, twine one leg around his, and grab his head with both hands to pull him into a kiss that I figured would make him see stars, if not actual galaxies.

The elf in me wanted to distance myself from the situation and analyze just what it was that made Paen so attractive to me, but bless my dad's mortal genes, there was enough of him in my chromosomal makeup to let me ignore the elf part and go into a full swoon of delight when Paen's lips touched mine. That touch was brief, but I didn't mourn its loss because what followed was enough to have my shoelaces melting.

It started out like a regular kiss—our lips were there, smooshing up against each other, tongues present but not yet engaged. There was a sense of aroused excitement with the first couple of passes of lip action, followed by a tentative, questing touch with the tip of my tongue. Paen's tongue answered, and suddenly he wasn't just kissing me, he was feasting, supping on my mouth, drinking me in like I was the source of all being. His body was hard against mine, but it wasn't an unpleasant sensation—far from it. While he was busy making love to my mouth, my body curled around him, trying to get closer still.

Wanting more, I poured into him the feelings he was arousing in me, the sensations he fired up deep inside me, the desires and wants and a whole slew of complex emotions that I couldn't even begin to imagine. I flooded him with what I was feeling—and he froze.

Is something wrong? I asked as his body turned into a statue. He pulled back, looking down at me with his quicksilver eyes, now so bright I swear I could read a book by them.

"This is not really an appropriate place to continue," he said, answering, but not really answering, the question I had mind-zapped him.

"Oh." I looked around at the dimly lit stairwell. "You're right, it isn't. Shall we go up to my apartment?"

He stepped back and indicated I should precede him. Speed on stairs has never been my forte, having inherited my father's tendency to clumsiness, but I made it up this flight in record time. I hurried into the apartment with an excuse on my lips for Clare to explain why I was dragging Paen off to my bedroom, but there was no Clare to be seen. Nor Finn.

"Huh," I said, peeling off my jacket and tossing it on the coat-tree. "I wonder if she and Finn went out?"

Ethereal giggling, followed by deeper, more masculine laughter, drifted out from behind the closed door to Clare's room.

Paen cocked an eyebrow at me. "I would say they stayed in."

"Geez!" I said, looking for a moment at Clare's door. "They just met! And now they're in there going at it like bunnies?"

The other eyebrow rose.

"We're different," I told both eyebrows. "She's not conducting an experiment, she's just giving in to her libidinous faery nature."

"Elves don't have a libido?" he asked, taking off his coat.

"Of course they do. They're just not as flighty as faeries. They don't feel the need to have sex on a daily basis, as most Fae folk do. They are circumspect. They have restraint. They can wait for the proper time and place, and most importantly, the right person to come along before they . . . *rawr!*"

Paen reeled back a few steps from the impact of my body being flung onto his.

"I want another one of those kisses," I said, wrapping my legs around his waist.

"Circumspection and restraint having gone out the window?" he asked as he hoisted me a little higher, staggering ever so slightly in the direction I pointed.

"I'm also human," I mentioned, nuzzling his neck as he struggled to open my bedroom door.

"Would you mind . . . thank you."

"So very polite. I love the Scots," I said as I reached behind me to open the door, closing it as Paen carried me across the threshold.

"Our politeness is just one of our attributes." He stopped a foot into the room, looking around it in surprise.

"My mother's idea," I said, unhooking my legs so I could stand. "She and Dad went to Africa last spring, so for Christmas last year she hired a decorator to come in and redo my bedroom. Don't let the malacca and mosquito netting fool you—the bed is quite sturdy."

"And the elephant head?" he asked, looking at the wall above the headboard.

"Fake. Mom wanted to get the real thing, but I had to draw the line somewhere. There's a matching foot basket I use for trash around here somewhere."

"I see. And the machete is for . . . ?"

I picked it up and gave it a twirl before hacking at an aggressive palm that blocked the path into the bedroom. "The plants are very real, and were tended by my mother before she turned them over to me, so they grow like crazy. I'm dreading what will happen this summer, once some actual sunlight gets to them. There, I think you can get by. Mind the rhino."

"Bench?" he asked, eyeing the large wooden figure that lurked in the shrubberies my mother insisted live in my room.

"Yup." I skirted a faux-leopard rug in order to fling a few dozen accent pillows off my bed. "You can ride him, too, but he's not very comfortable. I use his horn as a backscratcher when I have an itch I can't reach. So . . . um . . . here we are. Do you want to get naked?"

Paen thought for a moment. "Do you?"

"Well . . ." I looked at him, really looked at him. He wasn't movie star handsome, but I liked his face. It was a typical Scottish face, kind of long, with interesting cheeks, and a jaw that made my knees go a bit melty. His eyes were unparalleled—going from dark, cloudy grey-almost-black, to a silver so bright it came close to scorching me. I was still more than a little bewildered by my instant attraction to him, but there was no denying it was there. So where was the harm in giving in to it? "I think I'd like you to be naked first, and then I'll get naked later."

"That hardly seems fair," he said, frowning just a

little. "You'd have me at a disadvantage if I was nude and you weren't."

"You saw my boobs already. That gives you a point up on me—all I did was get to feel you."

"I didn't see your breasts. I saw your bra."

"With my boobs in it. It's the same thing," I argued.

"Is that really an important distinction?"

I wrinkled my nose as I thought about that. "Well . . . not in the world peace sort of sense, no, but I'm trying to establish my footing with you. I'm a bit nervous."

"And you are taking advantage of that fact by dictating to me a bizarre set of rules you just thought up?" Paen may have been grumbling, but he kept unbuttoning his shirt.

"Maybe. OK, I am. You got away with all that experiment stuff, so I'm going to be the rulemaker. Rule number one is that you get naked before me."

"Do you have body issues?" he asked, shucking his shirt.

It took me a minute to answer. I clutched the malacca, mosquito-netting-wrapped bedpost to keep from running over to touch that magnificent chest again. "Just the usual. Nothing out of the ordinary. Why, do you think I should have body issues?"

"No," he said quickly as I looked down at myself. "I just wondered. So many women seem to be unhappy with themselves, it's refreshing to find one who isn't."

"Oh. Well, as far as that goes, I'd like pretty much everything improved, but since that's not going to happen without a new set of genes or a really expensive plastic surgeon, I'm resigned to living with this body."

"It's a very nice body," he said politely, sitting on the rhino's back to pull off his shoes and socks.

"Thank you. I wouldn't mind being taller than five foot four, having bigger boobs, and less in the hip and thigh area, but eh. I can live with myself."

"That's a good attitude to take. I never understood women who feel driven to surgical enhancement to match a society's ideas of beauty."

"Well, I did have my ears bobbed," I reminded him, watching with interest as he stood back up and put his hands on his belt.

"Yes, but I assume that was to lessen the taunting that you must have undergone as a child."

"Yup. Although my dad says he thinks my mother's pointy ears are sexy. He likes to nibble on them. Mom says that to an elf, ears are an erogenous zone, but I've never found that to be true."

He unbuckled his belt, dropping it and the sporran on the chair. "Would you like me to nibble on your ears?"

"They're not pointy," I answered, a little shiver of mingled anticipation and excitement doing a number on my nervous system. "Are you purposely stalling? Are you not dropping kilt because you suddenly realize that making love is a hundred times better than just plain old fucking?"

"No," he said, his hand on the waistband. "Why, are you having second thoughts?"

"You asked me that before. I said no then, if you recall."

"That's right. Well . . ." He hesitated for another

moment, then with a quick move unbuttoned his kilt and let it drop to the floor. He wasn't wearing underwear, something that mildly shocked me. "There. I'm naked and you're dressed. Now it's your turn."

"Don't rush me," I said, not sure where to look first. Oh, OK, I looked there first, but just because I wondered. But once that curiosity was satisfied, I gave the rest of him the once-over. "I'm guessing you have no body issues whatsoever."

"You guess wrong. Are you going to just stand there and stare at me?" he asked, picking up his kilt and neatly folding it to sit on top of his shirt.

"I'm an elf. I'm a visual person. I like looking at you."

"You're human," he said, marching over to me and pulling me up against his naked body. "You're also one of the sexiest women I've ever met, bobbed ears and all. Now take off your clothes before I rip them off."

"Oooh. Aggression. Dominance," I said, my breath catching as my hands slid up his ribs. He was warm, hard, and male. My senses went into overload as I rubbed myself against him, stroking all that lovely flesh.

"Does it arouse you?" he asked, nibbling a path up my neck toward my ears, his hands moving down my sides, around to my butt.

"Not really—oh dear god!"

I've had boyfriends who've done a little earlobe nibbling before my mind took its usual coital walk, but never has anyone ventured beyond earlobe territory to the rest of my ears. When Paen bit gently down on the top of my ear, I just about passed out from the bolt of arousal that zapped through me. My legs literally shook from the tremors of pleasure that were coursing down from the touch of his mouth. "Rip them off!"

"Hmm?" Paen asked as he nibbled the top arch of my ear. My knees buckled.

"Rip my clothes off! Right now!"

He pulled back a little to look at me. "You want me to rip your clothes off?"

"Yes! Right now! Rip them off, then ear me again!"

"I thought you didn't find aggression and dominance—"

I slapped a hand over his mouth. "Too much talking, not enough action."

"Very well," he mumbled under my hand. "But I want you to remember that the destruction of your clothes was your idea."

In the end, he didn't rip my clothes off, although he did help me out of them in a time that would do a quick-change artist proud.

"There, I'm naked. Now do my ears again!" I demanded, lunging at him as I kicked off my underwear.

He chuckled as I turned my head for maximum ear position. "Changed your mind about ears being sexy, have you?"

"You have *no* idea," I said, quivering as his hot breath touched my ears. Something occurred to me then. As his tongue swept a long stroke up the side of my ear to the top, I sent him the sensations of sheer, utter arousal that he was generating, alongside a hunger that I hadn't known existed in me. For a moment I could feel an answering hunger in him, and then gently I was closed out, as if a door had shut between us.

Stop doing that!

"I thought you liked this?" he asked, nipping my ear. Every bone in my body turned to pudding.

I do. I mean stop shutting me out of your mind. It's not fair. I'm willing to let you into mine. I just want you to feel what I'm feeling. I want to know what it is that I do to you, too. Why won't you let me in?

He stopped nibbling long enough to take one of my hands, place it on his belly, and slide it down the intriguing trail of hair that led to points south. "Does that answer the question of what you do to me?" he asked as my fingers closed around his erection.

Only partially, I answered, wanting more from him, but unable to express what I wanted without sounding like an idiot. I wanted to tell him that I needed some sort of emotional attachment, but I knew what his answer to that would be. And since I had agreed to his ground rules, I couldn't change them now.

I'd just have to make him realize how shallow sex was without anything behind it, my inner elf decided. The human in me wanted to point out that most men were completely and utterly happy with nothing but a physical relationship, but I squelched that thought. Paen wasn't most men. He was different, in more ways than the obvious. He was so . . . needy. He needed someone to show him how much more there could be to life.

"I'm going to lick you from head to toe," he mumbled against my neck, his voice thick with desire as he backed me the couple of steps to the bed. "Then reverse the route until I end back at those tasty little ears of yours."

"Sounds like a plan to me," I agreed, grabbing a foil packet from my nightstand drawer before beating back the mosquito netting and getting into the bed—without allowing his mouth to break contact with my skin—as gracefully as possible.

One eyebrow twitched at the sight of the foil packet.

"For later," I said, pulling him down onto me.

"We don't need that," he said, his tongue making a swipe across the top of my ear. I shivered with ecstasy and rubbed my hips against his erection. "You're immortal."

"No, I'm half elf. That means I have approximately double a human life span, but I can still get diseases. Not to mention pregnant. And since I'd like to avoid both at this time, we'll just have to do this my way."

"If you insist," he said, pausing to suck his breath in when I trailed both hands down his sides to find the proof of his interest again.

"No more ears. I'm on the verge of an orgasm now, and I don't think I could stand much more," I told him as his head dipped toward mine.

"As you like. No. No more of that right now, either," he answered, plucking my hands from his crotch.

"Am I too rough?" I asked, worried for a moment that my (relative) inexperience was causing me to do things wrong.

"Not at all, but tonight is for you. I want to give you pleasure, and if you keep touching me that way, it'll all be over and I'll just go to sleep."

"You're a vampire!" I said, nipping his shoulder. "You're supposed to be above that sort of mortal behavior."

"I'm also male," he said with a grin that made my toes curl. "Let me do it my way this once. Let me give you pleasure."

"You can try, but no promises I'll be here to enjoy it."

His head dipped again and he took one of my suddenly impudent nipples in his mouth. "We'll see."

Streaks of pleasure blossomed in all sorts of interesting spots, making my body hum with interest.

Unfortunately, my brain had other ideas. The feeling of disassociation washed slowly over me, a feeling that I knew would end with me drifting off while my body enjoyed the benefits of Paen's attention.

"No!" I yelled, desperately trying to grab his head to anchor myself. My hands drifted bonelessly to the bed despite my efforts to fight the lethargy that filled me. "No, dammit, not this time! Paen, stop! It's not working . . . god damn it all!"

My being floated gently out of my body, hanging over the figures on my bed for a moment, just long enough for me to appreciate the fact that Paen might be a vampire, but he had the nicest ass I'd ever seen on a man. While I sobbed in silent, impotent rage at being taken away against my will, I drifted out of the room and into our living room.

Which was in the process of being burgled.

"Paen!" I shrieked, trying to grab the doorframe as I drifted through the room toward another. I dog-paddled wildly to get myself back into the living room, somehow managing to keep myself from being sucked into the tiny kitchen. "Clare! Burglars! Help!

Someone! Oh, this is just fine and dandy. Son of a poodle, what *are* you?"

A glimmer of light from a streetlamp that peeked in through the blinds touched on the dark figure of a man as he moved around the bookcase where we stuffed bills and assorted items of a sundry nature. At first I had thought it was someone intent on robbing us, but the light revealed that this man evidently had six arms. As I watched, he flitted from one object in the room to the next, examining everything almost soundlessly—almost, because each time he moved an item to look at it, there was a soft pattering sound.

"Look, I don't know what you are, but I don't want you here. So leave and . . . hey!"

A loud groan audible from Clare's room caused the whatever-it-was to pause for a moment before it started toward her bedroom door. I lunged toward the figure, but it passed right through me, sending me spinning toward the other side of the room in a cold eddy of air. I screamed silently in sheer frustration at my helpless state. "Stop it! You can't go in there! Clare! Something's coming in! God damn it! Paen! PAEN!" *Paen!*

Samantha?

There's something out here, something cold. And it's going into Clare's room—

I didn't even have time to finish thinking at him. In the time it takes between seconds I was back in my body, naked and extremely warm.

And alone, the door to my room slamming back against the wall.

Be careful, I yelled, grabbing Paen's shirt and yanking

it on over my head as I ran toward the door. *It's got six arms.*

"It doesn't have any now—it's gone." Paen's voice rumbled out of the darkness of the living room. I felt along the wall for the light switch, but he was right— the room was empty of all but him. He started toward me. "Are you sure you saw—"

"Yes, I'm sure I saw him. It. Whatever."

He bent to pick something up.

"It had six arms and moved really quickly, like he was being fast-forwarded. It was really creepy, and I couldn't do a thing to stop it—what's that?"

"Stones," he said, an odd thoughtful look on his face. I touched them. They were small and round, as if they'd been washed up on the shore, about the size of a penny.

"Stones? Where did they come from?" I looked around and noticed a couple more near the bookcase. "What the heck?"

"They're apports," Paen said, turning as Clare's door opened. I flung myself forward to stand in front of him as Finn loomed in the doorway, a sheet wrapped around his waist, Clare peeping anxiously over his shoulder. "The being you saw was a poltergeist."

Chapter 7

"Is something wrong? We heard noises," Finn asked from Clare's doorway, grinning when he noticed Paen was naked and I was wearing his shirt. "Ah. Never mind, then."

"Sam? What are you doing?" Clare asked.

"Standing in front of Paen. He's naked," I said, a little annoyed that she didn't have the decency to look away. "Do you mind? Stop ogling him and look at your own. No, wait, don't."

Clare frowned. "You're not my mother, Sam. If I want to look at Finn, I will. You have your own boyfriend—you can't tell me what to do with mine."

I waved that away. "I'm not talking about that. We have poltergeists!"

"*What?*" she shrieked, trying to push past Finn. He mumbled something over his shoulder at her. She disappeared for a moment to reappear in her silk bathrobe. I snatched a pillow off the couch and shoved it at Paen before running to my room for his kilt.

"Sorry, it must have fallen into a plant," I apologized

as I dusted off the kilt, blocking the view of him long enough for him to put it on.

"Poltergeists? We have poltergeists? You mean like the little blond girl in the movie?" Clare asked, going straight for the bouquet on the bar that marked the division between the living room, and kitchen. She popped a couple of lilac blossoms into her mouth.

"She was an actress, not a poltergeist," I answered, slowly walking around the room, picking up small stones. "This was a man. Or man-shaped. And he had six arms."

"Six arms? Definitely a poltergeist," Finn agreed. "Did he leave apports?"

Paen held out his hand. His brother took the stones and nodded.

"What's an apport?" Clare asked, munching lilac. "Six arms? Are you sure, Sam?"

"Six arms are kind of hard to miss," I said, bringing back a handful of stones to Paen. "They look the same."

"They are. An apport is the result of a poltergeist manifesting physical energy. I'd heard of them, but never seen one until now," Paen answered.

"They look like normal stones," I said.

"They are normal. It's a physical reaction to the poltergeist interacting in our world. Did you find them around the things you saw him touch?"

I nodded, rubbing my arms, cold with fear, the remaining chill of the poltergeist, and most of all, from the loss of Paen's body next to mine. "What does a poltergeist want with us? I thought they just inhabited old houses?"

"I have no idea what he wanted, but I'm going to

find out," Paen said grimly, handing me back the stones as he strode over to the phone in a swirl of pleated blue and green plaid.

"Who are you calling?" I asked, half joking. "An exorcist?"

"No, someone better," he answered, asking the directory assistance for a number. He wrote it down, punching in a new number as he added, "I'm going to call a Guardian."

"Oh, no," Clare gasped, her eyes widening, a lilac blossom halfway to her mouth.

Goose bumps marched up and down my arms as Paen held a quick one-sided conversation with someone. I slumped down onto the couch, watching him worriedly. I might not have had too much experience with dark beings, but even I had heard of Guardians. They were badass warriors, protectors of the portals to hell, the people who wrangled demons and their ilk. Guardians were good guys, but they were also seriously powerful people who were single-minded in their duties, and didn't particularly care who got in their way while they performed them. Jake told me once he'd been called in to assist a Guardian with an algul (night-feeding ghoul) who'd kidnapped a living child. The Guardian was evidently perfectly happy with using Jake as a sacrifice in order to destroy the algul, but fortunately, he had managed to escape the experience with his life intact (although he had nightmares about it for six months afterward). "Er . . . is it absolutely vital to have a Guardian? I could try scrying the location of the poltergeist—"

"No!" shouted Clare. "Gods above, Sam, the thought

of what would happen if you should try to tap into the dark powers . . ." She shuddered eloquently.

"Much as I'd like to see you scry, it won't be necessary in this instance," Paen said, hanging up the phone before quickly entering yet another number. "An acquaintance of mine just gave me the number of a Guardian who is in the area, and might be willing to help us—assuming you don't mind a second late-night visitor?"

I glanced at the clock. It was now the third hour of deep night, and I was getting pretty tired. Still, the thought of poltergeists marching around our apartment gave me the willies. "Go ahead and invite him here. The sooner we can get this over with, the better."

Luckily the Guardian Paen called was not put out by being called in the middle of the night. She was also not what I was expecting. Less than an hour after Paen called, she was knocking at our door, a warm, friendly smile on her face as she greeted me.

"Hullo, I'm Noelle. I understand you're having a bit of a poltergeist problem?" the petite, red-haired woman asked.

"Uh . . . yes, we are. Please come in."

We'd used the time it took for Noelle to arrive to get dressed, search the apartment for more apports, and do a little research into poltergeists. Unfortunately, there wasn't a lot of information to be found online.

"Hullo," Noelle said, giving everyone a smile as I performed introductions. "Ooh, a Dark One. And a Moravian. How interesting that a poltergeist would make an attempt with you here."

"Thank you for coming so quickly," Paen said, shaking her hand. "We're lucky that you were available to help us."

"My pleasure. I'm in the area researching the migratory pattern of Celtic werefolk, so this makes a nice change of pace. Might I see the apports, please? They should give me an idea of the type of poltergeist we're dealing with."

I frowned at Paen as Finn handed the Guardian the collection of small stones.

"What?" he asked quietly.

"How does she know what you are just by looking at you? Is there some sort of a sign that I missed?"

"She's a Guardian," he said blithely.

"Yeah, but she doesn't look so badass to me— whoa!"

Evidently Noelle's appearance was misleading. In the time it took for me to have the brief exchange with Paen, she finished looking at the apports, recited a couple of words, clapped her hands, and whammo! The poltergeist suddenly appeared in front of her. He looked even creepier in the light, his body movements fast and jerky, like he was on videotape being run at twice the normal speed.

"This is a minor poltergeist," Noelle told us when Clare gave a little scream and ran to hide behind Finn. "An apprentice, by the looks of him. He hasn't mastered the skills of appearing human or controlling apports yet. What's your name, poltergeist?"

Several loud raps answered her question. Noelle nodded, as if she understood the odd answer. "Very well, Reuben. How were you made?"

Two raps sounded.

"Is it talking?" I whispered to Paen, moving until I was right next to him.

"Evidently. I've never seen a poltergeist before. This is fascinating."

"Yeah, fascinating," I muttered, wishing for a moment that the poltergeist and Guardian were gone so we could go back to our previous activities. Maybe if I meditated first, I'd be able to ground myself enough to stay in my body?

"I see." Noelle glanced at Clare, then over to Paen and me. "As you know, there are two breeds of poltergeists, orthodox and mundane."

"Ah," I said, trying to look savvy with the whole poltergeist thing.

Evidently Noelle saw right through my attempt. "Orthodox poltergeists are born, while mundanes are made poltergeists, generally by the cursing of a demon lord. It seems Reuben here was cursed by Oriens. He was, in fact, a faery before he was cursed."

"Don't you say it!" Clare said, pointing a finger at me.

I grinned, but said nothing.

Noelle calmly examined the poltergeist. "Do you know what I am?"

He rapped out an answer.

"Then you know that I am perfectly capable of conducting an exorcism if necessary," Noelle said calmly, sketching a couple of wards on him.

A barrage of agitated rapping met that statement. The poltergeist himself blinked in and out as if unable to contain his emotions.

"Just so," Noelle said, nodding again. "I hope it

won't come to that. It really would be best if you would cooperate with us by answering our questions."

The poltergeist knocked twice.

"Excellent." Noelle turned to where I was clumped up against Paen's side. "I think we're ready to proceed."

"Er . . . forgive me for asking, but do all poltergeists talk by making rapping noises?" I asked.

"Oh, heavens, no. Only the inexperienced ones. A truly old poltergeist could pass for human if he wanted. Reuben here is a very young one; I'd say about twelve or so."

There were three raps.

"I stand corrected—he's fifteen. What questions would you like me to put to him?"

"Samantha?" Paen deferred to me. I flashed him a grateful smile that he hadn't tried to usurp my authority, straightened up, and gave the poltergeist a firm look.

"I'd like to know why he was here searching the flat."

Reuben rapped out an answer. I looked at Noelle for a translation.

"He says he was sent here to find something."

"What?" I asked the poltergeist. "Who sent you? And why were you going into Clare's room?"

More rapping. Noelle listened for a moment, her eyes narrowing as she concentrated. When Reuben's knocking came to an end she blushed a bit, answering us without meeting our eyes. "He says he was sent by Pilar to find a statue of a bird. I won't go into why he was going into Clare's room other than to say apparently Reuben has some voyeuristic tendencies."

"Ew," I said at the same time Clare gasped in outrage. "Who is Pilar?"

Noelle listened again to the raps. "All he's saying is Pilar is the one who hired him. I don't think he can answer the question, Sam. I doubt if he knows more than that." She lowered her voice. "I don't think he's particularly bright."

Reuben rapped once.

"This is the second mention of that statue," Paen said thoughtfully, giving me a curious look. "I'd like to see it."

"It's locked up at Mila's sex shop," I reminded him. "We can see it tomorrow if you think it has some bearing on things, although I don't see how it's anything but a coincidence. An odd one, to be sure, but still a coincidence."

"Possibly. It's difficult to tell," Paen said.

"Is there anything else you can tell us about Pilar or why you were sent here?" I asked Reuben. The poltergeist shimmered a second or two before answering.

"He says no. He was summoned by Pilar, given instructions to search your flat, and sent on his way."

"What does Pilar look like?" Paen asked.

Noelle translated the answer. "Medium height, dark hair and eyes. He had a monkey with him, a small monkey."

"A monkey?" I gawked for a moment.

"How very odd," Clare said, peering around Finn's shoulder to look at Reuben. "The man who shot me had a monkey. And you said you saw a monkey before, didn't you, Sam?"

"Yeah. What sort of a monkey was it?" I asked the poltergeist.

"Small monkey," came the answer.

"Was its name Beppo, by any chance?" I asked, aware that Paen had moved away from me and was looking out the window to the street below.

"Yes."

"Oooh," Clare said, coming out from behind Finn. "How eerie is that?"

"Not terribly eerie," I answered, nibbling my lip for a moment. "But I'm willing to bet my entire savings that this Pilar guy is one and the same as our two monkey men."

Noelle looked surprised. "You were shot?" she asked Clare.

"Yes. My Versace is completely ruined," Clare answered, her chin rising in a militant manner. "I'd like to meet this Mr. Pilar again. In a closed room. Just him and me and a garden hose."

Noelle squinted for a moment at Clare, and then nodded. "Oh. Faery. That explains it."

"I am not!" Clare protested.

We all ignored her. A few more questions determined that Reuben had no more information for us, so Noelle dismissed him with the warning not to come back. She warded the doors and windows as an additional line of defense.

"It won't keep out a really powerful being, but it should help keep out any statue-seeking poltergeists," she told us as she was leaving. She paused for a minute at the door, tipping her head to the side as she considered the four of us standing in the living room. "Does this remind anyone of a movie?"

"Eh?" I asked, confused, my attention divided

between making plans and watching Paen look out the window.

"A bird statue that everyone seems to want, a private investigator named Sam, a partner who was shot—doesn't that ring any bells with you?" Noelle asked.

"No," Clare answered, frowning.

I smiled at Noelle, having watched more of a classic movie channel than my cousin. "Just call me Bogey."

She laughed and wished us all luck, leaving with a little wave.

"Now what do we do?" Clare asked, looking from Paen to Finn to me.

I stifled a yawn. "I'll check the databases for any information on a man named Pilar, especially in relation to objets d'art. You can—"

"Go to bed," Paen interrupted, finally turning away from the window. He picked up his coat, giving me a long look as he did so. "It's late. You're tired."

"I'm not," I started to protest, but stopped when Paen tipped my chin up so he could look deep in my eyes.

His thumb stroked over my cheek briefly. "Now there are dark circles under your eyes. You need to sleep before you try to do any more investigating."

"Bed! What a wonderful idea. I wholeheartedly endorse it," Clare said, pulling Finn backward into her room. "We can work in the morning. Or later in the morning, since it's morning now."

"You're leaving?" I asked Paen, a little shaft of pain turning in my chest. "I won't deny I could do with a little rest, but I thought you . . . I thought we were going to . . ."

"Your flat is well warded, and Finn will protect

you both from anything that manages to get past them," he answered, giving his brother a quick nod before the latter was hauled into Clare's room, the door slamming behind them.

"I don't need protecting by any man," I said grumpily. I wanted to pretend it was because I was annoyed at all the distractions, but the truth was that I didn't want Paen to leave. There was something about him that felt so . . . right. Like we fit together seamlessly. "Besides, I think Finn's attention will be elsewhere."

"Regardless, you need sleep, not sex."

"Maybe I need both," I said a bit tartishly, annoyed with his high-handed attitude.

He just gave me a look.

"Oh, all right, I admit I'm a little tired, but in defense I'd like to point out that the activities in which we were engaged ended up with me drifting off just as I've done every other time."

"I'd only just started," Paen said, looking annoyed as well. "I didn't have a proper chance."

"Mmm. Well, guess the point is moot since you're ordering me to bed." I started toward my bedroom, pausing to look back as he opened the front door. "Mind if I ask what you're going to be doing while the rest of us are sleeping?"

"Yes, I do," he said, closing the door firmly behind him.

You rat fink, I yelled at him, only just refraining from slamming my bedroom door.

He smiled. Right into my head. It was such a sweet, gentle brush against my mind, I thought for a moment that I'd imagined it.

Chapter 8

"There you are. I wondered if you were going to show before noon." I smiled at Clare as she bustled into the office, a fresh bouquet of mixed flowers in her hand.

"Of course I'm here! Where did you think I'd be?" She plucked out the remains of yesterday's mostly eaten bouquet and took the vase down the hall to the bathroom for fresh water.

"Well, given that you and Finn were at it all night, I'm surprised you're here at all," I said when she returned.

"Hmph," she snorted, plopping the fresh flowers in the vase. "You're just jealous because your boyfriend left you and mine didn't."

"I don't have a boyfriend. Paen is not a boyfriend. He is a client. I admit we have a personal situation going on, but it's nothing permanent."

"So you say. What have you been doing this morning, Miss Productive?"

I tossed a folder onto her desk, stretched, and looked out the window at a rare sunny May day.

"Quite a bit, actually. I ran out to Mr. Race's house first thing this morning to see what it knew about his manuscript, but came up empty there."

"Was it like Finn's castle?" she asked, leafing through the pages of the report I'd typed up and printed.

"No, the house remembered a manuscript, but the memory was fuzzy, as if it was from a long time ago. The housekeeper let me look around, but there wasn't anything else to pick up. I did get the name of the appraisers who worked on Mr. Race's collection a few years ago. I was just about to drop by their offices and see if I couldn't wheedle a peek at their report on the manuscript, but if you don't have other plans, perhaps you could do that while I go talk to the local expert on mages."

"Mages?" Clare's nose wrinkled as I scooped up my purse and jacket. "Why on earth do you want to talk to someone about mages?"

"Read the second report. While you've been romping away half the morning in bed with Finn, I found a morsel of information about the Jilin God statue. Turns out it's older than I thought—and has mystical origins. There are not a lot of details about it available—"

"You can say that again," Clare interrupted. "I've researched that thing for three days now without finding so much as a solid description of it."

"—but I did find an obscure reference to a mage who supposedly possessed it before it disappeared. It's not a big lead, but other than scrying, it's the only avenue I have to pursue right now."

Her eyes got huge. "You're not going to scry, are you?"

"Stop looking so frightened. I told you I had it

under control," I reassured her. "But just to make you rest easier, I'm going to have Jake with me when I try it. Just in case."

"Oh, Sam, I wish you wouldn't—"

I let her work it out of her system (there's nothing quite as pathetic as a frustrated faery), but in the end, did what I had intended to do all along. I did admit there was some validity to her concerns, however, and swore to be careful and to not scry without a spotter. "Jake'll be there for me," I told her as I was leaving.

"I just hope that's enough," she said darkly.

I hurried down the stairs and out onto the street, stopping when Clare leaned out the window to bellow at me, "What about the statue? I thought we were going to look at it?"

"Later!" I waved frantically at her to hush up, glancing up and down the busy street. No one seemed to pay us any attention, but who knew what interested ears might have caught that?

The mage expert lived on Cockburn Street, in a very chic area full of cafés, exclusive shops, and snooty galleries. The apartments, like the other businesses, were housed in a connected line of grey stone, steep-gabled Victorian buildings. I located the correct apartment, pressed the appropriate buzzer, and gave my name. "Hi, I'm Samantha Cosse. I called earlier."

"Ah, Miss Cosse, yes, of course I remember you." The disembodied voice of a man came out with the tinny quality so peculiar to intercoms. "Please come up."

I glanced at the sign reading CASPAR GREEN and noted the apartment number, opening the door when it buzzed at me. Two minutes later I found myself in a sunny peach and cream sitting room, enjoying a brief burst of sunlight while sipping a cup of India tea and nibbling on a tart lemon cookie.

It was perfectly normal-looking, peaceful even, except for one thing—my elf warning system was going off like mad. Something was not right in this room. Something was definitely not right.

"How can I assist you?" Caspar asked, holding out his hands in a gesture of generosity.

I rubbed my arms, trying to quell the goose bumps that marched up and down my flesh. "Er . . . this is going to sound very rude, and I apologize in advance for that, but you don't happen to have anything demonic around, do you?"

"Demonic?" he asked, looking startled.

"Yes. Something that a demon has touched, maybe?" I suggested, looking around the flat. Nothing looked out of place—the sitting room was flooded with sunlight, the peach walls catching the light and turning it warm and soothing. Regardless of that, I felt chilled, as if the air was refrigerated. "Perhaps something that's been charged with a dark power?"

Caspar looked around as well. "I am a bit taken aback by that question. I have no demonic object, nor any object that has powers, dark or light."

"I'm sorry, I didn't mean to insult you," I said hurriedly. "It's just that something is pinging my Otherworld radar."

His face, unremarkable except for a pair of extremely bushy black eyebrows, mirrored surprise. "Your Otherworld radar?"

"That's what I call it," I said, smiling and trying to

analyze the feeling that something was wrong. "But I have to admit that sometimes it's a bit off."

"Indeed," he said politely, offering me the plate of cookies again. "How is it I can be of help to you?"

"I understand you have an academic interest in the history of mages," I said, hastily swallowing a mouthful of cookie. Nothing makes quite such a dashing impression as spewing cookie crumbs all over the place. "I'm interested in the man who may be connected with a manuscript called the *Simia Gestor Coda*. Have you ever heard of him or it?"

Caspar sat back in a peach-colored chair, his brow furrowed and fingers steepled as he thought. "The *Simia Gestor Coda*. Hmm. The name is somewhat familiar, but not something I remember much . . . ah. Wait. I have it. The *Coda* concerns the origins of several races—Dark Ones, Fomhóire, and Ilargi are what I remember, but there may be more in the manuscript."

I licked lemony powdered sugar off my lips as I pulled out my PDA, relieved that my long shot had turned out so well. "Fomhóire I've heard of—they are the Celtic branch of faeries, yes? But I don't think I've ever heard mention of Ilargi."

Caspar waved an elegant hand at the plate of cookies. I shook my head, taking notes on my PDA as he spoke. "I believe the Fomhóire would be very surprised to find themselves called faeries, but that is neither here nor there. The Ilargi have Basque origins. They are reapers, of the moon clan."

"Oh," I said, a little chill going down my spine. Reapers I'd heard of from my Diviner studies—they are beings that light the way of the dead. Not someone you want to hang around. "Do you happen to know who wrote the *Coda*? Thus far I haven't been able to find out any information regarding its author, or more than a vague skeleton of its history. I know it was connected with Marco Polo somehow, and it disappeared approximately three centuries ago, but that's about it."

"I wish I could help you, but alas"—Caspar spread his hands again, showing me they were empty—"I know little more about it than you. I do not know who authored it, although I have heard the name of Samaria Magnus mentioned in connection with the *Coda*."

"Samaria Magnus?" I asked, making a note of that name for further research. "A woman?"

"No, it was a false name, one taken to protect the identity of the individual from charges of heresy. No doubt his origins were in Samaria. Magnus was a common surname adopted by mages over the centuries."

"Ah. That makes sense. So this Samaria Magnus wrote a manuscript about the origins of a bunch of different people, and then . . . what?"

"No one knows. Both Magnus and the *Coda* disappeared for several hundreds of years. The latter made an appearance in the late seventeenth century, when it was the cause of much infighting between the mages of the time. But it, too, slipped from view. Few know it ever existed, let alone know much about it. I'm afraid that is the extent of my knowledge about both the *Coda* and Samaria Magnus."

"Well, I appreciate both," I said, tucking away my PDA and taking a sip of tea before setting the delicate china teacup on the table next to me. "There's not a lot to be found about it, but this should give me a little more to go on. Thank you so much for your time."

"It is my pleasure," Caspar said, escorting me to the door. "If I can assist you any further with mages, thirteenth century or otherwise, I am at your disposal."

He made me an elegant bow, his smile lingering in my mind as I tromped down the stairs to the street, aware by the prickling of my back that something wasn't as it should be. It wasn't until I was on the bus, halfway to Diviners' House, that something occurred to me—at no point during our conversation did Caspar Green express the slightest bit of curiosity as to my interest in Samaria Magnus or the *Coda*.

"What do you think that means?" I asked Jake a good forty minutes later, as we were on another bus, this one headed for Butterfly World, an insect zoo of sorts.

Jake looked pensive—not an unnatural state for a Diviner, but a stranger to his usually sunny countenance. "I'm not sure. It could be that he has no interest in the *Coda* or this mage, despite his academic studies."

"Or it could be something he's not telling me," I said. "My elf warning system was into the red zone while I was in his apartment."

"Your elf warning system is notoriously unreliable," he answered, giving me a look.

"It's not unreliable. Just a bit . . . touchy."

"Touchy? Like the time you swore your room was haunted, and you conducted nightly séances to try to contact the haunting spirit?"

I looked out the window and tried my best to ignore him.

"You had everyone up for three nights in a row, convinced that your room contained a poor, lost spirit who was stuck in this dimension, unable to get to the next, isn't that right?"

It's amazing how hard it is to ignore someone sitting right next to you.

"You even demanded that Brother Immanuel conduct a ritual of purification in your room, in an attempt to help the spirit on its way."

I gritted my teeth.

"And what was it that turned out to be inhabiting your room?" Jake asked, laughter rife in his voice.

I turned around just enough to glare at him. "You know full well it was a mouse, so stop smirking. I never said my elf sense was very highly attuned. I just said it's there, and it warns me about things."

"Not always Otherworld things, though," Jake pointed out gently.

I let that go, partly because he was doing me a favor in agreeing to monitor me while I scryed, but mostly because he was right.

"Tell me again why we're doing this at Butterfly World?" Jake asked as I paid our entrance fee (Diviners take a vow of poverty not to purify their souls, but to keep them from being tempted to divine locations of material goods that could make them impossibly wealthy). He looked with interest at the brochure that was given to us with our admittance tickets. "Will we have time to see the poison arrow frogs and the royal python?"

"If you're good, yes. And we're here because this

is the sunniest, warmest place in Edinburgh, thanks to their industrial-strength sunlamps. I think the jungle area is going to be our best bet," I said, consulting the giant map posted at the entrance. "Hopefully we can find a quiet, out-of-the-way corner where no one will bother us."

Jake followed docilely as we entered what looked like a huge, outsized greenhouse, happily perusing the informational pamphlet. "Did you know that the life span of your average butterfly is only a fortnight? There is one type, a zebra butterfly, that can live ten months, though."

"Fascinating." I paused for a moment to get my bearings, a little thrown by the mass of color flitting around. There must have been two or three hundred different types of butterflies—some brightly colored, others in camouflage, and all of them swooping around in a never-ending palette of color. The air was thick and humid, heavy with the scent of damp earth and sickly sweet flowers. I started sweating almost immediately. "Look, behind that clump of palmish whatever, next to the big machine. That looks like no one goes there."

"Probably because it's off the pathway," Jake remarked as I leaped over the low barrier intended to keep people out of the tropical foliage.

"Yeah, yeah. I'm not going to do any damage. I just want a little privacy."

Luckily the group of kids in school uniforms that had arrived before us sucked up the attention of the Butterfly World attendants, leaving us able to slip behind a dense clump of palms in a corner of the building. I pulled a lap blanket out of my backpack and spread it out on the moist earth, glancing up for a moment at a sunlamp that beamed its rays down on us. It wouldn't have done as a substitute on its own, but since it was sunny outside, the combination of artificial and real sunlight was enough to power my elf cells.

"Right. If you'll sit there . . . mind the butterfly . . . I'll sit across from you, and I think we should both be hidden from view by anyone on the path." I gestured to a spot. Jake obediently sat down cross-legged on the blanket, looking expectant.

I settled myself in a pool of sunlight, pulling a soft leather bag from the backpack, carefully removing from it both my black mirror bowl and a small flask of water. I held the bowl up so it shared the sunlight with me, closing my eyes as I allowed the sun to soak into my being, merging with my essence, becoming something new, a bright, shining light of everything that I was. Concentrating fiercely, I poured the light into the black abyss of the waiting receptacle.

What in god's name are you doing? a startled, somewhat panicked voice asked.

Paen?

What are you doing to me? Stop it! Stop filling me with that blasted light!

I'm not filling you with light. I'm charging a scrying bowl.

You may think that's what you're doing, but you're damn near blinding me.

Don't be ridiculous. How can charging a bowl spill over onto . . . hey! You're talking to me!

There was a long pause before Paen sighed resignedly into my head. *Where are you?*

Butterfly World. Why?

I'll be there as quickly as I can.

You're welcome to watch, of course, but there's no need for you to be here. I've brought my Diviner friend Jake along to keep me from sucking all the tourists into another dimension.

Paen sighed again.

That was a joke. Seriously, there's no need—

I'll be there. Don't scry without me.

Paen's presence withdrew from my mind, leaving me with the feeling of loss. "Well, crap."

"Eh?" Jake asked, still looking expectantly at me.

"One of my clients wants to watch the scrying," I said, setting the bowl on my lap.

"Why didn't you say that before you dragged me in here?" Jake got to his feet. "How long will this client be? Will I have time to take in the scorpions?"

"I don't know where he is. Hang on, I'll ask." I reached out with my mind, holding an image of Paen, bringing up all the confused morass of feelings I had about him. *Where are you?*

On the way. I should be there in about ten minutes.

"Go look at the scorpions," I told Jake. "Come back in about fifteen minutes."

"Erm . . . Sam? I didn't see a mobile phone there." Jake looked a bit perplexed.

"Oh . . . well . . . this client just happens to be telepathic," I said, trying to avoid specifics.

"Righto." He toddled off without any further questions. That's one of the things I liked about Jake—he didn't sweat the little stuff.

I debated just going ahead and doing the scrying without waiting as ordered by Paen—after all, I am a take-charge sort of person, and he was paying me to do a job—but in the end I justified a wait as something that would be courteous and professional. Not to mention the good five minutes I spent flat on my belly hiding from the group of Scottish horticulturists who were grouped just on the other side of the clump of palms that screened me from the walkway, examining the leaves with a closeness that almost led to my discovery.

Where are you?

Butterfly house, off to the left of the entrance, north corner, hidden behind a sturdy clump of palms.

Could you have chosen a brighter spot? I don't think this sunlight is quite *enough to fry me to a crisp.*

I didn't know you were coming to the party. There's a shady spot just behind me, covered by an energy curtain and hidden behind a big misting pump, if you want to risk that. I have to stay in the sun. It powers me.

The palms in front of me rustled as a black shadow streaked into the corner made dark by an overhead curtain, and a lurking machine that churga-churgaed away quietly to itself.

What are you doing?

I smiled at the peevish note in Paen's voice. Poor man, all this sunlight had to be uncomfortable for him.

Listening to the butterflies argue.

A meaningful pause filled my head. *Butterflies argue?*

Oh yeah. They're really actually quite cantankerous for such pretty things. Always getting into fights with each other.

I see. Is this an elf trait, or have you just lost your wits?

I gave him a mental eye roll. *Look, I don't pick on you because of the way you were born, OK? So don't give me any grief about being able to understand butterfly. And while we're on the subject of different—what made you change your mind about doing the mental thing with me?*

A sigh emerged from over my shoulder, in the vicinity of the misting machine. I smiled straight ahead at a couple of startlingly blue mortho butterflies that were flitting around taunting each other.

"Are you going to try scrying now?"

"As soon as Jake gets back from looking at creepy-crawlies. Are you going to avoid answering my question?"

"Yes."

"Why?"

"Because I don't wish to answer it. How long will the scrying take?"

"Probably not too long. Why are you so adamant about avoiding the fact that we can mind-talk?"

"Why are you so desirous of doing it?"

I shrugged, still watching the butterflies as one took offense to a slur and attacked the other. "I've never had this ability with anyone. It's pretty unique. I just don't understand why you're so freaked about it—oh, hi, Jake."

"Don't tell me, you're talking to the butterflies?"

"No, to my client, Paen Scott. Paen, this is Brother Jacob, one of the Diviners who used to teach me."

Jake glanced around quickly, giving me a worried look. "Erm . . . Sam . . ."

"He's behind the machinery," I said, waving at the big misting machine. "He's a Dark One. Sunshine is a no-no."

"Ah," Jake said, squinting at the machine. "Pleasure."

"Likewise," came Paen's voice from behind the machine. "Can we get on with this? I have a tip I'd like to discuss with you, Samantha."

"Tip? What tip? About your statue?"

Paen said nothing.

"Fine, be mysterious." I sighed, picking up the black mirrored bowl in one hand, the flask of springwater in the other. "Hopefully this won't take very long."

Scrying isn't my forte. I came to that conclusion some ten minutes later, when I was trying to decipher the images that flashed in my mind while covered with hundreds and hundreds of squabbling butterflies. An image of the gold bird statue popped into my head for a moment. Clearly I had statues on the brain. I closed it out and focused my thoughts on the monkey statue before looking into the bowl.

"What exactly do you see?" Jake asked, batting at a couple of butterflies that left me to investigate him.

"I see the statue," I hissed through my teeth, experience having proven that opening your mouth to speak while covered in butterflies is not a good idea. "It's a black monkey all right. Smallish, kind of ugly. Has a really big . . . er . . . masculine attribute. Looks Pagan rather than Chinese."

"Where is it?" Paen asked from the cover of the misting machine.

I shook my head to dislodge a couple of the butterflies that clung to my eyelashes, and looked deep into the reflective water held in my scrying bowl. It was a bit difficult to scry because the butterflies, evidently attracted to me while I was doing my sun elf thing, were flitting around in front of the bowl, but I managed to see past them, past the surface of the water, deep into that twilight place between realities also known as the beyond.

"It's in a dark place. Closely confined in some sort of sarcophagus or something like that. Maybe a tomb," I said, sending the mental picture of it to Paen. "There's a definite feel of it being held in a confined, protected place."

"A tomb? What tomb?" he asked.

I shook my head. "No idea. I can't see its location beyond the fact that it's entombed. All I see is the statue itself."

"Er . . . Sam? I hate to hurry you, but I think you should try to wrap this up," Jake said, his voice worried.

"Why?" I asked, my vision still turned inward, trying to pull out of the tomb to see where it was located.

"Because you're starting to emit light, and there's a lorry-load of butterflies heading this way that look like they aren't going to be content with just fluttering merrily around you."

I pulled back out of the scrying vision and glanced down first at myself, where tiny little pinpoints of sunlight were bursting out of me. "Wow. I'm in sunshine overload . . . holy moly!"

Heading toward us in a veritable tidal wave of brilliant color, every butterfly in the whole of Butterfly World was zooming straight at me in one solid mass that knocked down everything and everyone in its path. People screamed and threw themselves to the floor as the swarm flew at us. As if that sight wasn't frightening enough, the butterflies' chant of "Drink the light! Drink the light!" turned my blood cold.

I dumped the water out of my scrying bowl and leaped to my feet, snatching up my backpack before throwing myself through the palms, butterflies falling off me as I bolted for the door. "Run! Run for your lives! Killer butterflies!"

Chapter 9

"I don't believe I've ever run across a butterfly I'd classify as murderous," Paen commented a few minutes later. He stood in the shadow of an overhang of a maintenance building, clad in the same ankle-length black coat and hat that he'd worn to my office.

"Yeah, well, you didn't hear those little monsters chanting about *drinking* you." I stopped brushing off the butterfly dust—which Jake helpfully informed me was actually miniscule scales off the butterflies' wings—and scrunched my nose. "Why was I emitting light? I've never done that before."

"You've never channeled power from the sun before, either," Jake said, watching Paen with bright, interested eyes. "You probably pulled more than you needed, and it had to go somewhere."

I patted my torso, still a bit weirded out by the experience. Unlike Clare, I was not immortal, nor did I recover quickly from wounds. The fact that sunlight could burst out of me without doing damage relieved my mind on one level, and disturbed me greatly on another. I'd have to worry about it at another time, though. Right now I had more important concerns. "Whatever the reason, I'm glad it's done. I'm just sorry I couldn't pinpoint the location of the statue."

"You have no idea where it is?" Paen asked.

"Somewhere fairly close, that's the only sense of location I got."

"Close meaning Edinburgh? Scotland? The planet Earth?"

"Very funny," I said, walking toward the parking lot. I stopped and looked back at Paen, still standing in the shadows. "Mind giving us a lift back to town?"

He angled his hat so it shaded his face, stuffed his hands in his pockets, and strode past me into the sunlight. Jake and I followed, hurrying to keep up with Paen's long-legged stride.

"The answer to your question is this area. I think. Lowlands of Scotland. Somewhere around here, there's a tomb holding that statue. Any obvious spots you'd like to search first?"

"No," Paen said, turning his back to the sun so he could open the car door. I noticed for the first time that the windows of the car were heavily tinted. From the inside, they appeared normal, but anyone standing outside it saw windows almost as dark as my scrying mirror. "But I have information that may make such a search moot."

"Really? What sort of information?" I asked as I got into the car, claiming the front seat while Jake took the rear. I scooted around on the seat so I had my back to the door, able to see both men. "What did you find out?"

Paen's gaze flickered to the rearview mirror for a moment.

He's absolutely trustworthy, you know. You can say anything you want in front of him. He won't repeat it.

I could feel Paen hesitate, unwilling to share information in front of a stranger.

I know it's asking a lot, but I trust him with my life. You really don't have to worry about anything you say in front of him getting spread around.

"There was a demon waiting for me outside your flat when I left this morning," he said finally, evidently deciding to trust us both.

Jake's eyes widened.

"It's not like it sounds," I said hastily, giving Paen a small frown. "We didn't have sex."

"We didn't?" Paen asked.

"No, we didn't!"

"We were both naked," he pointed out. "And you begged me to make love to your ears."

Jake's eyes practically bugged out.

"Paen's blowing this totally out of proportion," I told him, waving a hand at my would-be lover. "The ear sex thing was unexpected. And just so you know, all he did was bite my ears. There were no ear-to-genital encounters. That's just creepy."

"I think this is probably none of my business," Jake said, looking oddly delighted. He kept shooting little questioning looks at Paen, then grinning at me.

I frowned in return. "True, so if Mr. Blabberfangs there doesn't mind, we can move on past the fact that we were naked and indulging in a little ear make-out session, and get to the point." Unbidden, my gaze dropped to Paen's lap. "Er . . . point of the conversation. You saw a demon?"

"Yes. On the street. It was waiting for me. It said it

had been sent by its master, the demon lord who demanded the statue. The demon said that there was a man in Edinburgh, a theurgist who has an interest in art from the Dark Ages. This man evidently has information about the statue, and possibly knows where it is located."

"Oooh, good clue, even if it does come from a demon," I said, pulling out my PDA to take notes. "What's the name of the guy?"

"Owen Race. Professor Owen Race."

I almost dropped my PDA. "Huh?"

Paen didn't seem to notice for a second or two that Jake and I stared at him with mouths hanging open in surprise. "What? Do you know him?"

"Kind of," I said, choking slightly. "He's a client. Jake referred him to me."

"Client!" Paen looked as surprised as I felt. "What did he hire you for?"

I bit my lip (a bad habit, but one I am unable to stop). "I can't tell you. That would be violating my ethics. It's not to find your statue, though, I'll tell you that."

"I appreciate that you wish to adhere to client confidentiality, but I must insist on knowing what work Owen Race has engaged you to undertake."

"Insist away. You are a client—I respect your right to privacy. Likewise, I respect Mr. Race's. I'll go so far as to assure you that my job for him has nothing to do with your statue, but that's all I'm saying."

"That's not good enough. There may be a connection that you don't see," Paen argued, turning onto a familiar street.

"Might I remind you that I'm a professional?" My

frown got a little tighter. "I'm not a complete idiot, you know. I can tell the difference between a job locating a stolen book and one to find a missing statue."

"Stolen book? What book was stolen?"

I growled to myself.

"I think this is where I get off," Jake said, evidently sensing the coming argument. He waited until Paen pulled past a zebra crossing and hopped out, poking his head back into the car for a moment. "Nice meeting you, Paen. Thanks for the entertainment, Sam."

"Bye, and thank you for all the support," I said, upping my frown at Paen to a full-frontal glare. "I'll let you know later how things turn out, OK?"

"It's a deal. Later."

Paen drove off, heading not toward my office as I wanted, but into the newer part of town where our apartment was.

"You're taking me home? I don't want to go home. I have work to do at the office," I said. "There's a little business about your mother's soul, remember?"

"Of course I remember! How could you possibly imagine I'd forget something like that? I am, however, capable of dealing with more than one situation at a time. Since we are going to continue to work closely together, I think it's appropriate to discuss a few things regarding our personal relationship." Paen's jaw was set as he whipped us around a corner.

"Oh. That makes sense. But we can talk at the office."

"Finn is there with Clare."

"So? I bet if we tried hard, we could talk with them there anyway."

"Would you also like to have sex with them there?"

My lips formed an O. I was about to protest that I wasn't interested in having sex with him, but the truth was, the idea was more than a little intriguing. Just the thought of his hot breath on my ears made me shiver. "Um. No. But it's the middle of the day, and I have work to do. I hate to waste time."

One of his eyebrows rose. "I have heard sex referred to as many things, but a waste of time is not one of them."

"You're not planning on sexing me up, then trying to worm out secrets about Owen Race, are you?" I asked, sudden suspicion causing me to narrow my eyes. No wonder he suddenly was interested in doing the sheet tango.

Paen turned onto my street and headed for the tiny lot behind my building. "The thought had crossed my mind, yes."

"Ha! I knew it. Well, it won't work."

"That was my conclusion as well. You are too honorable to do such a thing."

I basked for a moment or two in the warm glow of his approval, frowning when I realized that his tone added a different interpretation to the statement. "So why are we going to my apartment if you know I don't kiss and tell?"

He shot me a look that had every cell in my body clamoring for action. "I desire you. I believe you desire me. That emotion is impairing my ability to function. I need that ability to continue directing the pursuit of the statue. Therefore, a lovemaking session will do much to clear both our minds. Consider it work therapy."

"Whoa, wait a second," I said as he slipped the car into my parking spot. I put my hand on his arm, holding him in the car when he would have jumped out. "Your desire for me is impairing your ability to function? What's that all about?"

He frowned. "Surely you understand the power of desire? You said you feel an attraction to me."

"Yes, I do. But I don't have to give in to that attraction."

"Don't you?" he asked, getting out of the car, suddenly flooding my head with the emotions he felt during our previous almost-sex session. Hunger was uppermost in his emotions, but it wasn't just a hunger for blood—it was a need for something to fill the gaping hole inside him. It was a silent plea for light to fill his darkness, for someone to take away the pain of utter loneliness, the hopelessness that seeped into every corner of his being.

He needed love.

He needed *me.*

"OK," I said, dropping all objections as I leaped out of the car. We made it to the door of my apartment before I gave in to temptation and flung myself at him, kissing the breath right out of his mouth.

"You're good for someone who hasn't had a lot of practice," he admitted three minutes later, when I retrieved my tongue and broke off the kiss long enough to get the door to the apartment unlocked.

"I'm inspired by the subject," I told him before racing to the bedroom. I yanked off my jacket en route, simultaneously beating back the shrubberies in my room and hopping on one foot while trying to pull off my shoe. Without thinking, I yanked open the blinds to let the sunshine in, stopping for a moment to soak up the wonderfully warm rays before turning to see what was keeping Paen.

He was pinned up against the door, his shirt in one hand, the sunshine lapping at his shoes.

"Oh. Sorry about that. It's instinctive," I said as I angled the blinds to limit the sun to an area directly in front of the window.

"So I gathered," he answered, whapping at a narrow-leafed Australian Tree Fern that was infringing on his personal space.

I got both shoes and socks removed, and peeled off my jeans, standing for a moment with them in my hand, the sun warming my back as I looked at Paen. There was a lot of him to look at, too, what with that glorious bare chest right there for me to ogle. I gave in and had a good ogle, then managed to get my mind back to the question uppermost. "Foreplay or no?"

He stopped mid-unzipping. "Pardon?"

"Are you going to get naked now? Or just torment me with that chest first, driving me to a frenzy of lust-crazed wantonness that will make me rip the rest of your clothes off?"

He looked down at his chest. "You want to rip my clothes off just by looking at my chest?"

"Very much so."

"It's just a chest. Skin and hair."

"Oh, I beg to differ." I tossed aside my jeans and walked over to where he stood in a shady patch, stroking my hand down his chest from his clavicle to his sternum, following the lovely, sleek trail of hair that led straight down his belly and disappeared into his pants. "This is not just skin and hair. This is no mere chest. It's chest deluxe. Chest supreme."

He gave me an odd look, a mixture of disbelief and amusement. "You're a strange woman."

"So it's said. I know a good thing when I see it, however," I said, pulling my hand back with an effort. "So, did you want to dally with a bit of foreplay, or just go straight for the meat-and-potatoes thing?"

He dropped his pants. "What do you think?"

"Whoa! You've been anticipating," I said, admiring the view as I backed up a few steps. I pulled off my sweater and dropped it onto the chair so I stood in the sunlight clad in nothing but my underwear and bra. "OK. I'm good with that. Investigating to do, people to see . . . and evidently, penises to ride. Do you like oral sex?"

"Do you always talk so much during lovemaking?" he asked, an odd look on his face.

"Not normally."

He looked thoughtful for a moment. "Are you still nervous?"

"Maybe a little. In case you haven't noticed, I tend to blabber when I'm nervous."

I've never met anyone like you before, Paen thought. I don't think he intended me to hear him, but I grinned anyway as I did a sinuous little dance in the sunshine while slowly removing my bra.

Good. This'll be new territory for us both. Kind of puts us on equal footing.

"Is equal footing that important to you?" he asked, taking an aborted step forward, stopping because his toes hit the pool of sunlight that surrounded me.

"You hack your way through the foliage and I'll

meet you at the bed," I told him, giving in to the energy that flowed through me from the sunlight. I'm not very adept at dancing, or singing for that matter, but put me in the sun and I feel an indescribable rhythm, kind of like those solar-powered, highly annoying desk toys that weave and bob endlessly until you throw them against the wall or dump them in a dark closet.

"You're going to dance now?" Paen asked, having fought his way through the plants to the bedside. He was watching with interest as I slipped one side of my bra down in a sunny parody of a striptease. "Not that I mind. You're very graceful. And I enjoy looking at your breasts. As well as the rest of you."

I did a few slow-motion hip moves as I shimmied out of my bra, turning to slide my hands down my breasts, along my hips, to the lace bits of my underwear. "I don't normally do this in front of people, but the sunshine makes it hard for me to stand still."

"Take your time. I'm enjoying the show."

I smiled coyly over my shoulder at him and skinnied my way out of my undies, tossing them over my head like they were a bridal bouquet.

"Do I get to keep them?" Paen asked when I turned around. He held my underwear in one hand.

"If you really want, you can. Or you can keep me, instead," I said, slinking my way over to him.

"Hmm." His thumb rubbed over the satin of the underwear. "They're warm, silky, and very feminine."

I smiled as he tossed them aside and pulled me up against his chest. His body was hard and unyielding as I rubbed myself against him, my soft, smooshy parts very different from his solid, flat lines.

"But you're warmer, silkier, and infinitely more feminine. I choose you instead."

"Sounds good to me. Oh, wait . . ."

I slipped away from him to dig a packet out from under my pillow. "Now or later?" I asked, holding it up.

"Might as well be now. I don't think I'll be able to stop once I get started," he answered.

I had to remember for a moment how to breathe at the promise that showed in his eyes, but got the condom on him in record time, and flung myself against him to enjoy the tactile experience of his flesh against mine. "Oooh! Man alive, it's going to be all over for me if you're going to do that!" My legs went boneless as he nipped the top of my ear with his sharp canines.

"There's not a large enough supply of blood for me to drink from this spot," he murmured, his tongue licking away the sting.

I almost came right then and there.

"Dear god in heaven, don't do that!" I yelled, jumping backward, the backs of my knees hitting the bed so that I went sprawling across it.

"Enough earplay?" he asked, looking down at me.

My body quivered. All of it, every last single inch of it, quivered and twitched and tingled at the look in his bright eyes, so light they all but burned my flesh. "I don't think I can take any more eargasms right now. I really want to experience the regular kind, if you don't mind."

"Very well. Perhaps you would prefer this, then," he said, kneeling next to the bed, spreading my legs so he was positioned between them.

"Oh, man," I said on a half gasp as he rubbed his cheeks on my inner thighs. One minute I was me, Sam, a half-elf private detective with a secret addiction to greasy hamburgers, and the next I was a shining orb of rapture, as bright as Paen's eyes, my whole body attuned to every move his mouth made against me. He nibbled, he touched, he probed, his tongue swirled a tango of delight against sensitive parts that suddenly roared to life with a demand to be taken to heaven and back. Without conscious thought, I opened my mind to Paen and shared it with him, shared the ecstasy and euphoria and glory that was his mouth on my tingling parts. He adjusted his angle of attack, and sent me flying . . . right out of my body.

"Dammit, no! NO! NOT NOW! Aaaaaaaaargh!" I all but sobbed as my conscious being parted with my body, and started drifting around the bedroom, at the mercy of the dancing motes of light. "God damn it! DAMN DAMN DAMN!" *Paen, help me!*

The scene below me was arousing, enticing, sexy as hell . . . and I wasn't there to experience the joy I knew Paen was bringing to my body.

Why is this happening? Why isn't it different with you? Why? I wailed.

Come back to me, Sam. Share this with me. Feel what I feel.

Before the words finished rolling around my head I was back in my body, just in time for the glorious Technicolor orgasm that swept over me. I screamed his name as he slid up my body, the pleasure he felt as his teeth sank deep into my breast almost as great as the pleasure he'd just given me.

Our minds merged, his exhilaration feeding mine until it spiraled into something more profound than anything I'd ever felt, a feeling that doubled, trebled as he moved against me, thrusting hard into me as he released my breast to bite hard on my shoulder. Pain flared bright for a moment, then dissolved into rhapsody, so mind-numblingly overwhelming that I could do nothing more than clutch his back as his body moved against mine, the sensations of him moving hard and deep inside me joining with the sensations he felt as he both gave and took life.

It was the experience of a lifetime, and one that seared itself onto my soul as he took me to another orgasm, one that triggered his own, the echoes of both rolling around our joined minds, the light from the being we made together filling every corner of darkness within him, bursting out until we *were* the light.

That was . . . dear god, are you still breathing? . . . that was the most amazing thing I've ever felt. It defies description. It was so astounding, I want to dance and sing and cry with the beauty of it. Paen—you're absolutely amazing. You pulled me back when I had left! Twice! No one has ever done that even once! I think I may faint. Or do a backflip. I can't decide which.

Paen lifted his head from where it had been nestled against my neck, his back covered in a sheen of sweat, his dark curls tousled, his eyes fading from brilliant, blinding silver to a rich grey. "I told you so," was all he said, a smile curling his lips.

I laughed as he kissed me, a kiss so tender it brought tears to my eyes.

"Smugness ill becomes you," I said as he rolled off

me to lie next to me on the bed. He peeled off the condom and tossed it into the elephant-foot trash can before collapsing, exhausted. "Besides, I know you felt the same thing I did, so don't be pretending it was just another day at the office. Ow. Are you OK?"

Paen looked down at himself as I stroked a hand down his chest. The whole front of his torso, from groin to collarbone, was bright red.

"You look like you're sunburned or something. Does it hurt?"

He touched a red spot on his stomach, looked at his hand for a moment, then narrowed his eyes as he reached out and cupped one of my breasts.

"Um," I said, a little ripple of happiness sweeping through me.

He pulled his hand back and showed it to me. His palm was beet red. "It's you."

"Me?" I asked, looking at my breast. "I'm turning you red?"

"You're giving me a sunburn. I can feel the sunlight in you when I touch you."

"Well, how do you like that? I didn't do this to you before. It must be because I got all charged up in the sun." I pressed my hand for a couple of seconds to a non-burned spot on his side. When I removed my hand, a faint pinkish image of my palm remained. "Whoops. Sorry about that. Does it hurt?"

"No," Paen said, lying back, his eyes closed. I could feel him concentrating, focusing his mind. As I watched, the redness washed away on his chest and stomach, as if someone was wiping it off. Only his penis remained startlingly red as it rested against his thigh.

"Wow, it even went through the condom. You can heal yourself, too, huh? Not going to do that as well?" I asked, looking at it.

It twitched. "No. Stop looking at it."

"Why?" I couldn't stop myself. It was fascinating how just looking made it start to stiffen up again.

"Because I don't have the energy to make love to you again right now. Not if you want me to be of any other practical use to you today."

I smiled at his penis and gave it a quick pat that I hoped wouldn't scorch it any further, and rolled onto my side so I was lying close to Paen, but not actually touching. "That's OK, I'm still recovering as well. That was the most amazing, most sensual, most . . . *profound* experience of my life. I had no idea it was possible to take intimacy past the physical level and into the spiritual. I feel as if I'm seeing you for the first time, Paen. And I'll always be grateful to you for making my first *real* time so absolutely, mind-numbingly wondrous. Is sex always like that?"

"No," he said abruptly, changing the subject. "I wish to meet Owen Race. Get dressed and let's go see him."

I sighed. "So much for pillow talk, eh?"

Chapter 10

"So, about this whole Beloved business—I'm a bit confused. What exactly is she other than someone who gets your soul out of hock?"

"It's not important."

Paen sounded downright grumpy. He looked even grumpier, having insisted on driving to my office since I refused to take him out to meet Owen without making sure it wasn't going to cause problems. Now we were smack-dab in the afternoon commute traffic, stuck in an impossibly slow line of cars that inched its way past a three-car accident that managed to block traffic in both directions.

"Look, it's going to take at least half an hour to get to the office—we can sit here in silence, fuming about the traffic, or we can chat. I vote chat."

Paen looked like he wanted to argue, but evidently he realized the truth of what I said, because he relaxed his death grip on the steering wheel and said, "I don't mind talking, but there are many other subjects of conversation other than Beloveds."

"Yeah, but none that you try to avoid so hard."

He shot me a look. "You're not going to let this go, are you?"

"Nope." I smiled. "I'm known for my persistence. It's why Jake thought I'd be a good private investigator. So you might as well give in to the inevitable and tell me what I want to know."

"You're the most stubborn woman of my acquaintance."

"I know. It's one of my charms. About the Beloved?"

He sighed and gave in. "A Beloved is more than just a soul-saver. She becomes a Dark One's life, the sole focus of his attention." He gave a little disgusted snort. "In other words, he becomes a shallow parody of what he used to be."

"I don't think that's very fair of you to say. I personally think it's really romantic that a man would love a woman so much that he'd devote his life to her."

"That's because you're a woman," Paen said, scowling in the side mirror at a bike messenger who smacked the side of the car as he passed. "The relationship between Dark One and Beloved is totally one-sided; she redeems his soul, binding it to her for eternity. There's no reciprocal binding, just him bound to her. If she dies, he fades away to nothing, but a Beloved can live on forever without her Dark One."

"I find it hard to believe that anyone who goes to the trouble of fetching a soul for someone else wouldn't feel some sort of affection for that person. So I'm sure it's not quite as one-sided as you make out."

"You don't know anything about it," he said with

a touch of churlishness that I found oddly endearing. I was beginning to suspect that Paen was arguing to convince himself rather than me.

"No, I don't. Why don't you tell me more about it?"

He shot me a wary look. "Why do you want to know about Beloveds?"

"Oh, I don't know. Partly curiosity. Partly because I like you and I'm interested in your history, and what makes you tick."

His eyes lost their guarded appearance.

"That, and I think there's probably a good chance I'm your Beloved, so I'd like to know what the job entails."

"I knew it! I knew Finn would fill your head with all sorts of idiotic ideas! You are not my Beloved!"

I laughed at the outraged expression on his handsome face. "Prove it."

"What?" We moved forward a few feet. Ahead of us, at the next intersection, a bevy of police cars and aid units were clustered, sorting out the victims and damaged vehicles, hauling away both to their respective destinations. One policeman was directing traffic around a tow truck, up onto the sidewalk, and down onto the street a few feet past.

"Prove to me that I'm not your Beloved."

"How the hell am I supposed to do that?" he asked, giving me another annoyed look.

I leaned to the side and kissed him. His eyes flashed quicksilver at the touch. "Sorry, I just couldn't resist. You're very kissable, you know. It makes my stomach do all sorts of things whenever I give in to temptation."

His gorgeous eyes narrowed at me. "You're trying

to use your female wiles on me to make me tell you what you want to know, aren't you?"

"Are you kidding? You knew the same wouldn't work on me—there's no way I believe I could sway you with sex."

"That's good, because I couldn't be swayed," he said, looking forward as someone four cars ahead was waved through the intersection. "That doesn't mean you can't kiss me, though."

I smiled and sat back, startling him into giving me a look from the corner of his eye. "As for how you can prove to us both that I'm not your Beloved . . . is there a test or something? Or is a woman, pow, just born your Beloved?"

"There are steps that must be gone through to culminate in a Joining," Paen answered grudgingly after a few moments of pregnant silence.

"Finn said something about that. This Joining thing is what gets you back your soul?"

He nodded.

"Gotcha. What are the steps?"

We moved forward another car length. Outside the car, the hum of idling traffic made a dull background to the excited chatter of bystanders watching from behind the yellow accident tape. "The first step is the marking."

"Right. Finn said that could be a psychic thing?"

"The second step," Paen said, ignoring my comment, "is protection from afar."

"Hmm." I tapped my chin. "That sounds very chivalrous. Kind of like you were watching out for someone when she needed you?"

"Possibly," he allowed.

"So I'm two for two, then."

He turned to give me a look that by rights should have sent me screaming. I just wanted to kiss him again, instead. "How do you reckon that?"

"You pulled me back when Pilar was threatening me while I was astralling the first time. That's protection from afar."

"Of a sort, and it was purely unintentional."

I laughed. "Don't sound so grumpy about it. You did pull me out of a bad situation, and I'm grateful for it. What's the third step?"

"The first exchange. And before you ask, that means an exchange of body fluids."

"Ew," I said, wrinkling my nose. "Oh, wait. Does French kissing qualify as an exchange?"

"Yes," he said, his jaw tight.

"Three down, how many left?"

"There are seven steps altogether, and those first three are just coincidences, no more."

"Fourth?" I asked, watching as an aid car pulled out with its sirens and lights screaming a warning.

"Fourth is the Dark One giving the Beloved the means to destroy him."

"Hmm," I said, tapping my chin again as I eyed him. "Like giving her a stake or something?"

He didn't answer, just tightened his jaw even more.

"Or could it be something as simple as telling her enough information about him that she could use it to bring about his destruction if she so desired?"

"You can't destroy me," he said, not answering the question.

"Wanna bet? I'm willing to wager that if I don't

find that statue and your mom loses her soul, you'd be pretty destroyed."

He didn't say anything to that, either.

"Paen—" I leaned over until he made eye contact. "I will find it, don't worry. I'm not going to let your mom lose her soul."

He nodded abruptly.

"This is like pulling teeth, so we might as well get the worst over with. What are the fifth and sixth steps?" I asked as I resumed my seat.

"A second exchange, and help in overcoming his darker self."

"Hmm. Second body fluid exchange, check. But overcoming your darker self . . . hmmm."

"As you now see, you have accomplished some of the steps, but not all of them," he said, moving forward another car space.

I don't know about that—I'm thinking that overcoming your darker self can mean a lot of things.

Such as?

Well, admitting someone into a previously-held-private area of your life.

I could feel him frown as he thought about that. *In what way do you think I've allowed you further than any other woman I've had sex with?*

How many of them did you mind-talk with?

He withdrew—not physically, but mentally—but before he did I got a sense of shock as he realized the truth.

"So that's five and six done. One's left, right? What's that?"

Deep within him, emotions warred so strongly I

felt them even with a few feet between us. "The seventh step is an exchange of blood."

"Blood, huh? I'm not into that, but I suppose if it doesn't have to be a bloodfest, I could tolerate it. Let's do it."

He gave me a look like I'd just suggested he strip naked and dance on the roof of the car. "You can't be serious."

"Sure I am. If it will get you back your soul, then it would be worth it to me to put up with a little blood."

"You have no idea what you're saying," he sputtered.

"In fact, I do. But according to you, I'm not your Beloved, so it shouldn't matter. I think. What happens if we do the seventh step and I'm not your Beloved?"

"Nothing happens, but you aren't—" he started to say.

I took his hand and pulled off my jacket the Celtic cross brooch my mother had given me for Easter. Before waiting for him to protest, I jabbed the tip of his finger with the pin, taking the end of his finger into my mouth to suck off the bead of blood that appeared there.

"Sam, no!" he yelled as I wrinkled my nose at the coppery taste of blood.

"Seventh step," I said, putting my thumb over the spot on his finger to stop the bleeding. I squinted at him, surprised to see that nothing looked different about him. "Um. Does it take a while for your soul to come back?"

"It would be instantaneous if you were my Beloved," he said, pulling his hand back.

"Oh. Rats."

"Rats?" he asked, looking a bit surprised. I didn't blame him—I felt a bit surprised by my disappointment that I hadn't turned out to be his Beloved after all.

"Yeah. I'm sorry I couldn't help you. I really thought I could."

The silver light in his eyes narrowed. "You want to become my Beloved?"

"No, not really." Pain flashed over his face so quickly I wasn't sure if I really saw it or was projecting. "That is, I want to help you. I like you, Paen. I like you a lot. I know you pooh-pooh any sort of emotional attachment in your lovers, but some level of it is important to me. I care about you. And I'd like for you to have a soul. So in that sense, yes, I was willing to be your Beloved in order to do that. But if you're asking if I'm madly in love with you . . ." I bit my lip.

"Well?" he asked, trying not to look interested but failing badly. Evidently he realized that as well because he gave up the pretence. "Are you madly in love with me?"

"I am not head over heels in love with you, no," I said carefully, honesty being one of my rules. I avoided thinking about the fact that chances were good I was soon going to be in that state.

"Ah." Deep within him, for just a second or two, disappointment added to the blackness that threatened to engulf him. "That's good. I'm not in love with you, either. But as for the other . . . er . . . I like you as well."

"Right. So we're both on the same channel, then."
Ahead of us, the cop waved the car in front and us
through the intersection. Paen shifted, a tiny frown
pulling his eyebrows together.

"Exactly."

"And I'm not your Beloved."

He was silent for a second longer than I thought he
would be. "That's correct."

"Sorry about stabbing your finger."

He made a little gesture waving it away. "It's nothing."

Silence filled the car as we made our way down
Princes Street and turned onto the street where my
office was located. I directed him to the loading zone
spot along the side that Mila had told us we could
use.

"You sit tight and I'll go unlock the side door," I
said, pointing to the unmarked door along the side of
the building. "It's faster than going in the front way,
and if you run, you shouldn't get too much more
sun."

"Thank you," he said, his eyes brightening as I caressed his cheek.

"You're still a bit sunburned," I said, rubbing my
thumb on his cheekbone.

"It was worth it," he said with a hint of a grin, and
something within me burst into glorious existence.

"Yes, it was." I got out of the car before he noticed
that I was being flooded with strong emotion.

"You are *not* falling in love with him, so stop
thinking you are," I lectured myself sternly as I
marched over to the door and unlocked it. I waved at
Paen, holding the door open as he jumped out of his

car and bolted toward me. "He's a vampire. You can't save him. He doesn't believe in love. He's totally wrong for you, totally—*ack!*"

Call it elf sense, call it heightened awareness, call it Sally if you like, but something sent my peripheral awareness into overdrive as Paen ran toward me. The world suddenly downshifted into first gear, time expanding so that everything seemed to be moving in slow motion. Paen loped across the tiny parking area, his hat angled to protect him from the sun. Beyond him, a dark-haired, familiar man rose from where he'd been hiding behind a large square trash bin, his arm swinging up in a slow arc as he shouldered a lethal-looking crossbow, turning his body so the metal bolt was aimed to intersect Paen's path. Next to him, clinging to the trash bin, a small spider monkey in a green striped suit sat busily unwrapping what looked like the remains of a candy bar.

"Noooo!" I screamed, even my voice sounding drawn out as I threw myself forward. I intended to push Paen out of the way of the bolt, but as I lunged toward him, my feet leaving the ground in a leap of distance they would never again surpass, the thought flashed through my mind that despite having just met him, despite the fact that he alternately aroused and frustrated me, despite the fact that we were clearly not in the least bit suited for one another—despite all that, I was willing to do whatever it took to save him.

Even at the cost of my own life.

Paen yelled my name as the bolt slammed into my shoulder, knocking me backward, flinging me up against the concrete side of the building. Hot, sickening pain swept through me, causing the world to spin off its axis. Paen roared something I couldn't make out, catching me before I slid helplessly down to the ground.

The last thing I saw before blissful oblivion took me in its arms was Paen's face, his eyes so dark they looked black.

"You've got your soul back," I said.

Chapter 11

"Well, all I can say is it's lucky you're immortal." The voice cut into the black abyss in which I was floating. It was female, familiar, with a posh English accent . . . ah. It was Clare speaking. To whom was she speaking, I wondered?

"Hrng," a voice answered her. It, too, was female and familiar. I racked my brain for a moment to place the voice, realizing with a shock it was mine. "Narf?"

"You see? I told you she would be fine. Elves can survive all sorts of injuries." Clare's voice was rife with authority. "You're worrying about nothing, Paen."

A dark Scottish voice rumbled around in my head, deep as the ocean and soft as velvet. *Sam? How do you feel?*

Confused, I answered, smiling at the voice. *When did you drop Samantha and start calling me Sam?*

He sighed. *Is that really important?*

Kind of. It's a sign of intimacy.

Sweetheart, we've been about as intimate as it gets, and you're making a big deal about a word?

You called me sweetheart! I said, my toes curling with sudden pleasure.

"I can see that I am worrying about nothing. Sam, you can open your eyes now. The bolt is out of your shoulder."

Bolt. Shoulder. The man who tried to kill Paen!

"Ack!" I squawked, my eyelids snapping open as I sat up. "Paen, are you—holy moly! What happened to you?"

A sudden zing of pain in my shoulder tried to claim my attention, but the sight of Paen standing in front of me, bloody and beaten, overrode all other concerns. The left side of his face was bloodred with what looked like a nasty burn, his eye swollen and starting to turn dark, a cut on his temple responsible for the blood cascading down the other side of his face. One arm hung limp, the sleeve of his long coat was shredded, while the entire front of his shirt was covered in dirt and blood.

"We were ambushed. How do you feel?"

"A lot better than you look. Your poor face! Your poor . . . um . . . what else is hurt on you?"

"Nothing. I'm fine," he said, waving away my concern with a nasty-looking metal bolt. He saw me looking at it and quickly tossed it into the garbage.

"OK. What's going on here?" I asked, looking from Paen to Clare and on to Finn, who was standing to the left. Finn also looked worse for wear, although not nearly as hurt as Paen. "Why are you guys so beat up? What happened to Pilar? And why am I sitting here now with just a dull ache in my shoulder rather than being rushed to the hospital to bleed to death like any normal person would do?"

"Oh, Sam," Clare said, shaking her head as she wrung out a washcloth over a small bowl. She dabbed gently at a swollen spot on Finn's cheek. "You never *were* normal. Now you're less so."

"Pot calling the kettle black," I said, shifting my gaze from her to Paen. My heart dropped a little at his battered face. I slid off the desk and ever so carefully touched his reddened cheek. "Sunburn?"

"Amongst other things. The man who shot you attacked me with a two-by-four as I was trying to bring you inside. You're sure it was Pilar? I didn't see him clearly."

"I'm sure. Beppo was there, too." I took one of Clare's cloths to hold on the wound on his temple.

"Finn got the crossbow away from him before he could stake Paen," Clare said proudly.

"That's nice of him. Can you heal this?" I asked Paen.

"Yes. How is your shoulder? Did you hit your head?" He flinched as I tried to dab up the blood, taking my hand in his to stop me. *No fussing.*

Why? I like fussing over you.

Why do you like doing that? he countered.

I don't know. Because it makes me feel— I stopped before I could say something I wasn't prepared to admit to myself yet, let alone him.

Aha! I knew it! You're falling in love with me, aren't you?

Would I do something like that to you? I asked, innocence brimming out of me.

He gave me a dark look. Gratefully, I let the matter go.

"I'm OK, and yes, I hit my head, but only just a little," I said, rubbing a knot on the back of my head. "What did Clare mean about me being immortal? I'm not immortal. I never have been. I just have a longer life span than most people."

"It'll stretch into centuries now," Finn said with a slight smile.

"I'm lost. Why on earth would you think I'm immortal?" I asked him.

He raised his chin and sniffed the air. "Believe me, I know. Welcome to the family."

"Huh?" He just smiled at me. I turned back to Paen, who was standing with his eyes closed, concentrating fiercely on healing his wounds.

"You're Paen's Beloved," Finn said. "Thank you for that, by the way. It's nice to see him with a soul."

"Yes, it is," I said, watching as the redness in Paen's face faded slightly, the wound closing itself. The swelling in his eye went down enough for me to see a bright silver glint when he opened his eyes to meet my stare. His new soul shone like a miniature sun within him. "You want to explain all this to me now?"

"Not really, but I suspect you won't allow me to get away without an explanation."

"Damn straight," I said, crossing my arms and leaning my butt against the desk. "I'm all ears."

A little zipper of excitement had me quivering for a moment as he glanced at my ears, but I pushed that down as something to indulge in later.

"We were attacked, evidently by your old friend Pilar. You foolishly threw yourself in front of a bolt meant for me. While I was trying to carry you inside,

Pilar attacked again. Finn got the crossbow from him, but couldn't stop him from cracking me a few times with a hunk of wood while I was trying to protect you. He left before Finn could disable him. It's noon now, or else Finn would have been able to track him. Everyone is fine. End of story."

"Oh, not even," I said, my arms still crossed. Paen's eye was almost down to normal, and although he was still covered with blood, at least the gaping cut on his temple had closed up and stopped bleeding. "I have lots of questions, like why Pilar would switch from attacking Clare to you? That question aside—"

"You are absolutely certain it was Pilar? Finn had never seen him before today, and I didn't get a good look before he attacked me," Paen asked, interrupting me.

"Yes, I'm sure it was him, although I didn't get a good look at him since I was too busy trying to shove you out of the way. Back to major confusion—your brother says I'm your Beloved, but we tried those seven steps, and you didn't get your soul back. What changed?"

"You sacrificed yourself for him," Finn said, stealing a kiss from Clare, who was bustling around gathering up bloody cloths. "It's necessary for a Beloved to be willing to sacrifice everything in order to redeem her Dark One's soul."

I narrowed my eyes at Paen. "You left that out of the list of steps."

He shrugged. "I didn't think it was pertinent."

"You didn't *think*—" My tiny little hairs on the back of my neck hackled up.

He held up a hand to stop the coming diatribe. "I meant that I did not think it was pertinent in the steps to Joining. My father said he hadn't been Joined until Mum offered herself up in his place, but I didn't connect that with us."

"So I was right after all," I said, feeling a warm glow of happiness at the thought of Paen having his soul back.

"Yes, you were right." He avoided looking at me, as if he wanted to hide something.

"Well, don't thank her or anything, brother," Finn said, rolling his eyes. "Talk about ingratitude."

"It's all right, he doesn't have to thank me." I examined his face, looking for some other sign that we were now bound together. There was nothing, no miraculous . . . something. I had no idea what I was expecting to see, but I felt a strange sense of loss that the indescribable something wasn't there. "I told him I would be happy to help him regain his soul."

"Yes, but—"

"Leave it, Finn," Paen said, shooting a look full of unspoken comment at his brother. "If you're feeling better, Sam, perhaps we can move ahead with our previous plans?"

The sense of something missing heightened. "Sure. Um. Just a second . . . I'm sorry, I guess I'm a bit more addled than I thought. We're Joined now, right?"

"Yes," Paen said curtly, using one of the damp cloths that Clare left to wipe the blood off his face.

"So I'm . . . what? I'm a vampire?"

"No, you're a Beloved," Finn answered, smiling when Paen scowled at him. "Someone has to tell her, Paen, and it's clear you're falling down on the job."

"I'm just trying to get a handle on this," I said with a faint apology. "I'm not a vampire, but I'm . . . what exactly? Still me or different?"

"You're no different than you were with the exception of being immortal," Paen said, tossing the now soiled cloth in the trash.

"Paen, that's not really fair . . . right. None of my business. You two work it out yourselves," Finn said, holding up his hands when Paen shot him yet another potent glance. "I'll just say this, Sam—there are three sorts of Moravians: Dark Ones, who have no souls until redeemed, Moravian men like me who were born with a soul, and females, who all have souls. Beloveds are more or less the same as female Moravians."

"Ah. Do the women . . ." I picked up a staple remover and made biting gestures toward my neck.

"Drink blood? They can, but they don't need to in order to live like we need to."

"That sounds rather unfair," Clare said, patting Finn on the arm as she made pouty lips. "All that biting you have to do that they don't."

He grinned at her. "Ah, but you like it when I bite you."

"So the females and down the line Moravians have souls, but the Dark Ones don't? Why are the males and females so different?" I asked.

"Ask him," Finn said, nodding toward Paen. "He's been researching the history of our people for decades."

"It has to do with the manner in which the first Dark One was created," Paen said. "No one knows for certain just how he ended up damned, but I hope to uncover the details soon."

"Ah. Sounds fascinating. But about this immortality thing—that's like payment for giving you back your soul?" I asked.

"Of a sort, yes. Any other questions?"

One. Why aren't you happier about getting your soul back?

I told you before—I don't need a Beloved. This changes nothing between us, Sam.

Oh, I thought it did, but this was clearly not the best moment to have a discussion about the new definitions of our relationship, so I let his comment slide and went over to my own desk, pulling out my phone book. "I'll call Mr. Race and see if he has time to talk with us."

"Thank you."

"Mr. Race? Our client?" Clare asked as she reclaimed her desk. Finn spun her client chair around so it was backward and sat next to her, allowing her to murmur soft little things to him every now and again.

Paen explained what he had been told while I worked my way through the hotel hierarchy of voice mail to leave Owen Race a message. I was just finishing when he picked up the phone, somewhat breathless. "Hello? Miss Cosse? Sorry, I was just coming into the room when I heard you leaving a message. Have you found it?"

"I'm sorry, no, I haven't. Not yet, but I'm working quite hard on it. I wonder if it's possible to set up an appointment to meet with you?"

"I don't suppose there's any chance of you coming to London for a few days?"

"I'm sorry, but that's out of the question," I said

firmly, wondering why he wanted to see me so badly. "Unless you have a solid lead indicating the manuscript is in London, that is. Do you have such a lead?"

There was silence on the other end of the phone. "No," he said finally, regret audible in his voice. "I don't have a lead."

"We are working as hard as possible on it," I reassured him. "I believe you said you'd be returning to Edinburgh at the end of the week?"

"Yes. I suppose I could come home early. Since you refuse to come to me, I shall have to, shan't I?"

I didn't roll my eyes. I wanted to, along with wanting to point out to him that in this day of instant technology, on-site research all over the globe was not necessary, but I kept that to myself, as well. "I don't intend to rush you, naturally, but if you *were* coming back to town—"

"I will return tomorrow." His voice was clipped, as if he was biting off the words.

"Great. Can we meet as soon as possible once you return?"

"That would be agreeable. I am free in the early afternoon."

I raised my eyebrows at Paen, who was listening in on Clare's phone. He nodded.

"Yes, that would be fine."

We set an appointment time for early afternoon, and I hung up after reassuring him once again that we were on the case, and hoped to have results in the very near future.

"In other words, you lied to him," Clare said, frowning at me. White clouds suddenly appeared to darken the sun.

"I did not lie. I can't lie, remember? We *are* on the case, and I fervently hope and pray we'll have results in the near future. And stop clouding up the sky. We get little enough sun here, I'd like to enjoy it while I can." I paused a moment, glancing at Paen. "I can still go out in the sun, right? Beloveds don't burn easily, do they?"

"No. I told you—nothing other than your mortality has changed."

"Whew. I don't think I could do without sunlight. Let's go back a couple of minutes—why is Pilar after your blood now?" I asked Paen.

"I have no idea. Perhaps he wasn't really after me?"

A little chill sent goose bumps down my arms. "In which case, it means he's willing to kill anyone in order to get that statue."

"Why don't we take a look at it?" Paen suggested. "You said it's locked in a safe?"

"Mila has it in her office downstairs."

"I'll get it," Clare said, jumping up. "Mila knows me."

"As your sworn bodyguard, I will assist you," Finn said, following her to the door.

She cast a hesitant glance at the window. The sun was still shining brightly. "You don't have to. It's not that far."

"No, no, I want to. It's my duty."

"But I don't want you to get burned . . ."

"It would be worth it. Come on, let's go." Finn pushed her toward the door.

She paused a moment, then gave in. "All right, but we'll go the back way. There's less outdoor time that way."

I gnawed my lip as the door closed behind them. "You think it's OK to let them go off on their own with a murderous Pilar lurking around?"

"Yes. Finn will let me know if he needs help." Paen didn't look the least bit concerned. It went a long way to calming my jangling nerves.

"I suppose so. I don't know why he was so anxious to go with her. It's just downstairs . . . oh. The sex shop?"

He smiled. "That would be my guess."

I tipped my head as I looked at him with a critical eye. "You should do that more often."

"Reveal to you the unsavory side to my brothers?"

"No. Smile. It looks good on you. It makes me go all girly inside when you smile."

His smile faded, his eyes turning dark. "Sam, I don't like this."

"You don't like me complimenting you?"

"No, I don't like you falling in love with me." He crossed his arms over his chest and loomed over me, clearly trying to intimidate me.

"I never said I was falling in love with you."

"You didn't deny it, either."

Despite my tall parents' genes, I'm not a tall person, which leaves me a tad bit resentful when I'm loomed over. I stood up and faced him. "You want me to do something elfy to you?"

He frowned. "You're changing the subject."

"Yes, of course I am. I learned it from you. You want me to or not?"

"Do what? Curse me?"

"No. This." I leaned against him, closing my eyes, breathing deeply as I allowed my soul and his to merge. We were still Paen and Sam, but now we were one being made up of two. As we bonded into something new, I reached out with my inner elf, searching for the entry point. I found it and pushed through, pulling Paen with me, causing the world to shift slightly. It was as if everything had been ever so minutely out of focus before, but now everything was sharp and correct. "Welcome to the beyond."

"Beyond?" Paen asked, looking around my office. "The shadow world of the elves?"

"Well . . . kind of. Elves live here, but so do others. Faeries, for one."

His gaze touched the familiar objects in the office. "It doesn't look different."

I smiled. "My mother chose this building for our office. She's the original feng shui-er. Or rather, the first to do the elf version of it. She chose this location because it is in what the elves call a founded place—one fundamental to the world, rich in the essence of the beyond. Sympathetic to elfkind, in other words."

"Ah. I wondered why you chose Scotland to live if you needed sunshine. We're not known for our overabundance of sunny weather." A smile flirted with his lips.

I went all melty inside at that smile, but I tried to keep things light. "Any sunlight is good. It doesn't have to be a gloriously sunny day like today. The reason you don't see anything different in the office is because this building stands on land that is founded, but the area down the block isn't. If you can risk a peek out the window, you'll see the difference."

Paen used a folder to angle the sun off his face as

he opened a window and poked his head out quickly. A low whistle of surprise followed.

"Pretty freaky, huh?"

"Different. It looks . . . unpleasant. Disjointed. Harsh."

"Yeah, it does. That's what our world looks like to elves who walk in the beyond."

Paen closed the window, looking thoughtful. "That would explain why there are so few of them around."

I nodded. "Only the ones like my mother who are comfortable in the mortal world live outside the beyond. The rest prefer this world, where they can avoid anything upsetting, and stay in founded areas."

"Understandable." His lips pursed. "How do we get back?"

I smiled. "Worried I'll leave you here?"

"Hardly." This close to him, and with my elf senses running amok in their native environment, I could feel every emotion in him. His face held polite interest, but inside him, curiosity was driving him nuts. "I'm merely curious. I had no idea you could bring a non-elf into this world."

"I've never been able to before, and yes, I've tried. I think it's because now we're bound together." I slowly backed up a step, pulling my soul from his, shifting us back into our reality.

"Interesting," he said. "You said elves are not the only ones who can enter the beyond?"

"Any Fae being can. Others as well—mages, for instance, can, or so I've been told. I've never seen any there, but to be honest, I've only been there a couple of times. I prefer this version of the world. Now, about your need to smile more . . . maybe you just need a massive influx of kissing?"

"We weren't talking about me smiling—we were talking about you falling in love with me, and why it's a bad idea," he said, not moving when I leaned into him and gave his chin a flirtatious slurp.

"No, we weren't. I haven't said one single word about being in love with you. Kiss me, dammit!"

"Sam—" Paen stopped me from lunging at him. I was teasing him, but I could see in his eyes—I could *feel* inside him—that he wasn't responding. "I'm quite serious. I can't allow you to continue down this path."

"You can't *allow* me . . ." I stopped, disbelief twisting painfully in my heart. "Oh. I see how it is. You have your soul, so you have no further need for me. I was just a means to an end, wasn't I?"

I pulled away, turning my back on him so he wouldn't see the tears that suddenly made it difficult to see. I felt betrayed, hurt, used. I knew that was unfair since he'd made it clear he hadn't been looking for a serious relationship, yet I felt like so much had changed in the last few hours. After what we'd been through together, how could he still want to close me out?

"I never asked you to redeem my soul for me." Paen's voice was filled with regret, but nothing else. "I am grateful than you did, more grateful than I can possibly express to you, but gratitude is—"

He didn't finish the sentence. He didn't need to, I could hear the words as if he had spoken them. Gratitude was all he was prepared to offer me.

He was right. I knew that. But it still cut me to the bone that my newborn feelings for him were unrequited.

"Fine," I said, blinking rapidly to disperse the tears. I wanted to say something more, something sharp that would make him hurt the way he hurt me, but two things held me back—it wasn't a good business practice to hurt clients, and I couldn't hurt him even if I wanted to. That realization struck me like a wrecking ball—I wasn't falling in love with him; I'd gone right ahead and done it. At some point in the last few hours I'd gone from self-sufficient Sam, to needy, dependent Sam . . . and the man to whom I'd offered my heart didn't want it.

Chapter 12

Grief swamped me, so strong that I could taste its bitterness on my tongue.

"Sam," Paen said, taking a step closer to me. "I never meant for you to be hurt. I thought you understood the sort of relationship I could offer—"

Voices outside the door interrupted him before he could say something that would have me bursting into tears. Clare and Finn came into the room, laughing, Finn holding the shoebox containing the statue, while Clare, with a guilty look cast my way, hustled a bag from Mila's shop into a drawer in her desk.

"We got the statue. We had a peek at it in Mila's office—it doesn't look important at all to me," Clare said, the cheerful smile on her face fading when she looked first at Paen, then me. "Sam? What's wrong? Are you crying?"

"No, of course not," I said, desperately trying to blink back the tears as I frowned out the window.

"Yes you are, you're crying!" She rounded on Paen, a fierce expression on her face. "What did you do to her?"

"Me?" Paen asked, looking surprised. The boob. "I haven't done anything—"

"Leave him alone, Clare." I managed to swallow the lump of pain in my throat and turned to face the room with what I prayed was a placid smile. "It's nothing important."

"It is so important if he's made you cry," she said, looking militant as only an outraged faery can. She turned back to Paen with narrowed eyes. "What did you do to my cousin?"

"You didn't—Paen, tell me you didn't start spouting that rubbish about not needing any woman," Finn said, looking closely at him. "Oh, Christ, you did. When the hell will you learn—"

"This is none of your business," Paen interrupted, his eyes starting to flash blackened silver.

Finn took a position right in Paen's face, clearly furious at his brother. "It is when you're hurting the very same woman who saved your bloody soul for you!" he shouted.

"Guys, it really isn't—" I started to say.

"I never *asked* her to save my bloody soul!" Paen roared at his brother. The noise startled us all into silence for a moment. Everyone looked away as I took the shoebox from Finn and pulled out the statue.

"That was fun, but we have more important matters at hand than a broken heart," I said, setting the statue on my desk.

Clare gasped. "He broke your heart after you redeemed—"

"Enough," I said loudly, giving my cousin a warning look. "Can we move on, please? Anyone have

any idea why this statue is so important that someone is trying to kill for it?"

Four pairs of eyes turned to the statue.

"It's rather attractive, in a cheap knockoff sort of
way," Clare said, her head tipped to the side as she
pondered the statue.

Paen picked it up and examined it. It looked just
the same as it did the first time I saw it—a gold statue
of a bird, some sort of stylized, vaguely falconish
bird, with a cruel curved beak, claws wrapped
around a stick of wood, the bottom of it flat, adorned
with a crude MADE IN TAIWAN stamp.

"It's heavier than it looks," Paen said, turning it
over. "This is brass?"

"I think so. It's certainly not gold."

"Hmm." He rapped his knuckles against the back
of the statue. "It doesn't sound hollow. Probably it is
plaster covered over with a thin veneer of brass.
That's a very common technique used by knockoff
artists."

"I wouldn't doubt it. It certainly doesn't look at all
valuable. Any bright ideas on what's so important
about it?"

Paen shook his head. "None. But I'm hardly an expert on art pieces, other than an interest in the Jilin
God."

"Maybe it's cursed," Finn suggested, taking the
statue from Paen. "Or maybe this isn't really brass.
What if it's gold made to look like brass? Or what if
there's a valuable jewel or something hidden inside
of it?"

"Ooh, I like jewels," Clare said, peering over Finn's
shoulder.

"Could be a secret drawer or something built into it," Finn said, pressing various parts of the statue.

Paen and I shook our heads in synchronized dis- agreement. "It's too solid for that," I said.

"Well, then, your guess is as good as mine," Finn said, admitting defeat. He handed it to me.

"My guesses aren't particularly good at all." I avoided looking at Paen, trying my best to ignore the dull ache in the region of my heart. Now was not the time to try to work out my feelings—with someone trying to kill one or more of us, I had to focus on what really mattered.

My broken heart sobbed a lament that was hard to ignore.

"I think you should have an expert examine the statue," Paen said, giving it a thoughtful look.

"Art expert, you mean?" I asked.

He shook his head. I tried hard to forget how silky his dark curls were as they brushed against my flesh, but the memory refused to be banished. "I was think- ing more about that Diviner friend of yours," he said with a long, unreadable look at me.

I didn't even try to reach out to his mind.

"Jake has already examined it. Kind of. He looked at the box and said that what was in it wasn't touched by evil."

"He might find more if he could examine the statue himself."

I thought about that for a few moments. "I sup- pose it couldn't hurt to ask him, although that's not really the sort of thing a Diviner does."

Paen glanced at his watch. "I have some estate

business to take care of at home. Will you be all right for a few hours if I leave?"

"Do you mean will I be shot at again by murderous villains who wish to steal my statue?" I risked a quick peek at him. His eyes were clouded and dark. I shrugged. "No idea, but now that I'm Miss Immortality 2006, it doesn't really matter, does it?"

"Sam—"

"I'll be fine," I said quickly, not wanting him to say anything that might set me off again. "Go do your stuff. I'll take the statue to Jake and see what he has to say about it."

"What would you like us to do?" Clare asked, waving her hands toward the desk. "Shall we compile a list of historic tombs in Scotland?"

"That would be helpful, although I'd suggest starting with this area first. If Owen Race does, in fact, have the Jilin God, it would likely be somewhere near his house, wouldn't you think?"

"We'll look up the history on his house and family," Clare said, hurrying over to her computer, snatching up a tulip as an elevenses snack.

"Great, then everyone's got a job," I said, packing the statue up in its box and stuffing it into my oversized bag. "We can meet back here for dinner, if you all like. Hopefully I'll have information about this statue so that we can figure out who wants it, and why."

Sam?

The soft brush of his voice in my mind almost brought me to my knees. I stiffened both them and my resolve, snatching up my coat and bag as I headed for the door. "See you all later."

Paen's voice was soft in my head, filled with regret. *I don't want to leave you feeling this way.*

I didn't answer him. There was nothing to say. Well, nothing he wanted to hear. On the bus to the Diviners' House, I thought of quite a few things I'd like to say to him, but my pride kept me from saying them.

"You've been dumped before," I told myself as I got off the bus and started off the three blocks to my destination. "It stings for a bit, then goes away."

"Rather like the bite of an annoying insect?" a man asked from behind me. Cold seeped into my skin, leaching all heat from my body.

I spun around and found myself facing the man who had tried to murder Clare and Paen, the same man who shot me, rifled Paen's desk, and menaced me so greatly that even seeing him in broad daylight on a busy Edinburgh street left me chilled and shaken. It was Pilar, and not even the sight of Beppo in cute pinstriped overalls could dilute the sensations of power and menace that rolled off the man. "You're Pilar, aren't you? What do you want with me?"

The man smiled. "In general, or at this moment?"

"Let's start with what you're doing now," I said, backing up a step.

His smile deepened. "You will come with me now."

"What do I look like, the world's stupidest person?" I asked, trying to bravado my way out of the situation. He reached for me, but I backed away, toward the road. "You think I'm going to go meekly with you so you can shoot me again? Think again."

"Mr. Green wishes to see you," Pilar said, gesturing with one hand. He must have had a taxi waiting, because one obediently pulled up directly behind me.

Beppo watched it all from his perch on Pilar's shoulder, his tail wrapped securely around the man's throat.

"Caspar Green? You know him?" I said, instinctively reaching out my mind for Paen. I stopped just before the words formed, flinching at the pain the action caused. It felt so wrong to not share something with him, but he'd made it perfectly clear that ours was a casual relationship at best. I was completely on my own—not a hideously comforting thought.

"He wishes to see you," Pilar said again, opening the door to the taxi, making like he was going to shove me in. I had a moment in which I could have resisted him and made an escape, but in the end, I allowed him to have his way. My curiosity got the better of me, and I figured so long as we were in a public venue, I'd be safe from any attempts he made on my life.

Public like a parking lot? my inner self asked. "Fine, but just so you know, I'm armed," I said, clutching my purse in a manner I hoped indicated some serious firepower.

He merely pulled back one side of his coat to reveal a smaller version of the crossbow he shot me with, and gave me a sardonic smile.

"You didn't have much luck with that earlier." I ignored the faint pull of pain in my shoulder. "Both Paen and I are still alive and kicking."

"I don't know what you're talking about," Pilar said, his eyes flat and black with denial.

I gawked at him for a moment, glancing at the cabdriver before saying in a low voice, "You're not going to try to make me believe you didn't shoot me a few hours ago, right? Not to mention shoot a few holes into my cousin a day ago? Because there's no way

I'm going to believe it wasn't you who shot Clare—
not that many people walk around Edinburgh with a
spider monkey on their shoulder—and I know you
were on the other end of that crossbow earlier today."

"You must have me confused with someone else,"
was all he said, and sat back, refusing to answer any
of the other questions I pelted him with on the ride to
Cockburn Street. Beppo tried to make friends with
me, but I was too upset and confused to do more than
shake his hand when he offered it to me.

Pilar was all but glued to my side as we walked upstairs to apartment 12-C, the building as elegantly quiet
as I remembered from my previous visit. The cold that
seeped from him was so great, however, I made sure to
put as much distance as possible between us.

Caspar opened the door with the same polite
smile he had when I last left him. "Good afternoon,
Miss Cosse. How nice to see you again."

"Thanks," I said, entering the apartment when he
waved me in, Pilar and Beppo hot on my heels. "If
it's not too rude of me to ask, why are you trying to
have my cousin and a friend killed?"

Caspar looked genuinely astonished, I'll give him
that. Either he was a hell of an actor, or he hadn't
asked Pilar to shoot Clare and Paen full of holes. For
a brief moment I wondered if I'd seen my attacker
correctly, but one glance at Pilar reaffirmed that he
was the man I'd recently stared down at the other
end of a crossbow.

"Miss Cosse, I must humbly beg your indulgence.
Am I to understand there has been a murder attempt
on your life?" Caspar asked, taking my coat.

"Um . . . yeah. Something like that," I said, deciding

not to say anything about Pilar. If he was acting on Caspar's request, then I wouldn't be telling him anything new. And if Pilar wasn't working with Caspar . . . well, that meant he had his own purpose in wanting us dead, and I'd have to find out just what that was. "I had no idea you and Pilar were . . . *acquainted*."

Caspar ignored the slight emphasis. "Ah, yes, Pilar and I go back many years. I've found it beneficial to employ him from time to time."

"Do you always hire someone to bring people to see you? I'd think a simple phone call and invitation would be less of a drain on the old expense sheet." I took the seat he indicated. The room was just as sunny as it had been earlier, but something in it was still rubbing my warning system the wrong way.

"Indeed, no. But I thought it expedient to have Pilar bring you himself. I know you are a busy woman, and what I have to say to you is of the utmost importance."

"Shoot," I said, then flinched. Pilar smiled a particularly unpleasant smile. The temperature in the room dropped a good ten degrees as he took a seat on a chair against the wall. Beppo jumped off onto a bookcase, and started examining a leafy spider fern. I pulled my eyes from the two of them to the pleasantly smiling man who was busy at a sideboard. "Er . . . go ahead."

"Might I offer you an aperitif first? Sherry?"

"That would be lovely," I said, matching his polite tone despite the fact that I'd more or less been hustled there by a murderous hired thug.

He handed me a tiny glass containing a few sips of dark sherry. "You're a plain-speaking woman, Miss

Cosse. I like that. A toast to plain speaking and congenial understanding."

I clinked my glass against his, taking a sip of the sherry. I'm not a big sherry drinker, but this stuff was downright nasty. I wondered for a moment if it could have been drugged, then put that wild thought down to having watched too many old black and white movies.

"You're also a minimalist when it comes to conversation," Caspar said, taking a few sips of his sherry.

"Not really. My mother taught me it was rude to chatter on about nothing when someone has something important to say."

"Forthright, and understandably so, given your heritage."

I raised an eyebrow. It was true my eyes had an elf tilt to them, but I hadn't thought my genetic background was so evident. I passed as purebred mortal just about everywhere.

Caspar continued without pause. "I admire a woman who knows the value of a conversation that does not include unimportant chatter. There are many arts that have been lost over the years; decent conversation is, to my mind, the most lamentable of them."

"Indeed," I said, smiling politely and wondering when he would get to the point. I decided to help things along a smidgen. "What is it you'd like to talk about?"

"I wish to talk to you about a statue," he said smoothly, sipping at his sherry.

He got full marks for taking me by surprise, but lost a few in technique. "A statue? A statue of a falcon, perhaps?"

"No. The statue I refer to is of a monkey. A black monkey."

"You wouldn't by any chance be referring to the Jilin God?" I asked, deliberately keeping my eyes on his. Caspar wasn't a fool. He would notice if my gaze suddenly shifted at the mention of the statue.

"You see?" He smiled as he sat back, his face full of satisfaction. "You are a woman after my own heart. You know of what I speak, and rather than wasting both our time with unnecessary denials, you come right out and put the subject on the table. Yes, my dear, I do in fact refer to the Jilin God. Am I correct in assuming that you represent the interest of an individual in the statue?"

"I have many clients," I said, well aware that I was exaggerating slightly. "Their interests are varied, but you can, for the sake of this conversation, assume that I am also interested in the statue."

"That is a curious choice of words," Caspar said, crossing his legs. "You say 'interested in,' but not seeking. May I deduce that you have possession of the statue?"

"You can deduce anything you like, but that won't necessarily make it true."

Caspar sipped at his sherry. "You dislike lying outright, I see. Another admirable quality. I dislike being lied to. I assume from your non-denial that you do, in fact, have possession of the statue, or at least you know where it is."

"I don't have it on me, no. But I might know where it is." That wasn't exactly a lie, I told my conscience— I did know it was in a tomb of some sort. I just didn't know where that tomb was.

He laughed. "You have the statue—pardon me, know where it is—but you have not yet handed it over to your client, Mr. Paen Scott? Excellent. We progress. I take it you have no other interested persons in the statue?"

"That's not necessarily true," I answered, wondering how he knew about Paen. I didn't look at Pilar, but I felt the heat from my body being sucked out as the cold that surrounded him leached the surroundings of all warmth.

"Is it not?" Caspar set down his glass to consider me. "Who else might you represent?"

"Well, for one, there's me," I said, smiling.

"Well done, my dear. The mercenary streak does you proud." I almost rolled my eyes at that, but managed to keep my face a polite mask of interest. "I do like a woman who isn't afraid to take care of herself before others."

I let my smile widen. It couldn't hurt for him to think I'd be willing to sell out Paen. He might be more forthcoming with his role in the whole mess if he thought I could be swayed to find the statue for him.

"Why don't you tell me a little about the statue," I suggested, settling back in the chair.

He pursed his lips and I thought for a moment he was going to refuse, but he made a conceding gesture and said, "I suspect you know as much about it as I do, but if it pleases you to pretend ignorance, I shall indulge you. The Jilin God statue is approximately so big"—he held out his hands about six inches apart— "made of ebony, commissioned from Gu Kaizhi, one of the leading artists of the fourth century. It was later given to Marco Polo upon his arrival in Peking by the emperor himself, but mysteriously was not included in the inventory Polo had conducted when he left China."

"Was it stolen?" I asked, pondering the coincidence of both the *Coda* and the statue having their origins with Marco Polo.

"Perhaps. The statue reappeared briefly in Venice in the early eighteenth century, and then passed through private families for several generations. It was known to be in Paris and the American colonies, but then it disappeared from sight altogether."

"Hmm. Why is it called the Jilin God?"

"The origins of the name are shrouded, but the statue itself depicts the monkey god Sun Wukong. Are you familiar with the legend?"

I shook my head. "I'm afraid my knowledge of Chinese history is pretty pathetic."

"Ah. That, too, is lamentable. Sun Wukong was the god of monkeys who escaped capture by Yan Luowang, the god of death. Sun Wukong not only escaped death, he also destroyed the books of the dead. He was called to heaven for judgment, and wreaked havoc there as well; his reign of terror finally ended when Buddha imprisoned him."

"Wow. So he represents, what, the ability to overcome death?"

Caspar nodded, looking pleased. "You picked that up quickly. Yes, the monkey god is a representation of the origins of many of the immortal races—he overcame death and imprisonment to end up a warrior against demons and evil spirits. Yan Luowang is said to have created the statue to hold Sun Wukong prisoner, but was unsuccessful. It is rumored that instead, he placed within its safe confines the secrets of the immortal races."

"Secrets like what?"

His shoulders rose in a slight shrug. "Just what secrets it contains is unknown."

"Hmm. But because of this, the statue is highly desirable?"

His eyelids veiled, the long fingers of his hand toying with the sherry glass that sat on a small table next to him. "It is treasured first for its artwork, second for the historical importance, and third and most importantly for the secrets said to be contained within it, yes."

"How much is it worth?" I asked, wondering why a demon lord would want the statue. Perhaps because it was valuable?

"Let us say that I am willing to offer you twenty-five thousand pounds for it, a fraction of its true worth."

I tried not to look stunned. Twenty-five thousand pounds! "What sort of fraction?"

"Its true value has never been calculated," Caspar said with a slight shrug. "But I can assure you that there are many who would pay almost anything to get it."

"And you?" I asked, relishing my role as double agent. "How much would you pay to get it?"

"I said I would pay you twenty-five thousand pounds."

I smiled and waited. He didn't disappoint me. "Naturally that could be considered a retainer. I would be willing to pay another twenty-five thousand upon delivery."

"I see. Well, thank you for the information," I said, gathering my things as I stood. "I will be in touch, I'm sure."

Caspar frowned. It wasn't a nice expression. "You have not said whether you were taking the job or not."

"Haven't I?" I tried my best to look innocent. "I'm sorry for the confusion—I've already been hired to find the statue for someone else."

"But I will pay you much more than he will—"

"That doesn't matter," I said, starting for the door. "I don't betray my clients' confidences like that, not for any amount of money. Thanks for the sherry and the conversation. You're right—it is a lost art."

"Pilar—" Caspar nodded toward me. His henchman leaped to his feet and started toward me.

"I wouldn't be so trusting of your little bullyboy," I tossed over my shoulder as I reached for the door. "Earlier, he—"

I didn't see it coming, didn't even have an inkling. My elf senses, usually so sharp (if not accurate) didn't warn me at all. Pilar grabbed me just as I was opening the door. One moment I was there about to tattle on Pilar to his boss, the next a massive wave of energy slammed into me, so powerful it knocked me clear out of reality.

Chapter 13

Um . . . Paen? . . . Paen? . . . Helloooo?

Sam?

Oh, good, I was hoping you didn't have your mental voice mail turned on.

My what?

Nothing. Little joke.

Very little.

Yeah, well, you try making a joke when you're caught between realities, and see how well you do.

A pause filled my head. *You're caught between realities?*

Yes. I seem to be stuck here. I was wondering if there was something you could do to help me out?

His silence was telling. *Where are you?*

I don't think I'm anywhere, to be honest. I seem to be nowhere, caught in some sort of a web between reality and the beyond.

Then how do you expect me to help you?

We have to pass through this to get to the beyond. I was hoping you'd merge with me, and that would pull me out. Kind of a reverse of what I did with you earlier.

Or it might just pull me in.

True. I hesitated, hating to ask him for anything, but not seeing any other choice. I'd been stuck here for the last couple of hours as I tried everything I knew to get out, to no avail. *Can you help me, please?*

He didn't answer, but I knew the moment he merged with me, the two of us like separate pools of mercury forming into one glorious entity. Joined as we were, I could feel everything he felt, and what it was he was thinking.

And he could do likewise.

He had to know I was trying to avoid confronting the emotions that swirled around in me, a vortex of love and anger and pain. But he said nothing as the merging pulled me back into reality, separating us into two people again.

I found myself standing in my office at the window, blinking at the bright afternoon sun that poured in and spilled into a warm pool on the floor. *Thanks, Paen. I appreciate that.*

I wish to talk to you about what's happened.

Sorry, can't right now. Things to do, places to go, people to curse.

What?

Nothing. Another little joke.

Sam—

Signing off for now. I'll see you for dinner later. Bye.

I'm just outside your office—

La la la, my fingers are in my ears and I can't hear you!

You're not listening to me with your ears, woman. I'll be at your office in twenty seconds or less, and then we will discuss the situation.

It wasn't easy to tune him out of my mind, but I

did it. I hurried out the front way so I wouldn't run into him coming in the back, my soul bleeding tears of anguish. I just about cried salty ones when I got to Diviners' House and discovered that the shoebox in my bag was empty.

"Sam? Are you all right?" Jake asked as I stared numbly at the inside of the empty shoebox.

"No, I'm not all right. I'm just about as far from all right as you can possibly get and still be alive. God damn it, Jake! Someone stole my statue!"

He gave me a thin-lipped look. "After what you told me about being shot by that man Pilar, I'd think it would be a relief to have it off your hands."

I narrowed my eyes as I thought back to the visit to Caspar's house. "I bet it was Pilar who zapped me. I bet he stole the statue while I was immobile between realities. How on earth am I going to get it back?"

"Why do you want it back? It sounds to me like it hasn't brought you anything but bad luck."

"It's mine," I said, putting the empty box back into my bag. "The demon gave it to me. Yes, by mistake, but both Clare and I were shot for it—that means I have the right to get to the bottom of what it is, and why Pilar wants it so bad. Thanks, Jake. Sorry to disrupt your day for nothing."

He saw me to the door, stopping me briefly as I stood on the doorstep, soaking in the warmth of the sunshine. "So, this thing with you and Paen—I can't tell you how happy I am that you've found someone at last. I wasn't sure about him, since Dark Ones tend to be a bit intense, but he seems like a nice bloke. I wish you both an eternity of happiness. One question—should I be buying a wedding present anytime soon?"

The sun went behind a cloud. Pain gripped my chest and didn't allow me to breathe. "No," I said, and left.

I was pretty much on autopilot all the way back to the office, finding my way to the correct bus, getting off at the correct stop, and walking the two blocks to the office without seeing, feeling, or registering anything around me. I was too caught up in my own misery to even notice the sudden bank of black clouds that started rolling in from the north.

"Life sucks," I said as I opened the door to my office. Finn and Clare, back from wherever it is they'd gone off to, looked up from her computer, questions evident in their expressions. At my desk, Paen sat, making notes on a notepad. I noticed he was left-handed, as I was. It warmed my heart for a moment before I remembered that as far as he was concerned, my heart could take a flying leap.

"You look horrible," Clare said, getting up to take my coat and hang it properly on the coat-tree. "Did Brother Jacob not have anything helpful to say about the statue?"

"What statue?" I asked, pulling the shoebox out of my purse and handing it to her.

She opened it. "I don't understand. Where is the statue?"

Grief built up inside me until I thought I'd break down into a good, old-fashioned elf-dirge. I'd lost Paen, lost the statue, and I wasn't the tiniest bit closer to finding either the Jilin God or the *Coda*. A big old pity party welled up inside me and whined to be set free. "The statue was stolen from me sometime while I was held prisoner."

It took only a few minutes to tell my startled audience the events of the last two hours, ending up with a brief rant against everything that had gone wrong of late. "I can't believe this," I said, storming around the office, waving my hands in the best drama queen fashion. "I'm known for my ability to find things. It's what I do best! Nothing has ever stayed lost once I've tried to find it, and yet here I am, employed to find two simple items, and I'm no closer now to finding their whereabouts than I was when I was hired, not to mention losing a third item I wanted to keep!"

Clare popped a lilac blossom in her mouth, her eyes huge as she watched me emote.

"I think you're allowing things to get to you," Paen offered, getting to his feet. He tucked his notebook away into his jacket pocket.

I pointed a finger at him. "You're a big part of the problem, buster."

He raised his eyebrows. "I fail to see how our personal situation—"

"I'm not talking about your commitment issues—I'm referring to the fact that you didn't tell me everything you knew about the Jilin statue. You willfully withheld information about it, information that might have helped me if I had known it two days ago." That wasn't strictly fair, but I was grasping at straws.

"What information?" Finn asked, frowning at his brother.

Paen frowned back at him for a moment before turning to me. "I told you everything I knew about the statue."

I marched over to stand in front of him, my hand on my hip. "Oh you did, huh? You didn't mention that the statue represents the origins of immortal races, and that it supposedly contains some big secret of how they were created. You didn't tell me that it was priceless, worth so much that someone would offer me fifty thousand pounds just to find it for him."

"Fifty thousand—" Paen grabbed the finger I was using to punctuate my sentences by poking it into his chest. I squelched the little tremor of pleasure that zipped through me at his touch. "Who offered you money to find my statue?"

"The mage expert I consulted earlier. It turns out he is also looking for the Jilin God, only he was a bit more forthcoming with information about it." I let Paen see the full extent of my discontent.

He glared right back at me. "I had no idea it represented the origin of immortal races any more than I knew it was priceless. I've done extensive research into the origin of the Moravians and never heard of it, so perhaps the information from your source is questionable. Who is this mage expert?"

"Possibly it's questionable, but it sounded like the truth. It would explain why a demon lord would want it—if it held secrets of the immortals, surely that would give a demon lord power over the various races?"

"It is within the realm of possibility, but just barely," Paen said, releasing my hand. "The expert's name?"

"Hmm? Oh. Caspar Green."

I thought Paen's eyeballs were going to pop out of his head.

"Who?" he roared.

"Caspar Green. Why are you so upset?"

"That's not a man, that's a demon," Paen snarled, slamming his fist into the wall. I flinched at both the hole he left and the red welts that appeared on his hand. "He's the one who is demanding I repay my father's debt."

It was my turn to do the eyeball pop. "You're kidding. Caspar is the one doing this? We're going to have to have another talk with him."

"Right now," Paen said, snatching up his coat and heading for the door.

All four of us trooped out and descended upon Caspar. Or tried to, at least. He didn't answer his door buzzer or the phone, and when Paen, driven by fury, scaled the outside of the building and deliberately broke into the apartment, he came up empty-handed.

"He's gone to earth," Paen growled a few minutes later, as I dabbed at the cuts on his hand made by the broken glass. "Search the flat. We may find something that says where he is, or what he's up to playing us against each other like this."

We found nothing. The flat was almost sterile in its pristine state, as if it were there for show and not really lived in.

"So what do we do now?" Clare asked when we returned disheartened to the office. She munched lilac blossoms like they were popcorn. "Just wait around for Caspar and Mr. Race to return? Do we have time for that? What if Mr. Race doesn't know anything about the statue? What if the demon who talked to Paen was wrong? What if Caspar won't cooperate?"

"Race is the only lead we have," Finn said.

"Yes, and we can't talk to him if we can't find him. Evidently he's en route, and no, he doesn't have a cell phone. I asked his housekeeper. So we're playing the waiting game for both him and Caspar."

"But we should be doing something!" Clare wailed, waving her hands around.

Paen jumped up from a chair and marched over to the window, staring out it with an expression of extreme frustration, anger, and a tinge of hopelessness that just about broke my heart.

I slumped into the chair that he vacated, the faint warmth left behind by his body sinking into mine until it made my soul want to weep. Life suddenly seemed so overwhelming, so bloody impossible. I had tried everything I knew how to do, and yet repeatedly failed. "This is beyond frustrating. Why can't I find that damned statue and manuscript? I've never *not* found anything I've looked for before, so why am I now having absolutely no luck? What is Caspar up to? Why is Race suddenly incommunicado when we need to talk to him? I tell you, it's enough to make an elf-girl cry."

"Poor sweet Sam," Clare said, gliding over to me. "Maybe you've lost your power?"

"Huh?"

Clare nudged the phone over so she could perch elegantly on the edge of my desk. "Because you . . . you know." She nodded to where Paen was standing at the window, careful to avoid direct light. "Maybe that caused you to lose your powers."

I pulled out a small mirror from my desk and checked. "Nope. Still half elf. And we were in the beyond today. I wouldn't have been able to do that if I'd lost my elfly powers."

"You went to the beyond?" she asked, slanting another glance at Paen. "Together?"

"Yes, not that it has any relevance to my sudden inability to find things," I said glumly; resting my forehead on the desk.

"But you lost that bird statue, too. That's incredibly careless and irresponsible."

I raised my head to glare at her.

"Which is not like you at all," she added quickly. "Perhaps someone has cast a spell or cursed you?"

"We'd see a curse, and surely Sam would be able to tell if someone cast a spell on her? Elves are notoriously hard to enchant," Finn said, taking his place next to Clare, and giving her shoulder a supportive squeeze.

As if *her* shoulder needed the reassurance that it was cherished . . . I dropped my forehead to the desk again. "I'm not cursed, and not enchanted. I'm just suddenly . . . ineffective. But that's going to change."

"You have another plan," Clare said, clapping her hands with delight. "I knew you'd come up with something, Sam. It's best not to put too much reliance on what a demon says. What are you going to do?"

"Desperate times call for desperate measures," I told the desk.

"I told you she wouldn't give up," Clare said to Finn. He started to protest that he never doubted me, but I held up a hand to stop him.

"I don't trust that demon who spoke to Paen," I said thoughtfully. "Not Caspar, the other one."

He half turned toward me. "Is there any particular

reason why, or do you just have a general distrust of demons?"

"The latter." I pushed Clare's hip off the desk and replaced the phone where I wanted it. "It's too pat, too convenient. It smacks too much of trying to divide and conquer."

Everyone looked at me.

"Don't you see?" I asked, waving my hands around in a vague gesture intended to convey coherence. "The demon wants to confuse us, throw us off the track by sending us on a wild-goose chase. And who does it want us to chase? Our other client. No, it just seems too coincidental."

"She has a point," Clare said. Finn nodded. Paen frowned.

I took a deep breath. "Since I can't seem to locate either object we were hired to find—nor hang on to a simple bird statue—I've decided that I'm going to engage the services of someone who can."

"Who is that?" Clare asked, blinking. "Brother Jacob?"

I shook my head.

"Another Diviner?" Finn asked.

I shook my head again, avoiding looking at the silent man whose presence behind me registered on every molecule in my body. "No. I'm going to have to bring in some big help. I'm going to consult a seer."

I thought for a moment that Clare was going to choke. "You're . . . you're . . . no, you can't! Finn, tell her she can't! Seers are bad!"

"They're not bad, they're just a bit . . . pricey. And Finn has nothing to do with the matter, so don't try to drag him into it," I said. "We were hired to do a job,

Clare, and we're going to do it by one means or another."

"But . . . a seer, Sam? That's even worse than a Guardian or a theurgist!" Clare, distraught, ran for her flower vase.

"I accepted the job. I don't have a choice in the matter."

"Paen?" Clare turned to him. "Don't you have something to say about Sam's plan to use a seer?"

"No," he answered, crossing his arms over his chest as he leaned against the wall. His eyes, normally so bright, were dulled like tarnished silver plate. "But only because the idea is so ridiculous it doesn't merit an answer."

"Ridiculous!" I gasped, sitting up straight.

"That's what I said. Anyone who deludes themselves into believing that they can consult a seer without paying an unthinkable price deserves the label of ridiculous." My gasp changed into an outraged huff. "You are not going to turn this over to a seer," he added, walking around the client's chair in front of my desk where his coat and hat lay. "I want to find this statue more than anyone, but not at the cost of others' lives. You're hungry and exhausted. You need food. I believe we can spare an hour to feed you and Clare while we discuss the next step."

"Correction—you can talk about it all you like over dinner, dessert, and the swivel hips of a troop of dancing girls. I, however, have work to do, and I intend to do it before the night ages any more."

"Sam!" Clare looked scandalized.

I sighed. She was right. Just because Paen had all but ripped my heart out and stomped it into nothing but a smear on the ground didn't mean I had to be rude. He was a client. A professional, rather than personal, demeanor was clearly called for. Henceforth, I would be the personification of investigative professionalism.

"My apologies, gentlemen. I didn't mean to sound so brusque. I'm sure you'll all have a lovely dinner, but I'm afraid I'm going to be a bit busy."

Sam, why are you doing this?

I glanced at Paen. "If you have something to say to me, please say it out loud. The mental broadcasting station has been closed due to FCC conflicts."

"You're not going to use a seer. I forbid it."

I gathered up my coat and purse. "You're my client, Paen, not my father." I was unable to keep from sliding him a hurt look. "Or my lover anymore, for that matter. Therefore, I'll do as I please. I'll see you all later. Enjoy dinner."

Paen blocked the way to the door. "Very well, since you insist on playing this game—if you will not respect my wishes with regards to the seer, I will fire you."

"Really?" I stopped directly in front of him, my body demanding I keep walking until it was pressed up against all those lovely hard lines of his. "You're willing to give up your mother's soul over this?"

He hesitated for a moment. "I don't believe that a seer is the solution. If I had, I would have consulted one myself. Seers are not always what they seem, and seldom give the help you need."

"Yes, well, the bottom line is that I said I'd find that statue in the amount of time you have left, and I intend to do just that. Now please step out of the way and allow me to do my job."

His jaw tightened. "I'm removing you from the case."

"Too late. I've accepted the retainer. I'm going to find the statue," I said, trying to step around him. He grabbed for my arm. I backed up until I was out of reach.

"Sam, you can't do this," Clare said, closing in on me from the other side. Her face was puckered with worry, the remains of a flower clutched in her hand.

"I can't? Watch me," I said calmly, determination seeping from all the gaping holes Paen had left in my soul.

"There's no way out of here," Finn said, moving so he stood next to Paen. "We're not going to let you endanger yourself with a seer, Sam. Come to dinner and we'll talk about it."

I smiled, just smiled at Clare and Finn. Paen I couldn't look at without wanting to scream, sob, and rip all his clothes off in order to have my wicked way with him. Instead of any of those, I reached out and found the opening to the beyond, slipping through it before anyone realized what I was doing.

I heard an echo of my name, but it was distant and tinny, as if spoken from a long way away. I had to pass through Paen to get to the door, an act that almost brought me to tears with the pain of rejection. For one brief moment, time held its breath as my soul merged with his. Like the other times we'd merged, it was so right, so perfect I didn't want to leave. For a moment, I allowed my love to shine bright. Paen reeled in surprise. With a cry of anguish that ripped from my throat, I tore myself away from him and left the office, waiting until I was at the edge of the founded area to slip back to reality.

Paen tried a few times to mind-speak to me, but I barely had the strength to walk away from him— there was no way I could argue my feelings with him. After our last merging, he'd be well aware of the depths of my emotions, and I knew he wasn't happy about them. In a move of sheerest self-preservation, I put up a mental DO NOT DISTURB sign, and blocked his mind from mine.

It took a good half hour of solid persuasion to get the name and phone number of an area seer from Jake, but after I told him I would rather sacrifice my own soul than lose Paen's mother's, he caved and gave it to me.

"Just remember that a seer's services come at an exorbitantly high price," he advised as he wrote out a name and phone number. "She'll ask you for something very precious indeed. I hope you're prepared to lose something that matters to you."

"I'm immortal now," I said, pocketing the slip of paper. "I can afford to lose a few years of my life."

"Just because the seer that Brother Bartholomew used demanded seven years of his life does not guarantee that's what this seer will ask of you," he warned, concern filling his eyes.

I gave his hand a squeeze and kissed his cheek. "Thanks for everything, Jake—both the name and the worry. But you can relax. I'm not suicidal, nor overly stupid. I'll only barter something that I can do without."

He shook his head as I left. "That's not how it works, Sam. Just remember that whatever the price she asks, it's bound to be too high. Try to get it down to something that won't deprive you too much."

I thanked him again and walked to the corner where there was a pay phone. Three minutes later I was running to a taxi stand, having managed to get an appointment with Kelsey Franklin, local seer.

Chapter 14

The ride out to Rosslyn Chapel, where the seer arranged to meet me, wasn't overly long, but it seemed to take a couple of lifetimes. I was nervous, unhappy about having shut out Paen, but determination to see the job through (not to mention a wee touch of pride) kept me from bolting as I paid off the taxi, and looked through the gloom at the old stone building in front of it. Scaffolding along one side indicated that some restoration work was going on. Heeding the seer's instructions, I walked around to the side, where she told me a door would be left unlocked.

I glanced at the sky as I stepped into the building, wishing for approximately the five hundred and seventeenth time that my personal magnetism didn't stop watches. I guessed it to be after seven, which left me roughly five hours until deep night. I'd have time to meet the seer, engage in negotiations, and hopefully run out to pick up the statue from wherever it was being held. If the demon who talked to Paen was right after all, and Owen Race had it . . . well, I'd cross that bridge when I came to it.

"Hello?" My voice was hushed and somewhat hoarse. I stepped into a side aisle of the chapel, goose bumps prickling on my arms as my footsteps echoed eerily on the uncarpeted stone floor. "Anyone here? Mrs. Franklin?"

My voice echoed as well, sending little shivers down my back as I moved toward the main aisle. The chapel was built of a beautiful cream stone, twin rows of tall, intricately carved pillars flanking the dark wooden pews that filled the center part of the chapel. Candelabras with electric candles stood at each pillar, lighting the chapel with a warm golden glow that extended upward, to the high gothic arched ceiling, also elaborately carved with faces, figures, and ornaments. No light shone in through the stained glass windows, but I could see that they would be beautiful in sunlight. I paused for a moment, focusing my thoughts, and allowed the essence of the building to tell me its story.

"Whoa," I said softly, closing myself off from it. "You've got a lot of history."

"It was built in the mid-fifteenth century," a voice said from behind me. I spun around to see a woman slightly older than me, with long, waist-length braids of red that bobbed gently as she walked toward me, pulling off her raincoat before setting it and her purse on the nearest pew. "Founded by Sir William St. Clair, the last St. Clair prince of Orkney. You are Samantha Cosse?"

"Yes, I am. It's a pleasure to meet you." I offered my hand, relieved to find that the seer was made of flesh and blood, not some cold creature of the dark powers. Although I'd never met one before, I'd heard stories of how powerful they were . . . and how that power could be turned against the person seeking their help.

"We are alone, so you needn't fear we'll be interrupted," she said, waving me into a pew.

"Er . . . you're sure no one will come in?"

"I'm on the board of the Trust that owns the chapel. It is closed at this time of night, so no one will disturb us," Kelsey said, taking a seat and folding her hands on her lap. She was rather brusque and businesslike, but didn't give off any vibes that set my warning system off, so I sat next to her. "You said you wished to patronize my services. What price are you willing to pay for them?"

I bit my lip. "I suppose money is out?"

She nodded. "My time is valuable. I expect to be paid well for it." She eyed me for a second. "You are part elf. In a normal situation, I would ask you for a score of years."

"A score?" I tried to keep from looking too surprised. "A Diviner who recommended you to me said he only had to give you seven years for your services. Has inflation struck or something?"

She didn't crack a smile, just looked at me with a vaguely impatient expression. "My fee is dependent upon the individual who seeks assistance. As one with elf blood, your life span is greater than a mortal's, thus you would be asked for more in payment. But as you are also a Beloved . . ." Her voice trailed off as she scrutinized me.

I was suddenly very uncomfortable, feeling no little bit like a butterfly that had been pinned and was being examined with a magnifying glass. Self-preservation in the form of a distraction from the unnerving examination had me asking, "How do you know I'm a Beloved?"

She gave me a dismissive look. "You seek an object of great importance."

"Yes, I do," I said, thinking of Paen's statue. Although I wanted to find Mr. Race's manuscript as well, the statue took precedence in my mind since failure would mean an unspeakable tragedy for Paen's mother.

"The price for my services will be your soul."

"*What?*" I shrieked, leaping up from the pew. "You want my soul?" *Soul, soul, soul,* echoed my voice on the high gothic ceiling. "You have got to be kidding! No one gets my soul, OK? No one!"

"You would sacrifice another for yourself?" she asked, raising one finely shaped eyebrow.

"I will *not* give up my soul," I said firmly, refusing to be drawn into a conversation about whether or not I'd sacrifice myself for Paen's mother. I'd already done it for him, and look where that had gotten me. "There must be something else I have that you want. Something of value."

"I do not make a habit of bartering," she said stiffly, but considered me for a few minutes. "However, in this case, I find you do have another valuable asset, one which I will accept in place of your soul."

"What would that be?" I asked, wary.

"Your immortality."

I almost laughed with relief. I never wanted to be immortal—giving that up would be no trouble now that Paen had made his feelings for me—or lack thereof—quite clear. "It's a deal."

Her lips pursed slightly. "You do not mind becoming mortal again?"

"No, I don't mind. I'm not really a Beloved. Well, I am, but I've kind of been fired from the job. So immortality is not needed or desired. I lived my whole life as a mortal—I don't mind being there again."

She looked like she wanted to ask something, but all she did was pull a pendant from under her blouse and hold it out toward me. A large amber teardrop gleamed in the light, glowing beautiful shades of reddish gold. "Swear to the terms, please. You must consent in order for the bargain to be struck."

I placed my hand on the pendant and swore to give up my immortality in return for the seer's help. A little buzz of electricity went up my arm at the oath, but that was all. There was no big thunderclap, no sound of trumpets from heaven, nothing.

"Is it done?" I asked, rubbing at the faint mark the amber had left on my palm.

"Yes. You sound disappointed. Do you regret the bargain already?"

I looked her in her cold blue eyes. "No. It's just a bit anticlimactic, you know? I don't quite know what I expected would happen, but I guess I felt there should be a little something to mark the event."

She was all business, not even giving me a friendly look or slight smile. "What do you wish to know?"

"Oh . . . um . . . what I want to know is who has the black monkey statue known as the Jilin God."

Her fingers stroked the amber amulet as her eyes lost their focus. Part of the reason seers were so respected (not to mention feared) was the fact that many of them tapped into dark powers to achieve their visions. Some had working arrangements with lesser demons; others used conduits like an amulet or reliquary that harnessed a dark power. I gathered by the way Kelsey touched her pendant that the amber stone in it acted as a conduit. "The statue you seek was last in the possession of the being known as Pilar."

"Pilar? Are you sure?"

She gave me a look that was answer enough.

"How bizarre. I had a feeling he wasn't mortal, but he has Paen's statue, too? Hmm. Where is Pilar?"

"He is at present nine miles distant, south-southeast."

Hmm. Nine miles meant he must still be in the greater Edinburgh area. But how did Pilar get both my bird statue and Paen's statue? And why would he want both? One was a valuable antiquity, the other a cheap Taiwanese knockoff. I shook my head, confused. "You said the statue was last in the possession of Pilar. Does that mean he no longer has it?"

"That is correct. It is no longer in his possession, although he was the last person to possess it."

"Which means no one else has it now," I said softly, thinking hard. "I bet he's hidden it away somewhere safe. When I saw the Jilin God, it was entombed, held in darkness, away from all light. Is it still?"

"Yes, it is."

"How can Pilar have hidden it somewhere if it's in a tomb?" I asked.

"The statue is not in what you know as a tomb per se—it is protected while it sleeps through the centuries, kept from sight so as to remain undisturbed."

"Oh." I thought about that. It fit what I saw when scrying—I just interpreted that protected, confined state to be a tomb. But if it wasn't in some sort of a big tomb, then what was it in? "What sort of object is protecting the statue?"

Her eyes snapped back to focus as she dropped the pendant. "You have asked five questions, and received five answers. If you wish more, you will have to pay me again."

"Wait a minute! You never said I only had five questions to ask!"

"And you never asked," she replied, gathering her raincoat and bag. "Do you wish to consult me again?"

I gritted my teeth against the expletive that wanted to burst out. There was no sense in being rude, even though I do think she could have warned me there was a limit to the number of questions I could ask. "No, thank you. I believe I have enough to go on."

"You have my number should you wish to contact me again to answer other questions"—she eyed me like I was a piece of dead fish at the fishmongers— "mortal."

I swore to myself all the way back to town, in between trying to figure out why Pilar wanted both Paen's statue and the bird one. Maybe he was a statue freak?

The lights, music, and chatter from Mila's sex shop spilled out onto the street as I approached my office, relieved to see the lights off upstairs. I had half expected Paen and the others to be lurking around the office waiting for me to return, but I guessed they'd done the sane thing and wrote me off to go have dinner.

So why did that thought depress me?

"I'm hungry, that's all," I said as I unlocked the door to the office and used the light from the hallway to find my desk. I flipped on the desk light. "I hope they're all having a fabulous time without me. Although it might have been nice if someone cared a tiny fraction enough to wonder if I'm all right."

"How about if someone cared enough to turn you over his knee and spank you as you deserve?"

Chapter 15

I jumped at the sound of the voice, clutching my chest as I spun around. A man stepped out of the shadows, his brows pulled together in a familiar scowl. "Dammit, Paen, just give me a heart attack, why don't you?"

He stalked out of the darkness like he was a lion and I was a particularly succulent bit of steak. "It wouldn't matter if I did. You can't be killed short of decapitation."

That's what he thought.

"Where have you ... what do you mean, that's what I think?" Paen stopped in front of me, his hands on his hips, his eyes glittering like polished silver.

I tried to gather the shreds of my dignity, giving Paen what I hoped was a coolly professional look. "I didn't say that to you. You read my mind. Since you dumped me so cruelly and heartlessly, we are no longer a couple, so I will thank you to stay out of there. As to where I have been, that, also, is of no concern to you except insofar as my trip has resulted in several good bits of information regarding your statue."

His eyes narrowed. To my surprise, he didn't seem to care about the statue. "I didn't dump you, either cruelly or heartlessly. You fell in love with me! You broke the rules of our relationship!"

I stepped forward until I was toe-to-toe with him, determined to give as good as I got. Oh, sure, being so close to him sent my body into ecstasy, but I ignored its demands in order to clear up a few things with Paen. "At no time did you state I couldn't fall in love with you."

"Aha," he crowed, triumphant. "You admit that it's true!"

"Yes, of course I admit, you great big boob! And how can you say you didn't dump me? You most certainly did."

His eyes glowed with silver brilliance. "I did no such thing. I would have been perfectly happy to continue our relationship within the terms to which we both agreed."

"You would, would you? Just casual lovers, getting together once in a while for sex, is that what you want? Are we back to fucking versus lovemaking?"

"Yes," he snarled, grabbing my arms. "That's all I want. To fuck the breath out of you."

My heart gave a leap despite the crudity of the words and temporarily overrode my brain. I leaned into Paen, every curve, every soft line of my body melting against his. The feel and scent and presence of him filled me until I knew, I *knew* to the very last beat of my heart, that we were meant to be together. Joined. One. "Tell me," I said against his lips. "Tell me that all you want from me is sex. Tell me nothing else matters."

"Nothing else matters," he said, his mouth possessing mine, his hands hard on my hips as he pulled me even tighter against his body. *Nothing else matters but you.*

His mind opened up to me, and I merged with him, my body desperate, my soul singing a joyous song of being as I felt the need within him answered in me.

Tell me I'm wrong, tell me you don't want this, I demanded, his mouth moving over mine in a way that made me even more desperate for him. I didn't just want his touch, didn't just crave his body—it was all of him, everything that was Paen that I hungered for.

You're wrong. I don't want this, he said, smiling into my mind. I pulled back from his kiss, sucking his lower lip for a second before releasing it. "I insist you do that more often," I told him, breathless and keyed up, my body humming a song of desire and love.

"Tease you or kiss the breath from you?" he asked, the corners of his mouth turning up.

"Neither. Both. And smile, too." I kissed each corner, giving them a little lick as well. "Paen, I truly am sorry. I didn't mean to mess up your life this way. I didn't mean to mess up mine, either, but dammit, somehow, in just a few days, you've made me lose all reason and fall in love with you. The physical relationship you wanted isn't going to be enough for me. I want you, all of you, not just your body. I want you in the morning when you're grumpy because you haven't had your morning cup of coffee—"

"I don't drink coffee."

"And I want you in the afternoon, when you're stubborn and infuriating—"

"I am never stubborn or infuriating!"

"And I want you in the evening, when you're demanding, broody, and sexy as hell."

"I sense a theme here," he said, pulling me back for another kiss. "It goes without saying that I'm not demanding, broody, or sex . . . er . . . all right, I *am* sexy as hell. I will concede that, but about the rest you are wrong."

I laughed, tears of happiness in my eyes. Inside Paen, instead of the cold denial that had claimed him before, there was reluctant acceptance and a begrudging admission that I meant more to him than he wanted to allow. There was even the start of something that felt warm to me, soft and enveloping, an emotion that made my heart sing. *I want all of you, Paen. Every last bit of you. That's the only way we'll work. If you can't give me all of you, we just can't continue on together.*

I will give you everything I can, he swore, and I believed him. I wanted to hear that he loved me as well, but I knew it was too soon for him. I sensed there were deeper emotions in him, but didn't push it. He needed time to come to grips with his change of heart.

His kiss was hot and deep, sizzling down to my toenails until I was one gigantic blaze of desire. *You are the most exasperating, frustrating . . . fascinating woman I've ever met. Lord help me, I want you as well. I need you.*

Sounds like we've reached a détente . . . Paen!

Hmm?

He backed me up against my desk, his mouth still on mine, his hands roaming my body, thumbs brushing my breasts for a moment before they moved lower, unzipping my jeans.

This isn't lovemaking.

No. I told you—I'm going to fuck the breath out of you.

Here? Now?

Here. Now. Any complaints?

No. But what if someone comes? I might be moderately scandalized that he wanted to do this in the office, but I was no fool—I happily kicked my pants off as he yanked my sweater over my head. This was no mere sexual act. It was fast, sweaty sex, but it was fast, sweaty sex powered by love.

I told you before that someone is going to come, he answered, grinning.

Promises, promises, I answered, my fingers hurrying down the buttons of his shirt. I purred as the shirt hit the floor, my hands spread across his chest, fingers splayed wide across his pectorals before inevitably, one hand followed the silky trail of hair down to his pants. "Oooh. Now I'm anticipating."

"Anticipating what?" His breath caught as I caressed the bulge behind his zipper for a moment, slowly pulling the zipper down, my hands sliding around his hips to push his pants off.

"You don't mind if I indulge in a little fantasy, do you?"

I swear, the glow from his eyes could light up at least half of Edinburgh.

"Sweetheart, you can do whatever you desire to me, but I don't want you feeling obligated in any way. We can take as much time as you . . . oh dear lord." Paen stopped talking but inside him, a thousand sensations were roiling in his mind. Excitement, arousal, passion, the warm fuzzy thing that looked so much like the beginning of love, and intense sexual pleasure crashed over me like a wave as I took him in my mouth. My body hummed even louder as the emotions built within him, growing quickly to something that almost overwhelmed Paen.

"I'm sorry," I said, pulling back for a moment to look up at him. "Was that too much too quickly? I'm sorry if I'm going about this the wrong way. I assumed more is better? Yes? No? Boy, I hate being new at this sort of thing."

He looked wildly at me, as if he didn't quite understand what I was saying. "You haven't done this before?"

"Well . . . I started to once, with my last boyfriend, Carl, but I zoned out almost immediately, and that evidently ruined the whole experience for Carl so I never tried it again."

"Sam?"

"Hmm?" I said, flicking my tongue across the end of his penis. I smiled at the zing of pleasure my touch sent shimmering through Paen.

"Let's not talk about your boyfriends now."

"OK. But one of them kept talking about me doing this . . ." I snagged my purse from the desk and dug out a tin of breath mints, popping a couple in my mouth. "This isn't too much, is it? I've always wanted to try this."

Paen's eyes grew big as I crunched the mints loudly, licking my lips as the minty sensation of a cold burn made my mouth tingle.

"You don't think you're going to—dear lord, you are. And it's your first time . . . good god, woman!"

"Less talking," I said, swirling my mint-coated tongue along the underside of his penis. "More moaning."

And oh, how he moaned. He sucked in huge quantities of air as I took him into my mouth again, so caught up in what he was feeling, of the added sensitivity the mintyness brought to the experience, that it was almost as if I was the recipient.

I laved the entire length of his shaft with my tongue. Paen's entire body trembled as the air hit his wet flesh, his eyes rolling back in his head when I clamped my fingers around the base and concentrated on a particularly sensitive spot on the underside. "This is amazing. So this is what you feel when we have sex? It's so different than what I feel, but I have to say, it's making me incredibly aroused. What happens if I try this?"

He lasted a whole second before he jerked me upward, spinning me around so I faced the desk, shredding off my underwear and unhooking my bra before I could even blink.

"This is what happens," he growled, bending me over the desk, his knee nudging my legs apart. I gasped from the dual sensations of the cold wood of the desk as my sensitive, tight breasts hit it, and the burning brand that thrust into my waiting flesh.

"Paen!" I shrieked, clutching the table, knocking the phone off as my body was rammed forward. "Condom?"

"Don't have one," he growled, pulling back. "Should I stop—"

"Never mind, we'll risk it this *oooonce . . . !*" My sentence ended on a slight scream as he lunged forward into me again.

"Too hard?" he asked, pausing.

"No! Harder!"

He grunted a happy reply, his hips flexing, his fingers digging into my thighs.

My flesh made a squeaky noise on the polished wood as he pounded into me. The pretty wire flower-embossed in-box full of letters and receipts slid off the desk, bursting into a shower of paper as it fell to the floor.

"Oh, my god, yes! More!" I gasped, arms flailing for something to hold on to as Paen continued to make my eyes cross with ecstasy. The wire flower pen holder that matched the inbox (both gifts from Clare) went flying, pens scattering everywhere. "More!"

"I'll give you more," he grunted, grabbing my hips and pulling upward to alter the angle of penetration. A small pad of sticky notes trembled on the lip of the desk, then fell to the floor just as I started to moan non-stop. He was deep inside me, hard and hot and invasive, but at the same time, so much a part of me that I wasn't sure which emotions, which sensations were mine, and which were his.

"Christ, you're tight," he groaned, thrusting forward.

"I Kegel. A lot. Oh, yes, right there, oh my goooooooooo . . ." My inner muscles, honed by years of doing Kegel exercises, cramped from the attempt to keep him within their grasp. The cold burn of mint went from pleasant tingles to wildly erotic sparks of electricity that burned brightly, so brightly I thought I was going to pass out from the experience. "No more! I changed my mind! I can't take any more!"

You can take it, he said, his voice rich with emotion. *You can take this and more.*

My back arched as he filled my head with the sensations he was feeling, wanting—no, needing—for him to take life from me. Our souls entwined as he shoved my hair aside, baring the back of my neck.

Please, god, do it, I begged, on the verge of mind-numbing rapture. His teeth pierced my skin, the sudden sharp pain merging with the pleasure the rest of his body was providing both of us as he pumped into me. Light, silver, pure light blossomed behind my eyes as I gave in to the sensations we shared, spiraling us both into an orgasm of blinding magnitude.

"It's a good . . . thing I have a . . . strong heart," I gasped long, long minutes later, from where I lay panting on top of Paen after he had collapsed into a chair. His chest, slicked with perspiration, rose and fell in a ragged rhythm beneath my still quivering body. "Because otherwise, I'd be dead in a week."

"It's good that you're immortal, then," he said without opening his eyes, his head lolling exhaustedly against the high back of the chair. I pressed a little kiss to the pulse that beat so wildly in his neck, freezing as what he said made a couple of synapses stand up and take notice.

"Bloody hell!"

His eyes opened to look at me with curiosity.

The enormity of what I'd done sank in at that moment. "I'm not . . . I'm not immortal anymore."

"What?" The word shot out of his mouth in a manner that might be said to be yelling. I matched the sudden frown that appeared between his eyebrows.

"I'm not immortal anymore. I used that to barter with the seer."

He stared at me in disbelief for a moment. "You saw a seer after I explicitly told you not to?"

"No, I saw the seer after you unreasonably ordered me not to. The difference should be apparent, even to you."

"Unreasonably? Is it unreasonable for a man to expect his Beloved to listen to him once in a while?"

I pushed back so I could really glare at him. "You de-Beloveded me! You told me you didn't want me anymore—oh, not in so many words, but you know what I mean."

"You used your immortality—the one thing I could give you—in exchange for information?" he asked, disbelief warring with pain in his eyes.

I rubbed my thumb along his jaw, sharing the anguish he felt. "You said we had no future together. I thought there was no reason for me to live forever if the man I loved didn't want me to share eternity with him."

"Oh, Sam—" Regret filled him, spilling over onto me. "I never meant for you to be hurt. I just . . . I didn't . . ."

"I know," I said, kissing his nose. "You just were a little commitment-shy. What changed that? It happened so fast—one minute you were yelling, the next everything went flying and we were using my breasts to polish the desk."

He groaned. "You're going to force me into a detailed discussion of my emotional state, aren't you?"

"Yup. It's every woman's right as soon as she knows she's snagged a man. The sooner you start, the easier it'll get. Now spill."

"I stopped pretending you weren't important," he said, trying to look pathetic. I kissed him just because he was so cute. "When you ran off earlier, there was a moment when you passed through me. I felt just how much I'd hurt you—and how much you loved me. No one but my family has loved me, Sam. I thought I didn't need it. I realized then that I was wrong."

"It takes a big man to admit he's wrong," I teased, squirming against his penis. My tone was light, but I let him feel how much joy his words brought to me.

His hands tightened on my hips. "Stop distracting me or I won't tell you the last bit."

I stopped and looked contrite.

"I told myself the entire time you were gone that I was just waiting around for you to return so I could fire you, and go back to my life. But then you walked in looking so warm, and beautiful, and sexy—and all I could think about was how right it was that you were here with me."

Tears formed in my eyes. "Oh, Paen, that's just about the nicest thing anyone has ever said to me. That's so sweet, and I'm so glad you got your head out of your ass and realized that I'm the best thing that'll ever happen to you."

He laughed and kissed me. "I know I can trust you to keep me humble."

"Of course, it's my job. Only . . ." I bit my lower lip until he gently freed it with a few soft strokes of his thumb. "Now I'm back to living a mortal life. I didn't mind that before, but if you're going to live for hundreds of years, I think I'd like to live them with you. Is there any way to get my immortality back?"

His arm tightened around my waist, pulling me closer. The regret that simmered in him rose up again until it made me want to weep. "No reasonable way, I'm afraid."

"Stop blaming yourself for this," I said, leaning back against his arm so I could see him without my eyes crossing. "You are not responsible for my actions."

"If I hadn't said I didn't want you as a Beloved—"

I put my finger on his lips. "Paen, it was my decision. I had the choice, and I took it. You are not to blame."

"I am as much to blame as you are," he said, his eyes going stubborn.

"Fine, we can share the blame, but that's not going to do either of us any good," I pointed out. His chest rose and fell beneath me in a slower rhythm as we both recovered from the lovemaking. "You said there's no reasonable way for me to get back my immortality—what unreasonable ways are there?"

"Any number, varying from becoming a demon lord—which I don't advise—to buying it back, which isn't likely since seers never part with those items they collect."

"Oh," I said, my hopes plummeting. The thought of growing old while Paen remained young and vital made my heart ache. "There's no other way?"

He hesitated. It was an almost infinitesimal hesitation, but his mind purposely went blank for a moment. "No."

I put a finger on his chin and turned his head so he was looking at me. His eyes were clouded and wary. "What?"

"*What* what?"

"Paen." I frowned at him. "I felt you deliberately not think something at me."

One eyebrow rose. "That is the most ridiculous thing I've heard yet."

"You know what I mean, so stop evading it, and just spit it out. What is the other way that you don't want to tell me about?"

He sighed. He sighed so deeply, it came from the very depths of his soul. "Anyone who is turned by a Dark One is made immortal."

"Turned?" I thought for a moment. "Oh, you mean made a vampire? You can do that? I thought it was just a myth or something."

He looked away. "Dark Ones can turn mortals. It doesn't happen very often since there is no real reason to do so, but it is within the realm of improbable possibility."

"But females aren't Dark Ones, so what do they turn into?"

"Moravians."

I thought about that for a minute. "Finn said a Beloved was more or less a female Moravian. So if turning would put me back there, then I say let's do it."

"No." He gently pushed me off his lap and started gathering up his clothes. Since I didn't want to be caught standing around naked and sweaty, I did the same.

"Why?" I asked, fingering my shredded underwear and wondering if I could staple it back together. "It sounds like the ideal solution to me. I'd be immortal again, and you said the females don't have to drink blood."

"You're not doing it and that's the end of the discussion." Paen turned his back to me as he pulled on his shirt.

I ground my teeth and pulled my jeans on without underwear (something I disliked, but I didn't have much of a choice). "You're being high-handed again. I really don't appreciate that."

"What did you find out about my statue?"

"And now you're changing the subject."

"What did you find out about my statue?"

I finished dressing, thinking several loud thoughts that he summarily ignored. "Fine, I'll talk about the statue, but don't think I'll forget about this. I'm thirty-three now—I want to be immortal while I still look halfway decent. Pilar had the statue last. I'm sure he's hidden it somewhere nearby."

"Pilar?" A frown wrinkled Paen's forehead. "Where is he?"

I pulled my sweater on and reached for my shoes. "Somewhere in the area, according to Kelsey the seer. Edinburgh, most likely."

"I thought you said he had your statue. He has both?"

Paen turned around, dressed, and watched as I slipped on my loafers. I gave him a brief recap of my conversation with the seer, ending with the question of why Pilar would want both statues.

"Unless," I said, stopping as I tried to fit together two pieces of the puzzle that didn't want to mesh.

"Unless the two statues are the same?" Paen asked, clearly thinking the same thing I was.

"Yeah, but how can that be? One is of a bird. We all saw it—it was definitely a falcon of some sort. Your statue is of a monkey. They don't look even remotely alike."

"You saw the statue as entombed, confined in a dark place," he said slowly.

I nodded.

"And the seer told you the statue was hidden from sight, protected while it slept."

"Yes. But the statue I had wasn't hidden from sight, and it wasn't protected, unless you call a shoe-box protection, and I don't."

"What if the Jilin God was held within the falcon statue?" he asked, his brow still wrinkled with puzzlement.

"Of course," I said, enlightenment finally dawning. "It's inside the bird! That's why I saw the bird statue when I tried to scry the location of the Jilin God. Now it makes sense why Pilar would do anything to get it—he must have known the Jilin statue was inside the bird, and wanted it for his own purposes."

Paen pulled on his long black coat. "Let's go get it back."

"What, right now?" I glanced at the clock. The trip back from the seer had taken me twice as long to return by bus as the trip out. It was now less than an hour to deep night. "I don't know exactly where he is. It may take us a while to track him down."

"The sooner we get started, the sooner we can retrieve that statue," Paen said, holding the door open. "You don't need to come if you are too tired."

"No, I'm fine," I said, getting my jacket and purse. "You're right. The sooner we have it, the sooner your father's debt can be paid, and the easier I'll rest. Let's go kick some whatever-Pilar-is booty!"

"You are a strange woman," Paen said as we hurried down the stairs.

"Why, because I'm proactive and independent? Because I take pride in my work ethic? Because I'll move heaven and hell to see a job done?"

"I was referring to the fact that you are willing to face a potentially lethal opponent armed with nothing more than a purse and a PDA."

I smiled at Paen as he held open the door at the bottom of the stairs, brushing my fingers across his jaw as I passed. "I have a secret weapon."

His eyebrows rose in silent question.

"I have you," I said, smiling, full of confidence. Things were looking so rosy for us—we'd worked out the worst of the relationship kinks, Paen's statue was within our grasp, and I was sure I would be able to talk him into making me a Moravian to regain immortality. I still had a longer than normal life span, but that wasn't going to cut it when there was Paen to spend an eternity with. "All in all, things are coming together nicely. Nothing can stop us once we put our heads together on it."

I really wish someone would stop me from making those sorts of generalizations. They're almost always wrong.

We found Pilar the second hour of deep night. We'd spent the last two hours trolling through the city, following mostly my instincts on where Pilar was, but whenever we'd arrive at a location (nightclub, store, two cemeteries, an all-night McDonald's, and Edinburgh Castle), we'd find he'd been there and left. Finally we lucked out and found Pilar at one of the oddities in Edinburgh—the Real Mary

King's Close, an underground historical site made up of a warren of several seventeenth-century closes (narrow lanes used as shortcuts that were "closed" in by surrounding multistoried buildings). It was reported to be one of the most haunted spots in Edinburgh, so several ghost-hunting groups and parapsychology devotees booked time in it at night. We slipped in at the tail end of a ghost-hunting group and made it inside without anyone the wiser, following as the group walked down several levels until we were deep beneath the modern streets. Narrow white stone walls and uneven dirt floors made every whisper echo, so we were careful to be as silent as possible.

"Are you sure he's here?" Paen asked me in a whisper as the group gathered around their excited leader in front of the remains of a store.

We clung to the shadows cast by reproduction seventeenth-century lighting to avoid being noticed. I rubbed my arms, understanding why people thought this area was haunted. The buildings in the close had been built over for a couple hundred years, but this part had been excavated and restored to what were pretty realistic historic conditions. It was dark, damp, cold, and smelly.

I shivered as cold fingers of air touched my neck, then closed my eyes and concentrated for a moment. "I think so. It feels like he's here. I think he's"—I turned, my eyes still closed, trusting my elf instincts to guide me—"that way."

We waited for the ghost chasers to hurry off for their ghostly hot spots before turning in the opposite direction.

"Which one?" Paen asked as we came to a narrow alley with three entrances. I ignored the door marked MR. CHESNEY'S DWELLING and entered the sawmaker's workshop next to it. The room was empty of everything but a few shelves and hooks on the walls, but a partially opened wooden door led to a room beyond. I pointed and started toward it, but Paen pulled me behind him, giving me a look that warned me not to challenge him.

I stuck my tongue out at the back of his head and followed closely on his heels.

". . . took it away from her when she was trapped in the web and hid it. Now I need someone to go in and get it for me. You're Fae, you should be able to retrieve it."

A couple of soft raps answered the man's voice that emerged from the workshop.

"The curse means nothing in this instance—once a faery, always a faery, even if Oriens did turn you into a poltergeist. It's a simple enough job—all you have to do is find the statue where I left it in the beyond, and bring it out to me."

Three sharp raps followed. Paen sidled around the door to peer into the room. I peeked over his shoulder, shivering again as the cold seeped out of the room and straight into my bones. Pilar stood in the middle of the room, his hands on his hips as he faced a familiar poltergeist.

"Don't be a fool—you know I was born of dark powers. I can enter and leave the beyond, but I have no power there, so you're going to have to be the one to fetch the statue. Just don't cock it up! I want something done right for a change."

Whoa. It doesn't sound like he has the statue. At least I know I didn't lose it. He must have taken it without me knowing when I was trapped between realities, hauled it farther into the beyond, then not been able to get it out again.

Paen gave a mental shrug. *However it got there, it's to our benefit that he can't retrieve it easily.*

A couple more knocks answered Pilar.

"Don't be foolish," he snarled at the poltergeist. "It's not that easy to lift a curse, you know. The offer is simple—you bring the statue out to me, and I'll find a Charmer to lift the curse. Take it or leave it."

It sounds as if he is having difficulties finding someone to bring it out, Paen said.

I'm surprised he thinks a poltergeist can. Everyone knows beings born of the darkness have no powers in the beyond.

Reuben rapped out an answer that had Pilar snorting, "No. No one else knows where that half-breed elf was. It's safe enough until you retrieve it."

If Reuben was cursed to this state, it means he wasn't born into it. It's probably entirely likely that he would have his full powers in the beyond.

I suppose, although there wouldn't be much he could do there even with them. I've never heard of a faery who was cursed, but I don't get around much in the Fae world. Regardless, what are we going to do now?

Find out just where it is so you can get it yourself. Paen stepped into the room, his wide shoulders filling the narrow doorway. "Lost the statue, did you? That's too bad. Sam would like it back."

Life suddenly took on a very abstract quality. In the fraction of a second after Paen's words were spoken, Pilar spun around to find himself face-to-face with an angry vampire. But what he did next took us both by surprise. Rather than attacking Paen, or challenging him, or even laughing a mocking, superior laugh at Paen's bravado, he did something entirely different.

He killed me.

Chapter 16

A voice screamed in the small, closed room, echoing over and over and over again, a horrible sound that made my brain hurt. It was only after the screaming stopped and Pilar stepped back from me that I noticed he held a knife in his hands. A knife covered in blood right to the hilt.

Warmth seeped into my sweater as an odd gurgling, rasping noise seemed to fill my ears. Paen roared a curse and tore off the poltergeist from where he was clinging, just as if he was nothing more than a troublesome burr. Reuben went flying across the room, hitting the wall with a solid thunk. Paen looked startled for a moment as one of Reuben's arms remained in his grasp, but he threw down the limb as he lunged for me, his beautiful silver eyes almost black.

Beyond him, Pilar fled the room, an injured Reuben crawling out after him, leaving a trail of oily black blood and apports.

"They're getting away," I tried to say, but something was wrong with me, something was very wrong. I couldn't speak, and my brain apparently had shifted into slow motion again. My legs buckled and I fell backward against the wall, Paen catching me before I could hit the floor. *Paen?*

Dear god, don't speak. Don't move, Sam. It'll be all right. It's a lot of blood but I'll stop the bleeding somehow.

His eyes were so full of horror, they made mine blur with tears. I tried to touch his face but my arms didn't seem to work. *Paen?*

I'll call Finn. We'll get you help. There's a hospital nearby. Don't leave me, Sam, just don't leave me. Swear you won't leave me.

I won't leave, I started to say, but stopped because it wasn't true. The room telescoped, Paen at one end and me at the other, moving farther and farther away from each other until it seemed we were at opposite ends of a long tunnel.

Paen, where did you go? What's happening? Why can't I move?

Sam, damn you, don't leave me! There were tears in his voice that spoke in my head, tears and anguish and pain so deep it cut through my soul. *Hang on to me, Sam. Stay with me. Don't let go.*

I don't seem to be able to . . .

I drifted backward, as if my astral body had gone flying again, but this was different. Sheer terror filled me as I finally understood what was happening. I struggled to keep from drifting, but I was powerless. *Paen! I don't want to go! Please don't let me die! I love you! I don't want to leave you!*

I won't let you go, sweetheart, his voice answered in my head, distant but calm, reassuring. *Forgive me, Sam.*

Forgive you for what? I asked, sobbing tears of

agony. I wanted to scream and yell and fight, railing against the cruelty of fate. Now that I had found Paen, now that he had accepted me and we had a life in front of us—for however long—it wasn't right that I should be torn from him. *Paen! Please! Help me!*

Forgive me, my love.

Pain blossomed deep within me, a horrible, rending pain unlike anything I'd felt before, and for a moment I was thrilled to feel anything, because it meant I wasn't quite dead yet. Paen's silver eyes burned into mine a second before his teeth flashed and a streak of pain shot through my chest, a strange lethargy washing over me. He was feeding off me, drinking my blood, taking into himself everything I was, and had, and ever would have, leaving me . . . empty.

He dropped me, let the hollow shell of me flounder and sink into a black abyss, and with one last heartrending sob of sorrow, I was no more.

Sam?

Hmm?

How do you feel?

I'm not sure. Am I sleeping?

Yes. Wake up now.

All right.

I opened my eyes. We were still in the storage room beneath the streets of Edinburgh, faint light coming in through the opened doorway. An odd wind seemed to be howling somewhere in the distance, as if a storm was building. Beneath me, the ground was wet and sticky with blood. My blood.

"I'm not dead?" My voice sounded choked, hoarse and rough.

Don't speak out loud, not yet. Give your body time to heal the injury on your neck.

Memory returned to me. *Pilar stabbed me?*

Slashed your neck. He cut your jugular, damn near decapitating you, otherwise I would have rushed you to the hospital. But there was no time, Sam, no time. You were dying. You were leaving me and I couldn't stop it.

The wind picked up, its shrieks painful to my ears.

But I'm alive now, I said, still confused about what happened. So much of it was a horrible blur in my mind.

Paen said nothing, just watched me with a face that bore so much guilt, I wanted to weep for him.

I held out an arm. It was shaky and covered with blood, but it was my arm. *See? I'm here. I'm alive. I'm* . . . I stopped, horror crawling over my skin as I realized what was wrong. The wind that roared so loudly it hurt my ears wasn't coming from outside. . . . It came from within me.

From the place my soul used to reside.

"Sweetheart, if you keep trying to scream, you're going to bring the ghost hunters down on us, and you really do need to rest in order to heal up that neck wound."

The horrible rasping, squeaking noise that was my attempt to shriek in horror stopped. I slumped back against the wall, panting with the effort and stress. "Where's my soul?" I croaked.

Pain darkened his eyes, pain and regret and pity. For me. "I'm sorry, Sam. It was the only way I could save you. I had no choice. It was either turn you or let you go, and I couldn't do that. You may hate me for the rest of your life, but at least you're alive. And I swear to you, I'll find your soul and restore it to you."

"Turn me?" My voice was still hoarse, but growing a bit stronger. "You turned me? You made me a female Moravian?"

"Yes," he said, watching me carefully.

I shook my head, wincing slightly at the pain in my neck. "No. When I was a Beloved, you said that was the same thing as being a Moravian. But I had a soul then. I don't now. Where is it? Who has it? I want it back!"

"There is a price for everything, Sam," he answered, his eyes sad, so very sad. "The price of turning a person is the loss of their soul. That's why it's so seldom done—the cost seldom outweighs the act."

I digested that. I was weak from the loss of blood, hungrier than I knew was possible, but inside me, I was hollow. Empty of everything but that damned endless wind. Paen had done this in order to save me, in order to keep me alive. But was it worth the cost?

"Am I immortal again?"

His thumb stroked over my knuckles. "Yes."

"Can I get my soul back?"

"I'm . . . not sure." He didn't even try to disguise his hesitation.

"Has it been done before? Has someone who has been turned reclaimed their soul?"

His eyes were so polished, I could almost see my reflection in them. "Not that I know of."

A tear rolled down my cheek. "I know you wanted to keep me alive, but Paen . . . I don't want to spend eternity without a soul."

He pulled me into his arms so my face rested against his shoulder as I sobbed. His voice was rough with emotion, but thrummed inside of me like a thousand strings set vibrating. "I swear to you that you will have your soul back. I swear that on my own, Sam. You saved me when I needed you, now I will save you."

A soul means different things to different cultures. To most, it's the thing that makes us more than just sentient, the part of us that lives on when our bodies fail and turn to dust. As Paen drove me home, I came to realize another function of a soul—it connected us to humanity, made us a part of a common experience. Empty as I was inside, I watched dispassionately as people hurried through the streets of Edinburgh. I felt detached from them all, an observer who found them interesting, but not particularly of any value. I didn't care about them.

With one exception.

Looking at Paen brought tears to my eyes. Not tears of sorrow or self-pity—I had shed the last of those crouched on the floor of Mary King's Close. What made Paen different from the rest of the world was his soul—it shone so brightly around him, giving him a corona of warmth and love that drew me like a moth to flame. I wanted to be close to him just to bask in the glow of life that radiated from him. Touching him, being pressed up against him made the howling inside me die down just a little, and warmed a tiny fraction of my cold being.

"How did you live like this?" I asked him as he helped me up the stairs to my apartment. "How did you live so long without going mad?"

"I didn't know anything else," he answered, his lips brushing my temple. "Until I met you."

Paen insisted I rest and have a cup of tea. "You've lost a significant amount of blood," he said as he tucked a blanket around me where I sat curled up on the couch. "In addition, your body is using up a good deal of energy to heal your neck. You'll need fluids and sugar to help regain blood and finish the healing."

I touched my neck, pleased to see that my fingers came away without any fresh blood on them. The wound was slowly closing, the bleeding having stopped a short while before. Tea didn't sound the least bit appealing. I craved protein instead. "What I could go for is a steak. A nice big, bloody ste—" I stopped, appalled with the image in my head, my skin crawling at the thought of what I'd become. "Dear god—am I craving blood?"

"I don't know. Are you?" He plugged the electric kettle in and rustled around the kitchen, finding mugs, the milk, sugar, and tea biscuits.

"You needn't sound so unconcerned about it. This is a big deal to me," I said rather snappishly (allowable, I felt, given the situation).

He shrugged and brought the tea things out to the table next to where I sat. "It's not a big deal to me. I am and always will be a male Moravian—I must take blood from others, or I'll die."

"Well, I hope you're not peckish now, because this diner is closed for repairs."

He smiled and went to check the water. "I'm hungry, but I can wait."

"For how long?" I touched my neck again. It was hot, as if the skin was feverish.

"For however long it takes. Here." He thrust a cup of heavily sugared tea in my hands. "Drink."

"Sam? Is that you—oh, good, you came back." Clare traipsed out of her room, her long silk bathrobe almost exactly matching the shade of the pink rose she absently carried. "Finn and I were wondering when you would be ba— Goddess above! What happened to you?"

Clare stopped in front of me, striking a dramatic pose with her hand to her throat as she stared at me in horror. Behind her, Finn emerged from her room, tucking his shirttail into his pants. He, too, froze when he saw me, quickly turning his gaze to Paen.

"I turned Sam," my lover said simply, sitting down next to me. "The man who had been trying to kill her was finally successful. Or he would have been if I hadn't turned her."

I gave both startled faces in front of me a wan smile, waving Paen on when he offered to tell the recent events.

"We will find your soul," Clare promised when he was done, my hand clasped between hers as she sat at my feet, the remains of a mostly eaten rose on her lap. "I have absolutely no doubt that we'll find it. Is there a soul repository of some sort?"

That last bit was addressed to Paen. He shook his head. "Not as such. Her soul exists still, but it is held in the Akasha."

"Akasha?" Clare asked, puzzled.

"Limbo," I said, my voice still husky. "You know the Akasha—it's the place where faeries are sent as punishment."

The glare she shot me was fulminating but short-lived. "How do we find Sam's soul?" she asked Paen. "Do we just go to this Akasha limbo place?"

"You could go, but Sam couldn't, and only she or I could reclaim her soul."

"Then you go get it for her," Clare ordered, giving my hand another supportive squeeze. "We'll wait for you."

Paen rubbed a hand over his face. He was tired and hungry, facts I knew without even touching him. But his light and warmth drew me. His arm wrapped around me, holding me tight as I snuggled up against him, soaking in his heat with a relieved sigh. "It's not that easy. Beings of dark origins cannot enter the Akasha."

"Sam isn't dark—she's an elf, a sun elf," Clare pointed out.

"She was. She's Moravian now, and more importantly, soulless. All beings without a soul are by their nature dark. She can't enter the Akasha unless she has a soul, and she can't get her soul unless she can enter the Akasha."

I pushed myself tighter against him, half wishing I could crawl inside him to where that glorious soul glowed with life and love and everything that had been stripped from me.

"You can get it, then," Clare said, her face taking on a stubborn look. "You have a soul now, so you can enter this Akasha."

Paen shook his head. "I have a soul, but my origins are still dark. I was born without a soul—I will always be tainted by that, at least so far as the Akasha is concerned. I am forbidden entrance."

"Well then, what are we going to do?" she wailed,

her big blue eyes swimming with tears. I felt mildly upset on her behalf. She seemed so distraught.

"Tell her about your project," Finn said, taking a seat in the chair opposite. Clare abandoned me for him, curling up in his lap with a distressed look on her face.

"I've spent the last forty or so years researching a rumor I heard long ago. It concerned a manuscript that detailed the origins of the immortal races."

I pulled back enough to look up at Paen, surprised by the words that echoed ones I'd heard not so many hours before.

"What does that have to do with recovering Sam's soul?" Clare asked.

Paen's eyes were bright with determination. "Somewhere in the information about the origins of the Dark Ones are details concerning how a soul may be restored without the means of a Beloved. What would work in that case for a Dark One should also work for Sam."

"Are you sure this is a manuscript?" I asked, a vague sense of curiosity flickering inside me. "Not a statue?"

"No, it's a manuscript. Sixteenth century. It was named *Simia Gestor Coda* because the mage who wrote it supposedly had a fascination with monkeys."

"But," I said, my mind grinding to a halt, "I know about the *Coda*."

"What?" Paen whirled around to stare at me. "How?"

"It's the manuscript Owen Race hired us to find. He said it was stolen from his house."

Paen swore passionately. "I've been searching for it for almost forty years!"

"Is anyone else curious about the coincidences here?" I asked. "The Jilin God—"

"Is a statue of a monkey, yes," Paen answered. "I noticed that as you have, but the two are separate objects, related only by the fact that both share a common theme."

"More common than you know," I said, then told him what I had learned on my first trip to Caspar's house.

He was pacing the small area in our living room by the time I finished. "Why didn't you tell me this before?"

I held up my hand and ticked off the reasons. "Trapped in the beyond, lost the bird statue, meeting with seer, murdered by Pilar, resurrection. Besides, you never asked me."

He glared at me. I shrugged. "All right, that wasn't fair, but to be honest, there has been so much going on, I didn't think of telling you about an item I'm trying to find for another client."

"Owen Race," Paen said as he paced by me.

"Yes."

"The same man who was said to know where the Jilin God was."

"Yes. Oh." I frowned as I glanced up at him. "You think he's involved with Pilar, don't you?"

"It makes sense that he could well be involved, yes."

"But you said Pilar was in the employ of Caspar Green," Finn pointed out. Clare nibbled on a rose leaf.

"Yes, but Caspar wanted the statue at all costs," I

said, pieces of the puzzle starting to slide together. At least a few of them were. "Pilar knew I had the bird statue, but he evidently didn't tell Caspar that."

"He was acting on his own," Finn said, nodding.

"Or on someone else's behalf," Paen corrected.

"Like Owen Race's," I said.

"He's a double agent?" Clare asked, her eyes huge. She turned to Finn. "This is so exciting! It's just like a spy movie!"

"The Jilin statue and the manuscript are clearly tied together," I said slowly, watching Paen as he paced. He was thinking like mad, too. "You never heard reference to a statue when you researched the manuscript?"

"No, never. That's why I'm so surprised now— I've never seen mention of any other object in connection to it. But the coincidences are too striking to not mean something. Just what, though, I'm afraid I don't know."

"Mr. Race might know how they're related."

"Yes, he may well. He seems to be the mysterious figure behind a number of things," Paen said.

I glanced at the clock. "It's a little after two—is that too early to drop in on him?" I asked the room in general.

"I think we should," Clare said, getting off Finn's lap. "Right now! Client or not, it would serve him right if he's been hiding something from us."

"The sooner we can talk to him—and get the statue back—the better for Sam and Mum," Finn said, getting to his feet as well. "I say let's do it."

"No. Sam needs rest," Paen declared, stopping in front of me. I looked up to his face. His eyes were glittering brightly, and not just with concern. "She's been through hell tonight. A few hours' rest won't make a difference to Mum or the *Coda*, but will do much to help Sam recover."

His scent teased me almost as much as his warmth and light attracted me. I got to my feet with languid grace that was only partially due to weakness, a slow smile on my lips. "That sounds like an excellent idea."

"But—" Finn started to protest.

Paen's hand was warm on my back as he gave me a gentle shove toward my bedroom. "Sam needs time," he said. "We owe her that much."

The door to my bedroom closed on Finn's protests. I flipped on the light and frowned. The jungle of plants that inhabited my room looked more like a wasteland blighted by some horrific pesticide. Everywhere I looked were dried, brown fronds drooping lifelessly over the sides of containers, dead stems standing stiff and brittle, and spotted yellow and brown leaves carpeting the floor so completely that it was almost invisible.

"It appears my plants don't approve of the new me," I said as I stepped over a sagging palm frond.

"So it would seem," Paen said, watching me as he leaned against the door.

"What's it going to be?" I asked, striking a pose next to a draped swatch of mosquito netting. "Fucking or lovemaking?"

"Which do you prefer?" he asked, his face unreadable.

I shrugged. "Doesn't matter to me. I enjoy both."

That got him moving. He strolled across the

detritus of plants to where I stood, wrapping one hand around my neck, his thumb brushing my pulse point. "Sam, I know what it's like. I lived as you are now for almost three hundred years. But you were right when you told me there was more than just sexual gratification to be had from a relationship."

He was so warm, so alive, the light of being shining so brightly from him I just wanted to rub against him like a cat and bask in its rays.

"Remember how it was," he said softly, his hand caressing my neck now. "Don't let that memory slip away. Hang on to what you felt with me before."

Inside me, the howling wind rose until my eyes burned with tears. "I don't want to live this way, Paen. I hurt inside. I feel so . . . distant. Separated. Alone."

You have me, sweetheart, he said as I wrapped my arms around his waist. His arms closed around me and I drank in the glorious warmth that emanated from him, both physically and spiritually. *I won't let you go, Sam. You managed to find a way into my cold, bleak heart, and I'm not going to let you leave me now.*

You say the nicest things, I said, burrowing myself closer to him. *But there's way too much talking going on here, and not nearly enough lovemaking.*

His lips closed over mine in the sweetest kiss it was possible for me to imagine. *Made your mind up, then?*

Yes. I want you to make love to me, Paen. I want you to show me again just what a wonderful thing we have together. I want you to remind me how beautiful your new soul is. I want you to save me from this coldness inside. Love me, Paen. Please, love me.

The tenderness with which he disrobed me, kissing every inch of skin exposed, almost undid me. But I decided equal time was only fair, so I concentrated on making him squirm with want as I removed his clothes.

"I thought I was supposed to be making love to you," he said, his voice strained as I cupped both hands around his erection.

"We're taking turns." I flicked my tongue in his ear and bit the lobe gently, suddenly pulling back in surprise. "Paen?"

"Not really, no, more of an ache, a good ache, but if you continue to stroke me like that, I'm not sure I'll last."

I let go of his penis and blinked a couple of times before saying, "Heh. Joke. Kiss me."

His eyes lit with mingled humor and arousal. "Ah, you wish to role-play? Normally I prefer to be the aggressor, but if it will please you, I suppose I can give in to your demands."

The touch of his mouth on mine sent familiar zings of pleasure through me, heightening my anticipation of the moment when I would taste his desire. I couldn't wait and slipped my tongue into his mouth, teasing his until it followed mine back into my mouth.

"Ow!" His head snapped back in surprise.

"It just happened," I said, running my tongue carefully over the unexpected sharp, elongated points of my canine teeth. "When I bit your ear, suddenly these . . . they just were there. Where did they come from? Why do I have them? I thought you said I didn't have to drink blood? Can I get rid of them or am I stuck with them? What am I going to tell people?"

He laughed, pulling me close against him, kissing me again, but carefully this time. "You're Moravian now, sweetheart. You have the sharp canines because you can, if you choose to, drink blood. Your body will process it and use it as fuel just as it does food. Your body is low on blood now, and wants you to take in more. That's why they manifested—you can pull them back if they bother you, otherwise they will be gone when your body no longer craves blood."

"But why did they pop out now?" I asked, flinching when the point of one of my new fangs pierced my tongue. A bead of blood welled up, sharp with a copper taste, no different from any other time I'd bitten my tongue.

"Sexual arousal is closely linked to bloodlust. Your body is craving both from me. Do you want me to feed you?"

"Blood?" I asked, half repulsed, half intrigued by the idea. "I don't know—it's never been anything that's attracted me, but . . ." I stopped, unable to put the strange new feelings I felt into words. My blood did nothing for me, nor did I particularly enjoy the drop of Paen's blood I'd tasted when we Joined, but now the thought of taking into me his life force was strangely compelling.

"It's an acquired taste," he said, a wry smile on his lips. "Why don't we give you a little taste without demanding too much?" He nipped the tip of his finger until a couple of drops shone vermilion against his skin.

"Ready?" he asked, giving me his finger.

I eyed the blood on it. "I don't know if I'll ever be ready for this," I grumbled, but took the tip of his finger into my mouth, rolling my tongue around it, the drops of blood spreading quickly. There was no bitterness, no coppery blood taste—just a spicy, heavy flavor reminiscent of mulled wine. *Oh! It doesn't taste like mine at all. This is good! Is this what it's like for you, too?*

Only with you, love, he answered, gently pulling his finger from my mouth.

"Why only with me?" I asked, licking my lips, the taste of him still lingering. A need for more rose inside me with a roar that almost drowned out the endless howl of torment that the loss of my soul had left, but I fought it down, forcing the fangs back into normal canines. Paen was hungry, too, and couldn't afford to lose blood any more than I could.

"You're my Beloved. Your blood is like ambrosia to me."

"Oh," I said, flattered. I stepped back to the bed, assuming a seductive position in the middle of it. "I'm sorry I can't be your smorgasbord tonight. I can feel how hungry you are. But perhaps we can take your mind off of that for a little bit?"

"That, sweetheart, won't be difficult to do." The bed dipped as he joined me, kneeling next to me. "I believe it's my turn again, yes?"

"Oh yes," I said, letting him roll me onto my back, pulling my legs so my calves rested alongside his thighs. I wanted to caress the arousal that waved so happily at me, but lay back when he ordered me to stop distracting him.

"You're bossy," I said, squirming as his head

dipped down and he swirled his tongue around my belly button.

"Yes, and you like it."

"Not really." His tongue licked a path up toward my breasts. "Oh, all right, just a little."

"Just a little, hmm? So if I were to tell you that I was going to suck your delicious breasts until you were on the verge of coming, at which point I concentrated my attentions on those highly sensitive ears of yours, what would you do?"

"Breasts," I gasped, digging my fingers into his shoulders and pulling him forward. "Ears! Right now!"

"And who is the bossy one now?" he asked just before taking the tip of an aching breast into his mouth. His hand slid over to my other breast, his fingers ignoring everything but the tight nipple that was demanding equal time. I'd never thought my breasts were particularly sensitive before, but the feeling of his hot mouth and dancing tongue changed my mind. He sucked, he licked, he teased and tasted and tormented until I was writhing beneath him, wave after wave of pleasure rocking my body.

"Have you ever thought of piercing your nipples?" he asked, grinning wickedly as he paused a moment while paying equal attention to my second breast. His fangs flashed in the soft light, his eyes glowing with arousal and want and, yes, love.

"No!" I shouted, arching my back so my breast would receive what it wanted. "Yes! Do it! Hurry, before I die!"

The moment before he bit the very tip of my nipple was excruciating, not with pain, but with anticipation.

When his teeth nipped my breast, the sharp burst of pain melted almost immediately into something akin to a drug rush as he sucked off the resulting drop of blood, his tongue swirling over the abused flesh like the softest velvet.

It was heaven, it was ecstasy, it was absolutely the most divine feeling I'd ever experienced . . . until he shifted and his mouth touched my ears at the same time he entered my body. I screamed, my hands digging into his flesh as he filled me with more than steely flesh—he filled the empty spaces inside me with happiness and warmth . . . and love. It was like a brilliant ray of sunshine piercing a stormy sky.

My fingernails raked down his back as I grabbed his butt, shifting my hips and pulling him deeper. "I want you inside me!" I cried.

"Sweetheart, if I was any more inside you, I'd be coming out your mouth," he said, moaning as I wrapped my legs around his hips and thrust up hard as he bit the top of my ear.

"I want you in me. I want all of you in me," I begged, the world starting to come apart as a familiar rush of rapture built. Unable to stop myself, I bit his shoulder, not a love bite, but one intended to draw blood. As my teeth pierced his skin his back arched in surprise, pulling away from me. I threw my weight onto him, sending him falling over backward onto his back. I knelt for a moment to drink in the sight of him. He was so beautiful, so masculine, but it wasn't the outside of him that I craved—it was his heart and soul and very being that I wanted.

He growled at me, actually growled as I crawled up his body, my breasts brushing the wet length of his penis. "Sam, I told you, I like to be the one in charge."

"Fine," I said, pausing to bite his hip. He gasped in surprise. I smiled as I licked up the drop of blood that welled from his skin. I flicked my tongue over first one nipple, then the other. He held his breath for a moment, clearly wondering if I was going to bite his nipple as he had done mine. I smiled reassuringly at him for a moment, then leaned down and bit an area on his rib cage. "Order me what to do, then."

He shivered as I sucked a couple of drops of blood, then without a word pulled his legs up to provide a backrest for me, grabbed my hips, and before I could do so much as utter a gasp of my own, impaled me. "Love me!" he demanded, pulling me down for a kiss, his hands urging me into a fast rhythm. I bit his tongue.

"Sam!" he snarled, pulling back. I leaned forward and bit his lip.

"I love you, Paen. Now fill me! Fill every inch of me. I want all of you!"

His mind flooded me with the emotions and sensations that racked him, the light from his love almost blinding me. I felt the elation he experienced when I bit him, and without considering the wisdom of my actions, nuzzled aside his hair and bit down on the muscle that joined his neck to his shoulder. He groaned something that sounded like an apology, then pain burst hot in me, on the same spot where I was drinking from him. His orgasm exploded to life, sending wave after wave of intoxicating rapture through both him and me, triggering my own as we each simultaneously gave and received life.

He filled me, completed me, made me whole again . . . until I came back to earth, and found myself just as hollow, just as empty as I had been before we started.

Paen held me tight while I wept through the long, dark hours of the night.

Chapter 17

"What's first?" Finn asked without any prologue when Paen and I emerged from my bedroom several hours later. "The statue or the manuscript?"

"Manuscript," Paen said at the same time I answered, "Statue."

The love of my life glared at me. "We'll find the manuscript first. You need your soul."

"We'll find the statue first," I said, ignoring his scowl to pour myself a cup of tea from a lukewarm pot and scrounge a piece of toast from the breakfast remains that Finn and Clare had left scattered over the table. "My soul is already gone, but your mother's isn't."

"We still have a day left—" Paen started to say.

I shook my head and interrupted him, speaking around a mouthful of cold toast. "You said yourself my soul is tucked away somewhere on the Akasha. It's not going anywhere, but Paen, your mother's is in danger. And my darling, you and I both know how horrible it is to live without it. I wouldn't want her to have to go through this hell."

His frown deepened until it was as dark as his eyes. Begrudgingly—his reluctance to postpone the hunt for my soul something I cherished close to my heart—he agreed. "But only because it's likely the two things are related, and if we find the statue, we should find if not the *Coda* itself, information about where it is."

"That makes sense," Clare said, pushing around a small mound of scrambled eggs with her fork. I looked at Finn, and was struck for the first time by something that hadn't occurred to me.

"You can eat food? People food, that is, rather than just . . . people?" I asked.

He grinned. "I prefer the latter, but yes, I can eat food. Clare insisted I'd fade away to nothing unless I had something other than a liquid breakfast."

"Oh." I looked at Paen. "Can you eat something other than blood, too?"

"If I had to, yes."

I spread a little grapefruit marmalade on a bit of toast. "Good. I was worried that since I was a few quarts low, you'd have to go elsewhere to have your breakfast, but if you can eat real food, that's perfect."

He shook his head. "Sam, food provides us with no nutrition. Finn and I need blood to survive. I'll just wait until you have fully recovered before I feed."

You fed off me a few hours ago, I pointed out.

Just a few mouthfuls. His voice was tinged with regret. *I'm sorry about that—I didn't intend to take any of your blood until you've recovered from the loss, but you drove me into such a frenzy it was all I could do to keep from taking more than I did.*

"I can feel how hungry you are, Paen," I said, accepting a plate of fresh eggs from Clare. "I don't particularly like the thought of you snacking off of someone else, but this is a bit of an unusual situation, so you've got my OK to round up some breakfast."

"No, I can't," he said, going to the window to carefully look through the blinds.

"I appreciate that you don't want to do the fang sink with anyone else, but I have a feeling we're going to need your strength today. So go on out and find someone to feed from. Just don't enjoy it too much."

Clare rolled her blue eyes and went to get her coat and purse.

"You don't understand. I can't feed from anyone but you," Paen said, watching out the window.

I moved over to see what he was looking at. It was raining again, a cold, dark, nasty rain that almost exactly matched the cold, dark, nasty emptiness that resided inside of me. "You can't? Is this some sort of a Beloved thing?"

"Yes. When I said a Dark One can't survive without his Beloved, I meant it. Once he finds her, human blood taken from anyone but a Beloved is poison. Likewise, the Beloved's blood is unacceptable to any other Moravian."

"Whoa," I said, a chill going down my arms. "So if I had died when Pilar tried to kill me . . ."

"Paen would have died as well," Finn said, standing to stretch. "Which is one more thing I have to thank you for, Sam."

"I thought you were immortal?" I asked Paen. "You'd die without me? Really die?"

"Eventually. It isn't a quick or pleasant process, but it is inevitable."

"Who thought up these rules?" I asked, exasperated. I didn't mind thinking that Paen would mourn me for a long time if I died, but I didn't want to be the cause of his death.

"I hope the answer to that is in the *Coda*," he said, dropping the blinds to face the room. "Have you finished?"

"Eating or asking questions?" I stuffed a last forkful of eggs into my mouth, washing it down with cold tea.

"Both."

"Yes, I'm done. Let's go find Pilar and get the statue."

"We must also have our revenge for the dress he shot!" Clare said. "It will never recover, poor thing. This evil Pilar person must pay for that crime, and for shooting you, as well, Sam."

"Nice to know I come in second to a dress," I told her as I grabbed my bag and a jacket.

"Well, it *is* a Versace," she pointed out.

"What's the plan?" Finn asked, waggling his eyebrows at Clare. "I take it you want us to do some investigating?"

I looked at Paen. His eyes were dark with introspection. "I think it's best if they tackle Reuben while we go after Mr. Race and Mr. Green, don't you?"

Paen nodded his agreement, still rubbing his jaw.

"So you're going to meet with Mr. Green while we're doing what with the poltergeist, exactly?" Clare asked as we left the apartment and headed down the stairs to the outer door. We stopped at the door so the men wouldn't have to stand around out-side while we made the last of our arrangements.

"You're going to find Reuben. It shouldn't be too hard—Paen ripped off one of his arms, and there can't be that many five-armed, former faery polter-geists around here. Here's the address of the Guard-ian we used the other night. You and Finn help her question the poltergeist about the whereabouts of the statue."

She put her hands on her hips in a faery version of pique. "Why do we have to question Reuben about where it is? You're the one who lost it."

"Stop being so snippy. Lives are at stake!"

She sighed. "I know. But that poltergeist makes me uncomfortable."

"I'm sure you'll be able to cope with him just fine. As for why you need to question him, I have no idea where the statue could be. It was taken from me, and could be anywhere in the beyond. I didn't have it when Paen pulled me through the only entrance he knew. But Pilar has no doubt told Reuben by now, so your job is to get that info from him." I glanced at the watch on her wrist. "We still have an hour before the appointment with Owen Race, so I think it's proba-bly best if we talk with Caspar Green about what he knows first, then go out to Race's house. Does that sound all right to you?"

"Yes. I have a few things I'd like to say to Mr. Green," Paen said, flexing his fingers.

I smiled at him. Amidst the horrible cold and tor-ment that raged around inside me, he brought a little spot of warmth and happiness that gave me the strength to go on.

"What if they won't tell us what we want to know?" Clare said, her brow puckered. "That poltergeist didn't look terribly smart to me."

"We'll cross that bridge when we get to it," Paen said, looking grim, his voice even grimmer. "We aren't powerless."

Clare murmured an agreement, and with that, we separated, Finn and Clare going off to see what they could find from the poltergeist while we headed to Caspar's apartment. To my surprise, he seemed to be expecting us.

"Good morning, Miss Cosse. What a pleasant surprise. And Paen Scott! Welcome to my humble home. It is indeed a pleasure to see you both again. I take it you have come to deliver the statue to me?"

"Not quite. We've come to talk about a few things with you," I said, sitting when he gestured toward a peach love seat. "Not the least of which is your choice in employees."

"Why did you try to hire Sam to find the statue when you knew I was already searching for it?" Paen asked abruptly, every line in his body radiating anger.

"Ah. I thought perhaps you might put things together. Please, Paen, take a seat. There is no need to be uncivilized about this. You are naturally upset by what would appear to be some sort of trickery on my part, but I assure you that there is none intended."

Paen snorted something rude under his breath, but sat down next to me.

Do you believe him? I asked Paen

No.

Good. Neither do I. He's lying. All my elf senses are tingling.

Sweetheart, I'm beginning to believe your elf senses are easy tinglers. But I agree—he's not telling us the truth.

"The situation is a little more complicated than I originally led you both to believe," Caspar said, making another of those hands-spread-in-honesty gestures that I didn't for a moment buy into. His face was blank, unreadable, although he seemed to be watching us with sharp, dark eyes. "In hindsight, I am perhaps a little guilty of muddying the waters, so to speak, but I assure you that everything I told you, Paen, and you, Samantha, was the absolute truth. The demon lord Oriens *has* called the statue due as payment for services rendered to Sir Alec."

I shot Paen a questioning look. *Your father is a knight?*

Baronet, Paen said, his arms crossed over his chest as he waited for Caspar to continue.

So, someday when your father decides he doesn't want the title, you'll get it?

Eventually, yes. He will pretend to die of old age in a distant location, and I will take over the title until he has passed from mortal memory, then we'll reverse the procedure. It's worked quite well the last few hundred years.

Let me get this straight—you're a brooding, sexy titled Scottish vampire?

Paen shot me a quick puzzled look. *What's your point?*

Nothing. But remind me to write a book about you someday when this is all over. I bet women would eat you up with a spoon.

"Are you finished?" Caspar asked politely, brushing an infinitesimal bit of nothing off his knee.

"Sorry. I didn't mean to stop you. Please, continue.

This is fascinating," I said, blushing a little at being caught mind-talking to Paen.

Caspar smiled, and I swear if I had been mortal, I'd have lost a couple of years off my life at the sight of it. "I have been remiss in congratulating you on finding your Beloved, Paen. My felicitations."

Paen was made of sterner stuff. "What exactly haven't you told us about the statue?"

"So forceful, so blunt and to the point," Caspar said, the creepy smile still on his lips. Something about him had changed since I last saw him. Before, he seemed like a relatively pleasant, if a bit intense, man. Now I could swear I felt tendrils of dark power snapping and crackling around him, as if he sat in the middle of an electrical charge. "You two will do well together, I think. The information I perhaps unwisely kept from you is in regards to the statue's origin."

I thought back to our last meeting. "You said that it had been commissioned from a Chinese artist and later given to Marco Polo by the emperor."

"As indeed it was. But the person who commissioned it . . . well, there is no avoiding this revelation. The person who commissioned the statue was none other than myself."

Now, that took me by surprise. I don't know what I was expecting him to say, but it wasn't that he was the one behind the creation of the statue some two thousand years ago. "So the statue was originally yours. . . . Wait a minute." I dug through my recent memories and came up with something that didn't make sense. "You told me that the statue depicted Sun Wukong, the monkey god."

"As indeed it does," Caspar agreed.

I looked at him, a sense of dread building inside me until it was so great it spilled over onto Paen. He took my hand in his, rubbing his thumb over my fingers. *What's wrong, love?*

So many things, I don't know where to start. "You also said that the person who ordered the statue created was the god of death."

Paen's thumb stilled. Outside the room, the normal sounds of Edinburgh traffic faded away until it was as still as the room in which we sat.

"That is so," Caspar said finally, a tiny muscle twitching in his eyebrow the only sign that he was less than pleased that I had such a good memory.

"You are Yan Luowang, the god of death?" Paen asked.

"It is one of my names." Caspar made an odd sort of dismissive gesture with one hand. "Not one that I have used for some time."

"You're a god of death," I said, stunned. "A Chinese god of death. A real, honest-to-god god. Of death."

"God of the fifth hell, if I remember correctly," Paen said softly to me before frowning at Caspar. "But you told me you were an alastor. How can you be both?"

Caspar's shrug was a thing of elegance. "One does not reach heights of godhood without earning such a position. I rose through the ranks, naturally. I began as a mortal, became an alastor due to the intervention of a vengeful god, and eventually assumed the mantle of god of death. To be honest, it sounds much more impressive than it was."

I had an epiphany at that point. I'd like to think it

was my own razor-sharp brain putting facts together, but I suspect it was my elf side seeing beyond the obvious. "You're also Oriens, aren't you? You're the demon lord who wants the statue."

The muscle in his eyebrow twitched twice before he got it under control. "How perspicacious of you. I see I underestimated you, my dear Miss Cosse."

Paen rose slowly to his feet. Fury rose in him, hot and red, and I knew he was going to lunge at Caspar, intending to punish the demon lord for threatening his mother. I couldn't let him do that, of course— even if Caspar didn't *seem* like one hell of a badass power, he was. I grabbed Paen's arm and dug my feet in. He snarled an epithet into my head. I held firm. *No, Paen. You can't. I know you want to stop him, but even if he looks human, he's not. He's a death god. You can't beat him up.*

"Interesting," Caspar said, watching Paen's struggle to contain his anger. "But counterproductive. I can't help being who I am any more than you can, nor do we have the time to waste in trivial shows of anger."

"Trivial!" Paen growled. I held on with both hands, murmuring soft words of reason into his head.

Caspar waved away Paen's objection as if it was a pesky fly. "Time is running out. If you do not bring the statue to me before midnight tonight, I will be forced to take what payment I can for your father's debt."

"You bas—"

I slapped my hand over Paen's mouth, oddly enough agreeing with what Caspar was saying. *My darling, my sweet, sweet Paen, I would like nothing more than to see you rip him to shreds, but he's right. We don't have the time to waste hours arguing. We have to find that statue. Now.*

We wouldn't be in this position if he hadn't invoked the debt! Paen snarled.

I know. And I agree. But there's nothing we can do now but find the statue and give it to him. So let's put aside the fact that Caspar is the source of all the trouble, and get the damned statue.

"I see you have reasoned with your lover," Caspar said with another cold smile as I half shoved Paen back into the love seat. "My estimation of you rises even more, Samantha."

I whirled around and made the meanest eyes I could at him, letting him see in them the extent of my feelings. "I swear to you by all that is holy in this world and the next, you will pay for all you have done. You have threatened the family of the man I love, and I will never forget nor forgive that."

His smile dimmed a couple of notches.

I took a deep breath and slowly let it out. "Am I correct in assuming that you still do not know where the statue is?"

"If I knew that, it would be in my possession this very moment," he said dryly. "Should I find it, I will naturally excuse the debt, but as I have had no luck finding it thus far, I am forced to rely upon one of you to bring it to me."

"Who is Pilar?" I asked, sitting next to Paen, my hand possessively on his leg. The muscles of his thigh were tense and tight, as if he was poised to spring. "Or rather, what is he?"

"Pilar?" Caspar looked surprised by the question,

he looked truly surprised. "Pilar is a minion, a kung, a water demon of low caste. He should not concern you."

He doesn't know Pilar knows where the statue is. Do we tell him?

No. We need it to fulfill the debt. There's no guarantee that he will consider it met if he finds the statue first.

There's something we're missing here—he's a demon lord, god of death, and who knows what else. But he can't find one little statue?

A slow smile curled Paen's lips. I was glad he wasn't smiling it at me. Caspar's smile might have taken a few years off my life, but Paen's promised retribution at any cost. *He's weakened. That's why he's appearing in mortal form—I'm a fool for not realizing that. The statue must be a source of power to him, and without it . . .*

Before I could read the intention in Paen's mind, he was across the room, holding Caspar off the floor by his throat. "You will pay."

"You cannot harm me," Caspar choked out, the power crackling around him as it built up. "All you can do is guarantee your mother will suffer as your Beloved has. Now release me, Dark One, before I lose my temper."

"Let him go, Paen. Let's just get this over with so we can do our job."

Paen released Caspar. I stood next to him, a united front. "Right. Why do you want this statue so badly?"

Caspar adjusted his tie and brushed out the suit jacket that had been slightly wrinkled when Paen grabbed him. "It is my statue, as I have explained. I commissioned it. It was stolen from me and given to the emperor. All I seek is to have my property returned to me."

"You told Sam the secrets of the origins of the immortal races were held within it. Is that true?"

"I did not lie to her," Caspar said with an evasive air.

Are you thinking what I'm thinking? I asked Paen.

That it's too much of a coincidence that the statue should contain the same information as the Coda?

Yep. I'm thinking there's more there than meets the eye.

"Where is Pilar now?" Paen asked Caspar.

The latter frowned. "Why do you wish to know about my minion? He is nothing, a weak kung, of no relevance."

"He's also murdered my Beloved. I have a score to settle with him," Paen said.

"And yet she still lives. Would you waste your time on something so immaterial as revenge?" Caspar asked, clearly surprised.

"We also think he might know something about the statue," I said, stepping lightly over the truth. "We'd like to talk to him. He might give us a clue."

"Pilar? Hmm." Caspar closed his eyes for a moment, the dark power aura around him suddenly snapping out feelers, as if he was sucking in power from the surroundings. Paen pulled me backward, out of reach of them. Caspar's eyes opened, anger visible in them. "He does not answer my summons."

I didn't look at Paen, but my fingers tightened around his. *Pilar has double-crossed him.*

So it would seem.

"Where is he now?" Paen asked again.

"I do not know," Caspar admitted. "He is a water

demon, so he must go to ground near the water, but I do not know his location at the moment. I will, however, have a few things to say when I find him."

"Let's get out of here," I said to Paen, my senses going nuts in the power-charged room. "I can scry Pilar's location."

"You have twelve hours," Caspar said as we brushed past him. "I must have the statue by the first hour of deep night, or your mother's soul will be forfeit."

Paen's arm shot out so fast, I almost didn't notice it. Caspar did, though. Paen's fist slamming into his nose drove the Chinese god of death backward into the wall, the impact of his body hitting it sending several delicate china cups to the floor. Caspar slumped down the wall and joined them.

"Oh, that was smart—just break the nose of a demon lord," I told Paen as we left the apartment. "Like he's not going to get you for that?"

"It was worth it," Paen said with a smile.

"Let's see if you're saying that later on tonight." I looked at his watch. "Oh, good, we're not late for the appointment with Owen Race. Let's hope the seer was right, and he does know exactly where the statue is."

"I don't doubt that the seer was correct," Paen said, getting into the car. "It's what Race will want in exchange for that information that worries me."

I slid in next to him, pointed out the side of his face was burned, and waited the few minutes it took for him to fade the burn away. "As I see it, we have an excellent bartering point. And since it is a good guess the statue and the *Coda* are tied together, it seems to

me he'd want to help us find the statue so we can figure out where the manuscript is."

We drove the short distance to Owen's house
without saying much more. Paen was apparently
busy with his own thoughts, while I tried to digest
the fact that Caspar had so deceived us. On the way
there, I made a list of things we wanted to ask, but it
was of little use.

"He's not here?" I asked the housekeeper as Paen
and I stood in the hallway of the big old house. "Is he
going to be back soon? We had an appointment to
meet him this morning."

"He said nothing to me about that," the housekeeper said, plainly wishing we'd go and leave her to
her work. "The last I heard from the professor he was
in Barcelona, and wasn't expected to be back for several days."

I looked at Paen as the door closed behind us
while we stood on the front steps. The sky was black
and sodden, rain falling in an endless misery. "He's
gone?"

"Evidently," Paen said, turning up the collar of his
coat. "I think we should—"

He stopped abruptly, grabbing my arm in a grip
that was almost painful.

"What? What is it? What's wrong?" I asked, a sudden chill brushing me.

He hauled me forward to the car, jerked the door
open, and shoved me inside.

"Hey!" I said as he slammed the door and raced
around to the driver's side. "What gives?"

He started the car and jammed his foot onto the
accelerator. "It's Finn."

"Oh? Are they interviewing the poltergeist?"

"They were," he answered, his voice deep with anger.

What's wrong? What's happened? Why are you so mad?

Paen spun the car around an intersection, blithely disregarding both traffic safety and all applicable laws. *It's Clare. She's been kidnapped. By a small, dark man with a monkey on his shoulder.*

Chapter 18

"Where is she?"

Paen pulled up in front of a small, comfortable-looking bed-and-breakfast. Finn dashed from the protective shadowed doorway to the car, climbing into the backseat as I asked my question.

"I don't know," Finn answered, his face bloodied and black with anger. "The bastard grabbed her as we were talking with Reuben. I don't know what the hell he is, but he has some serious power at his control. He slammed me up against the side of the building before I even knew what was happening. I think I was knocked out for a few minutes, because when I came to he was shoving Clare back into her car. I tried to go after them, but didn't make it far on foot. I can promise you this, though—when I find the slimy wanker, I'm going to beat the living shit out of him."

"Sam?" Paen asked, waiting for me to tell him which direction to go.

"I'll try, but no promises." I closed my eyes and cleared my mind of everything until it was as blank as a clean sheet of paper. My thoughts went to Clare, visualizing her, drawing from within all the emotions that represented her. I saw Clare as a child at a birthday party, happy and laughing; Clare as a teenager on a double date, gorgeous and poised next to my gawky, awkward self; Clare as she was last week, helping me move furniture around the dusty, dank office, happy and excited and talking non-stop. I held all of those memories and emotions tight inside me, and used them to find where she was.

"To the east," I said, looking in that direction. "She's to the east of the city."

Paen pulled out a map from a pocket on the door, spreading it out on the steering wheel. "Can you pinpoint where?"

One possibility jumped out at me. I didn't hesitate as I tapped my finger on a large beige shape. "Dunstan Moor. I just bet you he's taken her there."

"Why?" Paen asked. "Why would he want to kidnap her in order to take her to a movie set?"

"It's not the movie set that's the attraction," I said, making shooing motions until Paen pulled out onto one of the major arterials leading to the east. "It's the lodestone."

"The what?" Finn had used a couple of tissues from my purse and wiped up most of the blood that had streaked down from a cut above his eyebrow, but he still looked pretty grisly, especially in the gloomy afternoon light. Like Paen, he had shadows under his eyes, making me wonder how much sleep the two had during the past few nights.

"Lodestone." I fell silent, wondering if it really was just four days ago when Paen had walked into my office. *We're running out of time.*

I know. The pain and regret was in his voice, seeping through despite his attempts not to worry me.

I don't want your mother to have to experience this, I said, rubbing a hand on my chest, as if that would ease the constant agony of howling wind that seemed to tear me apart from the inside out.

I know you don't, love. I don't want you to have to live this way, either. We'll find the statue and the manuscript. Don't worry.

"Lodestone like the magnetic stone?" Finn asked.

"That's one meaning of the word, but in the Fae world, it also refers to a location that is strong with the magic of the beyond, a place that draws elves and faeries. It's like a doorway between realities."

"Something like the place your office is located?" Paen asked.

"Like founded land, only multiplied by about a thousand times. Lodestones are treated as holy places, as sanctuaries where only the most ancient of rituals are held. There are only three in the UK."

"And Dunstan Moor is one of these lodestones?"

"Yes. I felt it when we were there the other day, but didn't think much about it. That's why Uilleam and the other ghosts had such a strong presence—the land itself was founded, making it possible for them to be more than just an apparition in our reality."

"You think Pilar has taken Clare there?" Finn asked.

I shrugged. "It's the only logical place I can see he might want to go to in this area. Although he's a demon, and as such can't use the lodestone as a doorway, it's conceivable he could tap its power by means of some being who could, like Reuben . . ."

". . . or Clare," Paen finished the sentence.

I nodded.

"What did you find out from Reuben?"

"Nothing," Finn answered, disgust evident in his brown eyes. "It was a complete waste of time. He was clearly afraid of Pilar, and had been in hiding since Paen ripped off his arm." Finn paused for a moment. "Did you know that a poltergeist can't function without his arms?"

"Er . . . no," I said, sidetracked for a moment into wondering if they could do the starfish thing and grow back their limbs.

"Well, according to Noelle, they can't. That's why Reuben was hiding from Pilar. He couldn't go into the beyond with one arm missing."

"Odd," Paen said.

I nodded. *That pretty well sums up the entire last five days.*

The rest of the trip was accomplished in near silence, our speculations of what Pilar might be trying with Clare too troublesome to put into words. We broke some serious traffic laws as we raced into the Lammermuir Hills, passing through gently rolling hills, small farms, and endless stretches of land dotted with sheep. The sky was black as huge, ominous clouds gathered to block the sun until it was almost as dark as night. Paen followed the signs pointing the way to Dunstan Moor, pulling in at the same viewpoint where we'd parked a few days before. Although night was almost upon us, the sun sinking behind the hills surrounding the area, huge arc lights lit up the ground beyond the cluster of trailers and collections of small tents used to house wardrobe and makeup personnel.

"Looks like they're filming again," Paen said as he helped me over the guardrail.

Sounds of men yelling, assorted deathly screams, and the inevitable clash of metal confirmed Paen's guess. I glanced at the field where the mock battle was taking place, then scanned the people outside of the range of the camera. No familiar shape caught my eye.

"To hell with them, I want to know where Clare is," Finn grumbled, following after us as we made our way down the low hill, angling slightly away from the bright lights.

I stopped for a minute and tried to locate Clare using my elf senses. I couldn't feel her presence specifically, but I had a hunch we would find her where the lodestone's strength was the strongest.

"I think she's over there," I told the two men, pointing to a small rocky cliff that rose behind the trailers. I started forward through the wild moor grass, heather, clumps of bracken, and occasional bluebell that made up the terrain.

"Sam," Paen said, taking my arm so I couldn't go any farther. "Stop. We need to have a plan of action."

"Plan of action? We're going to rescue Clare, find out from Pilar where the statue is, and then we'll get Clare to get it for us," I said, a little bit annoyed at the delay.

"Pilar has Clare," he pointed out, his eyes almost as dark as the falling night. "We can't just charge up and demand he hand her over."

"Sure we can. Once he sees the two of you, he'll realize he's outnumbered."

Paen shook his head. "He's murdered you, shot Clare, and thrown Finn aside as if he was a feather."

"Well then, I'll . . . I'll . . . I don't know. I can scry something. That might help."

Paen just looked at me.

"OK, so maybe it won't help," I said, throwing up my hands in exasperation. "You two are just going to have to be all manly with him. You're big, bad, immortal vampires. Do the creatures-of-the-night thing on him."

"Sweetheart." Paen sighed, releasing my arm. "I might have an exaggerated idea of my own strength, but even I don't believe we can overpower him by ourselves. He is a demon of immense power. It's going to take more than just the three of us and brute force."

"Well, this is just great!" I said, my hands on my hips as I turned to glare at Paen. "Why the hell didn't you mention this before we drove all the way out here?"

"You told me to drive. I assumed you would have a rescue plan. Since you don't, let us create one now."

I looked at Finn. "Is your brother always this annoying?"

"Yes," he said, grinning. "But since he's usually right, we tolerate him."

"Fine," I said, crossing my arms over my chest while giving Paen a glare that would have scorched a mortal man. "What do you suggest?"

Paen looked thoughtful. "It would help if we knew exactly what sort of weaknesses water demons have. Do either of you know?"

Finn and I shook our heads.

"Sorry, they didn't teach demonology at Diviners' school."

A burst of noise from the battlefield momentarily distracted Paen. "Hmm. Then we'll have to use what we have here. Sam, tell us more about this lodestone. Is there anything related to it that we can use to gain the upper hand on Pilar?"

I thought. "Well, it's like I told you—it's a sacred place to Fae folk. Not religious sacred, but one revered because it provides a natural bridge between the beyond and this reality."

"So you're more powerful here than you are any-where else?" Paen asked.

I shook my head. "The power contained in the lodestone is not one we can tap into and use—it per-meates the area, rather than people. That's why the ghosts were able . . ."

I stopped, my eyes meeting Paen's.

"The ghosts," he said, his eyes narrowing as he looked beyond me.

"You think?" I asked, not surprised that we'd had the same thought at the same time.

"Think what?" Finn asked.

"Are they here?" Paen asked, ignoring his brother.

I scanned the area. "Not sure. I need to open my-self up to the location to find them."

"What are you thinking?" Finn asked again. "What do ghosts have to do with anything? What are you looking for?"

"Are you sure they'll have a physical presence?" Paen asked. Finn punched him in the arm. "Ow. We're thinking the ghosts might be able to help us with Pilar. Now, stop beating me before I knock your lights out."

Finn grinned at him as I closed my eyes and

cleared my mind, preparing myself to listen to the site.

"Well?" Paen asked, clearly as impatient as I was to get on with things.

"I don't see . . . oh, wait. I think maybe over there." I opened my eyes and headed around the side of the trailer cluster to a flat area that stretched upward to a rocky cliff. "Hello, Uilleam."

The big Scottish ghost turned from where he and a few of his fellow countrymen were perched on an outcropping of rocks, evidently watching the battle scene being filmed. All the men wore the same disgusted looks on their faces.

I held out my arms for him as if I was welcoming an embrace. Uilleam's face lit up. His body did the shimmering thing as he allowed himself to be grounded, striding forward to me with a calculating look in his eye. I ran for Paen and held up a hand for him to stop before he could pull me into another ghostly kiss. "Up to you, master linguist. Let's see if they're interested in helping us fight for Clare."

Four minutes later we streamed over the rocks that marked the edge of the cliff, behind us an army of ghostly Scottish warriors, all of whom were aching for a good brawl.

"You know what this reminds me of?" Finn asked. "Something out of Tolkien. Paen could be Aragorn with his army of the dead, and you could be Legolas, while I am—"

"You are going to be one sorry Moravian if you continue with that analogy," I said, giving him a look that let him know I meant what I said. "I have no compunction about decking you if I have to."

Finn laughed, but the merriment dried up a few moments later when we reached the base of the cliff.

"Sam?" Paen asked, obviously hoping for some insight on my part.

"They're here," I said, holding my hands out, palms down toward the ground. "We're at the heart of the lodestone. I can feel they're here. There's something disturbing the grounding."

"Disturbing it how?"

I tried to locate the source of the disturbance, but the waves of power coming from the location itself were muddying the feeling. "Disturbing it. Making it not happy. I can only assume it's Pilar. Demons normally avoid places strong in power from the beyond, so it makes sense that such places wouldn't like them any more than the reverse."

"Then why did he bring Clare here?" Finn asked.

"Because it provides access to the statue, naturally," a voice called down from above us.

Uilleam shouted and pointed his sword at the cliff face. Standing on a ledge about halfway up, Pilar held a knife to Clare's throat. Beppo sat chirping on a rock next to them. The ghosts roared something that made the hairs on my neck stand on end, and started swarming up the cliff.

"No!" Pilar yelled down at them, dragging Clare backward into what looked like a shallow cave. "Call them off, or I will kill the faery."

"I am not a faery," Clare snapped, trying to glare at the demon who held her by the throat. "I am a lingerie model. There is a huge difference between the two things! Why does no one else see that?"

Paen shouted something to Uilleam. The ghosts

stopped their ascent, but they weren't happy about it, snarling and waving their swords around in a menacing fashion.

"She's a faery, she's immortal," I called up to Pilar. "There's no sense in threatening to kill her—you can't."

"I am *so* not a faery!"

"She'll be dead enough if I decapitate her," Pilar called back.

"Oh!" Clare yelled, looking even more indignant.

"All right, we've stopped the ghosts," I answered, moving a little to the side so I could have an unobstructed view of Pilar. Paen wrapped an arm around me and pulled me up tight against him. "Now, let's talk. Why do you want Clare? She doesn't have any powers except the ability to talk to flowers—"

"You are such a liar," my cousin gasped.

We all ignored her. "—and the ability to wear sackcloth and make it look good. So why do you want her, of all people?"

Pilar laughed. "I wanted her because I thought you were dead. But as you survived, you will do. I will exchange your cousin for you."

"You've got a deal," I said without hesitation, pulling away from Paen.

"Like hell he does," Paen snarled, pulling me back and stuffing me behind him. "You'll take me instead."

"Hey!" I said, slapping my hand on his back. "Less arrogance, if you please. He wants me."

"He's not getting you." *You don't honestly believe I'm going to allow a demon to take you, do you?*

He can't hurt me, Paen. I'm immortal now, remember?

He can decapitate you just as easily as he can Clare.
But he won't. He needs me.
It's a moot point. I'm not letting you sacrifice yourself.

"You may have your soul, Dark One, but you cannot enter the beyond on your own," Pilar said, jerking Clare closer. "Nor can your brother."

"I don't have a soul now, so neither can I," I yelled around Paen, up to Pilar.

"No, but you have a cousin who can," he said. "You will be a hostage for her."

"It doesn't matter who can enter what—Sam is here, and I'm not letting her go," Paen said, stubbornness positively rolling off him.

I thumped him on the back again. *Paen, truly I appreciate the anguish you feel at the thought of losing me, but I swear to you I'm not going to let him kill me. Again.*
No.
We don't have a choice!

"Then we appear to be at an impasse," Pilar said, glancing up at the sky. The clouds that had darkened the sky all day were starting to dissipate, little peeps of a quarter moon shining through the breaks. "It is almost deep night. Do you really wish to continue this stalemate until you run out of time?"

I pulled Paen until he was facing me. "We're out of options, sweetie."

His brow darkened, and I could feel the protests he was about to make. I laid a finger across his lips, gently brushing them away. "I know. I feel the same way. But I will not let Caspar have your mother's soul, not while it's within my ability to stop him."

His Adam's apple bobbed as he fought to keep his emotions under control. *I won't lose you again,*

Sam. I can't. You made me love you, dammit! You made me give up brooding, and sex without love, and happily going about my way without interference from anyone. You owe me!

I laughed, leaning into him to replace my fingers with my lips, offering him everything I had, pouring into him all the love I felt, accepting in return from him the radiant warmth of his soul, crested by a love so powerful it seemed to rock the world back on its axis. *I love you, Paen. I love you more than I ever imagined was possible for one person to love another. You are the sun to me, you warm me and give me life, and I could not exist any longer without you. But I have to do this. We have to save Clare and your mother, and if you can think of another way to do it, I'm all ears.*

Pain cut sharply through him, pain and regret, and anger at himself for not being able to save me.

But you did save me, I told him, drinking in his warmth as he pulled me up tight to his body. *You didn't let me die before, and I know you won't let me go now. No matter what happens, I know you won't let go.*

"I'll see to it nothing happens," he said grimly, pulling his mouth from mine. He half turned, calling over his shoulder to Pilar, "Release Clare, and you can have Sam and me as hostages."

Beppo jumped onto Pilar's shoulder. The demon seemed to consider Paen's offer for a moment before shrugging. "If you wish to offer yourself as well, I will not object. You may approach us, but only you two. No one else."

Paen had to have a short talk with Finn, Uilleam, and the ghosts before they would let us climb up to where Pilar and Clare waited. I got the feeling that unlike Finn, the ghosts weren't so much upset with Paen and me putting ourselves in potential danger as they were pissed at being done out of a good fight.

"You can fight later," I told Uilleam as I scrambled up a large rock at the base of the cliff.

"Do we have yer oath on that?" he asked, fingering the edge of his sword.

I looked in surprise at him for a moment. "You speak English?"

"We're dead, not daft," he said with a roll of his eyes. "We've naught else to do around here but listen to the tourists. At least, not until this lot came." He indicated the movie crew with a sweeping gesture.

"Oh. Right. Well, then, if you guys can just hold tight for a bit, I promise you we'll find someone for you to battle later. Pretend battle. No killing or anything."

The ghosts looked disappointed.

"Later," I said, giving Uilleam a warning look as I reached up to where Paen was waiting to haul me up a big rock.

We reached the outcropping where Pilar and Clare stood without any mishaps.

"Let her go," Paen ordered, nodding toward Clare.

Pilar smiled and released Clare, who took two steps to the side, then turned and slapped Pilar as hard as she could.

"That's for shooting my dress, you demonic twit!" she told him to his startled face before storming over to Paen and me.

"Her dress?" Pilar asked us.

I shook my head. "Honestly, you don't want to go there."

"It was a Versace!" came the outraged reply from where Clare was standing behind me.

Pilar closed his eyes for a moment, wearing an expression that was identical to one I'd seen frequently on Paen's face. I thought about pointing that out, but decided it wasn't something Paen needed to know at that moment. "If you don't mind, I'm rather anxious to have the Jilin God. Could we get on with it?"

"We can if you answer a couple of questions first," I said, taking Paen's hand. Just touching him toned down the howl of pain inside me that was my ever-present companion.

Pilar glanced at the sky again and gave another shrug. Beppo gave a little squeak and leaped from Pilar to Paen, quickly scaling his arm, jumping across him to land on my shoulder. I gave the monkey a stern look. "You didn't tell me you belonged to him," I said, nodding toward Pilar.

"He is a familiar—he does not speak," Pilar said, as if I honestly expected the monkey to answer. "What questions do you wish to ask of me?"

"Where is the Jilin God?" Paen asked, his fingers tightening around mine. Beppo wrapped his tail around my throat and began to pick through my hair, looking for mites.

"Within grasp in the beyond."

"Why did you zap me into the place between realities? Were you afraid of what I was going to tell Caspar?"

Pilar looked at me with unemotional black eyes. "I am afraid of nothing. It was not my intent to push you into the web; I simply wanted the statue. I didn't realize you had it until I touched you."

"Are you working for your master, or for yourself?" Paen asked.

You took my question!

There are plenty left for him to answer.

Pilar laughed. I didn't think demons could laugh, but he did, a mirthless, cold laugh, one that sent chills down my back. "I have no master."

"Wait a second—you do, too. Caspar said you were his minion, that he hired you to drag me in to see him, amongst other things. He's a demon lord, you're a demon—that makes him your master."

"Do you not yet understand?" Pilar asked, looking at me with an expression of something that looked a lot like disappointment. "The being you know as Caspar Green is not my master—he is my enemy. He tried to capture me, and failed. He tried to have me thrown down from the heavens, and failed. He has sought my destruction his entire life, and now he seeks to regain his former strength in order to rule this world. I am sworn to allow neither."

"But . . . you were working for him," I pointed out, wondering just how many surprises I could take in a one-week period.

Pilar gave me another disappointed look. "He did not recognize me in this form."

"Oh."

Paen's fingers tightened even more around mine until the grip was almost painful. "You are the sworn enemy of Yan Luowang, the god of death."

"Yes," Pilar said. I noticed he didn't give Paen a disappointed look.

"He attempted to have you thrown out of heaven,"

Paen said, and with his words, something struck a chord in me.

Figured it out yet, sweetheart?

Wait a sec . . . thrown out of heaven?

That's what he said.

I bit my lip as I looked closely at Pilar. He looked human, absolutely mortal, except for the cold that seemed to roll off him like a dense fog. "Caspar said you were a kung, a Chinese water demon."

"I am many things. That is just one part of what makes me a whole."

The pieces of the puzzle fell together with a snap that I could have sworn was audible. "Were you, by any chance, held prisoner in a stone prison for fifteen hundred years?"

Pilar smiled.

"You're Sun Wukong, aren't you? The monkey god? The subject of the Jilin statue? The one Buddha released, the one who became a champion against demons."

"And their lords. Now I seek to stop Yan Lu-owang, whatever the cost such an action may demand." Pilar made a polite little bow. "And you, Beloved, will do very nicely as the blood price."

Chapter 19

"I thought you were supposed to be the sacrifice?" Clare groused as she took my hand. "I don't see why I have to come along."

I looked beyond her to Paen, giving him a small, hopeful smile. He didn't return it.

"You have to pull me into the beyond. Evidently since I'm soulless, I can't enter or leave it on my own, but you can take me there."

"It's a ridiculous plan," she snorted, casting pathetic glances at Paen. "Don't you think it's ridiculous?"

"Very much so," he said.

"Stop doing that. Paen is on the edge as is," I whispered to Clare, jerking her hand to get her attention. "My hands are full trying to keep him from attacking Pilar, without you baiting him into an action we'll all regret."

"Well, it is silly. I don't know anything about this beyond place. I don't know why he thinks I'm going to be able to find the statue," she said, frowning at Pilar.

Beppo sat on his shoulder, making occasional

chirruping noises as Clare and I prepared to retrieve the statue.

"You do not have to find it. The Beloved will find it. She was born of the light; she will have powers there," Pilar told her for the third time. "Just do as you've been instructed."

"Yes, but it's all so very silly," Clare said, stalling like mad.

"Look at it this way," I told her. "At least if we die, we'll die together."

Her look of outrage would have brought a mortal to her knees. "I am not going to die!"

"I know that," I soothed, giving her hand a friendly squeeze.

"I should hope you do," she said, transferring her glare from me back to Pilar.

"Faeries can't die," I added, smiling at her outraged snarl. "Come on, Glimmerharp. Let's get this over with so we can take care of Caspar."

Clare swore colorful oaths at me as we turned and walked straight toward the rock face, where Pilar had indicated the nearest entrance to the beyond was. I was just about to ask her if she talked to her mother with that mouth when we hit a wall—or rather, I did. Clare passed through it, but I was held back by a field that didn't want to let me pass.

"Clare, you're going to have to pull," I said, pushing myself against the barrier between realities. "I can't . . . seem . . . to get thr—"

She wrapped a second hand around my wrist and yanked with a strength that was surprising. I was jerked clean through the barrier into the beyond, stumbling over a rock and falling to my knees, the shock of passing through it enough to strip the air from my lungs.

Sam? Are you all right? You disappeared. Paen's voice was warm and reassuring in my head, but it was different somehow—stretched, as if it came from a great distance.

I'm fine, I answered, getting to my feet, brushing the knees of my jeans as I took a quick look about. *Just a little shaky. I don't think that was the most graceful entrance I've ever made. Everything OK out there?*

Yes. Pilar and I are having a stare-down.

Who's winning?

He is. I don't think he has eyelids.

Maybe you should offer to arm-wrestle him, or have a spitting contest or something, I said, gathering up every warm emotion I could muster in the cold void of my soulless self, and sending them to him.

I love you, too, he said, and for a moment, he shared his warmth and light with me, reminding me again that I wasn't alone.

Clare looked around us. "This is certainly different. Where did all these trees and lovely flowers come from? And that brook? I know that brook wasn't there a few seconds ago," she said, pointing to a stream of silver that spilled over the rocks in a graceful display that promised refreshment and relaxation to any who paused to sit a while near it.

"You're in the beyond, now, Clare. Things are different here. Expect Disney music and dancing teacups at any moment. Put down that dove you found and come along. We have places to go, statues to rescue, demon lords to cream."

"Where exactly are we going?"

"To find the statue."

"I know that, silly," she said, snatching up a handful of wildflowers as I held out my hands, feeling for a familiar tingle that would herald a wrinkle. "But where is the statue?"

"Evidently where Pilar stashed it, somewhere around Caspar's apartment."

"Doesn't he know where he put it?"

"Yes, but things get shifted slightly in the beyond, so all he could say is that it would be somewhere near the apartment."

"But that's all the way back in town," she said, wandering over to where a silhouetted version of Pilar stood a few feet away from Paen. She waved her hand in front of his face. "They can't see us?"

"No. What you're seeing is the representation of him in the beyond. His aura is black because he has been tainted by dark powers." A little frisson of something went up my left hand as I felt along the rock face. I moved over a step, running both hands along the minute stream of power.

"Paen's aura isn't black," she said, looking at him. When you're in the beyond, people in the other reality appear shadowed slightly, as if you are viewing them through a thin veil, which I suppose is as good a simile as anything. "But he was cursed."

"He has a soul now. Ah. Here it is." I slipped my fingers into the stream, gently pulling it apart until there was a shimmering portal wide enough to allow a person through.

"The statue?" Clare asked, wandering over to me.

"No, the wrinkle. Come on, I don't know if it'll stay open once I go through it."

"Wrinkle? What's that?"

I hauled her in after me. It was like walking through a faint field of electricity. One moment we were on the side of a cliff in the Lammermuir Hills; the next we were standing at the end of the street on which Caspar's apartment was located.

"*How* did you do that?" Clare asked, quickly stuffing a petal in her mouth.

I shot her an exasperated look. "Didn't you ever watch any *Star Trek* shows? It's a wrinkle in the time/space continuum. Or something like that—I'm not quite sure what the technical name for it is. All I know is you can use the wrinkles to travel to another area in the beyond. You take that side of the street, I'll do this one."

Needless to say, Clare was too overwhelmed to do much but follow me as I searched the sidewalk and area surrounding the steps leading into Caspar's building.

"Crapbeans," I said, shoving a garbage can back under the stone steps leading up to the doorway. I dusted off my hands, giving the building a wary look. "I guess this means we're going to have to go inside."

"Oooh," she said, her eyes big. "Will he notice us, do you think?"

"I'm not sure. He's a demon lord, so he shouldn't be able to see into the beyond, but he's also a god, so who knows what the extent of his powers are?" I pushed down the feeling of dread that rose as I started up the stairs.

All right, sweetheart?

The warm glow of Paen's being filled me. *I am*

now, I answered, smiling at him but unable to stop the sharp pang of regret. *If only things were as they had been . . .*

We'll get it back, love. We'll get them both back, he promised me.

I took a deep breath, sent a heartfelt prayer to let us all get through this without any more tragedies being inflicted, and opened the door to the apartments.

"Don't you have to press the buzz . . . oh!" Clare sucked in her breath as she followed me into the building, rubbing her arms and shivering.

"We're not restricted by the boundaries of our reality in the beyond," I said, shivering as well.

Caspar's apartment might be on the third floor, but his presence turned the inside of the building black as night, seeping into every corner, filling it with a veritable miasma of dense, inky being. The only light we had was that coming off of Clare and myself—Clare's pure soul providing a halo of light around her, while faint sunlight seemed to gently glow from my skin.

"No wonder my elf senses were going berserk here," I said, rubbing the back of my neck where the hairs were standing on end.

Clare said nothing, but grabbed my hand. We climbed the stairs in silence, carefully making our way through the darkness, doing our best to search each inch of the landings, stairs, and hallways as we came to them.

"Well," I said what seemed like an eternity later as I stood outside a door labeled 12-C. "I guess we're going to have to go in and see if it's right under Caspar's nose."

"Oh, no," Clare said, backing down the hallway. "There is no way I'm going into that apartment."

"I don't think he can see into the beyond," I said, biting my lip. "We should be safe enough."

"No. Absolutely not. And I think you're insane for even thinking about going in there."

"Well, I'm not too wild about the idea myself, in case you hadn't noticed." I thought for a minute. "What we need is a distraction, something to grab Caspar's attention in case he can see us."

"How are you going to do that?" she asked, her face puckered with worry.

Paen, my love, we need some help.

I knew it! You're in trouble, aren't you? Tell Clare to pull me in—

We are not in trouble. We just need help. I need someone to capture Caspar's attention so we can check his apartment for the statue.

Paen created and discarded any number of objections to the thought of us going into the apartment, but he wasn't the man I loved for nothing. *Let me talk to Pilar.*

We huddled together in the darkness of the apartment hallway, vaguely aware when one of the mortal inhabitants passed by on their way to or from their homes, but mostly just aware of the profound sense of dread that seemed to soak into everything, ourselves included.

Go ahead, Sam, Paen told me eons later. *Noelle is conducting a ritual to summon Caspar. It should keep his attention off you, but she says you'll only have about five minutes before she has to stop the ritual.*

Perfect. Thank her for me, will you? Uh . . . you can't do the mind thing with her, can you? I asked, a little spike of jealousy going through me at the thought of someone else sharing something so intimate with Paen.

Ever hear of a mobile phone, sweetheart? he said, laughing into my mind.

I knew where Caspar was the second we slipped into the apartment. He was in the sitting room, the same lovely peach and cream room that had seemed so peaceful to me before, but was now a place of such horror my stomach clenched.

"Sam?"

The whisper barely penetrated the blackness. I turned back to where Clare stood in the doorway, her arms clutched around herself.

"I don't think I can go in."

I took one look at the terror in her eyes and went over to give her a reassuring hug. "It's OK. I've been here before, so it won't take me any time to go through the room I was in when Pilar zapped me. You just stay here, OK?"

"OK," she said, hugging me tightly. "If I was a faery—not that I am, but if I was—I'd rub magic faery dust on you to keep you safe."

I smiled and didn't point out the fact that the front of my shirt glowed with the incandescent light from the faery dust which had rubbed on me when we hugged. Instead I mentally girded my loins, marched over to the sitting room door, and prayed that Noelle the Guardian had enough power to keep a demon lord occupied while I stood only a few feet away from him.

I needn't have worried. Caspar was there in the room, standing in the middle, but he was frozen, as if locked in that position. Little curlicues of dark power snapped around him, but I clearly didn't register on his consciousness as I scooted around him, heading for the chair I'd sat on during my second visit.

The statue was tucked away behind a settee, still wrapped in the blue cloth. I snatched it up, uncovering just a bit of it to make sure it was really the statue before making a dash for the door.

Unfortunately, I forgot to watch where I was going, and tripped over a small footstool that sat almost hidden away under a table. Almost.

The statue flew from my hands as I fell to the floor, slamming up against the wall. My knees cracked painfully on the hardwood floor as I lunged forward to grab the statue before it could rebound, but to my complete and utter surprise, it didn't bounce off the wall like a proper brass statue of a falcon should.

Instead it shattered in an explosion of brass-coated plaster, the pieces of the bird falling into large chunks on the hardwood floor with several large thunks, the biggest of which was made by a small black statue of a monkey.

Caspar roared a scream of anger behind me as he broke the bonds of the summoning and spun around to see me scrambling madly toward the Jilin statue.

"You!" he screeched, his voice literally causing the windows to erupt into a thousand little shards of glass.

"Holy crap," I muttered, not taking the time to pick the monkey statue out of the debris of the bird— I just scooped it all up, hugged it to my chest, and bolted for the front door.

"Run, Clare, he's on to us!" I bellowed. She didn't

stop to ask who; no doubt she caught a glimpse of the monstrosity behind me.

Paen, pull us out, I yelled, my skin erupting into pain as Caspar's tendrils of power lashed out and caught me, holding me fast at the doorway.

"Noooooo!" Clare screamed, grabbing my arm to keep me from being pulled back in.

Bless his heart, Paen didn't bother with asking unimportant questions—he simply merged himself with me, filling me, holding me, binding me to him, and what was most important at that moment, yanking both Clare and me out of the beyond, back onto the cliff shelf on the Lammermuir Hills.

I threw myself into Paen's arms, unmindful of the sharp corners of the bits of statue I held clutched to my body, so grateful to be away from Caspar, tears mingled with the kisses I pressed to his face.

"Clare," Finn shouted from the plain below.

"I'm all right," she yelled back, going to the edge to wave at him. "But that demon lord was awful! He was the most horrible thing I've ever seen!"

Behind us, the stone groaned as if in protest.

"He was hideous, all black and twisted and misshapen!"

The sound of a thousand souls in agony ripped through us as the fabric of being was shredded.

"I think I would die if I were ever to see him again, he was just that awful," Clare called to Finn.

Caspar stepped out of the beyond, power coiled around him like snakes, writhing and twisting, snapping at everything they could reach. The ground shook, as if protesting Caspar's presence in such a sacred spot.

"I see you found my statue," he said, his voice filled with the promise of eternal torment. "I will take it back now, if you don't mind."

An immense cracking noise rent the air, causing everyone to cover their ears. The rocky shelf we stood on shattered, the stone crashing to the ground below, taking us with it.

Chapter 20

The silence that followed the roar of rocks and shrieks of the soft, squishy humans (or variations thereof) as they fell to the ground was almost as deafening in its absence as the sound was previously.

Samantha? Are you hurt?

I groaned and shoved a cantaloupe-sized bit of boulder from my arm before rolling off Paen. *My left wrist might be broken. It hurts bad enough that I may barf. Are you OK? Why did you grab me right as we fell? I must have crushed you when we hit the ground.*

I grabbed you so you wouldn't be crushed. Let me see your arm.

A red wave of pain and nausea threatened to overwhelm me as I struggled into a sitting position, my hurt arm held tight to my chest. "I'm fine," I told Paen as he tried to examine my arm. He had a nasty gash in his cheek that spilled blood down the side of his face, but he looked relatively all right. "Find Clare."

"Clare? Where are you, love?" Finn loomed next to me, hurling rocks aside as he searched for my cousin. "Can you hear me?"

"Of course I can hear you," came a muffled reply from about ten feet away. Finn gave a relieved shout and flung rocks willy-nilly until Clare's torso was uncovered.

"What about Pilar and Caspar?" I asked Paen as he turned back to me. The rear side of him was covered in blood, his shirt tattered and bloody from where he had hit the debris-strewn ground. Beyond him, Uilleam and the ghosts approached, leaping from rock to rock.

Paen snarled an oath as he helped me to my feet. "Who the hell cares about them?"

"Oh! Just look at this shirt! Just look at it! It's completely ruined!" Clare pushed aside Finn's helpful hand as she lunged a few feet away to where Pilar and Beppo emerged unscathed from behind a truck-sized boulder. I was glad to see that despite being bloody and filthy, Clare hadn't been hurt.

A state that would change if she had her way.

"This is the second outfit of mine you've ruined," she screeched at Pilar, snatching up a rock and brandishing it. "This shirt is raw silk, hand-screened by Donna Karan herself! And now it's totally ruined!"

"Clare, no, he's the monkey god! You can't hit a god!" I yelled, but not before she cracked Pilar upside the head with the stone. He stared in stark surprise at her for a moment, then threw his head back and roared his fury to the night sky.

"Christ on a handcar, I can't take her anywhere," I swore, starting toward her—but at the exact moment that Pilar turned his furious eyes to my cousin, an explosion sent us all ducking. Debris rained down upon us, rocks and sticks and chunks of earth pelting us without discretion, the air thick with the stink of demons as Caspar emerged from a pyramid of broken rock. Behind him, a good hundred or so demons swarmed out of the ground, leaping onto the nearby rocks, their shrieks cutting into the night.

"Sun Wukong!" Caspar bellowed, his face black with rage.

"Oh, shit," I said, watching in horror as Caspar flung open his arms and called up his demon horde.

"My feelings exactly," Paen answered, scooping me up in his arms and hauling me to the large rock Uilleam was perched on. "May I?" he asked, setting me down before holding out his hand.

"Sun Wukong, you have deceived me!" Caspar screamed, pointing at Pilar.

Uilleam grinned and yanked off the sword that was strapped to his back. Since he had another in his right hand, I guessed the second was a spare, for emergencies. "Aye, ye're welcome to Old Mab. She's got a wicked bite to her."

"Um . . . Paen . . ."

"As you deserved, Yan Luowang," Pilar called back to him. Beppo hopped off his shoulder as Pilar leaped a good eight feet onto the boulder nearest him, striking a dramatic pose as he addressed the enraged demon lord. "You have defiled this reality for long years. Now it is time for you to be sent back to the fifth hell where you belong!"

"Stay here where you're safe, love," Paen told me before nodding toward the demons climbing down the rocks. "Shall we?"

"Aye, we shall," Uilleam answered, then lifted his sword high as he gave a battle cry. The ghosts shouted in return as they ran forward to meet the on-slaught of demons, Finn and Paen at the front.

"This time, I will have my revenge," Caspar swore, lifting his right hand. Power crackled off it like miniature lightning. "This time, I will destroy you."

I closed my eyes for a moment and wished myself anywhere but here, about to witness the showdown of two ancient gods. I opened them again when I heard a chirruping—Beppo was picking through the rubble at my feet.

"Isn't this exciting?" Clare asked, coming over to where I was seated. "It's just like something out of *Lord of the Ri*—"

I shot her a look that stopped the words dead, and slid off the rock to carefully make the few steps over to where Beppo was struggling with a stone.

"You're too sensitive," Clare told me, then frowned at the monkey. "What's he doing?"

"I don't know, but I have a feeling—hey! Come back here with that! That's my statue!"

The clash of steel and screams of demons rose into a wave of noise as the ghosts and vampires met the attacking demons. I threw myself after Beppo, intent on retrieving the black monkey statue he'd found in the rubble, but at that moment, two bright lights hit the area, taking everyone by surprise for a second. The lights were blinding, causing me to stumble over a rock and hit the ground a second time.

"Cool, reenactors," a black silhouette with an American voice said from behind the huge arc lights.

Around us, the battle raged, the noise of it almost deafening.

"What are those ugly brown things they're fighting?" another voice asked.

A red wave of pain and nausea rolled over me as my bad arm smashed against a rock. I retched up my last meal, gasping for air, desperately trying to stay conscious as my body rid itself of everything in my stomach.

"Who cares?" the first voice answered. "Just film it, it's great footage. Watch your step, there's a woman puking right here."

"That's my cousin, if you don't mind," Clare said indignantly as she bent over me, pausing to ask in a much more civil tone, "Are you movie people?"

"Dude, check out the babe," the second man said, nudging the first with his elbow.

"I'm a model, not a babe," Clare answered, and despite her frivolous nature, ignored them to help me to my feet.

"Get the statue," I gasped, the world spinning around me as I tried to fight down another wave of nausea.

"What? Oh." Clare pointed at where Beppo was leaping from rock to rock, dodging the flying bodies and spinning swords to reach his master. "Too late."

"No, it bloody well isn't," I answered, staggering forward as best I could.

Sam! Stay where you're safe! Paen was next to a huge boulder, swinging a sword black with demon blood, one demon clinging to his side while two others rushed toward him. Behind him, Finn was fighting with a battle-axe, the two men protecting each other's backs. They used their weapons with such skill, and moved with such coordination—one swinging left while the other went right—I wondered if it was due to skill or experience.

That damned monkey has the statue. I'm OK, just take care of yourself. Above you!

Paen snarled an obscenity in my head as a demon threw itself down on him. I knew I would be helpless in battle with a broken arm, so I plunged forward, through the fringes of ghosts battling demons.

"That's mine," I yelled to Pilar as Beppo leaped up his arm, the Jilin statue in the monkey's furry little hands.

Pilar smiled as he took the statue from Beppo, turning to raise it triumphantly over his head. "Behold, Yan Luowang! The statue which you created in my image! It has returned to me at last."

"Nooooooo!" screamed Caspar from where he perched on a rock. His body twisted in anguish—or so I thought for a moment. As it continued to twist it grew, lengthening, folding up on itself, his features becoming misshapen parodies of a human face. I realized then that he was changing out of his human form, his true demon lord body being revealed. It was a horrible sight, so foul my eyes instinctively skittered away from looking at him. "Revenge . . . will . . . be mine!"

"Into this vessel you poured all your hatred, all your knowledge of the Old Ways. With its destruction, so shall you be returned to your origins. Return to the fifth hell, Yan Luowang! Return and leave this world in peace!"

"No!" I screamed, Caspar's anguished howl a horrible echo. I snatched up a palm-sized rock, took aim, and hurled it directly at Pilar's head. The piece fell harmlessly at his feet as he turned to look at me. "I brought it back! It's mine! You are not going to destroy it!"

"You will not win this time!" the horrible monstrosity that was Caspar screamed, and leaped toward us. Finn, Paen, and the ghosts all moved as one to stop him.

"Man, what's with ugly guy's costume? Someone's been playing way too much Dungeons and Dragons," one of the film people said.

"Dude," the other one said in acknowledgement, and turned the camera on the sight of the demon lord version of Caspar going down under a swarm of Scottish ghosts.

Pilar grabbed me by the throat and hauled me upward, until I was dangling a good six feet off the ground. "You dare intervene in a sacred duty?"

"It's my statue," I croaked, unable to breathe with the hold he had on my neck. "I found it first."

Sam! Paen shouted, evidently having just seen my predicament. I knew without looking he was hacking and slashing his way through the demons that were trying to free their master.

"It must be destroyed," Pilar told me, unmindful that I was turning blue. "It contains the source of his powers. Without it, he will be confined to hell, where he belongs."

"Can't . . . breathe . . ." I gasped.

"It was given to you by mistake," Pilar continued, just as if I wasn't slowly asphyxiating in front of him. "It was taken by Paymon, a rival demon lord, several hundred years ago. I knew Paymon would not allow Yan Luowang to have it, so I was content to wait. But

Yan Luowang is clever. He has gathered power over the centuries, waiting for the moment when he could steal the statue back. I bartered for it from Paymon before he could do so."

"I . . . can't . . . breathe . . ." My lungs ached to draw in a breath, but Pilar's grip on my neck prohibited any air from passing.

"Here come the Marines," one of the Americans called out as behind him, film extras ran to join the battle, yelling enthusiastically as they had been coached to do. I wanted to shout at them, to warn them that they could be killed, but there was no way I could do anything but dangle helplessly in front of Pilar. I clawed at his hand with my one arm, but he didn't seem to have any trouble at all holding me up for an extended period of time.

"As the servant of Yan Luowang, I was able to monitor his quest for the statue. It would be just a matter of time before the Dark One he charged with finding it would come to you, so I attempted to remove you from the scene by giving you another task, but you, foolish one, would not leave."

The screams of several men tore through the night as a veritable volcano of Scottish ghosts erupted off of Caspar, their bodies cartwheeling as they were flung high before plummeting back to the ground.

"Now, that is some quality battle choreography," one of the Americans commented. "No wires, yet. Impressive."

"You . . . Owen . . . Race?" Red spots started appearing before my eyes. My legs kicked madly as I tried to break the hold Pilar had on me.

"Instead, you intercepted the minion Paymon had

sent to bring me the statue, completely mucking up my carefully laid plans. Yes, I am Owen Race. I am also known as Samaria Magnus." Pilar stopped for a moment to narrow his eyes at me. "You are not a very good investigator. You should find some other form of employment."

"Sun Wukong, I will be—" Caspar went down again as a herd of movie extras flung themselves on him.

"Tried to . . . kill us?"

Pilar gave me another of his disappointed looks. "You do not know what will happen if Yan Luowang were to regain power. He would not be content to rule in Abaddon—he would lay claim to the mortal world as well. I would do anything to stop him, even if it meant killing innocents."

The red spots merged into puddles and formed interesting shapes as they danced before me. "Why . . . tell me?"

Between them, Pilar looked moderately surprised at my question. "It is traditional, I believe, for the villain to explain all his plans just before he kills off the pesky heroine."

"Not . . . pesky . . . *determined* . . ." I gave up fighting him, and hung limp from his grip, the burn in my lungs so great I just wanted the red blobby things to ease my suffering.

"You're not watching enough movies, demon. The audience always wants to see the hero win," a deep, masculine, angry Scottish voice said behind him.

"Dude, catch the guy on the rock with the bodacious sword!" a voice called out over the roar of the battle.

"Can't, filming the D and D guy. Look at him go! He's picking them off like they were fleas."

"Paen, no!" I managed to choke out, blinking madly to clear my vision. Paen had managed to get on the rock behind Pilar, and was in the middle of a downswing that, judging by the size of the sword he carried, likely would divide the monkey god.

Pilar swung around, his arm raised to block Paen's attack.

It was too late for Paen to stop the downswing, but he didn't even ask why I wanted mercy for the man who was currently choking the life out of me—he threw his body weight to the side so the sword struck Pilar at a different, less deadly angle.

"What is it about you and arms?" I asked, gasping in great lungsful of air as the stranglehold Pilar held on my throat was released by dint of Paen lopping off his arm. I rubbed my throat, wondering if I'd ever be able to swallow again.

Paen and Pilar stared at the gruesome member lying at their feet.

"Er . . ." Paen said, then looked at me. "Why didn't you want me to kill him?"

"You took my arm off!" Pilar said, his face filled with amazement.

"Because he's a good guy," I answered Paen hoarsely, wincing at the sound of my voice. Paen's eyes narrowed on my throat.

"Good guys don't try to throttle innocent women," he said, swinging the sword back up so the tip pointed at Pilar's jugular.

"You cut it right off. My arm, you cut my arm off." His nostrils flared as he raised his head to glare at

Paen. "Do you have any idea how long I've had this human form? Six hundred and twenty-seven years. I *liked* it! And now you've had my arm off."

"You were strangling my Beloved," Paen said, his eyes flashing quicksilver.

"She was trying to stop me from destroying Yan Lu-owang," Pilar replied, raising the statue over his head.

Caspar roared out something I didn't understand, charging straight at us, extras falling off him like confetti.

"Please, please don't destroy it," I begged. "We need it to fulfill a debt. Couldn't we have it just long enough to do that, and then you can use it to destroy Caspar?"

"No," Pilar said simply, and slammed the statue to the ground.

Existence hesitated for a moment. Everything, every living being, every inanimate object, every elf and demon and imp, even the earth itself paused for a moment as if to understand the implications of Pilar's action, then continued on as if nothing momentous had just happened.

But something did happen. The ugly, squat statue of a monkey hit the granite and mica and all the other minerals that went into forming the rocks and earth of the lodestone, and shattered into four pieces.

Caspar screamed and threw himself at us. I screamed (hoarsely), and stared with eyes filled with tears at the pieces of the statue. Paen lunged forward to stop Pilar, but the monkey god was too fast for him, leaping off the rock with a jubilant laugh.

Paen's beautiful silver eyes met mine, and I fell to my knees with the anguish I saw in them.

No. There has to be another way. This isn't the end.

It is, sweetheart. The debt can only be repaid by the statue, he answered, and grief so deep it seemed endless welled up inside him and spilled out onto me.

Caspar, in his twisted, horrific state, screamed in Chinese as he scrabbled at the remains of the statue. I grabbed one of the pieces, intending to brain him with it—not that I knew it would do anything to permanently harm him—when a thought struck.

"Here," I snarled, snatching up a piece of the statue and throwing it at him before reaching for another piece. "Here. And here, and here. You now have all the pieces of the Jilin God. The debt Paen's father incurred with you is now fulfilled! I demand acknowledgement of receipt of the statue before deep night!"

"You!" The twisted face of Caspar was a truly sickening sight to behold, but it was made almost unviewable by the hatred that filled it as his eyes raised to mine. Paen wrapped an arm around me and pulled me up so I was held tight to his body, his wonderful warmth soaking into me. "You think you have won, but you have not. For I have this!"

From the head of the monkey statue Caspar withdrew a small, rolled-up bit of parchment. "Behold, the *Simia Gestor Coda*! Into it Sun Wukong wrote all the knowledge of the ancients, all of my knowledge that he stole from me!"

Paen sucked in his breath, releasing me to lunge for Caspar, but the god of death leaped aside, holding the manuscript tightly. Behind him, Finn slashed through a couple of demons obviously intent on reaching Caspar, but it was no good.

"Now you will suffer as you have made me suffer," Caspar gloated, his body stretching into a thin, ribbony suggestion of a human. "You too will spend an eternity in torment, and when at last you decide to end your own agony, I will be waiting for you!"

"No!" Paen shouted, throwing himself onto Caspar.

Eerie, high-pitched, evil laughter was all that remained as Caspar succumbed to the inevitable and was pulled back into his domain in hell, taking the manuscript with him. The demons suddenly vanished, leaving the ghosts and extras fighting nothing more substantial than air. They all froze, and for a moment, there wasn't a sound.

"Dude!" a voice said in awestruck amazement.

"Did you get that?" a second voice asked.

"Er . . . get the big guy in the ugly costume and all those little brown guys disappearing?"

"Yeah."

"I got it, but no one is going to believe it."

Paen helped me to my feet, being careful to avoid jarring my arm. *Sweetheart?*

The howling wind inside me seemed a horrible parody of Caspar's mocking laughter. Pain twisted deep within, pain and despair and hopelessness.

Sam? Paen's fingers were warm on my chin as he tipped my head back so he could see into my eyes. *Don't cry, love. We'll find another way.*

"He's gone?" Finn asked, covered in black demon blood, panting as he stopped to help Clare over a gore-splattered stone.

"Ew," she said, prodding Pilar's detached arm. "That's just gross. So, we won?"

Two fat tears rolled down my cheeks. Paen pulled me up to his chest, but not even the lovely glow of his soul could warm me now. "I'm cold," I told him.

"I know, sweetheart. We'll get it back. If I have to go to hell myself, we'll get it back."

"Get what back?" Clare asked, her brow furrowed. "I thought we won."

I wrapped my good arm around Paen and held him tight, allowing him to pour into me all his love and warmth and everything that he was, but it wasn't enough. Sharp fingers of despair kept me tight in their icy grip.

"The *Coda* was lost," Paen said to Clare, but he never took his eyes off mine.

"Oh, the manuscript that's supposed to tell Sam how to get her soul back? But I thought that wasn't a sure thing?"

"It isn't . . ." Paen said, stopping before he could complete the sentence, his arms tightening around me.

I did the job for him. "But it was the only chance we had."

"Non-deities have such linear thinking," Pilar said, leaping over a few rocks to land a few feet away, Beppo clinging to his shoulder.

I wondered for a moment why I wasn't surprised to see Pilar wasn't affected in the least by losing an arm—then I realized I didn't feel anything inside that wasn't an all-consuming hopelessness.

"He does not have the *Coda*. There is no *Coda*. There never was. The manuscript he has is nothing more than a few scribblings I made centuries ago. It was intended to draw Yan Luowang out of hiding. And it succeeded."

Paen lifted his head from mine to look at Pilar, his beautiful eyes stark with loathing. "I will destroy you. I don't know how, but this I swear—I will destroy you for what you've put us through . . . for what you've done to Sam."

Not even the fact that Paen would undertake such an impossible task warmed me. I shivered, wondering if I would ever be warm again, and leaned into Paen, too exhausted even to think.

"She's diminishing," I heard Clare's voice say. The words were familiar, but they didn't seem to have meaning to me anymore. My focus was on the tornado of misery that ripped through me. "My aunt said something once about elves who diminish. They just sort of fade away until they are no more."

Sam, my love, hold on to me. Don't leave me now, not when I need you. I can't live without you.

Paen's words seemed to come from a long way away. I examined them, holding them, wondering why such beautiful words should mean nothing to me anymore.

The pain washed over me.

Hold on to me, love. I'll help you with the pain.

There was no sense fighting it.

You must fight it, Sam. Don't give in to it, don't let it sap your strength.

My ending had been written. How ironic that it would happen now when I had found the one person I was ready to give up everything for.

Dammit, Samantha, I will not let you go! You are a strong, smart, sexy woman and I will not lose you. Now fight, damn you! Fight for me!

"Can't you do something to stop it?" Clare asked, her voice thick with tears.

Pilar sighed, his voice as distant as everyone else's. "I've always found elves to be so melodramatic, but since she did stop you from slaying my mortal form, I will return the favor."

"You've done enough already," Paen snarled.

"Not yet, but I'm about to. This will accord us without debt on either side," Pilar said.

"What—"

I was ripped from Paen's side, yanked without ceremony from my existence to another one, a world filled with drifting souls and beings which had been caught there.

"Behold the Akashic Plain," a familiar voice said behind me.

Epilogue

"You already talked to him—why do you need to talk to him again?" I held the phone away from my ear for a second. "No, he's not going to change his mind. He's not that kind of man, and besides, he can't. I'm his Beloved. He can't impregnate me and leave me for someone else. Well, OK, he *could*, but he wouldn't because he's nice. And he loves me. A lot. He was going to destroy a god for me! Only a man head over heels in love would decide to do something so ridiculous."

My mother, never one to keep feelings to herself, unburdened herself of several items, up to and including the likelihood that the elf side of my family would look down on Paen because of his dark origins. "Like I care what they think?" I flinched at the barrage that followed that statement. "Sorry. Yes. Yes, I hear you. Yes, yes, yes. Huh? Of course we're going to get married! I don't know about Clare—she and Finn seem to be pretty tight. More than her usual boyfriends. I think they may be getting serious. We'll just have to see how that goes."

Outside, traffic hummed along merrily in another gloriously sunny—AKA rare—May day.

"No, you can't talk to him again, you've talked to him three times already today. Someone finally tracked down his parents, so he's telling them everything that's been happening. Yes, you'll meet them. Yes, they're nice. Mom—" I sighed and prayed for patience. "No, I won't let his mother help me pick out a wedding dress, OK? I have to go. No, now is not a good time to look into ear reconstruction surgery—I'm happy with my ears! Paen likes them, too. No . . . no . . . it's not a matter of money, I just don't want them re-elfed! Look, I really, really have to . . . Mom . . . Mom, Paen is stark naked with an erection that could bring down buildings, and he's calling for me. Gotta run! Love to you and Dad. *Again.* Bye!"

I clicked off the phone to the sound of my mother sputtering indignantly, rubbing my ear in an attempt to get feeling back into it as I leaned against the wall and stretched. I knew my mother was going to be excited by the news that I was now immortal (something she had been fretting over ever since I had my ears bobbed), and madly in love with a man who was just as crazy about me, but she was running amok with international phone calls. I had a suspicion she'd be dragging Dad over to Scotland in the very near future.

Still at it?

My toes curled at the warm, rich voice in my head. *Yes. It feels good. I like doing it. I may do it every single day from here until the end of our time.*

Paen sighed from where he leaned against the door. "How is your arm?"

I smiled at nothing and arched my back, relishing the absolute joy that sunlight on my skin brought, making me giddy from the power it fed me. I was clad in a rather risqué eyelash lace chemise . . . and nothing else. "Perfect. You were right—the sunlight did a lot to hurry along the healing process."

"I thought it might. Was that your mother again?"

"Of course. We'll probably hear from her another good dozen times today before she works most of the excitement out of her system. I liked your parents."

"Good. They liked you, as well. My mother says you're not to pick out a wedding dress until they get back to Scotland. She's excited about having a daughter-in-law and doesn't want to let any of the wedding planning slip past her."

I laughed. "That'll be a battle royal—my mom against yours. Oh well, we'll let them work it out. I don't really care so long as the end result is the same."

He raised an eyebrow. "Wild, unbridled wedding night sex?"

"No." I shook my head, to his surprise. "A passionate, romantic, wonderful beginning to our eternal wedded bliss."

He smiled.

"Followed immediately by wild, unbridled wedding night sex."

"Sam? Are you decent?" Clare's voice drifted in through the closed door. Paen edged past the pool of sunlight on the floor, grabbed my robe from where it lay over the wooden rhino, tossing it to me before he opened the door.

I sat up on the window seat where I'd been soaking up the all-healing rays from the sun, and watched with curiosity as Clare forged a path into the room. "We brought you some flowers—merciful goddess, what happened here?"

Paen handed her the machete. "It appears her plants are happy again."

"Good god, it's like a jungle," Finn said, only part of him visible as he fought his way past a particularly exuberant African oil palm. "I expect to see a lion or rhinoceros at any moment."

Paen moved aside to hold back a rubber tree leaf.

Finn laughed at the sight of my rhino. Clare disdained the use of the machete and beat her way over to my dresser, placing a large bouquet of hothouse flowers there, turning them until she was happy with the presentation. "Are you all better?"

I stretched in the sunlight, happiness welling out of me as I looked at Paen where he leaned against the wall, his arms crossed casually over his chest. Those lovely eyes of his were like sunlight on silver, shining back at me. "Yes, I'm all better now."

"Good. Is your mother happy about the wedding?"

"Very, although she is a bit annoyed we haven't actually set a date. I tried explaining to her that I only *just* forced Paen to his knees to propose, but you know how she is once she gets an idea—she doesn't much listen to anyone else."

"Well, she is an elf. You know how they are."

I sent Paen a mischievous grin. "Mom did say that she'd be perfectly happy organizing a double wedding, if you and Finn . . ." I let the suggestion fade to a stop, expecting one or the other of them to voice a negative exclamation. To my surprise, they just eyed each other for a moment.

"You never know," Finn said finally, with a grin that warmed my heart.

"I'm going to expect a lot more than a proposal in a car riding home from the scene of a demon attack," Clare informed him, then snatched one of the flowers from the vase and popped a petal in her mouth as she turned back to me. "Speaking of that, perhaps you can explain to me what exactly happened. Paen was too busy taking care of you after Pilar dumped you on the ground, and then Finn was bleeding and he had to eat, and those movie people wanted to talk to me about a possible role in an upcoming science fiction movie, and . . . well, with all that, I just never did find out what happened."

"Pilar took Sam to the Akashic Plain," Paen answered, a small smile making the corners of his mouth turn up.

Have I told you today how much I love you?

Yes. Seven times, as a matter of fact.

Ah.

It's not nearly enough.

I grinned.

"But how did he do that?" Clare asked, absently plucking a carnation from the bouquet and peeling off a few petals, which she promptly ate. "I thought it was impossible to get to the Akashic Plain?"

"Linear thinking," I said cryptically, and sent Paen a mental image of me stroking every square inch of him.

He straightened up. *All* of him.

"What?"

"Pilar is a god. There are places where deities can break the rules. The Akashic Plain is one of them."

Paen sent me back images of myself covered in whipped cream, and him with a bowl of strawberries.

I shivered, but not from cold.

"Oh. So he took Sam to the Akashic Plain to get her soul back, and then plopped her back in our reality?"

"Yes." I dwelled lovingly over what it felt like taking Paen into my mouth, of the scent and taste of him, of the joy I received in giving him pleasure.

"And he wasn't angry about Paen cutting off his arm?"

"Not angry enough to wreak any vengeance, no," Paen answered. He thought about nibbling on my ears. My entire body tightened in response.

"What about the statue? If it was a demon lord's statue, why didn't Brother Jacob see that? And why was the monkey statue hidden inside the bird one?"

"The bird statue shielded the Jilin God, making it impossible for anyone to detect its dark origins." I remembered what it felt like when Paen thrust hard into my body, causing every single one of my muscles to tighten around him.

"The demon lord who held it hid the statue within another one for security. He changed the outer statue's shape every so often, in case Caspar was on to it." Paen dwelled lovingly on the thought of my nipples.

I sucked in a breath, my body tingling like mad from his mental images.

"All right, that I understand, but what about your father? How did he get the statue?"

"Er . . . Clare, my sweet, I think we should be going now," Finn said, looking from me to Paen.

"But your father . . ." She popped another bit of carnation into her mouth.

I recalled what it felt like to ride him, our bodies moving together in a rhythm that swept us into ecstasy.

Paen lurched forward, stopping abruptly at the edge of the sunlight.

"I think they need some time to themselves right now," Finn said, shooting Paen a grin before swinging Clare up in his arms and fighting his way to the door. She giggled as he kissed her nose. "Actually, as it turns out, Caspar forged part of that receipt. He did help Dad find Mum, but the payment due was Dad's assistance in locating the statue, nothing more . . ."

"You do realize the irony of this, don't you?" Paen asked as the door closed behind them. He skirted the sunlight, stalking me as a predator would. I shed the robe, then, after a moment's thought, the chemise as well.

"The irony of you proposing to a sun elf? Yes, my darling Paen, I do indeed realize that I'm going to have to learn to love the moonlight."

"And I'm going to have to make sure the castle brings in even more profit than it does now," he said in a low voice filled with arousal as he pulled off his shirt and pants, standing naked just at the edge of the pool of sunlight.

"Really?" I admired him for a moment, merging myself with him, wanting to burst into song with the happiness I felt when our souls twined around each other and became one. "Why is that?"

"Sunblock," he growled, ignoring the sunlight as he stepped into it to scoop me up, carrying me to the bed. "I'm going to need lots and lots of sunblock."

Three months later the CEO of a UK-based company which produced sunblock, amongst other pharmaceuticals, happily reported to board members a quarter of record sales. He just couldn't figure out why most of the sales were concentrated around a remote Scottish town. . . .

Read on for a preview of Katie MacAlister's next
Aisling Grey, Guardian, novel

Light My Fire

Coming from Signet Eclipse
in November 2006

"I hate it when people do things like that," I grumbled as I slammed shut the door to Nora's apartment.

"What, act polite?"

"No, do that horrible foreshadowing thing that everyone around here seems to do." I tossed down Jim's leash and went to check Nora's answering machine to see if there were any messages from the shipping company. "Just once I'd like someone to walk up to me and, instead of predicting distaster or bad luck or any of the myriad other unpleasant happenings that have been predicted for me, say, 'Aisling, you're going to win the lottery today. Or lose ten pounds overnight. Or fall madly in love with the next man you see.' Anything but foreshadowing."

Jim sighed. "It's all about you, isn't it? Never thinking about anyone else, only concerned about your own happiness."

I glared openmouthed at the demon as a knock sounded on the door. I hurried toward it, glad I'd left the outer door unlocked for the delivery guys. "That is so totally off base, and you know it!"

"Fine, you want to be that way . . ." Jim scratched a spot behind its left ear and considered its crotch as it said, "Aisling, you're going to win the lottery today, lose ten pounds overnight, and fall madly in love with the next man you see."

I opened the door on the last of his words.

The man standing in the doorway raised an eyebrow. "Hindsight, so they say, is twenty-twenty."

My jaw dropped. My heart speeded up. My lungs seemed suddenly airless. And my stomach wadded up into a small leaden ball.

A small fire burst into being on the nearby area rug. Jim ran over to stomp it out.

"Drake," I said on a gasp, air rushing once again into my lungs. "What are you—"

"You are hereby summoned to attend a synod of the green dragons tomorrow. Attendance is mandatory." Drake slapped a stiff black portfolio into my hands and turned to leave.

"Hey! A synod? Wait a minute—Jim, there's another one near the curtains."

Drake spun around again, his green eyes blazing with emotion—eyes that I knew so well, that had once seemed to hold everything I wanted. But that was before he betrayed me. . . .

"Do you refute your oath of fealty to the sept? Do you refuse to honor your commitments, mate?"

"No," I answered, lifting my chin. I'd known all along that I was bound to the dragon sept that Drake ruled as wyvern. Even though we were no longer together, technically I was still his mate, and until I could find a way to undo that, I owed them my help when needed. I'd been braced and ready for this ever since I'd left Budapest. "No, I am not refuting my oath to the sept. I will attend the meeting as your mate. I simply wanted to know . . ." The words died on my lips.

He crossed his arms over his chest. "What did you want to know?"

Whether he missed me? Whether his heart hurt as much as mine? Whether he regretted betraying me the way he did? Those were the first three things that came to mind, but there were others. All of which were questions that I would ask over my cold, lifeless corpse. So to speak. Luckily, before I had to try to think of an impersonal question, Jim stepped in to the rescue.

"You really are going to have to get a grip on controlling dragonfire, Ash. Hiya, Drake. Come crawling back, did you? Man, you are so whipped." Jim shambled over to give Drake a quick sniff. "I never met anyone so completely— Fires of Abaddon! You don't have to barbecue me!"

"Don't set Nora's bathroom on fire," I warned as Jim raced off to put out the flames that burst into a corona around its head. I turned back to Drake, less worried about Jim's doggy form taking harm than about Nora's bath towels. "You get points for marksmanship, but lose on effect. Roasting Jim alive won't do anything but leave the scent of burnt dog hair hanging around the apartment."

Drake looked thoughtful as he rubbed his chin. "Actually, I was off. I was aiming for you."

My eyes opened wide as his words filtered through the sudden love/anger/sadness cocktail that had recently become my usual my emotional state. "You wanted to burn *me?*"

Drake moved so fast, it didn't even register in my brain. One minute he was standing several paces away; the next he was pushing me up against the open door, his body hard and aggressive, mine automatically answering by going all soft on him. "You cannot be under any delusion that you can simply walk away from me."

"I know I pricked your pride by leaving you," I said carefully, telling my body to stop mugging him and to behave itself so I could concentrate on reasoning with the most *un*reasonable dragon in human form that ever walked the planet. "But there is nothing more between us, Drake. It's over."

"It is not . . . over . . ." he growled, his lips so close to mine I could feel the heat of his mouth. The scent of him, spicy and masculine and uniquely Drake, went immediately to my head and made me giddy with want. But beneath that want, there was heartache, a pain so profound it all but crippled me for the week following our breakup. It had taken seven long days of nonstop sobbing for me to come to a point where I could get on with my life . . . without Drake at my side.

"Oh, man. He's going to pork you right here in front of me, isn't he? Jeez, and they say dogs have no shame."

"Demon, silence. And close your eyes," I ordered, unable to see if Jim followed my command, because Drake chose that moment to claim my mouth. He was a naturally arrogant, dominant man, and those qualities showed in his kisses. He wooed with a passion that left my knees weak and my toenails steaming. His entire body entered into the kiss he gave me, one hand sweeping up to cup my breast, the other sliding down my back to grab my butt, pulling my hips tighter against his.

Fire flamed to life in him, dragonfire, the familiar heat of it as welcome as manna as it roared through me, igniting my soul. My heart, my poor abused heart, wept with agony at the feel of him with me, joining our halves together in a way much more elemental than mere sex. It was as if our souls fit together, one completing the other, the two of us together forming one brilliant, glorious being that would burn together for all eternity. . . .

"No!" I cried, pulling my mouth from his. "You are not going to seduce me again! Dammit, you broke my heart, Drake. You can't piece it back together with glue made up of a few kisses and mind-numblingly fabulous sex! Over means over! I will honor my vow to the sept. I will present myself as your mate at the weyr and sept meetings. I will support your dragon decisions in any way I can. But I will not allow you to destroy me again!"

One of his long, sensitive fingers pushed aside my shirt to trace the rounded sept emblem that he'd branded into my flesh, marking me as a wyvern's mate. The emerald fire in his eyes slowly banked as he spoke. "You are mine, Aisling. You are mine today, tomorrow, and five hundred years from now. You will always be mine. I do not give up my treasures, *kincsem*. You would do well to remember that."

He stepped away, leaving me quivering against the door with so many emotions I couldn't begin to separate them. I clutched my arms around myself as he left, wanting to sob out my pain, wanting to follow after him and fling myself in his arms, wanting everything to be the way it was before he had stomped all over my heart.

That's how Nora found me a few minutes later, glued up against the door, slow, hot tears leaking from my eyes, dragonfire licking my feet.

"Hello, everyone. We're back a bit early. The kobold attack turned out to be a false alarm— Aisling? Oh dear, you're on fire again." Nora set down the dog carrier she used to transport Paco. She squinted, adjusted the bright red glasses that perched so jauntily on her nose, and touched a finger to my shirt as I stamped out the last of Drake's fire. "Dragon scales." Her eyes lifted to mine, considering me in the cautious, thoughtful way she had. "A dragon visited you? A *green* dragon?"

I swallowed back a big lump of unshed tears and pushed myself away from the door, staggering over to collapse on her couch, my pounding heart slowly returning to normal.

Nora looked from me to the door, tipping her head on the side to examine it. "Judging by the Aisling-shaped outline that appears to be scorched into the door, I'd say it was *the* green dragon who visited you. How is Drake?"

"As stubborn as ever. Oh, Nora. I thought I was past this!" Both Jim and Nora watched me as I slumped into a giant wad of misery. Paco, released from his confinement, ran over to wrestle with my shoelaces, as was his wont. "I am so ready to move on. Here you are, poised to start my training—oh, that reminds me, there's something I need to tell you about that—and whammo. Two minutes with

Drake, and I'm a mess. How am I ever supposed to get over him?"

Nora sat down next to me, her dark eyes watchful as they peered at me out of her glasses. "Perhaps you are not meant to get over him," she said simply.

"Huh? Not get over him? Nora, do you have any idea how crazy that man . . . dragon . . . whatever he is, do you have *any* idea how crazy he makes me?"

"You know, normally I just can't get enough of you whining about Drake, or crying over Drake, or ranting about Drake, or any of the other gazillion 'about Drake' things you constantly do because you're obsessed with the man but refuse to admit it, but since you insist on starving this fabulous form I've taken simply because I'm a few pounds over the standard Newfie weight, I just don't have the strength for it today." Jim turned around and marched off to the room Nora had turned over to me.

She raised an eyebrow at the retreating demon. "What's gotten into Jim? I know you and it have a special relationship, but I've never heard it be outright rude before."

"It's mad that I won't take it to Paris because Drake is there. . . . Although he's not there, he's here. So I guess there's no reason not to go visit Amelie, except now I have this dragon thing to go to." I sighed and slumped even more, feeling far from the confident, self-assured person I so desperately wanted to be. "Nora, do I talk constantly about Drake? I don't sound obsessed, do I? I just sound . . . weary, right?"

Paco pounced on the paper that had fallen from my hand. Nora got it away from him before he did any damage to it, smoothing the sheet over her knee as she sat next to me. "Well . . . since you asked, I'm afraid I'm going to have to agree with Jim."

"What?" I shrieked, sitting upright in order to glare. I didn't, of course—for one thing, Nora was my friend, not just my mentor, and for another . . . well, there was a pesky little voice in the back of my head that was whispering its agreement with both Nora and Jim. The roots of denial, however, were strong and difficult to dig out. "You think I'm obsessed with him, too?"

"I think you're in love with him, yes. And despite the differences you have, I believe you are meant to be together. Further, I believe that you know this, but are too stubborn to admit it to yourself."

There's nothing like a bit of plainspeaking to knock the wind from your sails.

"But . . . but . . ."

She shook her head, picking up the paper to glance at it. "I was going to address the issue with you in a few days, when we begin your proper training. A Guardian's strength comes from within, Aisling. To deceive yourself is to weaken your power."

"He betrayed me," I said, wanting to scream the words. "He broke my heart!"

"He betrayed your trust, yes. But you betrayed an oath to him. You both have to learn how to make compromises in order to happil— What on earth?"

The fury in her voice yanked me from the dark musings about my life. "Oh! I'm so sorry! That's what I was going to tell you, but then Drake came in and distracted me. A man named Mark Sullivan was waiting when Rene dropped us off at the door. He said he's with the Committee, and he's slapping a restraining order or something on you that says you can't teach me, because there's an investigation going on."

Nora nodded, her lips moving slightly as she read the letter.

"Rene?" she asked, looking up, a finger marking a spot on the letter. "You saw Rene?"

"Story for another day. Does the letter say what this is all about?"

She went back to reading, her face impassive. I hadn't known Nora long—it had been about a month since we'd met in Budapest—so I wasn't too good at reading her body language. There was no way to mistake the anger in her ebony eyes, however. They positively flashed black sparks as she crumpled the letter up and threw it on the floor for Paco to bat around.

I waited impatiently for her to say something. When she did, my eyebrows rose in surprise.

"The fools. The bloody ignorant fools. I've half a mind to curse the lot of them."

"I know how you feel. I was shocked when Mark said you were not going to be allowed to teach me. Why are they doing this?" I gave her arm a friendly pat as she looked blindly at her hands.

"It's Marvabelle, of course," she answered.

"Marvabelle? O'Hallohan?" I asked, even more surprised by the name she'd mentioned. "The Marvabelle who was in Budapest? The one with the wimpy oracle husband? The one who used to be your roomie when you were studying to be a Guardian? That Marvabelle?"

"One and the same." Nora jumped from the

couch, striding across the living room with her chin high. She turned and paced back. "She's had it in for me ever since we were recognized for stopping the Guardian killings. She warned me then she would not stand around watching me have glory she felt she deserved."

"*She* deserved! She did nothing to catch the murderer!" I got to my feet and stomped around in sympathetic indignation, keeping a tight rein on my anger lest it manifest itself again in dragonfire. "We did all the work! We figured it all out. All she did was get in the way."

Nora stopped pacing in order to grab my sleeve as I stomped by her. "To be honest, you did all the work, and you figured it out. But I thank you for your outrage on my behalf."

"That doesn't matter," I said, waving away her thanks. "What does matter is that Marvabelle thinks she can mess with you. Us. I didn't know she had this sort of clout with the Committee."

"Neither did I." Nora picked up a stuffed toy and managed to exchange it for the letter Paco was gnawing on. She smoothed out the letter and read it again. I peeked over her shoulder, my eyes narrowing at the officious language mentioning a complaint against Nora and the investigation that would subsequently follow.

"*In concordance with the precepts of the code of the Guardian's Guild, you are hereby ordered to cease and desist any form of Guardian training until otherwise notified, pending the outcome of this investigation,*" I read aloud. "Oh, that is such bull!"

Nora nodded, folding the crumply letter and setting it in a basket that held her correspondence. "I agree. But don't let it upset you. I have nothing to hide, and I have committed no violations of the Guardian's code. This is just a minor setback, and not worthy of our concern."

"Not worthy? It's utter crap, and I for one don't intend to sit around while . . ." I stopped at the determined look in her eyes. This was her profession, her life that we were discussing. Just because I wanted to punch the Committee in the nose for believing Nora could do anything unethical didn't mean I could act on those desires. "OK. Just a minor setback. Gotcha."

"We will begin your training tomorrow, as planned," Nora said firmly as she carried Paco's carrier to a closet. "Hopefully it will have the side benefit of helping you control Drake's fire."

"Er . . . I don't mean to question you, but didn't that letter say—"

"I do not intend to allow one spiteful woman to waste any more of our time than she has," Nora answered. She pulled a book out of the floor-to-ceiling bookcase that lined one wall and held it out for me. "Although it grieves me to do anything against the Committee's dictates, in this I know they are wrong. We will proceed as planned." She paused in the doorway to the kitchen. "Unless you have had a change of heart?"

I laughed so hard tears wet my eyelashes. "Nora, I've broken just about every rule there is. I don't know why you'd think I'd balk at breaking another one."

She smiled, warmth glowing from behind her glasses. "I didn't think you'd mind. I'll make an appointment with Mark to discuss the issue. Now, as for your problems with Drake—why don't we have a nice cup of tea and talk it over?"

Whether I wanted to admit it or not, Jim's (and Nora's) words had hit me hard. I raised my chin and shook my head. "No, I'm through obsessing and monopolizing the conversation and whatever else I've been doing over that annoying man. I'm just going to have to work things out on my own. Er . . . would it help if I talked to the Guardian people, too?"

"It certainly couldn't hurt. Don't worry about that now—I'm sure we'll get everything straightened out once I can sit down and talk to them. And as for you . . . Aisling, I didn't mean you couldn't talk to me about your troubles," Nora said, opening the shutters that closed off a small bar from the kitchen area. "I will always be here to listen to you if you need a friendly ear."

"Thanks. I appreciate that." I gathered up my things and the book she'd handed me, and glanced at the clock. "I'll let you know if I need a shoulder to sob on. Right now I have an outfit to pick out for tomorrow's dragon conference, a book of demonic class types to memorize, and a demon to appease. If I leave now, I think there's time for me to zip over to Paris and make it back by midnight. I'll bone up on the texts you gave me once I get back."

She looked skeptical as I rushed into my room, grabbed my purse and passport, and ordered Jim to follow me. "Aisling, you'd really go all the way to Paris and back in twelve hours just to make your demon happy?"

"Paris?" Jim asked, shuffling its way out to the living room. At the word, its ears pricked up, its eyes lit, and it suddenly looked a good ten years younger, not to mention five pounds lighter. "Did I hear that right? We're going to Paris? Right now?"

"Yes, I would," I answered Nora first. "You and Jim are both right—I have been obsessive and moody. I owe it a trip. By my voice, by my blood, by my hand, demon, I banish thee to Akasha."

Before Jim could do more than open its eyes wide with delight and surprise, it disappeared in a puff of black smoke.

"Man, that's a handy little spell," I said as I ran for the door, waving at Nora as I went. "See you later— I'll be back by midnight. Don't let the Committee get you down. It can't be anything serious or we'd know, right?"

Honestly, there are times when I think I should be teaching a class called Famous Exit Lines You'll Later Regret.